CROWD CONTROL

The ground began to shake in thunderous syncopation. The crowd swung toward the sound to see two Battloid-configured Veritechs—a VF-1A and a VF-1J—appear from behind a glass-and-chrome highrise.

"Now hear this," the pilot of the single-lasered VT said over his mecha's PA. "You are in violation of Executive Order Fifteen dash Seventy-Seven, which forbids any assembly undertaken without the prior consent of Governor Leonard."

The demonstrators booed at the mention of Leonard. "He denies us food, knowing that we'll protest," Seloy snarled. "Then he has the excuse he needs to deploy his mecha. Usurper!" she screamed in Zentraedi through cupped hands. "To show allegiance to Leonard dishonors all T'sentrati!"

The crowd of Zentraedi began chanting again. Max's heart began to race as the chant increased in volume, drowning out the dueling words of mecha pilots and sympathizers alike.

Suddenly then—incredible as it seemed—the two pilots opened fire on the crowd. From the VT's chainguns tore bursts of transuranic rounds as big as candlepins, any one of them capable of blowing the foot off a Battlepod . . .

By Jack McKinney
Published by Ballantine Books:

THE ROBOTECH™ SERIES:
GENESIS #1
BATTLE CRY #2
HOMECOMING #3
BATTLEHYMN #4
FORCE OF ARMS #5
DOOMSDAY #6
SOUTHERN CROSS #7
METAL FIRE #8
THE FINAL NIGHTMARE #9
INVID INVASION #10
METAMORPHOSIS #11
SYMPHONY OF LIGHT #12

THE SENTINELS™ SERIES:
THE DEVIL'S HAND #1
DARK POWERS #2
DEATH DANCE #3
WORLD KILLERS #4
RUBICON #5

ROBOTECH: THE END OF THE CIRCLE #18
ROBOTECH: THE ZENTRAEDI REBELLION #19

KADUNA MEMORIES

THE BLACK HOLE TRAVEL AGENCY:
  Book One: *Event Horizon*
  Book Two: *Artifact of the System*
  Book Three: *Free Radicals*
  Book Four: *Hostile Takeover*

THE ZENTRAEDI REBELLION

Jack McKinney

A Del Rey® Book
BALLANTINE BOOKS • NEW YORK

A Del Rey® Book
Published by Ballantine Books

Copyright © 1994 by Harmony Gold USA, Inc.

All rights reserved under International and Pan-American Copyright Conventions. Published in the United States of America by Ballantine Books, a division of Random House, Inc., New York, and simultaneously in Canada by Random House of Canada Limited, Toronto.

Library of Congress Catalog Card Number: 93-90967

ISBN 0-345-38774-0

Manufactured in the United States of America

First Edition: May 1994

10 9 8 7 6 5 4 3 2 1

For Michael Riccardelli—Zor Prime—faithful correspondent and provider of anime, comics, and rousing ideas for Robotech

ACKNOWLEDGMENTS

Since its inception, when Carl Macek restructured three Japanese *animes* to create the television series, Robotech has been an interactive enterprise. Comico Comics adapted the eighty-five original episodes, and Palladium Books provided additional details on characters, mecha, and chronology for the role-playing game. In adapting Robotech and the Sentinels for Del Rey Books, I incorporated material from the original scripts and the role-playing game; and in writing *The End of the Circle*, I tried to be faithful to Macek's vision. Eternity Comics has been doing the same in their adaptation of the Sentinels and in several spin-off series, incorporating material from the scripts, the role-playing game, and the novels.

For several years now I have wanted to chronicle the events that led to the launch of the SDF-3—to fill in the gap between book six of the original series and book one of the Sentinels. However, some of that story has since been detailed by Bill Spangler in "The Malcontent Uprisings," a series he wrote for Eternity Comics. In the interest of consistency and continuity, I have included some of Bill's plot elements in the present work (chiefly, the events of 2018—with all apologies to Bill for the changes I made). Several key Zentraedi characters sprang from his imagination, as did many of the Zentraedi terms. I am also indebted once again to Kevin Siembieda for his detailed descriptions of mecha and of the factory satellite, and to everyone at *Protoculture Addicts*, not only for keeping Robotech vital, but for publishing a magazine line devoted to mecha.

Continuity is what distinguishes Robotech from similar

(though admittedly more widespread) sagas like Star Wars and Star Trek. It has always been my belief that only *one* version of the Robotech story exists, and that we writers are mere chroniclers of that tale.

2015

CHAPTER
ONE

2015 began much as any other year in recent memory: a Zentraedi attack left yet a third version of Macross in ruins; friends died and were buried; and Rick Hunter found himself hopelessly conflicted, if not by love this time, then by rumors of promotion and his dark imaginings of things to come.

Altaira Heimel, *Butterflies in Winter: Human Relations and the Robotech War*

SPRING'S FIRST SUNRISE BRIGHTENED A BLEAK LANDscape, pockmarked with craters and crazed with fissures opened by weapons of destruction. In the Northwest Territory, where a rain of Zentraedi annihilation bolts had incinerated countless acres of fir forest and hardened vast expanses of sand to glass, stood thrice-born Macross City, Earth's burgeoning capital only three months earlier and now its most recent casualty of war. Hurricane-force winter storms had been no kinder to the place than Khyron had, and with the early thaw had come an understanding of just how much damage the city had sustained in the moments before its frigid burial.

From a rostrum that once had been a segment of elevated highway, a middle-aged man with a noticeable Germanic accent was addressing a sizable crowd of Robotech Defense Force personnel and civilians. The only way to tell one from the other was by the RDF unit patches adorning the sleeves of the soldiers' antihazard suits.

"The sudden deaths of friends and loved ones affect us more profoundly than the near death of an entire world,"

3

the speaker was saying. "And it is those loved ones—those teammates, techmates, and comrades—that we seek to honor today, on the occasion of this sad assembly."

His name was Emil Lang, and he was Earth's preeminent mathematician and physicist. Robotechnology's chief proponent for more than a decade, he was seldom at a loss for words, but much of his address that day had been written for him by Lisa Hayes. She was Admiral Hayes now, in the wake of the destruction of Macross City and the Superdimensional Fortresses 1 and 2, and the deaths of Admiral Henry Gloval and dozens of the RDF's highest-ranking officers.

Few among a crowd estimated to number ten thousand were aware that Lang's were borrowed words, though Rick Hunter knew as much, because he had been with Lisa when she composed them two months earlier.

"Lang wants to know what *I* would say if I'd been chosen to deliver the memorial," Lisa had explained at the time.

Rick understood how Lang might be nonplussed by the assignment; commo of the nontechnical sort didn't come easily to the Wizard of Robotechnology. And yet who better to memorialize Gloval, Claudia Grant, and the rest than the man most responsible for the reconstruction of the SDF-1? The Earthman most responsible, that was. To another went credit for the ship's original design and engineering: the Tiresian Zor, in whom Robotechnology itself had its beginnings.

Lisa's contribution notwithstanding, Lang's sentiment was genuine, and it spoke to everyone in the crowd. Several of Rick's closest friends had died in Earth's protracted war with the Zentraedi—some in deepspace, some in Earth's wild blue yonder—and each of those deaths had touched him more than the devastation visited on the planet as the culmination of that conflict. Rick was willing to accept that he, like so many of Earth's survivors, had been living in staunch denial of the cataclysm. But if that were true, then Khyron's surprise attack on the dimensional fortresses and the city that had grown up around them had constituted a long-overdue wake-up call.

Those sections of Macross that hadn't been atomized during the attack, had been rendered uninhabitable by radiation, thwarting early plans for salvage operations and memorial services. Readings hadn't subsided to safe levels until late February, and then there was the snow to contend with—snow that had commenced on the night of the attack and continued unabated for two months, almost as if nature had fashioned a microclimate to hasten the cooling. March's sudden melt loosed avalanches that had blocked the pass between Macross and Monument City and had turned the valley floors to sludge. Even now, Rick's Veritech—a VT-1S configured in Battloid mode—stood to its ankles in thick mud.

Rick thought the de rigueur antihazard suits a touch belated, given that one-quarter the city's population had been dosed with radiation on emerging from the shelters—Rick, Lisa, and Minmei more than most. In addition to the sixty-six hundred dead who had been aboard the fortresses or providing mecha support, over five thousand civilian residents had died, most within days, some as recently as that morning. Bodies had been retrieved by the planeload, but it had been decided that there would be no coffins. General staff's plan called for Lake Gloval to be filled in and made a common grave site—a shrine. Though a shrine none would dare visit for at least ten years to come.

Macrossers, however, were nothing if not war-hardened, and most would have braved the residual fallout suitless to honor those who had flown endless against-all-odds missions in their behalf. Rick would have numbered himself among that noble group, but as an RDF captain, commander of celebrated Skull Team, he was obliged to attend as both man and mecha—"crafted," as the Veritech pilots put it.

Skull—the lot of them in Battloid mode—was deployed along what remained of the concourse linking the downtown mall to the flight deck of the SDF-1's Daedalus forearm. Ghost, Vermillion, and Indigo teams were similarly arrayed along the parallel concourse that fed the Prometheus. Both appendages were actually Thor-class supercarriers that had been grafted onto the fortress some five years earlier, at the start of the War against the race of giant warriors known as the Zentraedi. Rick, seated NBC-suited and neural-capped inside Skull One's ultratech cockpit, was ten city blocks west of the slagged half-mile-high hulks of the SDFs 1 and 2; the former, dismembered and decapitated, was up to its chest in the mud-filled crater that had been the lake, the twin booms of its truncated main gun raised in a attitude of humble entreaty.

No more, it seemed to be saying to the early morning sky. *Let it end here.*

Looking west, Rick could see across the rooftops of block after block of burned-out buildings clear to the elevated roadway that was serving as a stage for the long-delayed ceremony. By telephotoing the VT's exterior-mount videocams, he could bring into sharp focus nearly every hooded face on the makeshift rostrum: Dr. Lang, Professors Lazlo Zand and Sheamus Bronson, Macross Council politicos Milburn and Stinson, Chief Justice Justine Huxley, and Mayor Tommy Luan. Elsewhere stood Brigadier General Gunther Reinhardt, generals Maistoff and Motokoff, full-bird colonels Caruthers and Herzog, and Major Aldershot.

Rick spent a moment contemplating his pending promotion and shuddered at the thought of being lofted into the numbing company of all that assorted brass. He would just have to decline any advancement in rank, he told himself. Appeal to the aging flyboy in Reinhardt by saying that while he was flattered by Command's confidence in his leadership abilities, his place was and would always be with the Skull.

He reasoned he had a good chance of pulling it off. Providing that *Admiral* Lisa could keep from getting involved.

"In conclusion, let us at least try to embrace a constructive perspective," Lang was saying. "Let us try to view the coming years as a bridge to the future, however uncertain. We are a forward-looking race, and it is our faith in the future that will guide us . . ."

Lang was finally winding down—and just in time, Rick decided. For what had begun as a remembrance of the dead had deteriorated into a eulogy for Lang's precious dimensional fortresses and his plans for constructing an SDF-3.

And so when Vince Grant succeeded Lang at the podium—towering over it—he concentrated on remembering his sister, Claudia. And when Lieutenant Mitchell took the microphone she remembered enlisted-ratings techs Sammie Porter, Vanessa Leeds, and Kim Young, all of whom Mitchell had relieved at one time or another on the fortress's bridge. Cat crew officer Moira Flynn read off the names of hundreds of pilots she had waved into battle, and Dr. Hassan, chief surgeon aboard the SDF-1, recalled acts of unsurpassed bravery.

And when Lisa Hayes spoke . . . Well, when Lisa spoke about what it meant to have served under Henry Gloval— the father she would have preferred—and about Claudia Grant, her closest friend and sister-in-arms, not even the MBS broadcasters could keep their deep voices from faltering.

"Skull," Rick barked into his helmet pickup, as sobs filtered through the tactical net. "Present arms!"

The crowds turned to the half-buried ships. The technoknights of Skull, Ghost, Vermilion and Indigo raised their autocannons in salute, Veritech teams screamed over the lake, disgorging payloads of hothouse flowers, and the massive guns of a dozen MAC II Destroids offered thunderous praise to the dead. A reclamation crew positioned on the rail-gunned shoulders of the SDF-1 unfurled a huge banner bearing the RDF insignia: an encircled, curved-sided diamond suggestive of a fighting kite.

Sunlight gleamed off the battered alloy surfaces of the SDF-1.

There had been talk of a closing address by Exedore, but the general staff had had a last-minute change of mind and the Zentraedi ambassador's shuttle flight from the factory satellite had been canceled. Khyron's raid—though in no way undertaken in the name of all the Zentraedi—had brought about a resurgence of hatred for the race with whom Humans were now forced to share the Earth. Bron, Rico, and Konda—the first of the aliens to defect during the War—had been ordered to remain in Monument City and satisfy their grief by watching live coverage of the funeral.

Their absence was nearly as conspicuous as that of Lynn Minmei.

Following the ceremony, Lisa came directly from Fokker Field, outside Monument City, to Rick's temporary quarters—even though her quarters were only a few blocks away in Monument's newest suburb, transported all but intact from Macross by a fleet of flatbed trucks.

"I don't want to be alone," she said when she arrived. "I can't be alone. Not tonight."

Rick held her and stroked her long hair. They went over the day's events and she cried in his arms; then Rick led her to his bed and tucked her in. Gradually, her sobbing diminished and she fell asleep, and Rick returned to the living room, planting himself by a fixed-pane window that overlooked Monument's distant high-rise skyline. He felt strangely separated from the world, insulated by the window glass as he had been by the faceplate of the thinking cap and the permaplex of the VT cockpit.

The walls of the small house were hung with photos of Skull One and of assorted mecha, and dangling from the ceiling were plastic models of vintage prop planes of the sort his father and Leo Epstein had so loved, some of them purchased at Bron, Rico, and Konda's kiosk in the Macross mall. In Lisa's quarters were her stuffed toy ostrich and an oval vanity mirror decaled with stars that had somehow survived Khyron. Mass-produced modular rectangles of plastic and lightweight alloy, the two houses were mirror images of one another but identical to dozens of others in the transplanted neighborhood.

In the kitchenette was the round table at which Lisa had composed the introductory remarks to Lang's speech. By the time she had finished, the notepaper was so tearstained that Rick had had to have the few paragraphs transcribed. He marveled at how fluently she could cry, at how deeply she could grieve, especially when there didn't seem to be a tear left in him. With all that had happened in the past five years, it had gotten so that death was only unexpected when its cause was disease.

Fortunately for the Human race, Earth was proving itself

immune to pessimism. In spite of what the War had wrought, the planet was healing itself. Angry sunsets and blood-red moons were things of the past, and songbirds had returned to a patch of forest in the hills surrounding Monument—Lisa's favorite spot for picnics. Conditions in the so-called Southlands were reported to be even better.

Monument City had been founded by a group of Zentraedi loyal to Breetai, the warrior giant without whose help the War would have been lost—without whom, in fact, the Earth itself would have been lost, rid forever of "Micronians," as the aliens referred to any race that failed to measure up to their forty-foot stature. The city lay to the southwest of Macross, across a now-tortuous landscape of eroded hills and precipitous outcroppings, and was in many ways an imitation of Macross, right down to the milk-carton skyscrapers, Quickform buildings, pedestrian malls, and crater lake. Save that the rusting ship centered in Monument's lake was a Zentraedi dreadnought that had driven itself, like a spike, partway into the ground—one of tens of thousands of disabled and depleted warships that had oriented on Earth in the final moments of the War and plunged toward it. Much of the planet's ravaged surface was an eerie Robotech boot hill studded with crumpled ships, too numerous to either bury or dismantle. Only time and the elements might remove them, though not in the life span of anyone then living.

With the unequivocal destruction of Macross—it would never again rise from its ashes—facsimile Monument had been forced to accept Macross's 100,000 refugees, much as Earth had been forced to accept the defeated and marooned Zentraedi. Thus, in the three months since Khyron's assault, Monument had swollen to over ten times its original size. There was no SDF-1 to supply the fabricators that had enabled Macross Three to flower overnight, but Macross's city planners—out of foresight or perhaps paranoia—had seen fit to construct Macross as a veritable transportable city. Indeed, the construction designs and materials developed for Macross had already been exported around the world, to wherever people were struggling to rebuild: to Portland, Denver, Detroit, Albuquerque, and Mexico in

North American Sector; to the Eastern European Commonwealth, Japan, India, Australia, and central Africa; and to relatively robust South America—the Southlands—whose cities housed the highest concentrations of Micronized Zentraedi—those of Human scale, whether by choice or design.

Monument had a mixed population of full-size and Micronized aliens, and despite the sudden growth and ethnic flip-flop, it remained essentially a Zentraedi city, governed by a council made up of aliens and representatives of the small but vocal group of advocates who had spearheaded the movement for autonomy from Macross.

Watching the lights wink on in Monument's towers, Rick wondered how much longer the city's most recent immigrants would be willing to live under Zentraedi rule. The War, after all, had been fueled by fears of alien domination.

When he went to check on Lisa, he found her sound asleep, covers pulled tight around her head like a hood. Gazing at her from the bedroom door, she seemed the same, plainly pretty, twenty-nine-year-old military brat he'd once called *an old sourpuss*. Same heavy locks of brown-blond hair, same pale complexion and slender figure. Not that he was all that different from the long-haired Veritech jock Lisa was always accusing of indulging in amateur heroics. But Rick knew that deep down they both had changed. Or had been changed by events. Who knew anymore?

Mostly, he was still trying to get used to the idea of the two of them as partners. They had only declared their love three months back, amid the searing flames of a city under siege—just when it had looked as if Rick and Minmei would be setting up house after five years of flirting with the arrangement. No matter that he had won Minmei by default; she had proposed to him, and no one could revoke that moment.

Minmei had moved into his Macross module, following her disastrous breakup with cousin, manager, and then love interest Lynn-Kyle. She was going to give up her career as a singer—as The Voice—and Rick, in turn, was expected to resign from the RDF. Minmei's formula for happily ever after: just the two of them, playing house, reminiscing about old times, going gray together. But all during that week they had spent together, in and out of each other's arms, Rick couldn't get Lisa out of his mind. He'd been between the two women for so long that the very idea of choosing one over the other . . . Well, maybe he needed confusion in his life, he'd told himself.

Unaware that Khyron was about to guarantee that.

Minutes before the Backstabber's assault, Lisa had stopped by the house to inform Rick, very matter-of-factly, that she was being transferred to the factory satellite. Once there, she was to assume command of the near-completed SDF-2, and of the proposed Expeditionary mission to Tirol, homeworld of the Robotech Masters. Realizing that she would be out of his life for a long time to come had almost been enough to drag a confession from him. But it was Lisa's follow-up that finally did the trick: she loved him, she said. She had always loved him. And she was tasking Minmei—*Miss* Minmei, at that—with taking care of him.

A scary thought, even in the best of times.

Lisa hadn't gotten a block when Khyron's cruiser had fired the first of its annihilation bolts, and there she went, hurrying right into the thick of it. Giving chase, Rick's first obstacle was Minmei, who threw herself in front of him, shouting, "You can't leave me like this. How can you even think of going back into space?"

He had stepped around her and dashed after Lisa, Minmei hot on his heels, intent on playing out their final scene to a backdrop fashioned in hell.

"If you really love him, you'll let him go," Lisa had told Minmei. "He's a pilot. Flying is his life."

"You call that a life?" Minmei said back. "Battle after battle until everything is destroyed?"

Rick chimed in: "We're fighting to preserve a future. Someday you'll understand that." A somewhat ill-timed remark, what with fire falling from the sky and much of Macross already in flames.

The look Minmei returned was pitying. "There is no future. And you're wrong, Rick, I'll never understand—not war, not love, not any of it."

But hadn't that been Lynn-Minmei's problem all along? Rick asked himself now. Her celebrity had so isolated her that she had no comprehension of the real world. Lisa, on the other hand, understood all too well.

"It takes a soldier to understand the bitter truths," she had said earlier that same afternoon. "People think that because Khyron is dead and spring has arrived that the RDF's work is completed. They're wrong. But it's always easier to pretend. Everyone's become a Minmei."

No wonder that he and Lisa were inseparable, Rick thought. And that he hadn't so much as spoken to Minmei since the attack.

The bitter truths many of Macross's hagridden inhabitants were ignoring were two threats that still lurked in the stars: one posed by the race that had bioengineered the Zentraedi—the Robotech Masters—the other posed by an equally fiercesome race known as the Invid, one of a host of enemies the Zentraedi had made during their period of empire building for Tirol. The SDF-2, the gargantuan fortress Lisa was to have commanded, had been built to address the first threat. As envisioned by Admiral Gloval, the members of the Expeditionary mission would sue for peace with the Masters in their own space, thus removing the Earth from danger. Now, though, with the SDF-2 about to be interred, hope for the successful execution of the mission had centered on the sole remaining spacefold-capable battlewagon of the Zentraedi armada: Breetai's flagship. From the flagship would be fashioned a new dimensional fortress, Lang's SDF-3.

There was no denying the necessity of the mission. Rick, in fact, had probably been the first to suggest using Breetai's ship. But lately he'd been regretting having opened his mouth. Why couldn't he have said, *We're just going to have to pray that the Masters and the Invid have better things to do than come looking for revenge.* Didn't it make more sense to get on with healing and repopulating the Earth instead of wasting time worrying about things that might not even happen?

Even so, he knew it was too late for regrets. There was no dissuading Lisa, in any case. She saw it as a sacred obligation to carry out the assignment Gloval had given her on the morning of his death. Rick could understand that, too, though it sometimes felt that his and Lisa's newly affirmed love was little more than an extension of that obligation. Something he and Lisa owed to Gloval, Claudia, Sammie, Kim, and Vanessa, all of whom had foreseen a Hunter-Hayes union long before either of them had.

The hand of fate seemed to be steering him along with forceful claps on the back. He was grateful for the shove that had landed him in Lisa's life, but he wanted to evade any jostling that might mean added responsibilities. He was comfortable with his captain's rank, and he knew that he was an able team leader. No need to overextend himself, or allow anyone else to. He simply didn't have what it took to command from a desk or from behind the shielded partition of some tech-heavy balcony in a war room.

CHAPTER TWO

Owing to certain remarks attributed to Admiral Gloval in the days preceding Khyron's raid [on Macross City], controversy has long surrounded the SDF-2. Gloval is claimed to have said that the fortress wasn't built as a vehicle for the Expeditionary mission [to Tirol]; instead, it was meant to serve as a decoy, to be used in the event that the Robotech Masters should come looking for Zor's original creation. Hence, the fact that while bearing a visual resemblance to its progenitor, the SDF-2 was incapable of reconfiguring from Attack mode, wanted a barrier system, and lacked any means of executing a fold. Drawing on [Lisa] Hayes's assertions [in her Recollections], several commentators have posited that Breetai's flagship was to have supplied the fold system for the SDF-2 once the two ships had rendezvoused at the factory satellite. While it is clear that Hayes accepted this as given, the evidence is inconclusive that such a transfer of technology was discussed, let alone planned. At the time, Lang was reluctant to tamper with the flagship's fold system or reflex engines, and the factory satellite itself was plagued with glitches. It is far more likely—and certainly more in keeping with the surreptitious methods of the REF—that the decoy SDF-2 was to have been dispatched from the Solar system by fusion drive, allowing the REF to focus on finding some means of refurbishing Zor's ship and employing that to reach Tirol before the Masters reached Earth.
Mizner, *Rakes and Rogues: The True Story of the SDF-3 Expeditionary Mission*

KHYRON'S CHRISTMAS EVE RAID ON MACROSS, launched as a prelude to his decisive assault, had already reduced much of the eastern part of the city to charred rubble: the industrial sector, the fuel-storage depot, and a residential area squeezed between the lesser lakes, one of which hosted its own spikelike Zentraedi destroyer—a *Thuveral Salan*. Portions of the Downtown Mall had suffered as well.

RDF Command had purposely allowed the Backstabber

to escape with a supply of Protoculture sufficient to revitalize his badly damaged cruiser, in the hope that he would quit Earth and fold for Tirol, presumably to inform the Robotech Masters of the defeat of the Zentraedi Grand Fleet. A costly miscalculation, to be sure, for just over a week later, Khyron returned to inflict his final vengeance on the Micronians who had won the War.

The cruiser had announced itself from twenty miles out, ten degrees southwest, with a plasmic eruption that obliterated the downtown center on its way to crippling the SDF-2. The unprotected ship immediately listed and toppled forward into the lake, incapacitated and aflame. Admiral Gloval countered with a surprise of his own by ordering the SDF-1 into the skies, reflex engines roaring, Hammerheads and Decas streaking from launch tubes, in-close weapons thundering away at the closing enemy ship. When brute servomotors had repositioned the titanic twin booms of the reflex cannon so that they were pointing straight out from the fortress's shoulders, Gloval issued the fire orders and the ship spewed a two-mile-wide beam of directed energy that flayed Khyron's cruiser and went on to burn a hole in Earth's magnetic envelope a quarter way to the moon. Gloval's was a brave though one-shot gamble, however, exhausting the fortress's energy stores; and, as devastating as it was, the blast failed to fully nullify the force field of the unstoppable battlewagon.

It will never be known who if any aboard remained alive. But someone or some mindless system steered the cruiser into a suicidal ballistic dive, even while the drained fortress was falling back into the lake, the booms of the main gun disintegrating on descent. The last words to reach the RDF's shielded command bunker in Macross City were Lisa Hayes's: *"Brace for impact!"* only moments before Henry Gloval and Claudia Grant forced Hayes into an emergency escape module and ejected her to safety.

Generals Reinhardt and Maistroff, eyes fixed on video screens in the bunker, had watched as the incendiary javelin that was Khyron's ship streaked between the main gun booms and sheared off the command tower before plunging into the lake. Knocked backward by the force of the impact, the SDF-1 seemed to go into spasms as it settled deeper into the now frothing water, liquid fire and massive steam clouds rising around it, throwing the winter sky into utter confusion.

And soon the snow began to fall . . .

"I keep thinking back to my first experience of this ship," Emil Lang was telling Lazlo Zand in the midst of their final tour through the corpse of the SDF-1, two weeks after the funeral ceremony. Lang's tone of voice was nostalgic, even mournful. He aimed a meaningful look at Zand through the tinted faceplate of the antihazard suit. "This ship changed my life, Lazlo."

Zand smirked and keyed the privacy communicator built into the suit's hood. "Safe to say it changed all our lives, Doctor."

Lang was chagrined, but only for a moment. A highly competitive colleague, Zand refused to grant that Lang might have been changed more than most—though Zand knew full well that it was true. "This was where Gloval ordered us to split into two teams," Lang went on, indicating a narrow corridor of glassy alloy. "Naturally, the ceiling was much higher then, and the ductwork is our own, retrofitted while we were returning from Plutospace."

Zand glanced around but said nothing. In the faint illumination provided by the bipedal drone-light that accompanied them, the corridor looked as if it had been finished in bold stripes, though in fact the stripes were scorch marks six feet wide.

Lang pointed starboard, to an enormous mass of slagged metal that had been a generator of some sort. "Gloval, Edwards, and I went this way. Roy Fokker led his group of marines along the port side."

Lang was a sturdy man of average height, normal looking except for his eyes, which seemed to be all dark, deep pupil, lacking iris or white. A souvenir from his initial penetration of the SDF-1 fifteen years earlier, when the ship was known as the Visitor.

The term *visitor* referred to the fact that the ship's seemingly calculated descent and controlled crash on Macross

Island hinted at the potential for an equally calculated lift-off at some future date. At the time, Lang had proposed calling it the *tease*.

Zand was bonier and slightly taller, with an unruly fore-lock of dark hair streaked with strands of premature gray. He was attached to the Special Protoculture Observations and Operations Kommandatura, and he answered directly to Lang. Laboratory-bound in Macross City's Robotech Research Center for the past two years, Zand had only been aboard the SDF-1 on one other occasion, and he suspected that Lang had deliberately kept him away from the ship. That he had been invited on this, the last tour before the fortress was to be buried, had only added to an ever-increasing feeling of vexation.

They had just traveled downship from the hold in which Macross Two had been housed during the SDF-1's journey home from the outer reaches of the Solar system. Further downship were the engine rooms and the now cold and hollow bellies of the reflex furnaces. Elsewhere in the ship, Dr. Bronson, Ambassador Exedore, and Breetai were searching for any Protoculture-driven components that might be usable for mecha reconfiguration—mechamorphosis. Though Micronized for the tour, Breetai was still a giant of a man, eight feet tall from the soles of his jackboots to the crown of the hastily fashioned cowl that covered the ruined side of his face.

Previous surveys had established that there was little worth salvaging from the fortress, or, for that matter, from the submerged SDF-2, which had been explored by teams of underwater specialists. The ship's mother computer, known as EVE, had been moved to the Robotech Research Center in Tokyo shortly before Khyron's raid; and most of the remaining systems were so damaged that the process of dismantling and removing them would have proven more costly than fabricating them from scratch in the null-g heart of the factory satellite. As well, there were health and psychological reasons for laying the SDF-1 to rest as expeditiously as possible.

"It was somewhere near here that Fokker's team was attacked by the mecha that killed Cesar Hersch," Lang said, several minutes further along. "When I think of all the men who died on even that first recon ... Jenkins, Caruthers, Lance Corporal Murphy ..." He stopped to look around and his words trailed off. "Colonel Edwards and I are the only ones left."

The story of that initial recon was well known among the elite science corp of the RDF: the reconfiguring ship, the encounters with forty-foot-tall mecha, the rewiring of Robbie the Robot, the attacks, the rotting carcasses of dead giants. However, the tale had been so exaggerated and flavored with anecdotes over the years that it had become difficult to separate what was true from what was legend. The story about Gloval's chronometer, for example. On emerging from the fortress, the team reckoned that they had been inside the ship for six hours, when in fact the recon had lasted only fifteen minutes. Then there was the oft-repeated tale of Lang's IQ-boosting encounter with a piece of alien technology.

Zand was obsessed with the story, and he made reference to it now, interrupting Lang's comments about Colonel Edwards. "I'd like to see where it happened, Doctor."

Lang's eyes narrowed perceptibly behind the suit's faceplate. "Where what happened, Lazlo?"

"The event that changed your life."

Lang nodded in revelation. "I'm afraid that's impossible."

"I thought as much," Zand said nastily. "I was simply wondering if it might not work a second time, on a second person. Or am I being impertinent by even asking?"

Lang planted his gloved hands on his hips. "First of all, to this day I don't know precisely which system I activated to generate the power surge. One minute I was listening to Zor's onscreen message of counsel, and the next thing I knew I was regaining consciousness atop Roy Fokker's shoulders."

He gestured broadly to an array of blackened modules and fused components. "I've spent fifteen years with this ship, Lazlo. I know it intimately, head to toe. But even at the end I could do little more than throw the proper switches—this one to fire the main gun, that one to effect a modular transformation, the other one to initiate a Daedalus maneuver. But ask me to explain how any of those systems worked, and all I can do is shrug.

"More importantly, Lazlo, when I say it's impossible for you to view the site of my encounter, I simply mean that nothing remains of the cabin where it occurred."

"Zor's quarters, I believe," Zand said. "The cabin you saw fit to make your own for all those fifteen years."

The helmet pickups amplified Lang's forced exhale. "I make no secret of feeling a sense of kinship with Zor—in attitude if not intellectual prowess. But I'm not being proprietary with the technology he bequeathed us, if that's what you're thinking. For God's sake, do you think I'm in favor of having this ship buried when we've barely scratched the surface in comprehending it?" Anger had crept into his voice. "My artificially boosted IQ is irrelevant. Besides, I have something of equal importance to show you."

Neither man spoke while Lang led the way through a labyrinth of corridors and down several stairways into an immense hold in the groin of the ship. The obedient dronelight trained its beam on a cluster of towering columnar containers, which Zand recognized as Protoculture conversion modules, supplying reserve power to the Reflex drives.

Protoculture was the essence of Robotechnology, its fundamental fuel, its life's blood. Believed to be derived from an alien plant known by the Zentraedi as the Flower of Life, Protoculture infused the inanimate with a kind of lifelike willfulness. It functioned as a mediator between animate minds and mechanical systems, imparting to the latter the faculty to shape-shift, to reconfigure. More, it had the power to perform that same magic on the fabric of spacetime, enabling ships like those that had carried the Zentraedi to Earth to fold near-instantaneously across distances of millions of light-years.

"What exactly am I supposed to be looking at?" Zand asked impatiently.

Lang gestured to an empty area in the center of the hold. "That was where the fold generators stood before our inadvertent jump to Plutospace."

"The ones that got away," Zand said, chuckling.

"I've been asking myself ever since where they vanished to, and whether someday they might not rematerialize, unbidden." Lang took a few steps toward the empty area. "Another reason I'm against interring the ship. Think what we could do if we had those generators now. Think, so to speak, of the *time* we could save."

Zand regarded him dubiously. "Am I expected to help you look for them?"

"Of course not," Lang said, storming away, then whirling on Zand in obvious agitation. "I want you to know if you *feel* anything from this space, or perhaps from the Reflex drives. Something unseen. Some lingering . . . presence."

Zand saw immediately that Lang was dead serious, so he shut his mouth and tried to attune himself with whatever it was Lang was sensing. But it was hopeless. He would never be able to feel what Lang felt—not without first having his own mind enhanced.

Lang was gazing at the Reflex array. "If I had another week, Lazlo . . . If Milburn and the rest of those visionless politicians could only understand . . ." The helmet pickups betrayed his private laugh. "I'd begin by dismantling each of these drives."

"Then you do have some idea of what you're looking for."

Lang snorted a laugh. "Not really. Perhaps something Zor concealed here for reasons we may never grasp. Something I fear will remain alive in this ship despite our best efforts to bury it."

In the Macross Council's transitional headquarters in Monument City, Council President Braxton Milburn was hurrying through the promotions in an attempt to move on to matters of more pressing concern. The unmistakable urgency in Milburn's voice grated on Lisa Hayes. Important moments should never be rushed, she thought, and this moment had importance written all over it.

"Captain Hunter," Milburn said in his signature Deep South drawl, "will you rise and approach."

Lisa's heart pounded. She glanced down the length of the

long table, watching Rick rise and give a smart tug to his uniform jacket before setting out.

Milburn, overweight and jowly, had the head of the table. On his right sat Brigadier General Gunther Reinhardt, bald and bearded, and across from Reinhardt, the preternaturally tall Philipe Longchamps. Lisa was seated midway along, on Reinhardt's side of the table, in among other council members and RDF officers. Those officers receiving promotions—Rick, Vince Grant, Jim Forsythe, and a dozen others—were assembled at a second table. The room's window wall looked out on the copse of Quickform skyscrapers that was the city center.

Rick looked dashing. His thick black hair was neatly tucked behind his ears, and the high-necked blue yoke of the double-breasted jacket brought out the sea blue in his eyes. Lisa could barely keep from grinning, though when she swiveled to face Reinhardt once more, a shudder of misgiving passed through her. Would Rick fit in among the general staff? She pushed the thought aside as quickly as it had surfaced. Of course he would; he was made to lead.

"Captain Hunter," Milburn said, rising from his chair when Rick had stepped onto the low platform that had been erected for the ceremony. "In recognition of countless acts of bravery performed in the service of the Defense Force, and in heartfelt appreciation of your contributions to the civilian cause throughout this difficult period of reconstruction, and lastly in acknowledgment of your donations to the design of the Expeditionary mission—notably in the aftermath of the destruction of Macross—we, members of the council and the RDF, wish at this time to confer on you a much-deserved and perhaps long-overdue promotion in rank."

Lisa grinned despite herself. She'd fought hard to bring this about for Rick, insisting that he receive at least some of the credit for proposing to use Breetai's ship in the mission to Tirol, and for organizing the relocation of Macross's uprooted civilian population. No sooner did Rick begin to speak, however, than her smile faded.

"Sirs, Council Members," he said, "may I first say how honored I am. But I would be, uh, remiss if I didn't address some of my concerns about this promotion. I'm proud of what I've been able to contribute as a captain, leader of the Skull Veritechs, but I feel that a promotion to full-bird colonel—"

"Captain Hunter," Milburn said, "I'm sorry to interrupt, but you misunderstand."

Rick's left brow arched. "Huh? Well, of course I meant to say *lieutenant* colonel. But that doesn't change my feelings any. Sirs. I mean, it's—"

"Mr. Hunter." It was Reinhardt now, wearing a look of mild bemusement. "We're going to have to keep interrupting if you persist in making mistakes."

All along the table, secret looks of amusement were exchanged.

"Not lieutenant colonel?" Rick said. "Then, sirs, I'm afraid I'm at a loss . . ."

Milburn cleared his throat with meaning. "No reason to be, Vice Admiral Hunter."

Everyone in the room rose and saluted, then broke into applause while Rick stood staring at the white command cap Milburn was proffering. Clapping louder than any of them, Lisa fought back an impulse to run to Rick and fling her arms around him—if for no other reason than to shake him out of apparent shock.

"Begging your pardon, sir," Rick managed at last, his voice cracking, "but I'm only twenty-three years old!"

Everyone but Lisa laughed.

"Age isn't a factor in these crucial times," Milburn said. "It's all about being able to lead, Admiral. To shoulder responsibility. To do the job that needs doing. And all of us in this room are confident you can do just that."

"But what job—exactly, I mean."

"Admiral Hayes," Reinhardt said, looking at her.

Lisa turned to Rick, all traces of the smile gone. She was the career officer now, as she had to be. "Admiral Hunter," she began. "It will be your responsibility to supervise and direct all strategic operations relevant to the Expeditionary mission, including but not restricted to the requisitioning of armaments and mecha, and the selection and tasking of all key mission personnel, who, from now on, will be known as the Robotech Expeditionary Force."

Rick was gaping at her. "But that's supposed to be your job, Lis—uh, Admiral Hayes."

Lisa squared her shoulders, faintly annoyed. "My job, as you refer to it, Admiral, will be overseeing the construction of those areas of the SDF-3 that will be allocated to the REF. Is that understood?"

Rick gulped and found his voice. "Understood, Admiral." He saluted, but refused to meet her eye while he was returning to his seat.

The promotions completed, Milburn directed everyone's attention to the next item on the agenda: plans for housing the Defense Force in what had been Monument's Excaliber base. Follow-up discussions centered on contingency plans for constructing an entirely new base should the Zentraedi-dominated Monument City Council object to the RDF's presence.

Lisa scarcely heard any of it, caught up as she was in mulling over new concerns about Rick. Had she made a mistake, not only in judging who he was but what he was capable of? Would the promotion become an issue in their private life as well?

It wasn't until Captain Rolf Emerson stood up to deliver his report that Lisa regained focus. Young, cleancut, and handsome, Emerson was in charge of liaison with RDF units in the Southlands. Lisa had met him through the Grants and liked him.

"I have troubling news," Emerson began, his fine features mirroring the gravity of his voice. "Khyron's death has had a significant effect on Zentraedi concentrations in the Southlands. Most refuse to believe that he's dead, and many of those that do, believe that the RDF purposely destroyed the cruiser to prevent him from leaving Earth.

"The point is that his death has given the so-called demobilized hostiles something new and powerful to rally around. Coupled with food shortages and a sharp increase in discrimination as a result of what happened in Macross, the situation has become volatile, and we're going to have to act fast if we want to diffuse it. I realize that food is in short supply here, but if the North doesn't at least share what it has with the South, we could be facing a full-scale uprising in a matter of months."

Emerson paused to catch his breath. "Khyron might be dead, sirs, but his spirit is very much alive."

"It's a piece of Khyron Kravshera's skull," Exedore said evenly. "From the right parietal region, I would venture."

Lang regarded their grisly find with a mix of awe and revulsion. Large as a dinosaur's bone, the blood-encrusted thing bore traces of long bluish hair. Lang was glad to be wearing the NBC suit, and doubly glad that nothing comparable—from Gloval, say, or Claudia Grant—had been discovered aboard the SDF-1.

Lang, Exedore, and Zand were in a previously unsearched compartment in the tail section of the Zentraedi cruiser. The ship's blunt bow was buried deep in the lakebottom sludge, but its clefted stern had been raised from the water by giant cranes set atop the backward-leaning shoulders of the SDF-1.

Zand's gloved hand lifted a stiff strand of hair, eight feet long. "Are you certain?" he asked Exedore.

"Quite certain, Professor. I had many dealings with the leader of the Botoru Battalion previous to his enlistment in the campaign to reclaim Zor's dimensional fortress. However, as to how this piece of skull landed here, so far from the ship's bridge, one can only speculate."

Sealed inside an unnecessary antihazard suit, Exedore was simply a small man, though in fact he was hunchbacked, almost dwarfish, with mauve skin, a misshapen head, and pinpoint-pupiled eyes. He had barely escaped Khyron's raid on Macross, having returned to the factory satellite a day earlier.

Lang had no reason to argue with Exedore's assessment of the skull, though unlike Exedore, he had only seen Khyron once, and onscreen at that: the previous year, when the Backstabber had issued his ransom demands for hostages Lynn-Minmei and Lynn-Kyle. Even so, Lang recalled Khyron's slate-blue hair, the mannered voice, the condescending laugh.

The two Humans and the Zentraedi were still gawking at the bone fragment when Breetai and Bronson, a mecha-design specialist, appeared from an adjoining hold. Breetai was carrying what might have been the pincers of a gigantic lobster, save that they had been fashioned from some unidentifiable barn-red alloy and were studded with a trio of huge, glistening claws.

"Something that might interest you, Doctor Lang," Breetai announced in booming voice, carefully setting the pincers down on the deck. "Something from Khyron's collection of war trophies." He gestured to the adjacent hold. "The body these were attached to is in there."

Lang circled the pincers, studying them in silence. "They share some similarity to the arms of Male Power Armor."

"As well they might," Exedore said with transparent amusement, "since they were modeled after our battle suits."

"Interesting," Lang said. "I know I've seen them before, but if they're not part of the Zentraedi's arsenal . . ." He started to shake his head in defeat, and then it struck him: *Zor* had shown them to him in the warning message he had programmed into the SDF-1's mother computer. Lang was getting his first up-close look at pieces of an Invid weapon.

CHAPTER THREE

LAPSTEIN: *Does the process (of Micronization) produce a change in consciousness as well as a change in size?*

EXEDORE FORMO: *Only that which might be expected from suddenly having to address the world as a five-footer after having known it as a forty-footer.*

LAPSTEIN: *Does one experience a sense of disempowerment?*

EXEDORE: *Not in the way you mean it. Micronization was always purposeful, something undertaken in service to the Imperative. As a result, one feels "weaker" to some extent, but never disempowered.*

LAPSTEIN: *What purpose did the Robotech Masters have in mind when they used Protoculture to encode Zentraedi DNA with the capability to reconfigure?*

EXEDORE: *I should think the answer would be obvious: Micronized, the Zentraedi could be shipped by the tens of thousands to areas of contest, and once there, returned to full size to carry out the Imperative to kill and conquer.*

Lapstcin, *Interviews*

SO EXTREME WAS THE PUNISHMENT VISITED ON EARTH during the conclusive battle between the RDF and the Zentraedi that vast stretches of continental coastline and shelf had been altered beyond recognition. From the command center of his boulderlike deepspace stronghold, Dolza, Commander-in-Chief of the Zentraedi, had ordered his battle-group captains to target only those areas found to be richest in Human life as revealed by the warships' bioscanners.

The South American littoral, no exception to Dolza's homicidal wrath, was in moments forever changed. Death dropped in oscillating cyan waves on Lima, Caracas, Bahia, Rio de Janeiro, São Paulo, and Montevideo . . . In hellish quanta, death rained down the triple spines of the Andes Mountains, from Bogotá to Quito to Cuzco, then east in a sweeping curve across Lake Titicaca to La Paz, Sucre, and Cochabamba, and south through Arequipa and Santiago to Bariloche. Once-grand capitals and high-valley colonial gems suffered more than they ever had from Earth's tectonic violence, crumbling into themselves like scraps of burning paper. Rivers and lakes surrendered to heat as searing as from an exploding star. Millions of lives were extinguished in the drawing of a breath, the blink of an eye.

But most of the continent's "Micronian" hot spots were oceanside, and much of the forested interior was spared, from Manaus on the Amazon River to as far south as the Chaco, in Argentina. And it was into this relatively cool and unscathed parcel of land, this enormous sunlit oval of uninhabited jungle, savannah, and turbulent rivers, that thousands of crippled Zentraedi ships nose-dived in the end moments of the War.

Most of the goliath alien clones who climbed from the wreckage of those ships soon died of blood loss, starvation, or illness. But some managed to find their way north across Central America into what had once been the United States. They traveled in groups a hundred strong on a pilgrimage of sorts, a journey meant to deliver them to the dainty feet of their idol: to Lynn-Minmei—Min*may*—the woman/ weapon who was largely responsible for their unprecedented defeat. In honor of her, many submitted to the process of Micronization, while others did so to renounce the counterfeit past that was their racial history. Those that chose to remain full-size were persuaded to lend their strength to the massive projects that typified the reconstruction, helping to reassemble factories, airports, and residential buildings—to put the planet back together. And indeed many, as a result, experienced a peace they had never known, a new security.

Others, however, within whom the Masters' embedded Imperative to kill and conquer burned strongest, left their jobs to wander the unpoliced, radioactive wastes, or to ally themselves with Khyron and eventually die with him in the skies over Macross.

By May of 2015, the only remaining full-size Zentraedi had been lofted to the factory satellite or were living in the

north—in Monument, Denver, Portland, or on the Arkansas
Protectorate. Their Micronized brethren, on the other hand,
were dispersed throughout the world; but nowhere were
their numbers greater than in the city-states and polities of
the Southlands, which had a long history of racial tolerance.

Karita was one of those who had come south in search
of what he hadn't been able to find in two years of living
in the north. Unfortunately, those who'd sung the praises of
the promised land had neglected to mention anything about
food shortages.

"I'm telling you people for the last time," a man was
saying in a pidgin of Portuguese and English from the hood
of an ancient gasoline-burning pickup truck, "let us pass—
now."

The pickup was the first in a convoy of food trucks
bound for the city of Cuiabá. But positioned between the
convoy and Cuiabá just now was a crowd of some sixty
hungry and disheveled-looking Zentraedi men and women.

"You have to learn to fend for yourselves," the man continued. "Our land is already overworked. The fields can
only yield so much. And we're not about to supply you
with food when there are children with empty bellies right
here in Mato Grosso."

Cuiabá, in southwestern Amazonia, was where Karita
had ultimately landed, dispirited and out of scrip after
countless weeks of hard traveling on river barges and de-
crepit buses and trucks. Fragile, narrow-faced, and white-
haired, he had been the tender of a sizing chamber aboard
Breetai's flagship, and one of the first to join the Minmay
Cult, founded by the defectors Rico, Konda, and Bron. On
Earth, after the defeat, he had worked for a time in a factory, installing Protoculture chips in mecha neurocircuitry
boards.

The man on the hood was thickly built and dark-
complected, the owner of a large ranch in the hills. "Clear
the road and allow us to pass. We don't want to have to re-
sort to force."

"And neither do we," a man answered from the
Zentraedi side of the crude wooden barricades Karita and
the rest had erected across the roadway. Tall and lean, with

dark hair and a full beard, he was not Zentraedi but one of those peculiar Humans who, for reasons seldom clear, had made a personal cause of the alien predicament. "We are assembled here in nonviolent protest of Cuiabá's discriminatory policies," he shouted in English, the second language of most of the Zentraedi present. "Ours is an act of civil disobedience. But yours is in violation of civil rights edicts issued by the Macross Council in 2013."

The rancher scowled in anger. "Macross is a memory, friend. And things have changed a lot since 2013. You want to champion their rights, that's okay with me. But do it someplace where there's food enough to go around."

Karita was sorry to see that the advocate didn't have a comeback line prepared. But what was there to say, really? Nothing had changed for Karita since the defeat. He'd known some wonderful moments in the north, especially the previous spring when he and thousands of like-minded Zentraedi had spent weeks following Minmei from arena to arena on her "People Helping People Tour"—Monument, Granite City, Portland, Detroit . . . But he had grown disenchanted with his life in Macross. Not that the work wasn't satisfying, but he was treated with such contempt by so many people. Once, the famous Veritech pilot, Max Sterling, had had to rescue him from a near beating by two racist RDFers.

But he and most of the others who had come south were not the disaffected—the malcontent—but merely the dispirited, shamed by defeat and now further shamed by having to subsist on the charity of Humans who were skilled in ways few Zentraedi could comprehend, much less imitate. Humans who understood the secrets of creating, manufacturing, and repairing; of working with domesticated animals and coaxing food from Earth's fecund mantle. So why was it so difficult for them in turn to understand what the Zentraedi were going through?

"You do have food enough to go around," the advocate responded at last. "It would just mean a little less for everyone at the distribution center. We're not asking for any more than an equal share, as is our right under the law."

"We?" the rancher said, switching to Portuguese. "Have you forgotten what planet you were born on?"

The advocate laughed in derision. "Planets, countries, cities ... Only a fool would make places more important than people. What matters is that all of us are *Human*!"

"I think I remember that one from Detroit," said the Zentraedi woman pressed against Karita's left arm, indicating the advocate with her chin while the crowds on both sides of the barricades exchanged threats. "He was always quick to step into our troubles."

Close fraternization between male and female Zentraedi was something Karita was still getting used to, but he had gotten to know this female along the route south. Her name was Marla Stenik, and during the war she had served Azonia, commander of the all-female Quadrono Battalion. Petite and blond, she had what Humans would consider boyish good looks.

Bagzent, the beefy, red-haired Zentraedi crushed against Karita's other arm, answered Marla. "You're right about him. He convinced the mayor to keep the sizing chamber in Detroit instead of allowing it to be turned over to the RDF."

Bagzent would know, Karita thought. Bagzent had quit his work in Macross to join Khyron at the crashsite of his cruiser, north of Detroit in the Canada Sector. There, Bagzent had undergone voluntary Micronization in order to take part in Khyron's raid on Detroit to steal the sizing chamber, only to end up incarcerated in that city by the RDF for more than a year. In false refutation of that past, a plastic miniature Minmei doll dangled from a thong around Bagzent's thick neck.

Marla had her mouth open to say something when two large though Humanlike forms darkened the sky overhead. Moments later, with a familiar roar, a pair of Battloid-configured Veritechs put down on either side of the convoy, close enough for the crafts' fusion-turbine foot thrusters to raise a swirling storm of small stones and dirt. The forty-foot-tall Robotech titans stood facing the Zentraedi cordon, autocannons in gauntleted hands.

"This food shipment is designated for the Mato Grosso

Distribution Center in Cuiabá," one of the pilots announced over the mecha's loudspeaker. "Since that center is under the jurisdiction of the RDF South, your interference violates RDF statutes and you will therefore be subject to arrest and possible imprisonment if you fail to disband and allow the convoy to pass. If you want food, report to the center like everyone else."

"And be told that there isn't enough to go around?" someone behind Bagzent shouted.

"You will be fed," the other pilot said when the crowd had quieted somewhat. "You have our word on it."

"We piss on your word!" Bagzent yelled.

The Battloids raised their weapons and took a ground-shaking forward step. Reflexively, the crowd backed away. Everyone grasped the futility of resisting. But even as the Zentraedi were beginning to disperse, Karita could hear the rumblings of malcontentism among the dispirited.

Bagzent's basso voice was loudest of all.

"It won't always be like this," he grumbled. "Every day the reconstructed cities of the north lose some of their trained Zentraedi workers to our cause. We may never learn agriculture or aquaculture, but we won't need to raise vegetables or fish once we've begun to *take* what we need."

For emphasis, he viced his big hand around the Mandarin-robed Minmei doll and squeezed it until it shattered.

"Miss Macross of 2010, pin-up and poster celebrity during the War, singer, actress, prototype for a line of squeezable toys and mechanical dolls, heroine . . . The first thing I want to ask is: What comes next for Lynn-Minmei?"

Minmei feigned a good-spirited laugh. "Katherine, you must be reading my mind, because that's exactly the question I've been asking myself for the past few months." She shook her raven-black hair for the number-one camera, but kept her blue eyes on Katherine's, since the idea of the interview—in the fin de siècle tradition perfected by Barbara Walters and Rachel Poriskova—was to beguile viewers into imagining that they were eavesdropping on a conversation between close friends.

In fact, Katherine Hyson and Lynn-Minmei had met only hours earlier, but Minmei already liked the young, telegenic MBS broadcaster and was eager to help Hyson's career along if she could. Conveniently, though the *M* in MBS had once stood for Macross, it now stood for Monument City.

"And have any answers to that question presented themselves?" Hyson asked.

Minmei adopted an earnest look. "Actually, I've been thinking of doing some television work."

It was Hyson's turn to perform. "I hope you're not planning a series of celebrity interviews . . ."

"No, I'll leave that to you, Katherine. What I'd like to do is find some way to use television to reach those areas of the world where people are still struggling to rebuild and make meaningful contributions to the future."

Katherine offered an approving nod. "Talk about meaningful contributions."

They were seated face-to-face on the spacious lanai of a house owned by Japanese friends of Minmei—the son and daughter-in-law of her aunt Lena's first cousin. The multilevel teak and glass house perched on the north shore of Kauai; the comfortable chairs were made of rattan; and the salt-weathered deck overhung the ocean. Hyson was a slim and pretty brunette with large green eyes under pencil-thin brows, and a rosebud mouth lipsticked in a pale shade that made Minmei think of Claudia Grant. Hyson had jumped at the chance of interviewing Minmei in Hawaii, and in gratitude had promised Minmei an entire hour of airtime rather than the standard twenty-two-minute segment.

"I assume that your reaching out will include singing," Hyson said now.

"Some, yes. But I'll never again allow my voice to be used as a weapon."

"Surely you don't regret what your voice accomplished during the War?"

Minmei shook her head. "But I had no choice in the matter then. All I ever wanted was to bring happiness to people. Singing is my way of communicating love. But instead I wound up bringing an army to its knees."

"Someone once said that celebrity chooses us, and not the other way around."

"I think that's true. And it often introduces the best and the worst things to one's life. When I read about celebrities who are troubled by stalking fans, I want to tell them what it feels like to have an entire *race* wanting to know your every move."

Minmei's sudden introspection was genuine, and Hyson pursued it. "Lynn-Kyle, your cousin and co-star in *Little White Dragon*, played a part in shaping your career. Why didn't that partnership survive?"

"Kyle was pushing me too hard to become political at a time when I wasn't ready for that. As I said, I only wanted to use my voice to bring joy to people."

"Was it an amicable parting?"

"Not entirely."

"Have you talked to him since?"

Minmei recalled the littered black-sand beach in Monument where they said good-bye. Where Kyle had accused her of being immature and selfish. "No, I haven't," she told Hyson. "I don't even know where he is."

Hyson was perceptive enough to move on. "I know that you fired your manager, Vance Hasslewood. Any new management on the horizon?"

"I've been talking to some people."

"Would Sharky O'Toole be one of them?"

Minmei rocked her head from side to side, evasively.

"Let's touch for a moment on your abduction last year by Khyron," Hyson said. "Is it true that he was immune to the power of your singing?"

"He told me that he despised my singing." Minmei laughed into her hand. "But he did say that I was a well-built little thing—if my feminist sisters will forgive me."

"What did you tell him?"

"I called him a big, overgrown clown."

Hyson's jaw fell. "Another first in your career. And did you actually see Khyron and Azonia kiss?"

"Yes, though I wouldn't call it a passionate kiss. Kyle and I both saw them. Azonia referred to it as a 'demonstration,' because that's what Breetai called it when he ordered

Rick Hunter and Lisa Hayes to kiss in front of him."
Minmei blushed and angled her face away from cameras
one and two.

Hyson was shaking her head in wonderment. "I want to
get back to Rick Hunter in a moment, but before that, why
do you think that Khyron . . . spared you and Kyle, even
when he realized that he'd been duped and that your rescue
was imminent?"

"Because it isn't the Zentraedi way to take hostages,
much less kill them. He never understood that the RDF
might lie to him about ransoming Kyle and myself with the
SDF-1."

"I see," Hyson said. "What are your thoughts about the
malcontents?"

Minmei handled the question easily. "I'm a Humanist,
Katherine; I don't react to groups, but to individuals. The
Zentraedi are stranded here, strangers in a strange land, and
I think we have to keep that foremost in mind before we
condemn any of their actions."

Hyson leaned toward Minmei, confrontational suddenly.
"But, Minmei, you're not sanctioning what they've done—
raiding food depots, destroying factories, wreaking havoc
on remote settlements?"

"It isn't my place to sanction anyone or anything,"
Minmei said. "I'm only saying that we have to sympathize
with the torment they're going through. Machines saw to
all their needs, and now we're the only ones they have to
turn to."

Hyson considered it. "Some might say that this sounds
like something you picked up from Lynn-Kyle, in his guise
as pacifist and advocate of Zentraedi rights."

Minmei frowned. "Kyle taught me many things. One of
which was to regard all worlds and all peoples as equal.
With the issues Earth is facing now, Humankind—Terran
and Zentraedi—can't afford to be divided."

"Are you supportive of the Expeditionary mission to
Tirol?"

"I'm one hundred percent behind it."

"Has the REF asked you to join the mission?"

Minmei smiled lightly. "It's going to be a diplomatic mission. The REF doesn't need an entertainer."

"Speaking of the REF, there's a rumor that you and Vice Admiral Hunter were engaged shortly before Khyron's raid on Macross."

"Let's just say that we toyed with the idea of marriage. But as much as I care for him, I couldn't allow him to resign from the RDF. Earth needs leaders like Rick, and I couldn't allow my own selfish needs to come first."

Hyson grinned. "The problems of two people don't amount to a hill of beans in this crazy world, right?"

Minmei frowned, missing what she knew was a reference to some old movie or song. "I guess so."

"So in the twenty-first century, it's *Rick* who gets on the plane to carry on the fight."

Minmei's look of uncertainty held. "Uh—"

"But the two of you have remained close friends?"

"Oh, we're the best of friends. I've always seen us as star-crossed, from the day the Zentraedi attacked Macross Island to reclaim the SDF-1."

Hyson gave the camera operators ample time to close on Minmei's flawlessly beautiful face. "When were your happiest times?"

Minmei thought for a moment. "Aboard the SDF-1, as strange as that might sound. Living in rebuilt Macross before the War had completely dominated all our lives. Before I was voted Miss Macross." She looked into the camera. "That's why I couldn't bring myself to attend the funeral last month. I prefer to live with my memories instead of burying them."

A full month of work by demolition and reclamation crews had reduced much of Macross City to rubble. Leveled were some sites that had appeared in three incarnations—on Macross Island, inboard the SDF-1, and under the Big Sky of the Northwest: the Hotel Centinel, which had hosted hundreds of celebrity fetes before and after the War; the White Dragon Chinese Restaurant, owned by Lynn-Kyle's parents, Max and Lena; the Kindest Cut Steak House, favorite haunt of the late Veritech ace Ben

Dixon; the Variations and Seciele Coffee Shops, where Lisa Hayes had passed many an off-duty hour; the Pub, where Roy Fokker and friends had partied hard to the fusion jazz of the Black Katz; the Close Encounters Video Arcade, where Max Sterling had bested Miriya Parino at *Veritechs*!; John's Cabaret, where Minmei had often performed; the Bamboo Club, where Rico, Konda, and Bron had first met "the terrible trio" of Sammie, Vanessa, and Kim; and the Onagi Central Theater, where the computer-generated Bob Hope/Bing Crosby film *Road to India* had been playing when Khyron attacked . . .

Immeasurable tons of irradiated wood, aluminum, steel, glass, plastic, and concrete had been bulldozed into the crater lake. Then additional tons of specially treated sand and gravel and lead pellets were dropped by formations of C-150 cargo planes, until the lake was completely filled in, and what had once been Macross was little more than an immense, vaguely circular plateau, from the center of which rose three tellurian buttes, marking the resting places of Khyron's cruiser and the SDFs 1 and 2.

It was Earth's newest national monument.

At the same time Minmei was being interviewed by Katherine Hyson, Rory Lightfoot, a barrel-chested operating engineer of Cree descent, was standing on the running board of his idling bulldozer, clapping dirt from his gloved hands and the durable thighs of his antihazard suit. He spent a long moment gazing at the tor that was the buried SDF-1, then turned to his partner, who was seated in the cab of the massive machine.

"I've got two last words for that ship," Lightfoot said over the helmet intercom. "Good riddance."

CHAPTER FOUR

Being inside [the factory satellite] is like being inside an inverted mechanized jellyfish with thousands of tentacles at work, building yet another mechanized behemoth inside its own monstrous belly.

Emil Lang's technical recordings and notes

T WAS A GLORIOUS JUNE MORNING IN THE NORTHWEST: not a cloud in the sky and the mountainsides verdant with burgeoning growths of lodgepole pine and western larch. Fencing the sinuous river that flowed north toward Monument City were cottonwoods and aspen. The gray, military limousine had the asphalt road to itself, save for the occasional double-trailered truck hauling goods south to Denver or Albuquerque.

Rick and Lisa were at opposite ends of the limo's roomy rear seat, turned away from one another. The tinted privacy partition was raised and conditioned air whispered from the vents. They both wore dress uniforms, though their white command caps sat on the deck of the rear window. Of the frowns they also wore, Rick's was the more pronounced.

"I suppose you would have rather walked to Fokker Base," Lisa said, looking over at him—her first words since the curt hellos they had exchanged when the chauffeur, a warrant officer, collected Rick at his house.

Rick glanced at her but said nothing.

"Well, not to worry, Admiral," Lisa said. "I'm sure no

one at Fokker will interfere if you decide to fly Skull One to the factory instead of riding the shuttle."

Rick swung away from the side window. For two months now they had been tiptoeing around the issue of his promotion, but enough was enough. "I have no problem with the shuttle, Lisa. But this—" He waved his hands about, indicating the limo. "This is what I object to."

"What are we supposed to do, Rick—take a bus?"

"I just don't like the message it sends."

"Stop being ridiculous. You think people are going to begrudge us a chauffeured ride to Fokker? They know we're on important business. If I were you, I'd be more concerned with the message your attitude sends."

"My attitude? Can you blame me? You *knew* I didn't want this promotion. Why can't you see my side of it?"

"Oh, I do see your side," she answered calmly. "It's just that your thinking is warped."

"What, suddenly I'm incapable of deciding how to live my own life?"

Lisa made a fatigued sound. "You're right, Rick, I had no right to speak up for you. Maybe you were better off as a captain." Her expression hardened. "Or maybe you should have married Minmei and resigned from the RDF altogether."

Rick winced. He had hoped that Lisa hadn't seen the previous evening's telecast of Katherine Hyson's interview with Minmei.

"Yes, I saw the program," Lisa continued before he could comment. "And I'm still furious about it." She mocked Minmei's childlike voice. " 'We toyed with the idea of marriage, but as much as I cared for him, I just couldn't allow him to resign. Earth needs leaders like Rick Hunter and I couldn't allow my own selfish needs to come first.' "

Lisa's head shook in frustration. "She seems to have conveniently forgotten what she said in Macross when she found us by the lake, holding each other and crying." Her eyes bored in on Rick. "Or have you also forgotten?"

"Well, there was a lot going on—"

"All of a sudden she knew from the start that you loved me, and she hoped you could forgive her for trying to make you something you weren't—and for her pretending to be something *she* wasn't." Lisa forced an exasperated exhale. "And I didn't hear her mention anything to Katherine Hyson about how she'd discovered that she wasn't really eager to be married after all." She did her Minmei impression again: " 'Music and celebrity are my life.'

"She's rewriting history to make herself look noble to her adoring fans. That way she not only ends up with the life she wanted all along, but she evades the guilt of depriving the world of a hero—meaning *you*." Lisa held Rick's gaze. "Just imagine how it would be if you had married her. Minmei off on tour somewhere, and you left with nothing but your little fanjet."

Rick held up his hands in protest. "You know I wouldn't have resigned. All I'm saying is that I never wanted to exchange my thinking cap for a command cap." He snatched the brimmed symbol of his rank from the rear window deck and turned it about in his hands. "Anyway, I'm not convinced the Tirol mission is going to solve our problems, Lisa. There's too much work to be done right here."

Lisa softened. "Rick, I told Admiral Gloval the same thing you're telling me—that we should concentrate on rebuilding the Earth to defend it against the Masters. But Henry was convinced of the need to confront them in their own space, even if it meant going to guns with them."

Rick eyed her askance. "What happened to our 'diplomatic mission'?"

"Henry said the time had come for us to leave our cradle behind and stake our claim in space. But we can only do that when we've made peace with the Masters—or at the very least seen to it that they can't wage war."

"All the more reason for me to have stayed a captain."

Lisa shook her head. "You sell yourself short—you always have. You're capable of more than piloting a mecha and racking up enemy kills, and the Earth needs all that you have to give."

"Now you're the one making me sound like a hero."

"I'm sorry, Rick, but you are a hero. I suggest you get used to it."

Rick laughed to himself. "You know what I remember

most about that last day in Macross? Your telling Minmei that if she loved me she would let me do what I do best."

"I meant what I said."

"Yeah, but what you said was, 'He's a pilot, that's his *life*.'"

Lisa was silent for the remainder of the drive to Fokker Aerospace.

Three hours after launching, the shuttle was entering the smallest of the factory satellite's five docking bays—a recent installation, necessitated by the confounding fact that the four principal bays responded solely to Zentraedi ships.

A lieutenant colonel was on hand to meet Rick, Lisa, and the thirty-eight other officers and techs who had filled the shuttle to capacity. A second colonel, at the controls of a four-seater cart, drove Rick and Lisa to a private cabin where they could rest after the flight and acclimate to the factory's slightly-less-than-Earth-normal gravity. En route, they rode past a series of enormous viewports that opened on the factory's null-g heart, where Breetai's three-mile-long, 270,000,000-ton flagship was docked.

A fully automated repair and production station, the factory was a marvel, even by Zentraedi standards. Rose-colored and radish-shaped, with fissures and convolutions suggestive of cerebral matter, it was some twenty miles wide and could easily accommodate 1,500,000 full-size Zentraedi. At the end of transfer-tube spokes issuing from its midsection were half-a-dozen secondary pods that were hollowed asteroids. When operational, the factory could effect interior and exterior repairs on as many as ten ships simultaneously. A *Queadol-Magdomilla* like the one Khyron had commanded could be refitted with weapons, replenished with Protoculture, and restocked with battle mecha in less than eight Earth hours. For the giant warriors in wait, there were vast holds designed for exercise, recuperation, combat simulation, and resizing.

The upper eight levels of the central body were devoted to living spaces and command and control of astrogation and fold operations. The capacity of each level varied, but the height from deck to ceiling was never less than two hundred feet. The lower eight levels comprised the factory area itself. At the heart of the facility, between the two sections, was the zero-gravity chamber where flagships were overhauled.

The factory had been won from Commander Reno two years earlier in a joint Zentraedi-RDF attack led by Breetai. After Reno's defeat, it had been folded to lunar orbit, then moved under conventional power to a Lagrange point, closer to the Earth. As late as the spring of 2014, the factory had been manufacturing partially complete Tactical Battlepods, though glitches had since forced its shutdown. Doctors Lang and Bronson were understandably eager to get the thing back on-line, but they hadn't a clue as to how to do so.

Rick and Lisa's escort reappeared after three hours to convey them to a conference room located in the factory's "six o'clock" pod, the only one scaled to Human size, though the main plant abounded in cabinspaces and passageways suitable for Micronized Zentraedi. Exedore, Bronson, Harry Penn, and several others were waiting at a massive round table, which had as its centerpiece a Zentraedi projecbeam port. Sundry Human-friendly computers and an array of flatscreens had been retrofitted along the short walls of the room. Most of the long, curving outer wall was given over to a blister port which looked out on Earth.

"Breetai, along with Dr. Lang and Professor Zand, will be attending as a telepresence," Exedore explained as he was showing Rick and Lisa to their seats. His white, tight-fitting RDF uniform had gold piping, and had been tailored in a way that minimized his physical deformities. The room's harsh lighting, however, only intensified the mauve tones of his skin and drew attention to his peculiar eyes.

"Ah, here is Lord Breetai now."

Rick and Lisa turned their attention to a large screen that dominated the room's rear wall. Breetai had had himself returned to full size since the downside surveys, and back in place was the alloy half cowl that covered the horribly scarred right side of his face. In place of the dead eye beneath the cowl was a shining light-gathering crystal.

"Can you hear and see us, Your Excellency?" Exedore asked.

Breetai's voice thundered through the speakers. "Perfectly, Exedore."

A tech made hasty volume adjustments while Exedore went on to explain that Breetai was speaking from his personal cabin aboard the flagship. Lang and Zand—communicating from the Robotech Research Center in Monument—came onscreen to the left of Breetai.

Sheamus Bronson asked that everyone break the seals on the security envelopes that had been distributed and familiarize themselves with the contents. The feasibility of utilizing Breetai's leviathan to reach Tirol had been assigned top priority.

"Based on the ship's performance during the raid on Reno's forces," Lang was saying a moment later, "I'm confident that we can execute a jump to Tirolspace without depleting the fold system of the Protoculture necessary to return us to Earth. That much said, readying the mission basically entails completing the retrofitting that was begun in advance of our capture of the factory."

The hopeful murmuring that erupted around the table endured only until Exedore spoke.

"While I'm hardly the one to argue with Dr. Lang's evaluation of the fold system, I feel compelled to state that a hyperspace jump undertaken without certain precautions will end in tragedy."

When Lang asked for an explanation, Exedore deferred to Breetai, who was stroking his square chin with the fingers of his left hand. "Dr. Lang, you have overlooked the fact that Commander Reno was expecting us when we folded to the factory. Dolza had of course informed him that I had become Admiral Gloval's ally in the fight for the SDF-1."

"But Reno and his forces are dead," Dr. Bronson thought to point out. His full beard, thick hair, and flaring eyebrows lent a disturbing intensity to an otherwise handsome face.

"If Reno knew, the Masters know," Breetai told him.

Lang was nodding his head. "The Masters will launch an

attack the moment the flagship defolds in the Valivarre system."

"Is there a way to make the ship unrecognizable to the Masters?" Lisa asked.

Exedore turned to her. "With the destruction of the Grand Fleet, the Invid are surely ravaging the Masters' empire and closing on Tirol. The Masters will be doubly wary of *any* incursions into the Valivarre system of worlds."

Zand started to ask if Exedore was suggesting they scrap the mission, but Lang cut him off.

"He's proposing that we alter the signature of the flagship to mimic one that the Masters would welcome. Am I correct, Exedore?"

"Correct, Dr. Lang. The best solution would be to restructure the ship along the lines of Zor's dimensional fortress. If the Masters can be deceived into believing that Zor's ship—"

"Impossible," Bronson said. "If we had twenty years, if we had a century, we couldn't redesign the flagship to reconfigure. We could barely get the SDF-2 to sit up straight."

Again, Zand started to speak only to be interrupted by Lang. "We might attempt to mimic the *look* of the SDF-1 in cruiser mode. Needless to say, we'd also have to alter the Reflex engines to produce a different energy signature . . ."

Rick broke the short silence.

"I don't see the point of spending years redesigning Breetai's ship on the *chance* that the Masters will be duped. We'd be better off using the time to rebuild the Defense Force. By itself, the flagship packs awesome firepower, and if we could get the factory to start producing Battlepods again . . . I mean, how can we be sure the Masters even know where to come looking for us? Breetai didn't tell them, and we don't know that Dolza did, even if he did tell Reno about Breetai's, uh, defection."

Rick was suddenly aware that everyone at the table, Lisa included, was looking anywhere but at him. "What haven't I been told?" he asked at last.

Lang cleared his throat. "It's nothing we know for certain, Admiral Hunter, but we suspect that we may have already furnished the Masters with Earth's location."

Rick turned to Lisa. "How?"

"By bringing to factory here," she said quietly.

Rick shut his eyes and shook his head. "Which means they'll be coming here if we don't go there."

"Most assuredly, Admiral," Exedore told him.

"Dr. Lang," Lisa said quickly, "I want your best estimate of the time required to complete the redesign."

Lang drew a breath. "We've learned quite a bit since Macross Island, Admiral Hayes. But this . . ." He paused for a moment, then showed the camera a determined look. "Assuming that we'll have the necessary funding and personnel, I'd say it can be done in three years. And I'm certain we'll be spending most of that time restructuring the bow of the flagship to conform to the twin-boomed design of the SDF's reflex cannon. It will be like fashioning a racing car from a block of wood, but in the end you'll have a fold-capable fraud to pilot to Tirol. I promise that much."

Zand, among others, looked dubious. "And just where, Dr. Lang, will the raw materials for this miraculous transformation come from?"

Lang's marblelike eyes glistened. "First, we'll have to strip everything we can from the Zentraedi ships that litter near space and stipple Earth's surface. Then, we'll have to cannibalize the unfinished Southern Grand Cannon." He uttered a short laugh and pressed the palms of his hands together. "We may even have to ready a mission to Plutospace to pick up those pieces of Macross Island we couldn't take aboard the SDF-1."

Downside, grouped around a simple, square table in a run-down motel several hours south of Monument City, Macross Council President Milburn met in secret conclave with Senator Stinson, formerly of Macross, Senator Longchamps, Human member of the Monument City Council, and General Maistroff and Colonel Caruthers of the RDF. The cramped and airless room was devoid of computers, flatscreens, or recording devices of any sort. There was a distant view of the Grand Tetons from a cracked and grimy picture window, but Milburn had ordered the window's heavy green drapes pulled shut.

"We can't go on living like we're diplomats on foreign soil," Milburn was saying. "There aren't perks enough to make the job worthwhile and we've got no room to maneuver. That's the hell of having devolved into polities, each ruled by its own council. Goddamned Lang and the rest of them . . . They should be down here building me a new city instead of playing space cadets in that miserable factory."

Longchamps leaned back in his chair and folded his arms across his chest. "Is this just a grievance session, Milburn, or did you have something constructive to propose?" A rangy man of fifty, he'd seen autonomy coming for Monument long before the Macross Council granted it, and had positioned himself as an advocate of Zentraedi rights to reap the rewards.

Milburn smirked in Longchamps's direction. "Keep your shirt on, Philipe, I'm coming to that." His gaze lingered on Longchamps a moment longer. "I recommend we put our heads together and compile a list of people we can trust in Detroit, Denver, Mexico, Brasília, and the rest. We then propose to all of them the formation of a new United Earth Defense Council, to which, naturally, everyone on our team will be elected. The people will back the idea. They crave united leadership. They want to believe some ultimate authority is looking out for them."

The always debonair Senator Stinson mulled it over and shook his head. "It'll never fly. A UEDC will conjure up memories of Russo and the mistakes he and his bunch made during the War."

"What mistakes?" Longchamps asked. "You think Dolza would have extended the peace pipe if the UEDC hadn't fired the Grand Cannon? The mistake was in not giving Dolza the SDF-1."

Maistroff glared at him. "Easy for you to say, Longchamps, safe and sound on Earth while Gloval and I were getting our asses handed to us every day."

Maistroff was a tall, humorless man, known to be something of a xenophobic martinet. As an air group officer aboard the SDF-1, he had occasionally relieved Henry

Gloval on the bridge, and had personally conducted the debriefing of Hunter, Hayes, Dixon, and Sterling after their escape from Breetai's flagship. He had also—much to his distaste—been the first to shake the hand of Micronized Exedore and to lead him on a tour of inboard Macross City. Maistroff would never forget the expression on the Zentraedi's face when he got his first look at a revealing poster of the suntan-salon spokesmodel, Miss Velvet.

Milburn was holding up his big hands. "Enough of this. What's done is done. If the UEDC won't work, tell me what will."

Longchamps thought for a moment. "Suppose we revive the United Earth Alliance?"

Stinson vetoed it. "Same Russo problem." He paused, then added, "Although you might consider using the United Earth Government. It not only has a better ring to it, but it harkens back to the days of the Global Civil War when everything was just as parceled up as it is now."

Longchamps steepled his fingers and looked at Milburn. "When you say only our players will serve on this new UEG or whatever it's going to be called, who exactly among the five of us did you have in mind?"

All eyes turned to Milburn.

"To be honest, I think I'd stand the best chance of getting myself elected. But if any of you gentlemen want a crack at it, be my guest. So long as the five of us share a common vision of the future." He glanced around. "Do we?"

"Of course we do," Maistroff said, answering for everyone.

Milburn smiled without showing his teeth. "Now, speaking of Russo, it might not be a bad idea to borrow his idea of uniting everyone around a common threat. The arrival of the SDF-1 and concerns about the coming of giant aliens worked to end the Civil War, but I doubt we can work the same magic with the Masters or the Invid. People are too preoccupied worrying about where the next meal's coming from to be worrying about aliens. Lucky for us, though, we've got something better to work with."

"The SDF-3," Caruthers said knowingly. Thin-lipped and

rather pallid, Caruthers had served as Maistroff's adjutant aboard the SDF-1.

Milburn looked at him and laughed. "The sooner that the SDF-3's completed and launched, the better for the rest of us." He put his elbows on the table and leaned forward conspiratorially. "I'm talking about the demobilized hostiles, the recidivists, the recalcitrants, the malcontents, whatever the RDF's calling them now. People are already starting to think of the Zentraedi as walking time bombs."

"Which happens to be an actual problem," Longchamps said, "as opposed to a perceived one."

Milburn nodded. "That's the beauty of it. Hell, *I'm* as worried about the malcontents as anybody. But the trick is to convince the RDF that a United Earth Government can take the problem off their hands. My—that is, *our*—first suggestion would be that all Zentraedi aboard the factory satellite, full-size or Micronized, must remain there."

"Might have to make exceptions for Breetai and Exedore," Stinson said.

Milburn waved a hand in dismissal. "Those two don't pose any threat. They're wannabes. As for the ones in the North American Sector, I say we herd any potential troublemakers onto the Arkansas Protectorate for safekeeping."

"Herd, how?" Maistroff asked.

"What's it matter? Offer them advanced training in technology or construction, free room and board, whatever it takes."

"And the Micronized aliens in the Southlands?" Longchamps wanted to know.

"A bit more problematic," Milburn admitted. "What would be great is if we could tag the troublesome ones and monitor them like we used to do with endangered animals."

Caruthers mocked the idea. "Shoot them with tranquilizer darts and clip tags to their ears, huh?"

Milburn glowered at him. "They're hungry, right? So what say we earmark some supplies just for them, and we get Lang or somebody to invent a kind of transmitter that can be introduced into their bodies when they eat. Then we use a specially equipped AWAC-EC-33 to plot their whereabouts."

Everyone paused to consider it.

"You know what we could do," Maistroff said, laughing and getting with the program. "We could loft a network of satellites—telecast satellites just for the Zentraedi—that would actually be our eyes in the sky."

"How so?" Stinson said.

"By encouraging the aliens to phone in requests for music or some other thing and plotting the sources of the calls."

Milburn was beaming. "I have a friend, Tom Hoos, who would be perfect to get this off the ground."

"Lang would never agree to it," Stinson said.

Longchamps cracked a smile. "I'll bet Zand would."

"I'll leave it to you to convince him," Milburn said. "In any case, the malcontent groups we can't tag, we infiltrate with Earth-loyal Zentraedi spies. Even the RDF would have to agree to that."

Stinson proposed using Miriya Parino but Milburn shook his head. "She's one I'd like to see tagged—her and her husband and that half-breed kid of theirs. It's suspicious enough that they've distanced themselves from the Expeditionary mission, but my sources report they're in the Southlands as we speak. For all anybody knows, they've been wheedling information out of Hayes and Hunter and passing it on to their Zentraedi friends."

Milburn rubbed his hands together. "Getting back to convincing the RDF of the need for this. What we do is go to them with a name to head up the surveillance operation. Someone Lang and Reinhardt can put their full trust in." He paused briefly. "My choice would be Niles Obstat. He had plenty of experience running intelligence operations during the Civil War, and he has just enough ties to the old UEDC to offset people's concerns about him going soft on the malcontents."

"Obstat would undermine us," Longchamps said. "It's true he had ties to Russo and Hayes, but he was pretty tight with Gloval."

"So then we partner him with one of our own," Milburn said, as if he had been expecting an argument. He stood up, went to the door to the adjoining room, and said something to the armed guard on the other side. A moment later, a tall man of fifty or so years entered the room. He was lean and square-jawed, and what could be seen of his long hair was sun-bleached blond; the rest was concealed behind an irregularly shaped black alloy plate that covered most of the right side of his skull.

"Gentlemen," Milburn said, "I'm sure some of you know Thomas Riley Edwards."

CHAPTER FIVE

Max and Miriya's marriage may have taken place in deepspace, but that didn't mean it had been made in heaven. Their arguments didn't center around sex or money, but around how best to raise Dana. This was made clear to Lisa Hayes aboard Breetai's flagship, during the joint Zentraedi-RDF mission to engage Commander Reno, then in possession of the factory satellite. Hayes and Hunter, along with the Sterlings, were in an aft cabinspace when Hayes asked if she might hold six-month-old Dana, and Miriya, in response, simply tossed the child toward her. Seated approximately ten feet away, Hayes had to make a desperate lunge for the infant and only just managed to catch her. In his log, Hunter relates how he had never seen a demonstration of Max's temper until that moment.

Theresa Duvall, *Wingmates: The Story of Max and Miriya Sterling*

THE DRY HEAT OF BRASÍLIA'S WINTER PEAKED IN JULY. Despite its almost-mile-high altitude in the lush, undulating uplands of the Sertao, the city baked under a merciless sun. It was hardly the best time for a visit, particularly if your plans called for putting yourself in a shadeless, forlorn plaza in Brasília's Zee-town, at the center of a protest demonstration. But there was Max Sterling, plum-tinted aviator glasses fogged, faintly blue hair plastered to his forehead, engulfed by a thousands-strong crowd of chanting Zentraedi.

"Why in the world would Seloy want us to meet her here?" Max said into Miriya's ear over the guttural anger of the chant. She was slightly to the left in front of him, facing the speakers' platform.

"I don't know why she chose this place," Miriya said over her shoulder. "It probably has something to do with whatever it is she wants to show me. She wouldn't go into details. It sounded to me like she thought the phone was bugged."

This much wasn't news to Max. He had been at home the previous week when Miriya had accepted the charges for Seloy's collect call from Brasília. But he had been grappling ever since with the implications of their short conversation.

"Seloy doesn't even have a phone to bug," Max said.

Miriya turned her head to frown at him. "She didn't say it was her phone. She said *the* phone—the one she was calling from."

"And whose was that?"

"For the tenth time— "

"And you're sure she didn't say anything else about this mysterious item?"

Miriya elbowed him lightly in the stomach. "If she had, Max, then maybe we wouldn't be here, would we?"

Max removed his glasses and wiped the sweat from his eyes. He knew Miriya didn't have any answers. It was only his edginess speaking, the all-too-familiar protest scene: the crowd of hungry and homeless Zentraedi; the oratory rhetoric of the advocates, demanding that the Zentraedi's civil rights be respected; the distorted sound system . . . And the barricades, of course, on the far side of which Max usually found himself, crafted in a Skull Veritech.

He congratulated himself on the decision to leave Dana behind in Monument, in the care of Vince and Jean Grant. Even if Jean did have her hands full with Bowie, her somewhat sickly infant son.

An ironic consequence of the War, Brasília had at last achieved status as a world capital, a position it had been denied when Rio de Janeiro, São Paulo, and Recife were vital cities. Together with Belo Horizonte to the southeast, Cuiabá to the southwest, and Buenos Aires in the Argentine Sector, Brasília was now a major commercial center, exporting goods to all parts of the Southlands. Some longtime residents still referred to it by its original name of Plano Piloto, but most of them would have been hard-pressed to outline the city's original bent-bow-and-arrow design. The so-called North and South Wings had lost their definition, many of the six-story apartment blocks—the *super-quadras*—were gutted, and the 5-mile-long, 750-foot-wide Eixo Monumental that had been the arrow was now a linear barrio of makeshift dwellings, stretching almost to the arrow's tip at Praca Dos Tres Poderes, which housed the Ministry, the Supreme Court, and the Governor's Palace.

It was Max and Miriya's third visit to Brasília, though this time they had arrived not by Veritech but by commercial hypersonic, in order to set themselves apart from the RDF. Not an easy accomplishment for the War's most famous and most infamous of mecha jocks. It had gotten so that Miriya couldn't venture out of the house for fear of being surrounded by reporters; and Max's modest, upbeat, middle-American manner of speech was being mimicked by every pilot in the RDF, much as an earlier generation of jet pilots had mimicked Chuck Yeager's drawl. Citing Dana as an excuse, he had managed to convince Rick Hunter to grant him extended off-duty time, though in fact he was still unsure about the barricade question. A staunch defender of the law, he also saw himself as a defender of the rights of Miriya's—and Dana's—people.

Many Zentraedi regarded Miriya, along with Exedore and Breetai, as *hajoca*—traitors to the Imperative. Those same Zentraedi, while in awe of Max's warrior skills, reviled him for having married a traitor. At the same time, many of his fellow Earthers reviled him for marrying an alien and, worse still, for fathering a hybrid. It ate at him to think what life would hold for Dana if the situation didn't improve. She was too young to feel the sting of discrimination, but it wouldn't be long before she began to grow aware of the stares and snide remarks—especially at the rate she was developing.

Dana was one of the reasons Max had been noncommittal about the Expeditionary mission as well. Societal pressures notwithstanding, there was Miriya's sometimes careless handling of her. Not for lack of love—for Miriya was learning about emotions—but through a seeming absence of any nurturing instinct. In the hardened, parentless manner the Zentraedi were raised, she would expect Dana to cope with whatever circumstances presented themselves.

Miriya would leave Dana unattended around sharp or hot objects, abandon her outdoors to rain or snow, and toss her about as if she were a stuffed toy. Nonviolent play and simple affection were alien notions to Miriya; and Max, as a result, had become more the primary parent and househusband than he would ever have imagined himself.

"There she is!" Miriya shouted suddenly. Her right arm was raised and waving. "Seloy, Seloy, over here!"

Max followed Miriya's wave and spied Seloy about thirty feet away, angling through the crowd. He grinned broadly. Whenever anyone asked him if he could provide living proof that Humans and Zentraedi were members of the same stock—and many did ask—he would always say, *One day, if you're lucky, I'll introduce you to Seloy Deparra.*

Admittedly, there were physical differences that distinguished the Zentraedi from Humans, though nothing as obvious as, say, the epicanthic eye fold or the Mongolian spot, nor as superficial as hair color or skin tone—especially among the Southlands' ethnic mix of European, Asian, African, and indigenous peoples. There was something about the texture of Zentraedi hair, the shape of the head, the bone structure of the face, the turn of the mouth, a slight knobbiness to the elbows, knees, and shoulders ... But Seloy Deparra was an anomaly. As lithe and as peerlessly athletic-looking as Miriya, Seloy had widely spaced, long-lashed eyes and a mane of blond hair even a shampoo model might envy. Her face was triangular and her cheekbones were wonderfully pronounced. She was a walking advertisement for the wonders of biogenetic engineering. But could anyone unaware that the Masters had grown her single her out as Zentraedi?

In spite of the heat, she was dressed in a white jumpsuit and ankle boots, and was carrying a large nylon bag over one shoulder. She moved furtively.

"You think that bag has what she wants you to see?" Max asked.

"How would I know?" Miriya said.

A former Quadrono pilot who had served under Azonia, Seloy had inserted the Micronized and weaponless Miriya into the SDF-1, back when Miriya was bloodlusting after Max instead of simply lusting. Following Dolza's Rain of Death, she'd spent almost a year in Monument City before heading south. And within months she had fallen in with some powerful people, though she had never named them.

Miriya and Seloy exchanged salutes, fists thumping their chests like ancient Roman soldiers.

"*T'sen* Parino!"

"*T'sen* Deparra!"

To Max, Seloy merely inclined her head. "*Par dessu*, Sterling."

"Hello to you, too," Max told her, smiling.

Without further word she led Max and Miriya back the way she had come, halting only when they'd reached the outer edge of the crowd. Once there, she opened the shoulder bag to reveal a dark-haired, sad-eyed male child of perhaps eleven months, wearing a dirty, tie-dyed Minmei Tour T-shirt.

Miriya stared at Seloy; then, in Zentraedi, asked, "Where did you get it?"

"It's mine."

Max's mouth fell open. "Yours as in property," he managed, "or yours as—"

"It's mine," Seloy repeated. "I birthed him."

"But who was the donor?" Miriya said.

"I can't reveal that."

Miriya's eyes grew wide. "A Zentraedi?"

"A Human."

Max understood more Zentraedi than he spoke, but words of any sort failed him now. Dana was believed to be the only offspring of a Human-Zentraedi union, and something of a fluke at that, owing to Miriya's years of contact with Human emotions and foodstuffs. That was the reason Emil Lang was so intrigued by Dana, and why Lang was often so sympathetic of Max's concerns. Lazlo Zand, as well; though Max sometimes thought that the professor's fascination with Dana bordered on freakish curiosity.

Seloy's earlier furtiveness returned. "The donor—the father is searching for me. That's why I chose a crowded place for our rendezvous. The child and I are in danger."

She had barely gotten the words out when the ground began to shake in thunderous syncopation: one, *two*; one, *two*; one, *two* ... The crowd swung toward the source of the sounds in time to see two Battloid-configured Veritechs—a VF-1A and a VF-1J—appear from around the corner of a glass-and-chrome office high-rise. Max noticed that the usual RDF fighting-kite logos had been replaced by unfamiliar eagles, proud and upright, displaying crests of crown, laurel, and solitary stars.

"Now hear this," the pilot of the single-lasered VT said over his mecha's PA. "You are in violation of executive order fifteen dash seventy-seven, which forbids any assembly undertaken without the prior consent of Governor Leonard."

The crowd booed at mention of Leonard. "He denies us food, knowing that we'll protest," Seloy snarled. "Then he has the excuse he needs to deploy his mecha."

"Usurper!" Seloy screamed in Zentraedi through cupped hands. "*Negronta!* To show allegiance to Leonard dishonors all T'sentrati!"

One of the advocates said something that got the crowd chanting again. "This was the work mantra of the T'sentrati at the mining base on Fantoma," Miriya shouted to Max, her eyes wild.

Max's heart began to race. The chant increased in volume, drowning out the dueling words of mecha pilots and sympathizers alike.

Suddenly then—incredible as it seemed—the two pilots opened fire on the crowd.

From the VTs' chainguns tore bursts of transuranic rounds as big as candlepins, any one of them capable of blowing the foot off a Battlepod. Hundreds of Zentraedi were instantly dismembered. When Max came to his feet, quivering with terror and disbelief, scenes of carnage met his eyes: blood, limbs, headless torsos ...

But the pilots' savagery had elicited a perhaps unanticipated reaction: death had called to the Imperative, death had galvanized the crowd into action. And so those nearest the Battloids launched an insane counterattack, charging forward, chanting *"Kara-brek! Kara-brek!"*—meaning death by honor. Though it might be suicide.

Again the VTs fired, and again hundreds—aliens and Humans alike—fell to the green-tinted concrete paving stones of the plaza. The Zentraedi front line had been decimated but the attack was only momentarily slowed. Like sharks in a feeding frenzy, the wounded picked themselves up off the blood-slicked ground and resumed the hopeless charge. Others further back in the crowd joined in, Seloy included, racing forward with the child still slung over her shoulder.

"Seloy!" Miriya shouted.

The VTs fired. Hundreds more fell. Max's eyes searched for some sign of Seloy or the infant, but found none.

From several directions at once appeared half-a-dozen Centaur tanks—decades-old things that rode on huge in-line sleds and were crowned with single-barreled cannons. They stopped for a moment, shimmering in the heat; then, without warning, they lurched forward into the crowd, leaving scores of crushed bodies in their scarlet wakes.

Max threw a bear hug around Miriya and began to drag her away from the tanks, out of the plaza, struggling against the force of the Imperative with each backward step.

CHAPTER SIX

Begun in the terminal phase of the Global Civil War (1996), the team of Moran and Leonard—aided and abetted by Lazlo Zand and T. R. Edwards—would endure for some thirty-six years, until their deaths at the conclusion of the Second Robotech War. Revisionists often dismiss the pairing as an extension of the Russo/Hayes apparat that emerged from the Civil War. But on closer examination Moran and Leonard seem to have had more in common with the Zentraedi leadership, whom they so detested. The author, for one, cannot read of Dolza's hatred for "Micronians" without being reminded of Leonard's hatred for "aliens"; nor of Cabell's detailing of the Imperative embedding process without thinking of Moran's "brainwashing" at the hands of Conrad Wilbur's Faithful.

footnote in Zeitgeist's *Insights: Alien Psychology and the Second Robotech War*

"**H**IS FULL NAME IS ANATOLE WESTPHAL Leonard," Brigadier General Reinhardt told the gathered members of the RDF Command in their new headquarters on the Excaliber base in Monument City. It was a little over a week since the slaughter in Brasília, and Monument had been experiencing nightly protest demonstrations by Zentraedi and their legions of sympathizers.

"Westphal was the mother's maiden name," Reinhardt continued. "French-German descent, titled and very wealthy. Father was English, brought up in the U.S. He bought and sold beef worldwide. Anatole was born in Paraguay in seventy-five, but raised in Argentina and all over Asia."

The room was a high-ceilinged octagon crowded with technology, and the conference table was horseshoe-shaped, with inlaid keyboards and data screens. Guards were posted at each of the four sliding doorways. Neither politicians nor scientists were present.

Reinhardt directed a nod to the elevated glass-fronted control booth and a quarter-scale holo of Anatole Leonard flamed from a floor projector in the horseshoe's hollow. The digitized image had obviously been generated from parade footage of some sort; the bearish miniature in ornate uniform was marching.

Leonard's bullet-shaped, shaved head made Rick think of Josef Turichevskiy of the old United Earth Defense Council, and he whispered as much to Lisa, seated to his right on the high-rank curve of horseshoe.

Reinhardt was pacing back and forth in front of the holo. "He's said to sleep only five hours a day so he can devote the other nineteen to hating the Zentraedi. He saw extensive action during the Global Civil War, first with the Neasian CoProsperity Sphere, then with the Factionalists. Embraced the technophobic beliefs of the Faithful during reconstruction of the SDF-1 on Macross Island.

"We haven't been able to determine where he passed the War, but he surfaces in Brazil after the Rain of Death and emerges as one of the Southland's chief reorganizers, personally overseeing the evacuation of Rio de Janeiro by leading over 200,000 survivors on a three-month march to Belo Horizonte and on to Brasília. A regular legend, even though he's thought of by some as an opportunist who isn't above cutting deals with gangs of bandits, vigilante groups, and mercenary armies. Lately, Aaron Rawlins and Krista Delgado have thrown in with him."

"More separatists," Major Aldershot commented, running a forefinger along the underside of his waxed mustache. Awarded a Combat Infantry Star during the Civil War, he had a prosthetic left arm and right leg. "Rawlins and Delgado may have held the fort during the SDF-1's absence, but when it came time to pull together and rebuild, where were they—down in the Southlands organizing private armies. Their thinking is medieval."

Several at the table were nodding in agreement.

Reinhardt went on. "To Leonard's credit, he has managed to maintain peace among hundreds of self-interest groups operating in that area of the Southlands. More importantly, he has the people's support because he's willing to take a strong stand on malcontentism. He claims that the Zentraedi provoked this latest confrontation."

Video footage of the riot ran on the inlaid screens, handheld shots of the charge and its bloody aftermath. Watching the tape, Rick recalled his standoff with a murderous crowd of Zentraedi in New Detroit years earlier. At issue was a sizing chamber Khyron had designs on. Lynn-Kyle had spoken for the Zentraedi, ultimately forcing Rick to yield to their demands that the sizing chamber remain in Detroit. Rick had been obsessing over his failure ever since. He asked himself now whether he would have fired on the crowd if they had attacked him.

"The death toll stands at one thousand one hundred Zentraedi, forty-four sympathizers, and eighty-six bystanders," Reinhardt said when the tape had ended. "Martial law is in effect in Brasília, Belo Horizonte, and Cuiabá."

Rick spoke up. "I'd like to know how Leonard justifies using armed response."

"The official explanation is that the VT pilots panicked."

"What about the pilots of those tanks?" Lisa asked. "Their action was calculated."

Reinhardt made his lips a thin line. "Leonard promises it won't happen again. His forces will not enter a region unless asked to lend support."

"His *forces*," Aldershot said. "He sounds more like a field marshal than a governor. What's he telling us here, that he's forming his own army? From what I hear, he fueled the riots by denying food to the Zentraedi."

Rick came to Aldershot's support. "Captain Sterling told the Brasília newspapers that the VT pilots fired without provocation. And I'm more inclined to believe him than I am Leonard or any 'official explanation.' "

"You raise an interesting point, Admiral," General Maistroff said from the other side of the horseshoe. "By going to the press with their account before reporting to us, the Sterlings—inadvertently, perhaps—have made things worse. No matter what their motive, their actions cast a shadow on their loyalties to the RDF."

Rick reddened with anger. "Are you saying we could have found some way to sugarcoat what happened in

Brasília? Eleven hundred Zentraedi died, but a lot more lived, and, regardless of Max's going to the media, my guess is that the survivors are *already* spreading the truth to every corner of the Southlands."

"And what about Miriya Parino?" Maistroff asked evenly.

"What about Miriya?"

"To many of her people, she's a traitor. Her stepping forth in their behalf now could be viewed as an attempt to proclaim her renewed loyalty to the Zentraedi cause."

Lisa shot to her feet, but when she spoke her voice was controlled. "I'm sure General Maistroff recalls on whose side Miriya Parino fought at the end of the War. But just in case he doesn't, let me say that she is as loyal to the RDF as either Breetai or Exedore. I caution the general not to go looking for ulterior motives where none exist. And I caution everyone here that any divisiveness at this time will sabotage all the good we've accomplished, as well as the work that remains to be done."

Maistroff took the rebuke in stride. Everyone else waited for Reinhardt to resume the briefing.

"Indirectly, the RDF is responsible for Leonard's rise to power," Reinhardt said after a moment. "We never bothered to oppose Senator Moran's appointment to the Southlands by the Bureau of Reconstruction Management. And we didn't question it when Moran, in turn, appointed Leonard governor."

No one in the room needed to view a holo of the silver-haired Wyatt "Patty" Moran or hear a summary of his earlier contributions to the UEDC. Russo, Turichevskiy, Hayes, Zukov, Blaine, and Moran were all of a type to shoot first and ask questions afterward.

"The point I want to make is that the RDF stands to bear the brunt of the backlash if any attempt is made to interfere with further demonstrations by the Zentraedi. Another incident like Brasília and we're going to be accused of seeking some sort of 'final solution'—that we're out to exterminate them, loyals and demobilized hostiles both."

He paused for a moment. "I suggest, therefore, that we give serious consideration to Council President Milburn's proposal that a new United Earth Government be instated, composed of elected officials representing all city-states, autonomous sectors, and non-aligned territories." Reinhardt's glance moved from face to face. "Let's hand the business of running the Earth over to them so we can concentrate on our priorities, which are the building of the SDF-3 and the launch of the Expeditionary mission."

"In other words," Aldershot said, "any future slaughters of the Zentraedi will be carried out at the behest of the UEG and not the RDF."

Reinhardt shot him a look. "There are no military solutions to the Zentraedi problem, Major. There are only political ones."

"Who's going to be our liaison with this new government?" Rick wanted to know. "We'd be fools to rely on politicians to make the right decisions."

Reinhardt turned to him. "Naturally, we would have to make certain that the RDF is fairly represented. We could support the appointment of Lang or Chief Justice Huxley. As for the hostiles, Milburn proposes that we designate Niles Obstat to head a special operations group to study the problem."

"Spooks," Aldershot said in disgust. "Spooks and spies and smoke and mirrors."

"Military intelligence," Reinhardt amended.

The major snorted. "God knows there's been little enough of that lately."

Long on a first-name basis with catastrophe, the survivors of Tokyo had rebuilt their city in half the time it had taken Lang's core of Roboengineers to transfer Macross Two from the bowels of the SDF-1 to the high plains of the Northwest. New Tokyo was not, however, the one-thousand-square-mile conurban sprawl it had been at the turn of the century, but a tidier place of some quarter million inhabitants centered around the rebuilt Imperial Palace and the moats of the East Garden. The Ginza and Akihabara districts—known respectively for department stores and high-tech electronics—had been rebuilt underground, as had much of the *shitamachi*, the downtown. But gone were the nouveau riche enclaves of Harajuku, Roppongi, and Shinjuku, with their sleek high-rises and Western-style restaurants. North of the Imperial center, in the War-leveled Bunkyo-ku, were parks like the Koishi-kawa Gardens and temples like the Gokokuji, where in summer one could still enjoy the omnipresent *me-me-me* chirring of cicadas.

Lang had always had a fondness for Tokyo and for things Japanese—noh dramas, kabuki, bunraku puppet plays, karaoke, and all-night beer drinking. He had been in Tokyo, lecturing on extraterrestrial observations, when the Visitor had made its controlled crash onto Macross—a happy circumstance that had allowed him to be the first scientist of any note to reach the Micronesian island.

Post–Global War Tokyo had been home to the only off-island Robotech Research Center, and it was to Tokyo that Lang had returned soon after the Rain of Death to get the center operational once more. There, in underground rooms as fortified as the data storage and communication bunkers that had sheltered the residents of Macross Three during Khyron's attack, were housed the still-undeciphered texts found aboard the SDF-1, including most of what had comprised Zor's electronic library. And it was to Tokyo that Lang moved what had been obtained during the early-spring salvage operations in Macross: crateloads of additional yet-to-be-deciphered texts, the remains of the Invid battle unit Breetai had discovered aboard Khyron's cruiser, and the peripheral systems of the SDF-1's so-called mother computer. Known also as EVE—for Enhanced Video Emulator—the quantum machine had, among other things, provided simulated sunrises, daylight, clouds, and sunsets for the besieged population of inboard Macross.

Lang attributed his failure to fully penetrate the computer to the loss of several key components during Breetai's attack on Macross. He suspected that some of those components had folded with the island to Plutospace and were there still, orbiting in ice. His push for a mission to Pluto had less to do with gathering parts for the SDF-3 than with retrieving EVE's missing subsystems.

"Coming here, I always feel like I've arrived home,"

Lang was telling Zand in the midst of their inspection tour of the refurbished facility. A quarter-mile along in the main corridor, they were on foot and dressed alike in long white jackets and hard hats emblazoned with the RRC insignia: the RDF fighting kite contained by a square. Lang was setting a brisk pace, leaving Zand to scurry at his heels, the ever-faithful and overeager pet.

"If it weren't for my duties aboard the factory satellite, I'd spend most of my time here." Lang paused momentarily to inspect a motion-sensor device affixed to the corridor wall. "And now, what with all this talk about a possible role for me in the United Earth Government, I won't even have the pleasure of dividing my time between Tokyo and the factory. I'll be forced to include Monument City as well."

"You could decline a seat in the UEG," Zand said, short of breath.

"Ha! If it was only that easy, Lazlo. As you well know, I'm no politician. But it's clear someone has to look out for the needs of the RDF. Besides, I can't in good conscience disappoint Reinhardt and the others by refusing. They're all too aware of the dangers of factionalism, and neither of them trusts Milburn to play fair and square with the military." Lang shook his head. "I've no real choice in the matter. But I do regret having to burden you with the increased responsibility of overseeing our research work on Protoculture."

"It's no burden, Doctor, no burden, I assure you," Zand said in a rush. "I welcome the opportunity, the challenge of it."

Lang nodded. "Without specimens of the Flower of Life or a functioning matrix, we haven't a prayer of producing Protoculture. Our one hope lies in being able to synthesize it. I'm certain that the key to that process is to be found somewhere in EVE's databanks, but they're impermeable without the components we lost in Plutospace." He shook his head in regret. "If only we hadn't been so panicked after the fold. Then, of course, there were the lives of Macross's fifty-six thousand to occupy us . . . And the

Zentraedi." He forced an exhale, as if to rid himself of the memory.

"In the meantime, Lazlo, we must concentrate on the decipherment of Zor's documents. But not to the exclusion of other courses of investigation, you understand. This Invid craft, for example. What we assume to be a lubricant may in fact be a crude form of Protoculture, an ur-Protoculture. And let's not forget our Zentraedi test subjects: Rico, Konda, Bron—"

Lang halted abruptly and whirled on Zand. "It gets into you, Lazlo. Above and beyond Protoculture's effects on mecha, even beyond its effects on the space-time continuum, there're its effects on *living things*. Exedore has told us what it did to the Masters, we've speculated on the effect the leaves of the Flower of Life had on Khyron, I *know* what it has done to me ... I'm talking about punctuated equilibrium, Lazlo, genetic and evolutionary leaps. One day you'll understand—you'll see for yourself."

They had stopped by the Plexiglas sliders that fronted the center's machine intelligence laboratory. Central to the space was the android, JANUS M, that had been created three years earlier by the center's cybertechnician team. Hope ran high of seeing the astonishingly lifelike "female" automaton begin to think for itself soon.

Lang was regarding JANUS M absently. "If the Sterlings could only be convinced to part with little half-Human Dana for a month or so of testing ..."

"Dana, yes," Zand said with obvious eagerness.

Lang eyed him guardedly. "You know, Lazlo, perhaps it's unfair of me to burden you with all this work when you've got your own projects to attend to."

Zand was shaking his head back and forth. "You needn't worry. I won't disappoint you. I'll—"

"My seating on the UEG certainly won't prevent Milburn and his gang from running things, in any case."

"You could find some way to keep tabs on them," Zand said. "Learn what they're plotting before they can carry it out."

Lang halted again. "Insert a spy into the UEG?"

"Why not? They've spied on us in the past."

"True. But who do we know with a talent for espionage and unrestricted access to Milburn's circle?"

Zand rubbed his chin for a moment. "How about Lynn-Minmei? She could finagle access if she wanted to. And I recently heard her say that she's searching for a new career. Maybe she'd be willing to add 'spy' to her resume."

Lang considered it for a moment, then laughed. "Nice try, but I don't think so. I'll grant that she's a decent actress, but she's utterly guileless. Our spy would have to have a broad amoral streak." His eyes drifted aimlessly to the android once more. "No, Lazlo, we would have to *create* the duplicitous personality we need."

CHAPTER
SEVEN

*A Zentraedi clone received his or her designation from a list of
300 primary names and 300 surnames, each of which was represented by a glyph or combination of subglyphs, for a sum total of
90,000 individual symbols, many of which were likewise the names
for so-called everyday objects—combat-related objects, in the case
of the Zentraedi. On its inception, each clone was subjected to a
regimen of neurotutorials, which rendered it—him or her—capable
of identifying its own name glyph, in addition to some five hundred
others. An "educated" Zentraedi—a* domillan *or advisor, such as
Exedore Formo, to mention one example—was capable of identifying, reading, as many as five thousand glyphs. Writing, however,
was a separate matter, rarely practiced, let alone mastered.*

Cabell, *A Pedagogue Abroad:
Notes on the Sentinels Campaign*

"THANKS AGAIN FOR ACCEPTING MY INVITATION,"
UEG Senator Milburn told Minmei as he escorted her from
the limousine to the majestic ballroom entrance of the Hotel
Centinel. "I'm sorry it had to be last-minute, but I didn't realize you were in Monument until yesterday evening."

"Don't be sorry, Senator," Minmei said. "I'm honored
you thought of me at all."

Milburn smiled charmingly. "Who doesn't think about
you, my dear."

For a moment she thought he was going to kiss the back
of her gloved hand. But instead he took hold of her elbow
and walked her through the glass doors and down the carpeted stairway into the foyer of the grand ballroom. Hotel
guests stopped what they were doing to stare at them, and
several people in the ornate foyer applauded. Milburn acknowledged them with gracious aplomb.

"I have to absent myself for a few minutes," he said
when they were well into the ballroom itself and swallowed

by the crowd, "but I'll catch up with you before long." He grinned. "You think you can handle it?"

Minmei returned the playful look. "I'll do my best."

She accepted a drink from a passing server and gazed around the room, at the Hollywood-style gilded columns and the chandeliers and the posh draperies, unimpressed by the money the Centinel's owners had lavished on the place. The same owners who had run the now-razed Macross Centinel. Although this third incarnation of the hotel—all within fifteen years—was by far the most out of touch with the times.

Nevertheless, in keeping with the stately, anachronistic miasma of the evening—it was official now; the United Earth Government, like the Hotel Centinel, was to be reborn—Minmei was wearing the gold lamé dress she'd worn three years earlier to the Sterlings' shipboard, outer-space wedding. And she had her hair styled for bygone times as well, bunned and braided like a Chinese princess.

She had returned to the mainland the previous week. Monument's warm weather was holding—it was downright hot for August—but she feared autumn would arrive in an unannounced rush. And just where had summer gone, anyway? Looking back on the months in Kauai, summer seemed like one long day of lounging in the sunshine, playing in the waves, drinking piña coladas on the lanai. She'd spent the past week with Lena and Max, at their small house in the Monument 'burbs where she always had a room and where many of her souvenirs and keepsakes were stored. She often thought of herself as their boomeranging child, a title that would never apply to their son, Kyle. And like a child, she'd secluded herself in her room, rereading yellowing letters and scrapbooked articles clipped from the *Macross City News* and answering fan mail received since the telecast of Katherine Hyson's interview. Minmei thought that she had come off reasonably well, in spite of the sloppy editing, though she wished she'd been more circumspect in talking about Rick.

She wondered now if Hyson was somewhere in the ballroom or whether Milburn had been able to keep the media away.

She spotted many old friends. There was Mayor Luan and his fusty wife, Loretta; nearby, Dr. Hassan and the always-affable Mayor Owen Harding of Detroit. Lots of folks she hadn't seen in years: sports figures, actors, promoters and performers she'd met during the post-War "People Helping People Tour." More than a few waved and smiled, and everyone was respectful of her privacy. There would be no autographs to sign, and no requests for songs, either, thank heavens.

Lang was to have attended, but Minmei had heard that he was still in Tokyo. She had hoped Rick would be there, but he wasn't. She hadn't seen him in more than six months now. She supposed he and Lisa were too busy . . . well, whatever it was they were busy doing.

Exedore was the only Zentraedi in the room, and hanging on his crooked arm was none other than the voluptuous Marjory Prix—the former Miss Velvet, now simply Velvet—former spokesmodel for a chain of suntan clinics in inboard Macross. Posters of the barely clad Miss Velvet had been second in popularity only to those Minmei had done to promote enlistment in the RDF.

Jan Morris was also there—yet another former celeb, now an author of occult books—on the arm of Monument Council Member Stinson.

So was this what happened to all former stars? Minmei asked herself. They became the appendages of aging dignitaries at stuffy affairs in opulent hotels?

Two days earlier she'd hired a pilot to take her and her teenage cousin Jason for a spin in the Ikkii Takemi–designed fanjet she'd won as Miss Macross of 2011. The pilot had flown them over the buried remains of Macross, now reduced to a monument to the past. As she herself was—

"Lynn!" someone called out.

Minmei turned to the cheerful voice and saw Jan Morris mincing toward her on stiletto heels. Blond and obviously fit, Jan looked better than she had in years. Certainly since the time they had literally bumped into each other at the premier of *Little White Dragon* and a tipsy Jan had almost spilled her drink all over Minmei.

"Lynn, darling," Jan said, kissing the air near Minmei's cheeks. "How are you? You look positively radiant!"

"I'm fine, Jan. Love your gown."

Jan waved a hand in dismissal. "I had to have it let out."

A tall, stoop-shouldered man with unsettling blue eyes had appeared out of nowhere and was standing alongside Morris. Jan introduced him as Reverend Houston.

"Reverend Houston wrote the introduction to my book, *Solar Seeds, Galactic Guardians*."

"Have you read or listened to the book?" Houston asked Minmei, turning those eyes on her.

"Not yet," she started to say.

"I suspect it will be of real interest to you—particularly after hearing what you had to say about wanting to make a contribution to the planet at this time in your life."

Terrific, Minmei thought. A fan of television interviews.

"You see, Corporeal Fundamentalism—the subject of Jan's book—is about allowing the universe to speak to you. It's about stretching out and locating your seed guardian and paying close attention to its messages of guidance." Houston sniffed. "In fact, we—that is, Jan and I—are putting together an infomercial to get the book the attention it deserves. It would be great to have you on our panel—and naturally we'd be willing to work out a fair participation deal."

Minmei managed a weak smile. "Thanks, but I don't know—"

"You wouldn't have to be spontaneous, if that's what you're worried about. We'll script the entire thing. All you'd have to do is tell us beforehand what points you would want to make about our troubled times."

"I'll think about it," Minmei said in a tone that made it clear she wouldn't.

"Could I at least send you a copy of the book—free of charge? Who's your agent?"

"I don't have an agent just now."

"Then I could send it to your home."

Minmei gave him the Monument address of Max and

Lena's Chinese restaurant and promised that she would *try* to read the book. She didn't make it three steps from Houston before someone else called her name. This time it was the stout, round-faced, and balding Samson "Sharky" O'Toole, one of the theatrical agents she was considering signing with.

"Lynn, fancy meeting you here," O'Toole said. Again, the air kisses. Fortunately, O'Toole was without his usual cigar.

"Saw you talking to Jan Morris and that Reverend Houston."

"The Reverend was telling me about an informercial they have planned for her book."

"The Reverend," O'Toole said, snorting. "For what it's worth, Lynn, don't get involved with those two. You lend your name to some wacko fringe cult, it can follow you for life and alienate you to a lot of your regular public. Happens all the time."

"I didn't commit to anything."

O'Toole nodded approvingly. "Can we talk for a minute?"

"Only a minute," Minmei said firmly. "I think I see Senator Milburn looking for me."

O'Toole followed her gaze. "Oh, so that's who you're with. Well, then, I definitely won't keep you. But you remember when we talked in Hawaii I told you I was going to do some asking around for projects that might interest you?"

Minmei inclined her head and tightened her lips. "Mr. O'Toole, before you say anything, I really haven't decided who I'm going to sign with."

O'Toole shook his head and held up plump hands. "No obligations, none at all. I just wanted to let you in on what I've been hearing." He lowered his voice. "You know about what went down in Brasília in July and about the protests here in Monument? Well, seems someone's come up with a way to begin talking directly to our—how shall I put it?— our new brothers and sisters. A satellite network meant strictly for the Zentraedi."

Minmei put a finger to her lips in thought. "That's a wonderful idea. But how does it concern me?"

"They're toying with calling it the Lorelei Network. And they plan to keep your songs in heavy rotation." He waited a beat. "So what I'd like to propose to them—with your permission, of course—is that you might be interested—just *interested*—in hosting a show on the station. You know, what I had in mind was a kind of talk show where you'd only take calls from aliens."

"Your name," Bagzent demanded of the green-haired Zentraedi standing before him at the crude table.

"Mouro Dann."

In a struggling hand, Bagzent added a name glyph to his long list of names. "Work experience, if any."

"A year of employment in Monument City," Dann told him, "two years in Detroit."

"Doing what?"

"Herding cattle in Monument. Clerk work at the armory in Detroit."

Bagzent's left eyebrow went up. "Fort Breetai?"

"That's right.'

"Any familiarity with Human weapons?"

"Some field experience with the Wolverine assault rifle and the Watchdog antimecha mine."

"Well, well, well," Bagzent said, sitting back in his wooden chair. "I guess that only leaves your feelings toward Humans."

Dann made a fist of his right hand, raised it to chest level, and rotated it in a quick, snapping motion.

Bagzent shot to his feet, thumping his chest in salute. "*T'sen* Dann!"

"*T'sen!*" Dann returned.

Bagzent directed him to a group of thirty or so male Zentraedi queued up at the entrance to a canvas tent. "Go there for food, and await further instructions."

Bagzent appended a formula of scrawls to Dann's name glyph as the new arrival was hurrying off. A pale-complected Zentraedi seated alongside Bagzent at the table took a puzzled look at the list.

"That makes how many today?"

Bagzent's brow furrowed as he counted. "Twenty-seven from the north, fourteen from the south—six of them from Brasília."

"Is that more than yesterday's count?"

"Almost two times as many." Bagzent clapped his partner on the shoulder. "If it continues like this, we'll soon have the army we need."

Their jungle encampment of tattered army tents and the thatch-roofed longhouses the aboriginals had taught them to make was on a black-water tributary of the Xingu River, fifty miles south of its confluence with the Amazon. The nearest Human population center of any appreciable size was Manaus, almost eight hundred miles west-northwest. The rainy season air was thick with moisture, heat, and mosquitoes: the sun had been out all morning, but storm clouds were building in the west, and the sounds of distant thunder rolled over the treetops.

The population of the camp had reached nine hundred and fifty, including the two-hundred-plus Humans who had thrown in with them: tribal Indians who knew how to hunt for game; former prospectors of gold, diamonds, rubber, and oil who knew the whereabouts of hundreds of supplies-stocked Zentraedi ships; army deserters, fugitives, and practitioners of sorcery and bigamy, all of whom had made the densely forested interior of the Southlands their home long before the Rain of Death. Many of the Zentraedi were no longer wearing Human clothes, but uniforms bearing the corrupted V-like sigil—the *Cizion*—that stood for the power inherent in the Imperative. Under huge nets woven from vines and creepers stood sixteen salvaged Battlepods, now dappled in jungle camouflage colors.

Bagzent and his white-faced partner were soon joined at the table by a dozen other Zentraedi, each representing a different rebel unit in the rapidly swelling dissident army.

"What news from north?" asked the leader of the Steel Wind, a brutish man with black hair to his shoulder blades.

Bagzent filled everyone in on the latest rumors. "A new ship is being constructed in the belly of the factory satellite—a deepspace battlewagon that will carry members of the RDF to Tirol to confront the Masters. Exedore, Breetai, and at least four hundred Zentraedi who have not been Micronized are lending their might to the project."

The leader of the Steel Wind torqued his right fist. "We shall live to see Breetai and the rest allowed to run."

"Death Dance," said another leader. "The *Kara-Thun* for Breetai and the rest."

"Yes," Bagzent said, grinning, "we have a separate list for those who have betrayed the Imperative, and to it we add names daily."

"Make certain Miriya Parino's name is on it," someone shouted.

"She leads the list."

"And Anatole Leonard."

"Already done."

Bagzent made a mollifying gesture. "Let the RDF and Breetai's forces busy themselves with work on their fortress, while we lay violent claim to the Southlands and prepare to defend ourselves against the Invid."

"You're deluded to think we can survive an Invid invasion, Bagzent." The speaker was the woman, Marla Stenik, a singleton, unaligned to any group. "I say we find a way to position some of our troops aboard the factory so that we can take over the ship when the time comes. We could return to Tirol as Khyron planned to do before he lost his mind and decided to attack Macross."

Bagzent bristled but kept quiet.

"Is Zor's ship destroyed?" someone asked.

"Not only destroyed but interred," Bagzent said.

"And what news of the Backstabber?"

Marla chuckled maliciously. "Khyron Kravshera is dead, you fool. Dead and 'interred.' "

"Khyron lives," Bagzent's second shouted. "He was seen a month ago in Brasília, and in Cuiabá only last week. He is Micronized and moves only by night. He is merely waiting for us to organize and demonstrate our worthiness, then he will reappear to lead us."

"Poor fools," Marla said, shaking her head in theatrical dismay. "Khyron was a coward. He fled the final battle to save himself. The new fortress is our salvation. If it's worthiness you're after, then take that ship and search for what's become of the Botoru Division cruisers that didn't crash on Earth. The crews of those ships could be anywhere in this system—on the Moon, or Mars—waiting for a sign from us."

"You take the ship, *T'sen* Stenik. We'll take revenge instead." The speaker's name was Salta. He stood seven feet tall, and, like Bagzent, he had been a member of Khyron's Seventh Mechanized Division. One of fifty who had agreed to remain behind on Earth while Khyron brought reinforcements from the Masters. Salta raised his massive left arm and pointed to the west. "Out there lies a forest of ships, each containing salvageable mecha."

Marla scoffed at the notion. "Out there lies a forest you can hide yourselves in when the RDF comes gunning for you with squadrons of Veritechs and Destroids."

"Ignore her," Bagzent said. "Let the female units make and carry out their own plans. For the rest of us, the first target lies to the north, just outside Cavern City."

"The site of the Southern Grand Cannon," Salta said.

"It is stocked with food and supplies—even reconfigurable mecha we will learn to pilot." Bagzant banged his hand on the table. "We will carry on Khyron's work. We shall be his fist!"

"Dana, I'm warning you," Miriya said. "Come back here and finish your supper or prepare to feel the sting of my hand on your backside."

When Dana stayed put and showed her tongue, it was all Miriya could stand. She left the table, scooped Dana up in her arms, and nearly slam-dunked her into her seat. "Now, eat, you little brute," she snapped. "Grow strong and healthy like a proper Zentraedi."

Max, in the kitchen with an armload of dirty plates, regarded the scene with time-tempered concern. It was only when he caught sight of Rick's troubled look that he figured he should say something. "Miriya, I think maybe she's had enough."

Miriya tensed. "She hasn't had enough, Max. Not until I say she's had enough."

Two-and-a-half-year-old Dana glanced from Max to Miriya and grinned ever so slightly. "I'm gonna eat it all, 'cause Daddy cooked it." She turned to Rick. "Mommy doesn't know how to cook."

"Sure she does," Rick started to say, when Miriya cut him off.

"Don't lie to her, Rick, I don't know how to cook."

"I only meant—"

"He only meant that you know how to cook some things," Max said, coming to his friend's aid. "You know how to use the microwave, and that's cooking, sort of."

Miriya fumed. "It doesn't bother me that I don't know how to cook, Max. I just don't want her lied to—about anything. Who she is, what she is, how she got here, or who cooks her meals. There's enough lying going on in this world already."

Rick lifted his eyes from the table to trade looks with Max. Max knew that Rick was remembering the time aboard Breetai's flagship when Miriya had thrown Dana across the cabin to Lisa.

"So, Rick," he said, sitting down, "you were saying about Leonard . . ."

"Uh, that the pilots that fired on the crowds in July are being court-martialed. Leonard has apologized for sticking by them earlier."

"Too little, too late," Miriya said. "He should resign or be removed from office for instigating the riots to begin with."

"An apology is a start," Rick countered. "And next time, he'll have to answer to the UEG for his actions."

Max shook his head. "Nothing will change, except for the worse."

Rick looked at both of them. "Come on, you two. What's with all this pessimism? We have to give the UEG a chance, don't we? I mean, it's basically a matter of food distribution—"

"It's not just the food," Miriya told him. "It's about jobs, discrimination, rampant inequality . . . And why should we give the UEG a chance, Rick? Has Milburn or Moran or any of them considered having a Zentraedi representative?"

Rick sat up straighter. "Cavern City and Zagerstown tried to elect Zentraedis. And what about Exedore? Or isn't he Zentraedi now that he's wearing an REF uniform?"

"Of course Exedore's Zentraedi. But Exedore doesn't speak for the dissidents, and that's where the problem is." Miriya wiped Dana's mouth, lifted her out of the seat, and set her on the floor. "Listen, Rick, I watched my closest friend die in Brasília, so don't you think I want to see things work out? It's just that I don't trust the UEG, and I'm beginning to think that there are no peaceful solutions."

"There are always peaceful solutions."

Max showed Rick a dubious look. "You've been spending too much time on the factory. All of you—Lisa, Gunther, Emil. You don't know what we've been hearing."

"Then enlighten me," Rick said, more harshly than he meant to.

"Sectorwide, Zentraedi are quitting their jobs and making their way to the Southlands to link up with bands of militants. They're even leaving Monument. And can you blame them? The place is beginning to look more and more like Macross every day. The Monument Council is ineffectual; the jump in Human population will probably mean the ouster of all Zentraedi representatives. Let's face it, we've occupied and taken control of their city, autonomous or not. Everywhere else in the world, the Zentraedi have been herded into Zee-towns or lured into captivity, like we've done with them in the Arkansas Protectorate or on the factory satellite."

"We're a team on the factory—Humans and Zentraedi."

"A team that has abandoned Earth," Miriya said.

Rick shot her an angry look. "You think I want to be up there instead of down here working out solutions? But we've got the mission to think of. Besides, up there is where the two of you should be—and Dana. Vince and Jean are joining us, and they're bringing Bowie. What more can you do downside?"

"Speak out for Zentraedi rights, for one thing."

"Maybe *you* should run for the UEG, Miriya," Rick told her.

"No doubt Milburn and Moran would love to have me

on the team. But no matter how I feel about Humans right now, I still don't think I'm xenophobic enough for them. Or for the Bureau of Reconstruction Management. Or for the likes of Governor Anatole Leonard."

"The UEG will keep him under control," Rick argued. "There won't be another Brasília."

Max shook his head. "It won't matter one way or another, Rick. Malcontentism is going to spread like a cancer through the Southlands and touch all of our lives."

CHAPTER EIGHT

The Faithful, a short-lived, quasi-NeoChristian religious move-ment opposed to reconstructing the Visitor, did not so much end with the death of its founder as go into hiding for ten years, to emerge as The Church of Recurrent Tragedies, headed by Bishop Gideon Nboto, the Sudanese former lieutenant to the Faithful's founder, Conrad Wilbur. By then, of course (2016), Nboto and his ally in technophobia, Joanna Ricter-Fields, had a new ship to carp about: the SDF-3. "The Tirol Expedition (sic) is nothing more than an attempt to divert us from facing the problems of housing, food, and medical care that plague Earth's despoiled surface," Nboto told the world in an interview with Katherine Hyson. "In its refusal to face the challenge of restoring the planet, the RDF and the REF are sentencing the rest of Humankind to eradication by alien inva-sion or extinction by nature itself."

Weverka T'su, Aftermath: Geopolitical and Religious Movements in the Southlands

GOVERNOR LEONARD STOOD IN THE BACK OF THE open-air limousine and waved to the crowds gathered along both sides of Exio Rodoviario, Brasília's principal north-south axis. In the pre-War days, twelve-laned Rodoviario had formed the curve of Brasília's bow and was the main artery linking the north and south wings of the city. Now, the once-grand luxury apartment buildings with their walls of plate glass were empty shells, gutted by the Fire of 2012, and the numerous overpasses and cloverleafs had been torn down to supply building materials for the *favelas* of the poor. Now, Rodoviario coursed through mile after mile of ramshackle slums, dusted red over the years by the pla-teau's mineral-deficient soil.

November's cool winds lashed Leonard's broad face and shaved skull. Pursuant to Leonard's orders, the limo's bul-letproof canopy had been removed and no armed guards were permitted to ride in the motorcade's follow cars.

He was king here, commander and king; and to impress that title on his subjects he wore an olive-drab, woolen coat, heavy with medals and braid and cinched at the waist by a wide, big-buckled leather belt. With him, though seated just now, were Joseph Petrie, his aide-de-camp, and Wyatt Moran, who Leonard knew as Patty. Leonard and the Mark Twain–mustachioed UEG senator went back twenty years, and it was Moran who had appointed Leonard governor of Goias District. Petrie, however—small-boned and square-headed—was a recent acquisition, procured principally for his skills as a hacker. Moran was dressed in a lightweight white suit ill-suited to the season; Petrie in a military jumpsuit whose zippered pockets were stuffed with electronic widgets.

Leonard was still basking in the afterglow of July's strike against the aliens. The offensive had sent a clear signal to the people of his city, and a clearer one to the Zentraedi, that displays of malcontentism would not be tolerated. As a result, there were no antigovernment slogans in evidence along the motorcade route—though in fact Leonard had had his agents sweep the area of subversives beforehand. RDF troops from as far north as Cavern City and as far south as Buenos Aires had been called in to enforce martial law.

By last count, some five thousand Zentraedi had fled the Goias uplands since July, leaving Zee-towns throughout the district abandoned and ripe for razing. Initially, Patty Moran had taken issue with Leonard's actions, but he had since come to recognize their brilliance.

"Remember on Macross Island, how they used their Destroids to gas us?" Leonard had said to the senator. "Those mecha put the fear into us, didn't they, Patty? So you might say that I've simply borrowed an old RDF tactic for dealing with dissention."

By "us", Leonard had meant the followers of Dr. Conrad Wilbur. Dubbed the Faithful, Wilbur's cult had seen the Visitor as a kind of Pandora's box, dispatched from hell to lure Humankind into worshiping technology over God. Both Leonard and Moran were followers, and though the aims of the Faithful had been underhandedly sabotaged by 2009, Wilbur's beliefs had been given new life by the

Church of Recurrent Tragedies, and heavy—if covert—funding by Leonard himself.

Leonard waved and smiled at a group of people atop what remained of a concrete overpass. "They're chanting 'Brasília is for Humankind; the jungles, for Zentraedi,' " he told Moran when Moran asked.

Leonard's barrel chest swelled. This was how George Patton must have felt after his World War II victories in Italy and France. Leonard had made a lifelong study of Patton, learning from Patton's military successes as well as his political failures. Perhaps to humble him, Patton's desk-bound superiors had kept him from being the first to enter and lay claim to defeated Berlin. But Patton needn't have listened to those REMF commanders. He had his own army by then, and that army would have followed him anywhere. Just as Leonard had now. And Leonard would do whatever he felt needed to be done to quash malcontentism, regardless of what the RDF or the newly formed UEG might have to say about it.

The freakish aliens were the scourge loosed by the Visitor, the defilers and destroyers of God's material domain. No one could argue that point now, not in the unholy light of the Zentraedi's apocalyptic Rain of Death. And those who had ushered in the apocalypse had to be returned to the darkness whence they came—if not hurled back into the black void of space, then chased into the dark, forbidding interior of the Southlands. Chased into the jungles in the same manner the godless aboriginals had been chased there by Brazil's God-fearing Portuguese and Spanish colonizers. Chased, contained, and eventually exterminated: by weapons, poisoned food, disease-impregnated blankets, whatever was required.

Where in the Bible did it state that Humankind had to share its garden with otherworlders? Soulless, biogenetically created ones, at that. Earth had to be cleansed of them if Humankind hoped to be redeemed, just as every individual had to be cleansed of sin before he or she could stand naked in God's light. Cleansed through the performance of degrading acts, if that was what it took: cleansed by whip, by slaps, by the piercing of body parts; made to crawl across splinter-laden floors to lick the high boots of the Cleanser, begging like a sick child for another taste of the strap, the pliers, the black stiletto heel . . .

The motorcade was slowing as it approached the intersection with Esplanada dos Ministerios, where Leonard was to address the crowds gathered on the red-earth walkways of Brasília's pedestrian mall. The limousine had begun to brake and Leonard was just lowering himself to the back seat when three men and a woman hurdled the barricades on the east side of Rodoviario and made a mad rush for the open-air car. Dressed in ragged clothing and black backpacks of some sort, the quartet was screaming, *"Kara-brek, kara-brek, kara-brek!"*

The Battlepods of Khyron's Fist launched their attack at sunrise, arriving from the east, with Earth's yellow star at their backs. The strategy of making tactical use of the rising sun would not have occurred to Bagzent, but the aboriginal called Narumi had convinced him to give it a try. Outgunned, the Human forces guarding the perimeter of the Southern Grand Cannon in the sector known as Venezuela were taken by surprise and easily overrun. Of the six Veritechs and six Destroids that had occupied the base only a week earlier, four of each had been ordered south to shore up Brasília's civil defense forces. And of the fifty RDF soldiers who would have been guarding the cannon on any given morning, thirty were on leave in nearby Cavern City.

The perimeter had been breached with a minimum of bursts from the Battlepods' particle-beam cannons. Bagzent was reminded of Khyron's minimal-fire, lightning-fast raid on the concert dome in Denver, when Lynn-Minmei and her lover had been taken hostage.

The Backstabber would be proud of Bagzent's action.

Bagzent sat at the controls of his Micronian-capable Battlepod; the tattoo-faced Indian guide had the copilot's seat. Narumi was the chief of his tribe, a position Bagzent equated with that of a brigade leader. Pairs of Zentraedi manned the other nine pods. They had left the Xingu River camp five days earlier, and in that time had run and hopped their way along one thousand miles of jungle trails, crossing countless rivers and ruined roadways, often at a rate of 175 miles per hour, or 250 horizontal feet per boostered leap.

Bagzent was attired in a burgundy command uniform and a green campaign cloak chosen from items found aboard a rusting Zentraedi cruiser Narumi had led them to. The choice was deliberate—burgundy and green were the colors Khyron had worn during the Christmas attack on Macross City. One of the Human outcasts allied to the Zentraedi had decorated the exterior of Bagzent's Battlepod with the glyph that now stood for Khyron's Fist.

The radio in the pilot compartment of the bulbous-bodied craft crackled to life. "Unit seven reporting," a Zentraedi voice said. "Bagzent, respond."

"Report, Salta."

"We're on the rim of the weapon. Communications and tram transport into the main shaft are disabled. We haven't encountered many soldiers, mostly technicians. The place has been stripped clean."

"Any resistance?"

"We killed six at the first security checkpoint, then four more in one of the tram cars. Units four, five, and six encountered resistance at the mecha field. Five and six are down."

"What's our body count so far?"

Salta was quiet for a long moment. "Twenty-one Humans, I think."

Bagzent grinned. "Keep up the good work. I'm leaving Qapai and the others here. Leave Aayth on the rim and rendezvous with me on level one in the weapon."

Much like its slagged counterpart in the Alaska wilderness, the miles-deep energy gun took the form of a gargantuan upside-down Y. Never completed, however, it lacked the enhanced-firefield lensing of the original—compensation for a network of satellite reflectors the UEDC hadn't gotten around to lofting, much less positioning.

Bagzent ran the pod from the high-voltage fencing at the perimeter to the ceramic rim of the weapon's maw, then simply leapt over the side, following the tramlines down the central shaft and utilizing the jump jets to control the speed and direction of the fall. Narumi howled with delight, and Bagzent, too, experienced a gush of renewed vigor, in spite of his Micronized size. *Oh, to be full-size once more*, he thought. *To occupy the pod in its entirety. To reunite with the Protoculture. To be one with the mecha!*

Moments later, at the base of the central shaft, the Battlepod dropped through a ragged, gaping hole in a concrete ceiling, opened by particle-beam cannon or perhaps by the passing of Salta's craft. Bagzent landed the pod on its reverse-articulated legs and traversed the exterior cameras across a supply room of some sort. Salta's pod was standing nearby. Ten or so Human techs were clustered in a corner of the room, cowering.

"Aayth is on the rim," Salta said. "No reports of further activity at the field. We've captured two mecha intact. Veritechs."

Bagzent nodded for the video pickups, then slowly walked the pod to within twenty feet of the Humans.

"We're not soldiers," one of the Humans said through cupped hands. "We're technicians, and we're unarmed."

"My people in Brasília were unarmed," Bagzent answered over the external speaker. "One thousand one hundred of them were blown to pieces."

A woman in a hard hat stepped forward. "We didn't have anything to do with that. We deplore discrimination of any kind."

"Is that so, Micronian? Then tell me, how many Zentraedi are employed here?"

The Humans regarded one another with confused misgiving.

"I thought as much," Bagzent told them. He enabled the twin autocannons that protruded from the base of the pod and swiveled the muzzles front and center. "Now, prepare to experience the wrath of Khyron's Fist."

Reports of the incidents in Brasília and Venezuela arrived simultaneously at RDF headquarters in Monument City at nine hundred hours local time, and by eleven hundred hours that same morning, members of the general staff were meeting in emergency session. Reinhardt directed the briefing from his customary place on the command curve of the horseshoe-shaped table.

Rick was late in arriving because of a call he had put through to Lisa at the factory. Already present in the room when he slipped in were Caruthers, Maistroff, Herzog, and Aldershot, along with their various aides and adjutants. Exedore was there as well, and, from the newly formed Special Operations Group, Director of Intelligence Niles Obstat and Deputy Director Dimitri Motokoff.

"First things first," Reinhardt said when Rick was seated. "One of the backpack bombs detonated early, killing all three male Zentraedi. The woman—a known sympathizer—survived, but she's not expected to live. Twelve bystanders were killed, and more than two dozen were injured. Leonard's driver was killed outright, and both Senator Moran and Leonard's adjutant sustained slight injuries. Leonard himself escaped without a scratch."

"I'm sure he'll take it as a sign from God," Aldershot muttered.

Reinhardt reserved comment. "At fourteen hundred hours Brasília time today, Leonard issued a proclamation naming himself field marshal of the Army of the Southern Cross. 'A mobile force'—I'm quoting Leonard here—'dedicated to stopping the spread of malcontentism in the Southlands.'"

Grumbles of disbelief rose from the table.

"I might add that he enjoys the full support of the people of Goias district. Senator Moran is pushing for UEG recognition of the Army of the Southern Cross as a legitimate organization. Which would, of course, entitle it to funding for weapons, bases, salaries . . ."

"A cut in UEG funds could delay the Expeditionary mission by years," Rick said. "Maybe scuttle it completely." Lisa and Lang would be crushed, he thought.

"It hasn't taken the UEG very long to subvert us," Herzog said. "Not that this comes as any surprise."

Reinhardt instructed techs in the control booth to display a map of the Southlands on the main screen. "Early this morning, the Zentraedi launched three coordinated strikes: against the Southern Grand Cannon, the commercial airport at Laago City, and the RDF armory in Cuiabá." Reinhardt's laser pointer projected green circles on the three sites. "They were successfully repulsed in Cuiabá, but they managed to hijack three jetliners and two Veritech VF-1As from Laago, and they presently occupy the Grand Cannon, with a force of eight Tactical Battlepods."

"Is one group responsible for all three raids?" Rick asked.

Reinhardt looked to Exedore, who was seated at the left foot of the table. The Zentraedi ambassador distributed reconnaissance photographs before speaking.

"An analysis of the hand-painted markings on the plastrons of the Battlepods indicates that three separate groups are involved." He held up an enlargement of a fistlike symbol. "This glyph, photographed at the Grand Cannon, is meant to be read as 'Khyron's Fist.'" He showed two more enlargements. "This one could be interpreted as either 'Metal' or 'Steel' Wind. And this felinelike third—from Cuiabá—is perhaps 'Jaguar Skull,' though it could have a more generic meaning, such as 'Cat Skull' or simply 'Predator Skull.'"

Maistroff was the first to respond. "Since when do the Zentraedi read *and* write—other than yourself?"

"A fair question, Colonel," Exedore said, turning to him. "And the probable explanation lies in the fact that many Zentraedi received instruction in glyphic reading from RDF trainers when it came to cataloging various objects, such as weapons and nutrients, obtained from the crashsites of Zentraedi warships."

"What's more," Niles Obstat interrupted, "they have Humans assisting them with jungle foraging and technical know-how. Most of them are escaped criminals and disenfranchised Indians. They don't give a damn about Zentraedi rights, but they do have their own reasons for wanting to topple the existing order."

Obstat was tall and balding, though not so much as Gunther Reinhardt. He went on to detail how the intelligence division had placed a Zentraedi spy among the rebels. The operative was a former aide to Breetai, who had been working at the factory when approached about the infiltration mission and had agreed to be Micronized. Thus far, he had succeeded in making one intelligence drop—during reconnaissance of the armory in Cuiabá—which contained information about the rebels' camp on the Xingu River, the resurgence of male-female segregation among them, the presence of as many as two hundred tribal Indians and outlaws, and a plan to turn the whole of the Southlands interior into a kind of Zentraedi control zone.

"Our operative was unable to pass along a forewarning about the attacks on the Laako airport or the Grand Cannon. But we're awaiting further drops from him."

"Fifty-six may have been killed in Venezuela," Reinhardt added. "But if there's a plus side, it's that most of the weapons and usable supplies had already been lofted to the factory." He paused for a long moment, then smiled ruefully. "Leonard has asked if we want his Southern Cross to spearhead the counterstrike."

"Like hell," Aldershot said, leading a chorus of denunciations of the governor.

Reinhardt made a placating gesture. "The UEG has sanctioned the use of force by the RDF, but we're to limit ourselves to the Cannon. Just to keep this situation localized, we'll let the Argentine Base handle the details. Rolf Emerson is in charge down there, but I want the Skull to carry out the raid."

"Why the Skull?" Rick asked.

Reinhardt averted his gaze. "A request from the UEG. For purposes of propaganda, I suppose. Officially, the Skull will be on temporary duty with RDF South. I've notified Captain Sterling that he's been placed in command of the team."

Rick was taken aback. "And Miriya?"

"The UEG prefers that Miriya be dropped from our combat roster. Right now she's more important to us as a role model than a VT pilot. A shining example of homemaker, mother, *former* freedom fighter ... The fully acculturated Zentraedi, or some such thing."

Rick raised his eyes to the ceiling. Wait till Lisa got word of this.

Reinhardt was frowning. "If it wasn't for Cavern City, I

don't think the UEG would have even sanctioned a counterstrike. The Bureau of Reconstruction Management recently appointed a new governor to Cavern—a woman named Lea Carson. And because of Cavern's proximity to the Cannon, Carson's asked the RDF to make a comprehensive study of the city's defenses. So as soon as this mess is cleared up, we're going to send someone down there." The general turned to his adjutant. "What's the name again?"

"Captain Jonathan Wolff," Reinhardt's aide supplied. "Academy graduate, trained as a VT pilot on Macross Island and a tank commander on Albuquerque Base."

Reinhardt nodded. "Wolff, yes. I've heard good things about him."

Aldershot drew attention to himself with a meaningful cough. "Getting back to priorities, General, it seems to me that the situation in Venezuela calls for more than a surgical strike. Now's the time to move against the Zentraedi's camp on the Xingu as well—before they go and cache themselves in the heart of Amazonia."

Rick spoke up. "That's exactly what we *don't* want to do, Major. Unless we're prepared to deal with rioting in every city between here and Brasília."

Aldershot smoothed the ends of his waxed moustache. "Begging the admiral's pardon, but I'd prefer a few weeks of riots to who-knows-how-many years of guerrilla warfare and low-intensity conflicts."

"The UEG has its own reason for limiting us to a surgical strike," Reinhardt said. He deferred to Obstat, who in turn deferred to SOG's deputy director. A man of average height and build, Motokoff had blunt features and a mass of dark curly hair that covered his broad forehead and ears. Head of CD forces aboard the SDF-1, he was also credited with the planning of Operation Star Saver, the rescue mission mounted to save Minmei and Lynn-Kyle from execution by Khyron.

"Our operative reports that the rebels are planning to hold summit talks in Cairo early next year."

"Summit talks with us?" Rick asked.

Motokoff shook his head. "Among themselves. Where each group can make its demands known to the rest. The organizers are the Quandolmo, which Exedore tells me means 'resurrected ones.' They seem to think that Cairo's high radiation count will keep us away."

"How are the Southland's groups planning to reach Africa?" Aldershot wanted to know. "By swimming?"

"That's presumably what the stolen jetliners and VTs are for," Motokoff told him.

Aldershot looked at Reinhardt. "And we're going to allow this?"

"The UEG has ordered us to allow it. It's their belief we'll stand a better chance of negotiating a truce once the hostiles have reached a consensus among themselves."

"They seek nothing more than chaos," Exedore said. "There can be no answering the demands of the Imperative, no lasting peace. Especially between such warlike races."

Rick tensed. "Exedore, I'm getting sick and tired of hearing that line from you. We are not programmed for war."

The ambassador inclined his head ever so slightly. "I'm sorry to say so, Admiral, but it is my belief that you simply answer to different masters than we do. Yours are within yourselves, a product of your upbringing, your animal ancestry, and the fight-or-flight biochemicals bequeathed to you by millions of years of hunting for food."

Rick shook his head. "What about Miriya Parino? She's overcome the Imperative. Even the UEG considers her acculturated. And what about you and Breetai and the others aboard the factory? If three hundred can do it, five thousand can."

"It's true that some of us have been able to keep the Imperative in check, Admiral. But I would never presume to say for how long. More importantly, Miriya Parino Sterling seems to be a special case—the one you might term the exception to the rule. She has even produced an offspring. As for the rest, no amount of exposure to Human emotions could efface the Imperative. Your own admirals Gloval and Hayes agreed with me, not only about the similarities of our warlike natures, but in regard to the odds against achieving any lasting peace. If memory serves, Gloval quoted the odds as 'nothing short of astronomical.' "

"Gloval wasn't right about everything," Rick countered.

"He speculated that the Zentraedi had fought among themselves early on, and you yourself have said that's wrong."

Exedore nodded. "Yes, Zor's documents make no mention of internecine warfare among my people. But that's all the more reason to fear us now. Shamed by defeat, we are easily swayed by the latent force of the Imperative. The Masters made certain that we were familiar with shame. Shame was encoded in us to act as an incentive for seeking revenge on those who shamed us."

"What do you see as the solution, Exedore?" Reinhardt asked disconsolately.

The Zentraedi thought for a long moment, then said, "If I were in your position, I would have all Zentraedi executed."

CHAPTER NINE

One clear indication that Protoculture had its own designs on the Human race is that it wouldn't allow Humans to journey too far from home until they were suitably prepared. Lang and Gloval's first fold miscalculation took them to Pluto instead of the Moon; one shudders to think where a second jump might have delivered them had not crucial parts of the SDF-1's fold system vanished during the space-time transit. Then there was the factory satellite, folded without incident to Earthspace, only to promptly shut down, never to fold again. Some have suggested that Protoculture could sense when it was in hands other than those of the Robotech Masters. Consider, however, the escape from Tirol that Protoculture engineered for itself through Zor, by compelling him to dispatch the sole existing Protoculture matrix far from the Masters' grasp. More to the point, consider how the matrix concealed itself from Lang and the rest, who never once thought of searching the SDF-1's Reflex engines. Not because Protoculture was waiting for Zor Prime or the Masters, but because it was waiting for the Invid Regis.

Mingtao, *Protoculture: Journey Beyond Mecha*

"**B**REETAI, I WAS HOPING YOU'D DECIDED TO BE Micronized for Christmas," Lisa said into her headset microphone on seeing him appear on the bridge of the factory satellite.

The Zentraedi commander faced the cameras that were transmitting his image to the factory's command bubble, some eight hundred feet above the floor of the systems-laden bridge. "As a gift to you, Admiral Hayes, or is it that you wanted me to portray Santa's Claws in some holiday pageant?"

"It's 'Santa Claus,' Breetai. And, no, to both your guesses. It's just that I don't think the sweater I knitted will fit you now."

Breetai's left eyebrow arched, and he loosed a meditative murmur that was closer to a growl. "I've little need of a sweater, Admiral. My uniform suffices for most thermal conditions."

Lisa started to explain that she'd only been joking, but thought better of it.

"Not the easiest person to banter with—even when he's our size," Jim Forsythe said into her ear. He muted the command bubble's audio feed momentarily. "Before he was shuttled down the well to assist Lang in surveying the SDF-1, I quoted him that old line from *King Kong* about having been master of his world only to be brought down by the little guys."

"What did he say?"

"That he was never the master of any world and that he had no objections to being brought down by the little guys because it didn't matter to him *who* piloted the shuttle."

Lisa pressed her fingers to her mouth to stifle a laugh. Her mistake for trying to be funny in the first place. And for continually erring by thinking of the Zentraedi essentially as giant Earthlings, when in fact they were as different from Human beings as Humans were from plants. They hadn't been born so much as grown, and they had been endowed by the Masters of Tirol with near-supernatural abilities, not the least of which was the capacity to venture suitless for brief periods into the airless frigidity of space.

Humor, in any case, was the ultimate test of one's understanding of an alien culture, and Breetai's familiarity with Earth's societies only went back three years or so.

While she was musing, Emil Lang entered the command bubble, looking clearly preoccupied. His pupilless eyes seemed even more inward-turning than usual. Lisa was aware of his concerns about reduced funding for the Expeditionary mission as a consequence of recent outbreaks of malcontentism in the Southlands. The irony was that the threatened cuts weren't originating with the United Earth Government but with the RDF itself, forced suddenly to reckon with the uncertain intentions of Field Marshal Anatole Leonard and his Army of the Southern Cross.

Lang looked tired as well, from his constant shuttling between the factory and Monument City—now to attend UEG sessions. Not to mention the side trips to Tokyo for meetings with Professor Zand and the staff of the Robotech Research Center.

"The others should be here shortly," Lang said absently, glancing at Lisa and Forsythe while flipping through a file thick with Most Secret documents. "Then we can begin."

The bridge was located on level eight of the factory's moonlet-sized main body. Nearly two miles long, including the lofty command bubble, it was an arena-wide highway of sensors, data posts, projecbeam screens, interface banks, holographic tactic tables, and communication modules. And yet the whole of it had been engineered for manual control by the Human-size Masters or—as Exedore had explained—by the various clone triumvirates that served them. Central to the command bubble itself was a strategic and tactical planning table of incredible size, capable of displaying transvid data, computer-generated graphics, superimposed holograms, and real-time or condensed target assessment and acquisition information on as many as 15,000 objects ranging over an area of 500,000 cubic miles.

On Lisa's first tour of the bridge two years earlier she had been awed by the sheer size of the place—a reaction she would have thought impossible after having spent so many years inside the SDF-1. But many sections of Zor's ship had already been resized by the time she was transferred to Macross Island, and the factory was in its original state when it had been captured from Reno: a weigh station for giants and their war machines. And while it was true that she sometimes wished Breetai would opt for permanent Micronization—she cared deeply for him, with or without a sense of humor—she understood the logistic need for having forty-foot-tall beings aboard.

As well as having had to adapt to interior spaces of mind-boggling dimensions, Lisa had also found herself becoming reaquainted with the loneliness of command. Not since Macross Island had so much been demanded of her, nor had she been so caught up in her work. She imagined that Rick was under similar pressures downside, but there at least he had the company of good friends. Lately, she had stopped thinking about the future, because all her thoughts led inevitably to a calculation of the time she might be forced to spend on the factory. Three years? Five years? With each punctuated by a lonely Christmas. Just now it was all she could do to find time for brief phone conversations with Rick.

One by one, Dr. Lang's "others" entered the command bubble: the saturnine and bellicose Harry Penn, designer of exotic mecha; congenial chief engineer Sheamus Bronson; the very reclusive Dr. R. Burke, REF captain, head of weapons research and development, and inventor of the Wolverine assault rifle and the Watchdog antimecha mine; Jevna Parl, the gnomish, Micronized adjutant to Breetai, and the only bald and bearded Zentraedi Lisa had ever seen; and Theofre Elmikk, Breetai's perpetually embittered lieutenant, who served as liaison between Lang's technical crews and EVA teams of full-size Zentraedi tasked with warship dismantlement and reclamation.

"Are we ready to record?" Lang asked the technicians when everyone was seated.

"Whenever you're ready, Doctor," one of them answered.

Lang cleared his throat. "December twenty-two, twenty-fifteen. Premission briefing on the bridge of the factory satellite." He started to name those in attendance but stopped when his eyes met Lisa's. "Isn't Admiral Hunter supposed to be here?"

"According to plan," Lisa said. "But General Reinhardt asked for his assistance in assigning personnel to the Argentine Base."

Lang's tone of voice turned acerbic. "Reinhardt should know better. We need Hunter here."

"Perhaps when the Grand Cannon is retaken," Lisa was careful to say.

"It's my understanding that the Army of the Southern Cross volunteered to handle the situation in Venezuela, and I don't understand why they weren't permitted to. If REF personnel are going to respond to every action initiated by a dissident group, this mission will never launch."

Before anyone could comment, Lang waved a hand in dismissal and resumed his introductory remarks.

"Fifteen years ago, when we got our first look inside the crashed SDF-1, we were presented with a picture of what we would have to confront in the event the ship's owners ever arrived to reclaim it. The weapons systems and the dead giants found aboard the ship altered our view of the universe, and led eventually to the development of the reconfigurable fighting machines that have come to be called 'mecha.' It's telling, however, that Zor's warning message contained no images of Zentraedi Battlepods or Power Armor, but focused instead on the primary assault vehicles of the Invid soldier, the *Gurab* and the *Gamo*. What with the Zentraedi defeat, Zor was correct to award the Invid central place. But the so-called Shock Troopers and Pincer Command Units are only two of several assault crafts the Expeditionary mission must prepare to encounter."

For the next five minutes, Lang led everyone through a computer-generated, table-displayed tour of the Valivarre system of planets, moving outward from sunlike Valivarre to the ringed planet known as Fantoma and the inhabited moon of Fantoma known as Tirol—a somewhat desolate-looking orb, with much of its topography muted by volcanic flows.

"One of the million questions I hope to have answered," Lang said, "is why, with half the galaxy at their disposal, the Masters have chosen to remain on Tirol. If we accept Exedore's statement that the Masters have no attachments to place, then it's unlikely they consider Tirol their home. Do you concur, Breetai?"

"I wouldn't know, Dr. Lang," Breetai answered from the bridge. "I have had few direct dealings with the Masters."

Lang nodded. "Exedore has also stated that the architecture of Tirol's principle city, Tiresia, approximates that of our own Greco-Roman period, with the addition of some ceramic or ultratech innovations, including an enormous pyramid called the Royal Hall. Can you verify this, Breetai?"

Breetai shook his head for the cameras. "I have never made planetfall on Tirol."

"No matter," Lang said. "Breetai may not have set foot in Tiresia, but he has been able to supply us with even more relevant data."

Once more Lang directed everyone's attention to the command bubble's data table, above which a series of holograms began to materialize: a hover platform surmounted by a kind of snowman-proportioned warrior robot; a huge robotic cat with alloy fangs and a segmented tail; other automatons, headless things with bulbous, armored torsos and insectilelike limbs and appendages.

"Bioroid hover," Lang said, motioning to the holoids. "Hellcat, Odeon, Scrim, Crann . . . These, apparently, were created by the Masters in anticipation of a Zentraedi rebellion, led by Commander-in-Chief Dolza, and for use by clones as a police force on occupied worlds. With Breetai and Exedore's help in interpreting some of the documents found aboard this factory, we will be able to supply specifications to Dr. Penn's mecha design group and Dr. Burke's weapons development teams." Lang looked at the two men. "I want to caution both of you about placing any confidence in our ability to get this factory on-line again. Consider it a very large hangar space. Even if we do succeed in identifying and eliminating the glitches, production will be limited to Tactical Battlepods. Officer's Pods were produced elsewhere."

Jevna Parl elaborated on Lang's statement. "This facility specialized in the manufacture of *Regults* with Esbelliben Protoculture drives. *Glaugs*—Officer's Pods, as you call them—have been in short supply since an Invid assault on the Roycommi Weapons Factory."

"Note to Admiral Hunter," Lang directed to the recording secretary. "Discuss project involving new line of tactical simulators featuring Invid and Masters crafts as opponents-slash-targets." He snorted. "Assuming the RDF's accountants will agree to fund such a project."

Lisa watched Lang's ire build. She thought she could read his mind. What was to become of the mission to Plutospace? The surveys of the Zentraedi ships crashed in the trackless forests of the Southlands? The operation directed at salvaging materials from the eighty-six Zentraedi ships a fleet of tugs were maneuvering toward the factory? . . . Where was the funding going to come from? And was there any truth to the rumor that certain high-ranking members of the RDF and the UEG were beginning to talk about an *unmanned* mission to Tirol—a kind of remote appeal for peace?

All at once, Lisa's duties felt light by comparison. And the more she thought about it, the better she began to feel—for Rick as well. Even if he had been shanghaied into contending with the Zentraedi uprisings, at least he was doing so from behind a desk instead of from the cockpit of a Veritech. Which left the heroics to be handled by some other hapless fighter jock. And Lisa free and clear of having to assume any of the blame.

In pre-War times, no self-respecting resident of Buenos Aires would have been lax in making plans to escape the city's heat and humidity at the end of the Christmas holiday. But now, those holiday destinations—the white-sand beaches of Punta del Este and Mar del Plata—were buried yards deep by what Dolza's annihilation bolts had blasted from São Paulo and Montevideo and the near-dead Atlantic had washed ashore. Powerboats, terracotta roof tiles, ornate windowframes, blocks of rebar-impregnated concrete, wooden furniture and doors, plastic goods, tires, the husks of automobiles and train cars, chunks of tarmac, trash, the remains of the dead—a littoral dump that stretched for hundreds of miles north and south of the mouth of the Rio de la Plata, Buenos Aires's shallow and befouled estuary. Post-Rain Christmas meant suffering together in the Plaza de Mayo, enduring the muggy heat and the merciless pollen count.

But what did complaining ever accomplish? Max Sterling had asked himself. Particularly when you understood how the world worked: You railed to your best friend and commanding officer about the political climate of the Southlands, and in return found yourself in the heat. But Max understood, or thought he did. There were plenty of pilots who could have led the counterstrike against the Grand Cannon. But Hunter obviously saw the assignment as a test of Max's loyalty. Rick was making him choose sides between the RDF and those Zentraedi who had reembraced the violent terms of the Imperative. It was possible, in fact, that Rick's message had an even more sinister meaning: his way of saying, either join us on the factory or consider yourself assigned to every counterstrike that comes along.

"Don't you dare think of yourself as one of Governor Leonard's assassins," Miriya had warned him at Fokker Base, with Dana in her arms, trying for all it was worth to tug at her mother's green hair. "You'll be up against a band of renegades, Max—Zentraedi and Human filth. I'd fly proudly at your wing if the RDF would allow me."

Her sentiments had eased what would have made for seven onerous airtime hours in Skull One—Rick's former VF-1S, the VT with the Jolly Rogered tailerons. On arrival at the Argentine Base there had been a couple of hours of rest for the whole team, then a bus ride into the city center, *tapas* at some bar on the Plaza de Mayo, a sneezing fit on the Avenida Nueve de Julio . . .

Miraculously, Dolza's Rain of Death had missed Buenos Aires, but the city had paid a price for being spared. It had become home to hundreds of thousands of refugees from Chile, southern Brazil, Uruguay, and Bolivia. The city's sizable Zentraedi population had come from the hundreds of ships that had crashed in the Argentine mesopotamia—on the forested plains of Chaco, between the Parana and Uruguay rivers—and the hundreds more that still stippled the pampas and the windswept plateaus of Patagonia. Unlike in Brasília or Belo Horizonte, however, in BA the Zentraedi had been welcomed—even the most recent wave of aliens fleeing martial law in the Goias and Mato Grosso districts.

At four in the afternoon on the day following his arrival, Max was back on base, sipping a glass of limeade on the veranda of the commander's house. The base was well away from the city, fifty miles west of the Avellaneda industrial center, where sundry animal products, like hides and wool, were processed before being shipped north. Max could make out mountains in the distance, eucalyptus and chinaberry trees in the middle ground, and the ruins of an old *estancia* on the far side of the VT landing strip. He was mulling over the upcoming mission when the commander strode onto the veranda.

"Captain Sterling," Max said, leaping to attention. "Reporting as ordered, sir."

"At ease, Sterling," the major said, motioning Max back to his seat, then extending a hand. "Honored to meet you in person. I'm Rolf Emerson."

Max shook hands. Emerson was fine-featured and solid-looking, and his baritone voice betrayed a slight Australian accent. "We have mutual friends in Monument City, Major—Lisa Hayes and Vince and Jean Grant."

"How is Admiral Hayes?" Emerson asked, pouring himself a glass of limeade.

"Frankly, sir, I haven't seen her in months. Not since she shipped for the factory."

"That monstrosity," Emerson said with patent disdain. He sat down and raised his glass in a toast. "To better days, Sterling." He took a long gulp and set the drink aside. "So what's your impression of BA?"

"Hot and crowded. But it's wonderful to see a city with most of its buildings intact."

"You're not kidding." Emerson's brown eyes appraised him for a moment. "Sorry you have to be down here for the reasons you are."

Max hid his true feelings. "About the mission—"

"Suppose we leave that for tomorrow's briefing." When Max gave him an uncertain look, Emerson added, "Having misgivings?"

"Some."

Emerson nodded. "I think I understand. But war sometimes throws us into peculiar circumstances, Sterling. I shouldn't have to tell you that. Hell, back in Australia, before the Visitor, I fought against the Neasians when they tried to march into Melbourne. Then, five years later, I fought *with* them when the Exclusionists had a go at the place."

"You were born there?"

"In Sydney, yes. I was fifteen when Macross Island became the center of the world. Me and a couple of friends sailed there all the way from New Zealand, just to get a look at the ship, but the supercarrier *Kenosha* had the place blockaded. Like nearly every other sixteen-year-old, I enlisted in the RDF in the hope of getting posted to Macross, but that never happened. Instead, I was stationed right in Sydney and assigned to cleaning up the mess the Exclusionists had left behind. How about you, Max? How old were you when the SDF-1 arrived?"

"Ten. When I heard about it I thought it was some kind of movie promotion."

A tall, dark-complected woman with handsome, angular features appeared on the veranda to refill the pitcher with limeade. Max watched her intently.

"Her name's Ilan Tinari," Emerson explained when the woman was out of earshot. "We came here from Australia two years ago, when my request for a transfer came through." He paused for a moment. "I lost my wife and our only child in the Rain."

"I'm sorry," Max said—the most oft-repeated phrase since the events of 2012. "Where did you two meet?"

"She became my chauffeur and bodyguard in Sydney when we were trying to pick up the pieces Dolza left us." Emerson watched Max for a moment, then said, "Go ahead, Sterling, say what's on your mind."

"She's Zentraedi."

Emerson smiled lightly. "You'd know, wouldn't you?"

"I only meant—"

"I know what you meant: that you generally don't see much fraternization between male RDF officers and female Zentraedi. Excepting yourself, of course. But you'd be surprised at the men I could name who consort on a regular basis with Zentraedi women."

Normally, Max wouldn't have asked, but it was plain from Emerson's expression that the major wanted him to.

"Anatole Leonard, for one," Emerson said. "Brasília's best-kept secret. But you didn't hear it from me. Besides, I'm not certain it's still going on."

Max was dumbfounded. "Then how can Leonard be so intolerant of Zentraedi rights?"

"He's a complex man, Sterling. I wouldn't even presume to be able to explain it. No more than I could explain how it is that I'm with a person whose race was responsible for the death of my family. Or that you're married to a woman whose people you're about to engage in combat." Emerson shrugged. "Maybe we should chalk it up to the confusion of the times."

At sunrise, in the small circular chapel that stood beside Brasília's Alvorado Palace, Anatole Leonard thanked God for protecting him from the aliens' bombs. Daily prayer had long been a ritual in Leonard's life, but the sunrise sessions had only begun a month earlier, on the morning following the assassination attempt.

As old as the city itself, the Alvorado was Leonard's place of residence. The work of governing the district was done at the nearby Palacio de Planalto; but Alvorado, on the shore of Lake Paranoa, was where he relaxed, prayed, punished and, yes, was punished in return.

He understood that the bombs had constituted a warning of sorts, one aimed at demonstrating how easily evil concealed itself in the world at large. He had been arrogant that November morning in thinking himself invulnerable, in relaxing his focus on the holy imperative to eradicate the malevolent spawn of the Visitor. And so God had arranged it that others should suffer in his place—the chauffeur, the senator, young Joseph Petrie, dozens of people guilty only of adoring him . . . God was clever that way, knowing that when it came to punishing Leonard for straying, no one took a stronger hand than Leonard himself.

But where was his physical tormentor? *Gone.* Missing for months now, disappeared into the city's slums with the great gift he had given her. Oh, how in need she was of a touch of the whip he had taught her to wield—a taste of the flame, a flick of the blade. *Satan's Whore!* he screamed at the memory of her. This wasn't the exquisite torture of being left chained to a bed, crazed for her slow return and promised forgiveness. This was abandonment, pure and simple, treachery of the highest order, and if and when he ever found her he would teach her new things about pain. Then, done with her, he would make her disappear for good. The way he had the doctors who had assisted him in impregnating her. The way he would do with Max Sterling and Miriya Parino should an opportunity ever present itself.

But until such time as his vengeful fantasies could be ful-filled, he could do little more than beg God's forgiveness and promise to expand his campaign against the wretched Zentraedi.

He began his penance but had only reached his fifth ren-dition of the Lord's Prayer when Joseph Petrie interrupted him with a whisper from the rear of the chapel.

"Senator Moran is here to see you."

Rather than check his watch, Leonard conferred with the light entering through the chapel's rose window. "At this hour?"

"He has someone with him."

"Someone I should know?"

"The senator seems to think so."

Leonard instructed his aide to show Moran and his guest to the breakfast room of the palace, then he resumed his prayers, punctuating them with bows of his shaved head and sharp, fisted blows to his massive chest. When he marched into the breakfast room forty minutes later, he was wearing his woolen uniform and shiny black jackboots.

Patty Moran stood up to greet him, supporting himself on the ivory-handled cane that had been his constant com-panion since the assassination attempt. Moran's blond, half-masked guest remained seated on the brocade chair. Leonard needed no introductions.

"Thomas Edwards," he said, genuinely surprised to find the man alive after some three years. "The last I heard you were at Alaska Base when the Grand Cannon was de-stroyed."

"You heard right," Edwards told him flatly.

Leonard was momentarily nonplussed. "But I thought Lisa Hayes was the only one who got out of there alive."

Edwards sneered. "Then I guess you heard wrong."

Leonard didn't bother to pursue it, knowing he would be lied to in any case. As far back as the Global Civil War, Edwards had enjoyed that kind of reputation: mercenary for the Neasians, "facilitator" for the World Unification Alli-ance, intelligence officer for the Russo-and-Hayes-run United Earth Defense Council ... "What brings you to

Brasília, Mr. Edwards?" Leonard finally got around to asking.

Moran traded amused looks with Edwards. "Thomas has a Christmas present for you, Anatole."

Leonard regarded Edwards and laughed. "Imagine my embarrassment—I must have overlooked your name on my shopping list."

Edwards went along with the joke, laughing out of the undamaged side of his once-attractive mouth. "Well, how about this," he said. "I give you your gift now, and I accept your IOU for mine."

Leonard straightened his smile. "I take that to mean you know what you want."

Again, Moran and Edwards traded looks. "Did I mention," the senator said, "that Thomas has been providing the UEG with some first-rate intelligence regarding the Zentraedi malcontents? Works very closely with Niles Obstat and Dimitri Motokoff, who personally brief the RDF on all developments."

Wearying of the game, Leonard nodded, then scowled. "Suppose we come to the point, Patty."

Moran started to speak, but Edwards cut in. "All I want for Christmas is the promise of a high-rank commission in the Army of the Southern Cross. Not now, and maybe not for years to come, but at my say-so."

Leonard stared at him in astonished disbelief. "You want to be a general in my army. In exchange for what?"

Edwards met Leonard's gimlet gaze. "A bit of intelligence that's going to put 'your' army neck and neck with the RDF." He paused briefly. "The only catch is that you have to be willing to travel to get the most out of it."

2016

CHAPTER TEN

"When it came to registering them [the Zentraedi], we found ourselves up against some real problems. Because only a few of them knew how to write the glyphs for their names, most of us had to come up with a spelling based on how they pronounced their names, which usually turned out to depend on which battalions they'd been attached to during the War, and so on. So what happened, was most of us [at Macross's Alien Registry Bureau] started making the names intelligible by using close-sounding words. I remember we'd go through different phases. Like one week we'd be into using names for office stuff or things you'd find around a house, and another week we'd be thumbing through a French or Arabic dictionary. Once, we even got over into Native American culture. I can't tell you how many 'Saloiois' became 'Seloy,' and how many 'Shaaynnas' became 'Cheyenne.' "

Unattributed source quoted in Tommy Luan's *High Office*

OUTSIDE THE DAUNTING ENTRANCE TO FOKKER AEROspace's Defense Force Administration Center, a military limousine was waiting in the snow. Fat flakes were melting on contact with the car's hot hood and piling on the epauletted shoulders of two soldiers standing guard. Christmas wreaths adorned with crimson bows hung in the tall windows on either side of the center's sliding glass doors, and holiday Muzak was wafting from speakers concealed somewhere in the Spartan vastness of the lobby.

Descending into the lobby by escalator, Rick asked himself if this was indeed his life or if he'd inadvertently wandered into some stranger's anxiety dream. Nothing felt entirely real, neither the limo nor the falling snow, and least of all the red-haired lieutenant with the document-stuffed attaché cuffed to her left wrist who recently had been assigned to him. Even now the young woman was chattering into his ear about scheduled appointments at RDF HQ in Monument City. Rick had a sudden urge to switch identities with her, though he understood that to be a product of his own dreaming.

Nevertheless, once the two of them had stepped from the moving stairway, Rick instructed the lieutenant to proceed to the car without him, explaining that he had matters of a personal nature to attend to elsewhere on Fokker Base, and that he would find his own ride into Monument City in time for the next appointment. The aide hesitated, but only for a moment, offering a crisp salute before hurrying through the sliders into the snow squall.

Rick waited for the limousine to move off, then walked across the expansive lobby to where a fighter-mode Veritech was suspended by monofilament cables from the arched ceiling. An inscribed brass plaque affixed to the belly of the fuselage explained that the mecha—the *Valkyre*—was the first-generation VF-1J Fokker Aerospace's eponymous Roy had flown during the War. The *Valkyre* had been moved from Macross City to Monument several weeks before Khyron's raid, first to the Mecha Museum on the Excaliber base, then to the aerospace base on the day of its official dedication. Rick had piloted the VT for a short period following Fokker's death, almost four years earlier. But it felt like yesterday, Rick frequently told himself, as he suspected would ever be the case.

The obvious reasons notwithstanding, the War against the Zentraedi had redefined the meaning of holocaust. Where survivors of previous wars or natural catastrophes had had to cope with deaths numbering in the hundreds or even the thousands, the Robotech War had left every survivor on Earth coping with the deaths of hundreds of millions. Every husband who had lost a wife; every parent who had lost a child; every child who had lost parents and siblings alike; every sole survivor of a village or a small city who had lost parents, siblings, relatives, and neighbors . . . The War had erased entire lineages from Humankind's family tree; worldwide, people were left family- and friend-less. *Less*.

Not a day passed that Rick didn't think about Roy—his best friend and confidant, his inspiration for stunt flying, his instructor in the mental and physical disciplines of mecha combat. Rick knew a lasting ache in his heart from not being able to talk to him. To some extent, Max Sterling had assumed the role of closest friend, but Rick and Max didn't always see eye to eye on judgment calls—the use of force against the dissident Zentraedi, for one thing. That was because Rick had, to some extent, *become* Roy—Roy as a career fighter jock. Besides, Max was too unassuming and even-tempered to ever replace impetuous Roy. Rick figured, for instance, that had Roy been around to talk some sense into him, he probably wouldn't have spent years bouncing back and forth between Lisa and Minmei. And Roy—a pilot to the last—would have stuck by him when Rick wanted to refuse the promotion. They might have ended up wingmen on the same VT team, perhaps in the Southlands, on the very mission to which Max had been assigned.

Max wanted to believe that Rick was responsible for the assignment, that it was blackmail of a sort, designed to force Max to choose between the REF or several years of pursuing malcontents through the Amazon rain forest. Opting for the former entailed leaving Earth; opting for the latter, the risks posed by daily combat. Either way, Rick would have preferred the luxury of a choice. And he had no illusions about malcontentism, as Max seemed to have. That the Zentraedi were Miriya's people didn't mean that they were her family. Like so many Earthers now, Miriya had no family. But should Miriya decide to accuse Max of crimes against her race, was Rick then entitled to hold Miriya—another of his closest friends—accountable for Roy's death? After all, it was the all-female Quadrono battalion that had carried out the raid against the then-grounded SDF-1 in which Roy, Kramer, and so many other Defense Force fighters had died. Miriya might have loosed the blue beam that brought the *Valkyre* down. In the same way, Rick might as well hold Lisa personally accountable for the burst of friendly fire that had left him critically injured during that same battle.

Circling the suspended Veritech, he imagined himself flying with the Skull again—flying, instead of attending briefings, reviewing dossiers, and arguing with government bureaucrats and number crunchers over each and every requested REF expenditure. But thoughts of mechamorphing with the Skull were simply more flights of fantasy. He was no longer a pilot; he was a public relations executive costumed in an admiral's uniform. He wanted to bitch about it to Lisa, but she was so seldom available she might as well have already left for Tirol. Bitching, in any case, wasn't what he was really after. He wanted to talk to her, friend to friend, and confide in her, lover to lover.

The squall had moved through by the time he stepped outside. He acknowledged the guards' salutes as he walked to the curb of the circular drive.

"Should I call for a car, Admiral?" one of the guards asked.

Rick had his mouth open to respond when a limousine pulled up alongside him and the driver's side rear window began to lower.

"Rick!" Behind the sunglasses and beneath the cowboy hat was Minmei. "Rick!" she repeated.

His look of disbelief gave way to puzzled surprise. "What are you doing here?"

She huffed. "Almost a year since I've seen you and that's what you ask—what I'm doing on base? Well, if you must know, I've enlisted in the REF." When Rick's jaw had dropped sufficiently, she added, "I'm only joking, Rick—though the REF could do worse than have me aboard."

"So then what—"

"I was with Colonel Caruthers. He's been giving me flying lessons. At least he was until the snow started. But, Rick, now I understand why you love flying. It's so fun."

"Yeah," Rick mumbled.

Minmei reached out the window for his hand. "I can't believe it's you. I've been meaning to call . . ."

"Me, too," Rick said quickly.

She grinned knowingly. "You've been busy. And congratulations on your promotion. The uniform suits you."

"More than the rank."

"How's Lisa? Is she here?"

Rick raised his chin to the overcast sky. "She's upside. On the factory."

"Will she be down for Christmas?"

"I doubt it."

"That's a shame." Minmei paused for a moment, then brightened. "Rick, are you busy right now?"

Rick checked his watch. "I have to be in the city by two-thirty."

"That's perfect, we have just enough time."

"For what?"

Minmei opened the door. "Get in, Admiral. Let it be my surprise."

They caught each other up on events of the past year while the limo carried them into Monument City. Minmei talked about her months in Hawaii and about having recently signed with theatrical agent, Samson O'Toole, who was negotiating a talk-show deal with the proposed Lorelei Network. The cowboy hat complemented the rest of her outfit of jeans, fringed jacket, and snakeskin boots.

Rick said little; each time he tried to respond to her questions, she interrupted him and brought the conversation back to herself. The limousine stopped in front of the restaurant Chez Mann.

"For old times' sake," Minmei said, slipping her arm through his as they were headed for the entrance.

The last time they'd been to Chez Mann she'd given him a scarf that made him look like some World War I biplane flyboy. They had talked about her career struggles, her problems with Lynn-Kyle, her desire to be finished with the "People Helping People Tour"—which the media had nicknamed the Grateful Undead tour. Minmei had had too much wine. Then Kyle himself had made an unexpected appearance, lecturing her about irresponsibility, tossing a drink in her face, tugging her from the restaurant. Seemed she'd kept an audience waiting somewhere, much as Rick had left Lisa waiting with a packed picnic basket at the Seciele Coffee House in Macross . . .

"Do you ever wish we could turn back the clock, Rick?"

"To when?" Rick nearly snapped. "I mean, when were things ever easy in our lifetimes? The Global Civil War, years of low-intensity fighting between the Internationalists and the Exclusionists, the War with the Zentraedi, Khyron . . ."

"You're right, I suppose. But I was happy aboard the SDF-1."

"I heard you tell Katherine Hyson that."

"It's just that so much has changed since then." Minmei stepped to one side to regard him. "Look at you, look at me."

Rick glanced over Minmei's shoulder and smiled. "Some things haven't changed at all." When she had followed his look and spied a group of teenagers approaching them, he added, "People still want your autograph."

Minmei started to say something when the leader of the teenage pack waved a piece of paper in the air. "Admiral Hunter," the youth asked, "would you sign this for me?"

Minmei laughed and Rick laughed with her. "See, I told you things have changed." She took hold of Rick's hand and gave it an affectionate squeeze. "Let's at least be friends like we were before. I've got no one to talk to, Rick."

Max felt a drop of sweat trickle down the side of his face from sideburn to jaw and work its way beneath the rolled-foam collar of the thinking cap. It was three o'clock in the morning on New Year's Day in Buenos Aires and the temperature outside the Veritech was fifty-nine degrees; inside the cockpit, though, with the permaplas canopy lowered and the air conditioning switched off, the ambient temperature was closer to ninety, and Max—not only in helmet but in multi-layered flightsuit—was dressed for Arctic conditions.

He opened the tactical net to take a quick roll call of Skull's elite, each pilot crafted inside his mecha on the Argentine Base jet strip: Ransom, Phelps, Fowler, Greer, Mammoth, Bell, Zotz. Lieutenant Ransom, presently at Max's left wingtip, was second in command and, along with Mammoth and Fowler, had flown with Hunter during the War. Bobby Bell was the youngest pilot, but Teddy Zotz—fresh out of Fokker Aerospace Academy and brother of Frankie, manager of the Close Encounters game arcade in Monument—was Skull's most recent addition. With the exception of Zotz, who was partnered with a VF-1A, the team flew twin-lasered VF-1Js.

"Preflight auxiliary checklist," Max said over the net. He flipped a series of toggles on the instrument console and watched the data-display screen for self-check responses. "Thermal shields—check; rad shields—check . . ." Telescopic enhancement, utility arms override, pilot seat hydraulic, radio/video feeds, collision warning system, canopy-ejection—manual, HUD mode control, threat-identity display, weapons-next toggle, laser targeting, interrogate friend-or-foe control display, countermeasures—electronic, chaff, flares . . .

The newer-generation Veritechs had sixty-seven controls, ranging from foot pedals to operate the legs to levers to activate the mecha's folding-torso system, though all were subordinate to the master control, which was the pilot's brain. Throwing the Guardian-mode lever without *thinking* the craft through the appropriate changes could land a pilot in serious trouble. The thinking cap was the material interface between Human and machine, but a thinking cap was only as efficient as the pilot who wore it. Mechamorphosis depended on a shrewd symbiosis between Human and mecha—or, depending on who you asked, between Human and Protoculture.

Piloting the VT in fighter mode, however, could be as uncomplicated as piloting a conventional craft—easier, since the Veritech's command computer was capable of not only executing perfect takeoffs and landings, but plotting courses, making necessary corrections, and tracking as many as fifty individual targets. Anything but biochauvinistic, Max had already instructed the computer to handle Skull One's takeoff and to plot the team's course north to the site of the Grand Cannon, in the Guayana Highlands of the Venezuela Sector—a distance of almost three thousand miles. Tasked, the computer informed him that their cruising altitude would be 35,000 feet, at a median airspeed of Mach one. Given the weather conditions, the estimated flight time was four hours and ten minutes; estimated time of arrival at the target was 6:40 A.M., Vene zuela-local time. Fuel was not a concern; a Protoculture-celled VT was good for approximately twelve years of continuous intra-atmospheric flying.

Max placed his gloved fingertips on the console keyboard and called up a map of the Southlands. The flight path would take them over the Argentine mesopotamia, the still-viable city of Asunción, Cuiabá, the forested interior of Amazonas, and Manaus, and on into the lost-world mesa region of Roraima. Darkness would mask the scarred landscape: the craters put there by annihilation bolts and fallen warships, the endless tracts of blanched forest, the burned and irradiated cities. Only the rising sun, blood-red behind a pall of lingering ash, would betray what had happened below.

Airborne, Max kept Skull One on autopilot, freeing himself to reflect on the past few days and perhaps think forward through the coming few. Anything to keep from thinking about the present.

Meeting and talking with Rolf Emerson had been an unexpected pleasure. Max hoped that Emerson and his companion would be transferred to Monument so that the friendship could continue to grow. A friendship between Miriya and the dark-complected Ilan might even be of some benefit to Dana; she would at least come to realize that the Zentraedi world didn't begin and end with Rico, Konda, and Bron. Alternatively, Max would have to see about getting Miriya to visit Buenos Aires to meet Emerson and Ilan, just to get things rolling. . . .

And he was going to have to confront Rick about pressuring him to join the REF. Max formulated possible replies and rehearsed some of the lines to himself: *I'm not a diplomat*, he would tell Rick. *And I refuse to sign on as a potential combatant against the Masters or the Invid—not with Miriya and Dana aboard.* And there was no way he would leave either of them behind . . .

Three and a half hours later, almost two hundred miles short of the Grand Cannon, Max established contact with Cavern City's RDF Base, employing a quantum-encrypted laser signal. The sun had been up for over an hour and the pale blue dome of the sky was brushed with crystalline cirrus.

"Skull leader to Cav City, requesting a news update. Anything to tell me, Control?"

Max waited for the on-board computer to decrypt the reply, hoping to hear that the situation had been resolved. But earlier intelligence reports remained unchanged: The Cannon was in the hands of no fewer than fifteen Zentraedi, armed with eight Tactical Battlepods. Mecha for mecha the odds were nearly even, but Skull had the advantage because the pods were manned by Micronized Zentraedi; even if the headless ostriches' weapons arrays were packing full plasma charges, they wouldn't be as maneuverable or in-close capable. Generally speaking, pods only succeeded through sheer numbers, in any case.

At one hundred miles out, Max again contacted Cavern City, but this time without running the signal through the VT's encrypter. At the premission briefing it had been decided that the Skull should attempt to lure the pods into an aerial encounter. Max was grateful for any strategy that kept him from having to hear the sound of pods running on their cloven feet—a grating, almost chain-clanking noise that still rattled him five years after first hearing it on Macross Island. Battlepods might be the grunts of the Zentraedi forces, but the strident sound of an overland charge by two or three hundred pods could unsettle even the most hardened RDF combat veteran.

From twenty miles out, Max could see the gaping high-tech maw of the never-completed Southern Cannon. With the IFF still silent, he went on the net to order the Skull into a low-vector approach. Then, at the fifteen-mile mark, the targeting computer chirped and the threat-assessment display screen filled with paint. Max emptied his mind of concerns for the future, and attended to the business of war.

"Six bandits at twelve o'clock," he sent over the net. "Enabling laser targeting and Mongoose heat-seekers. Prepare to break formation on my mark."

Max ordered video enhancement of the approaching mecha as electronic icons swung crazily through the onscreen targeting reticles. The sure-kill zone for most pods was behind and slightly below the juncture of the reverse-articulated legs, but none of the enemy were showing vulnerable profiles.

"Reconfiguring to Guardian mode," Max said, and, with a predatory bank, peeled away from the formation and fell upon the enemy.

Seloy Deparra stood at the port-side rail of the *Sin Verguenza* and swept her eyes along the Caribbean coast of what someone aboard the run-down trawler had referred to as Nicaragua. The sun was setting behind the shore's fringe of palms, suffusing the sky with shades of pink and purple. Seloy put her face into the wind and licked the sea salt from her lips. The four-day crossing from the ruined city of Barranquilla had been peaceful, but she was eager to plant her feet on dry land once more. The infant was quiet for a change, asleep in its basket, on its stomach with its legs bent and rear end raised. The boy child had spent most of the days and nights whimpering, either from hunger or some illness contracted during the arduous journey north from Brasília; Seloy couldn't tell which, and none of the Human crew had been inclined to come to her aid. Several times she had tried to get tiny Hirano to suckle at her breast, but her milk, which had never flowed strongly, had dried up.

"Once we're ashore, we still have a long trip ahead of us," Marla Stenik commented from a few feet away along the rail.

"How long?" Seloy asked.

"Freetown is almost a thousand miles northeast of our port of call. Figure on a week's travel."

"By ship?"

Boyish-looking Marla shook her head. "Overland. Perhaps on foot."

The two women had met in Barranquilla, where they were among a group of thirty-six Zentraedi—women, mostly—all seeking passage to the Northlands. It had taken Seloy six months to get that far, surviving on the scrip she had stolen from the child's father when, sick to death of the games she had been enticed to perform with him, she had left him to the luxuries of his Brasília palace. At the time she had little understanding of those games, though Marla had been helpful in explaining some of them since.

Seloy and the infant had gone into hiding after the May riots, then fled Brasília in the company of forty or so other frightened and equally disillusioned refugees. Never had the prospect of lasting peace between Humans and Zentraedi seemed more untenable. For a time, when she'd felt most vulnerable, Seloy had considered contacting Miriya, but in the end had decided that Miriya was better off thinking her dead. Hirano's father, obsessed with his search, would have inspected each of the dead rioters personally. And surely he was still looking for them. So it was better that Miriya remained ignorant of her whereabouts and plans.

She could only hope that the next team of assassins would succeed at their mission.

Midway into her sexual relationship with Anatole Leonard, she had begun to recall the rumors she'd heard about Khyron and Azonia in their final days, when the Imperative had broken down and they'd given themselves over to physical gratification. Seloy had had no inkling of the dangers of Human love, lust, or sexuality when she met Leonard; but she had been willing to give the relationship a try, as Miriya had with Max Sterling. Leonard, though, wasn't looking for a love partner but a disciplinarian—and who better to torture Human flesh than a Zentraedi? His addiction to pain and degradation had constituted an Imperative, of sorts, and so his desire to create a child with her had only confused her all the more. Particularly since the act was devoid of the intimacy Miriya had told her about. Instead, in keeping with the engineered thing that she was, she was artificially inseminated, rendered a mere piece of birth machinery. And when she learned late in her pregnancy—her body so altered she scarcely recognized it and her mind so warped by hormones that she couldn't think clearly—of Leonard's plan to keep the child for himself, she knew that she had to flee her royal prison and bear the child in safety. Two sympathizers, ignorant of her ethnic background, had midwived the birth and helped her to decide on the name, Hirano, which suggested a condition of being caught between opposing forces.

That first horrible night in radiation-poisoned Barranquilla, Marla Stenik had spied the infant and had asked Seloy why she was carrying the thing. Seloy had lied, answering that she had found the baby abandoned in Manaus. As to why she was carrying it, she said that the helpless thing had aroused her curiosity, adding that she felt no real attachment to it—which, in fact, was partially true. She marveled at the bond Miriya had apparently been able to form with her daughter, Dana.

During the sea crossing, Marla slowly revealed that two months earlier she had attended a rebel meeting in a jungle encampment well north of Brasília. Several hundred Imperative-driven Zentraedi and at least half that number of disaffected Humans had joined forces to launch raids on various Southlands cities and RDF installations. But Marla made it clear that she hadn't been encouraged by what she saw at the camp. While some of the Zentraedi had worked with Humans, it was obvious that they had learned nothing of Human culture or psychology. These were Zentraedi who still put their trust in Battlepods—as had the group known as Khyron's Fist, whose recent seizure of the useless Grand Cannon could only end in defeat and further shame for the Zentraedi race. Who would profit from their rashness, save for those who would die mistaken in the belief they had done so under the aegis of the Imperative?

Marla favored lofting a force of Zentraedi to the factory satellite and skyjacking the dimensional fortress under construction there. "The fortress is the key to our survival as a race," Marla had opined. She was certain that there were Zentraedi forces scattered throughout Sol's system of planets, waiting to connect with those whose warships had crashed on Earth.

Seloy and Marla's somewhat one-sided conversation had been overheard by two Zentraedi females, who had wandered over to introduce themselves. Vivik Bross was a small-boned, pixie-eared former Quadrono, while Xan Norri, with her high cheekbones and mounds of pale hair, could have sprung from the same clone queue that generated Seloy.

"I'm also in favor of infiltrating the factory," Bross said.

"Not to skyjack a ship that won't be spaceworthy for years to come, but to organize a network for smuggling mecha parts down the well to our beleaguered forces."

Seloy could still recall the amused look on Marla's face. "And just who among our 'beleaguered forces' has the know-how to make use of these mecha parts?"

Bross had pointed to Xan Norri. "She does."

Xan, it emerged, had worked closely in Macross City with a Human scientist named Harry Penn, who headed up the RDF's mecha design team. Penn had talked endlessly to Xan about the inner workings of Veritechs and Destroids. The war-widowered Penn had even confessed his love for her, begging that his secret be kept.

Xan's revelation had set Marla laughing. "I sometimes think that this thing the Humans call 'sex' is our real strength as female Zentraedi. Kissing with open mouths, touching, stroking body parts . . . Men will do anything for it. So it seems to me that the very weapon the Humans used against us during the War could be turned against them."

"Have you tried it?" Bross wanted to know.

"Of course I have," Marla told her. "How do you think I paid for my passage aboard this foul-smelling ship? And, trust me, I'm not the only one."

Seloy was struck by the fact that no one spoke for a long moment. Had exchanging sex for favors become a common though secret practice among Zentraedi females?

"So about these mecha you want to build?" Marla said at last.

"We've discovered a way to convert Female Power Armor into weapons of terror. We've already fashioned a prototype."

Seloy couldn't believe her ears. "The prototype is more powerful than Female Power Armor?"

Bross nodded. "It has three times the firepower, and it can be piloted by remote."

Even Marla was impressed.

"Our idea is to let the male groups attend to the actual combat," Xan went on. "They're reasonably good at it, and the fighting will keep them out of our way. They would never permit a female group to lead them, but I'm certain they'll have no qualms about being supplied with weapons that match the new Veritechs in missile strength and maneuverability."

"It's all about inciting terror," Bross added. "Humans have an inborn fear of haphazard violence."

Marla was shaking her head. "Even at its most efficient, a smuggling organization based on the factory won't be able to supply what you need."

"Only some of the parts would have to come from upside," Xan argued. "Protoculture cells, remorphing relays, that sort of thing. Otherwise, we have what we need right here on Earth. Aboriginals in the Southlands have been guiding the male groups to warships so concealed by the jungle that they haven't even been logged and plundered by RDF reclamation teams. Some are plunged to their stern thrusters into the ground, others are submerged in rivers. And in addition to the ships, we have a third source: a former Quadrono named Neela Saam, who is involved in the black market in Freetown, near the city of Mexico. That's where Vivik and I are headed, along with sixteen others aboard this ship."

Seloy was taken with Xan's intelligence and confidence. "Sounds as though you've already organized yourself into a band."

"We've named ourself the Senburu," Bross supplied. She lifted her shirtsleeve to reveal a crudely executed body marking, similar to the ones many Humans sported on limbs and torsos. The term *Senburu* meant "silent leadership"; the dye drawing depicted the face of a woman with a hand across her mouth.

"I want to join you," Seloy had announced, only to be ridiculed by Marla and Bross.

"The Senburu needs warriors," Marla commented, "not would-be *mothers*."

Seloy delivered her response with firm pride: "The infant is mine; I birthed it. His name is Hirano and mine is Seloy Deparra, former commander of the Lightning Brigade."

The mouths of her audience fell. "*T'sen* Deparra," Marla said with wide-eyed deference. "If I'd known—"

"How could you know?" Seloy had asked. "How could any of us be expected to recognize one another on this world, after what the Humans have done to us? We are ghosts of our former selves. But I promise one thing: that we can make them pay for their injustices."

CHAPTER ELEVEN

It never occurred to them [the Malcontents in possession of the Southern Grand Cannon] that the largely dismantled Cannon was worthless to anyone. So, the question frequently asked is why the RDF couldn't simply have allowed Khyron's Fist to remain where it was, rather than strike back, making martyrs of the Malcontents and ushering in the years of violence that followed. The answer, of course, is the same one invariably offered up as an excuse for responding to violence with violence: an example needed to be set.
Raphael Mendoza, *The Malcontent Uprisings*

"DO YOU HAVE A PASS TO BE ADMITTED ON base?" a corporal at Fokker Aerospace's intimidating front gate had asked.

"I'm Miriya Parino," she had told him, only to hear the question repeated with hostile impatience.

"You have a pass or not?"

"I'm Max Sterling's . . . wife," she managed.

The corporal had paled some, making rapid hand gestures to a security officer in the gate control booth. "I'm sorry, ma'am, uh, Mrs. Sterling. Pass right on through."

It wasn't the first time she'd been singled out for second-class treatment—the lustrous green hair consistently betrayed her—but the incident had left her feeling humiliated and angry, and Dana's insubordination was only making matters worse. The two of them were in the civilian waiting room of the Administrative Center, Miriya pacing back and forth in front of the tall windows that overlooked the jet landing field, Dana running circles around her when not climbing the seats, tipping over wastebaskets, and yelling at the top of her lungs. Elsewhere in the room were the wives, friends, and lovers of other Skull Team members: Sara

Mammoth; Greer's friend, Lee something-or-other; and Tom Foley, Jim Ransom's companion. Miriya liked Jim and Tom, individually and as a couple. Where heterosexual coupling was a source of confusion to many Zentraedi, homosexuality had a certain logic to it. Long segregated by gender, the Zentraedi identified with the concept of like-with-like, if not fully with the sexual component of the partnering.

Skull's retaliatory raid against the Southern Grand Cannon had been termed an unqualified success by the RDF: no losses for the team, and seven out of what turned out to be nine Battlepods destroyed. The other two had escaped. On learning of the success Miriya had examined her feelings. Certainly she felt something akin to relief knowing that Max was safe. But even though she was growing increasingly concerned for her fellow Zentraedi and increasingly distrustful of the motives of both the RDF and the UEG, she felt no sympathy for the malcontents who had died in Venezuela—neither pity nor sadness. Seven *Battlepods* had been destroyed. Not until that morning, during the ride to Fokker, had she stopped to think of the fourteen lost lives.

That in itself was unZentraedilike. The qualities of empathy and sympathy had not been written into the program the Masters had devised for their clone creations. Arrogance and aggression were the touchstones of Zentraedi character. Most lacked the ability to remember events from one moment to the next, so there was little sense of personal or racial history to their lives. They were empty shells, waiting to be filled and drained again and again. None, Miriya included, had the least idea of how old they were or just how long they might live under nonviolent circumstances. It was Dr. Lang's belief that, once inoculated against Earth's bacteria and viruses, a Zentraedi could live for hundreds of years. The challenge, however, was to create an inoculation against the persistent effects of the Imperative.

Miriya wanted a different life for Dana. That Dana was having an infancy and accumulating memories was a good beginning. Miriya thought often of the attack on the factory satellite, when she had held Dana aloft to Commander

Reno and proclaimed, "Behold the power of Protoculture!" Before she had any understanding of genetics, the power of biological reproduction, or the frailties inherent in Dana's Human side. She shivered when she reflected on the dangers Dana had been exposed to as a baby, with Max ever-patient and tolerant of Miriya's mistakes and inadvertent oversights. Did she love Dana? she frequently asked herself. Did she love Max the way Sara Mammoth loved her husband, Bill, or Tom Foley loved Jim Ransom? What had she been at the mercy of in inboard Macross when she had agreed to marry Max? Or had it been nothing more than a response to his having defeated her in hand-to-hand combat at the Peace Fountain? Would the Imperative someday reassert itself without warning, and might she then be a danger to Max or Dana? Again, she shivered. Perhaps Dr. Lang or Professor Zand could remove and banish Dana's Zentraedi programming. Hadn't Zand once mentioned something to that effect?

Her musings were interrupted by an ear-piercing squeal from Dana and the sight of Skull One roaring in for a landing on Fokker Field. The rest of the team followed, and everyone in the waiting room hurried to the window wall to wave to the deplaning pilots. Miriya scooped Dana into her arms and positioned herself among the group, the loving and vigilant partner. She watched Max climb down from his mecha, remove his thinking cap, and glance expectantly toward the waiting room. She smiled and waved a hello at him.

They embraced outside the door to the pilots' locker room. Max hugged Dana and lifted her over his head, making her laugh. He didn't offer details of the mission or his after-mission debriefing in Cavern City, and Miriya didn't ask. Instead, they kept things neutral by discussing the latest news.

"Things have gotten worse since you've been gone," Miriya said while they were walking to the bus stop. The Skull's easy win in Venezuela notwithstanding, the UEG was preparing to reestablish control over the autonomous Arkansas Protectorate, allegedly to safeguard Zentraedi citizens, when in fact the aim was to halt the emigration of

Zentraedi to the Southlands and to intercept any shipments of supplies to the malcontents.

"Settlements along the Arkansas border have enacted new measures against unlawful assembly," Miriya continued, "and the RDF has been given broad authority to conduct search and seizures."

"I'm sure those laws apply to Humans *and* Zentraedi," Max said.

"If that's true, why is the government offering economic incentives to any Zentraedi willing to submit to voluntary Micronization?"

Max glanced at her. "Sounds like the UEG is trying to turn Arkansas into a kind of Zentraedi preserve."

"That's exactly what they're doing." Miriya put a hand on his arm to arrest his motion. Dana was riding on Max's shoulders, banging her small fists on the top of his head. "I'm worried about Dana. You may think she's too young to understand what's happening, but she does."

"I know that. I'm concerned for her, too."

"Then do you think I should ask Lang or Zand to speak with her—just to explain things?"

"That's probably not a bad idea."

"I wish there was someone who could help me."

Max regarded her questioningly.

"I feel like I have to *do* something." Miriya shook her head in exasperation. "The rights of my people are being violated. I'm well-known, there must be something I can do." She held Max's troubled gaze. "And one more thing, Max. I want you to ask Rick to keep you off the roster for further missions in the Southlands."

"I can't ask—"

"Please, Max. A dishonorable end will come to any RDF officer assigned there."

"I hate it, Jonathan, I'm going to hate it here," were Catherine Wolff's first words on emerging from the military transport that had carried her, her husband, and their young son Johnny from the high desert of New Mexico to the suffocating heat of Cavern City, in the Venezuela Sector. A tall and strikingly handsome woman with long red hair and a cleft chin, Catherine was highly intelligent and always spoke her mind. "We're going to do terribly here."

Unfortunately, she was also in the habit of issuing dire pronouncements when faced with even the smallest of obstacles. But Captain Jonathan Wolff—her equal in looks, with slick-backed black hair and a natty mustache—had grown so accustomed to her moods over the thirteen years of their marriage that he scarcely paid them any mind. "Why don't we at least give the place five minutes before we decide," he suggested.

He had always been more adventurous than Catherine. His fondness for new places knew no bounds, and in point of fact he thrived in the heat and humidity of the tropics. Macross Island in the years before the War had been Wolff's fantasyland, and he would have given anything to have been aboard the SDF-1 when it had made its accidental jump to Pluto—Zentraedi attacks or no.

One of the first cadets graduated from the Robotech Academy, he had had every right to be aboard the ship. But just short of Breetai's attack on the island, fate had landed him on the RDF's Albuquerque Base, and it was there that he had met and married Catherine Montand. She had seemed daring at the time—a backpacker, a cyclist, an ace skier—but had since turned sedentary, rarely wanting to venture as far from Albuquerque as Santa Fe, let alone to the leading edge of the Southern Hemisphere. Eight-year-old Johnny, who had inherited his mother's nesting instincts, was angry at both his parents for having been forced to leave behind his friends and his favorite TV shows.

In the absence of jetways, passengers arriving at Cavern City Airport had to cross a stretch of blisteringly hot tarmac to reach the terminal. The Wolff family was struggling along with their hand baggage when a man in a lightweight suit hurried out to them from the terminal and insisted on carrying Catherine's bag.

"Captain, I'm Martin Perez, from Mayor Carson's office," he said, pumping Wolff's hand. In a courtly manner, Perez dipped his large head to Catherine, then ruffled Johnny's mop of dark curls, receiving a glower in return.

"Mayor Carson requests that you stop by the Cabildo—City Hall, that is—on the way to your quarters. If it wouldn't be inconvenient, of course. Lea—that is, Mayor Carson would like to welcome you personally. She would have met you here, but something came up at the last minute. Always a crisis, lately. I'm sure you understand, Captain."

Wolff grinned. "Sure, that'd be fine." He cut his eyes to Catherine. "You okay with it?"

"Whatever," she said, scowling.

Perez looked at each of them uncertainly. "Well, then, great," he said after a moment. "I have a car waiting out front—air-conditioned, for your pleasure—and I'll see to it that your baggage is delivered to your quarters. We can attend to immigration and customs later on."

The car was a twenty-year-old Toyota with nearly bald tires, a faulty muffler, and more rust than intact metal. The air conditioner worked well enough, but the windows had to remain open to keep exhaust fumes from fouling the cab. Perez did the driving.

The airport was situated north of the city on an expansive plateau. The two-lane road coursed through cattle-grazing land that had been hacked and burned from the surrounding forest. In the distance, in all directions, rose tall mesas with jungled crowns. Wolff, practically leaning out the window of the right rear door, was in his element, soaking in every detail of the landscape, nostalgic for New Mexico but at the same time excited to be beginning a new phase of his life. With a grandfather who had served in Southeast Asia, a father who had designed computer software, and a mother who been a photojournalist before settling down to newscasting on Macross Island, travel had been a major influence on his life. The elder Wolff had contributed to the creation of the machine language Emil Lang's cybernaut teams had used to interface with EVE, the mother computer discovered aboard the Visitor. It was on-island, at the Robotech Academy, that then-cadet Wolff had learned to pilot prototype Veritechs. But his first love had always been tanks and any sort of mobile battery—and it was Wolff himself, early in 1999, who had put in for the transfer to Albuquerque Base, which specialized in tank training.

Brian and Angelic Wolff, his parents, had died during Breetai's attack.

Except for the billboards and the ramshackle storefronts that lined the road, there were no signs of the city; then, suddenly, the road crested a slight rise and Cavern City was below, sandwiched into a cliff-faced ravine that was itself cleaved along its length by a deep, natural trench.

"I see where the place gets its name," Catherine remarked. She was seated at the window opposite Wolff's; Johnny, sullen, was between the two of them.

"Many of our citizens call it Trenchtown," Perez said, reacting only to the question and not Catherine's nasty tone. "You'll see as we descend that the buildings have been designed to harmonize with the ruggedness of the canyon walls. Much of the adobe is provided by the land itself. The same principle has been applied in several nearby cities, some constructed on the tops of mesas, others concealed in ravines such as Cavern's. The architectural style has been dubbed 'the Obscuro Movement.' "

"How interesting," Catherine said. "We'll make sure to visit each and every one of them, won't we, Jonathan?"

"I can assure you," Wolff said brusquely.

Perez smiled uncomfortably. "Because of its location, Cavern City has been attracting diverse groups of people—some from the Northlands, many from Amazonia and the Andes mountains, and quite a number of Zentraedi who escaped the tyranny of Khyron. And now—hopefully with increased RDF presence to discourage further acts of terrorism such as occurred at the Grand Cannon—we expect an even greater influx of immigrants."

"Zentraedi immigrants?" Catherine asked.

"Some, I'm sure. But have no fears, Mrs. Wolff, Cavern City has no malcontents. We all live in harmony—just like the buildings and the land."

Catherine regarded him in mild alarm. "Are you saying that the Zentraedi live among you?"

Perez nodded. "Over four hundred of them now. We're proud that no Zee-town exists in Cavern City."

"Terrific," Catherine muttered.

Hoping to change the subject, Wolff pointed to a dome-shaped structure, close to where the simplest of bridges spanned the city ravine. "What's that place?"

Perez glanced out the driver's side window. "Ah, that's the Church of Recurrent Tragedics."

Wolff lifted an eyebrow. "Some Southlands cult, right?"

"It's more than a cult—a religion I'd say. We also have our share of Interstellar Retributionalists, Catholics, Jews and Evangelicals. Cavern City is very multidenominational. If the Zentraedi had houses of worship, I'm sure there would be one here."

"The perfect community," Catherine said.

Perez gestured to a series of looming concrete trestles. "Soon to be our monorail," he told them.

Johnny perked up at the throaty sound of a motorcycle—a brand-new Marauder—as it roared past them on the highway. The rider wore a leather vest emblazoned with a serpentine symbol and the words RED SNAKES. "Bikers!" he said elatedly. "Maybe this place won't be so bad after all."

Like most of the buildings along Cavern's two-mile-long main strip, City Hall was a mix of adobe and plasteel, blockish and three-storied, with a rooftop tent of solar collector panels and the requisite microwave dishes. Perez left the Toyota in an elevated lot filled with electric vehicles parked in reserved spaces, then escorted the Wolffs upstairs to the mayor's office.

"You'll like her," he said to Wolff. "She has that Irish sense of humor."

On being admitted to the office, however, Wolff thought Lea Carson appeared anything but good-natured. In her antifashion hairstyle and suit, she looked downright belligerent.

"Wolff, glad to have you aboard," she said, stepping out from behind her desk to shake his hand. "I'll tell you straightaway, Captain, we've got lots of work to do here, so I hope to hell you're up to it."

"I'll do my best," Wolff said.

"You're right about that."

There were two others in the room, and Perez handled the introductions. Carson's director of emergency services, Rafael Mendoza, was a short, fair-complected black with somewhat squashed features under a tangle of henna-colored hair. Rho Mynalo was tall and thin, with shoulder-length brown-blond hair. He bore the enigmatic title "director of information" and wore a kind of uniform whose insignia seemed to be a corruption of the RDF fighting kite.

"Rho is Zentraedi," Carson thought to point out. "He's our liaison with the Cavern's extensive alien community." She looked at Wolff. "You'll be working closely with Rho, Captain. Any problems with that?"

Wolff shook his head. "None whatever."

"That's good, because the thing I want you to understand—the thing I want the RDF to understand—is that I refuse to run this city as a fortress. That's not to say that we don't need defenses, because we do—there are many dissident groups that refuse to believe that the Grand Cannon has been stripped of useful technology—but our goal is to discover some way of letting all people partake of this city, and I do mean *all* people. The way things stand, we have more Human agitators than Zentraedi. Rogues, foragers, fugitives from prisons destroyed in the Rain of Death . . ." She shook her head. "Then there's this motorcycle gang, the Red Snakes—"

"We saw one of them," Johnny exclaimed.

Lea glanced at him. "They're not very nice people, Johnny. Especially their self-appointed leader, a man named Atilla One." She waved a hand in dismissal. "But we'll go into all that some other time." She looked at Wolff again. "Captain, the thing to remember is that I didn't want this posting—I had my sights set on Ireland, but Senator Moran and the Bureau of Reconstruction Management didn't see things my way. I'm determined, nonetheless, to make the best of it, and I expect you to do likewise."

Wolff gave her his best glamour-boy grin. "Mayor, I'm made for this place."

Slowly, she grinned back at him. "You know what, Wolff—I believe you." She turned to Catherine. "I can tell that you don't share your husband's enthusiasm, Catherine, but all I ask is that you give it a shot. And if you're by any chance looking for a challenge, I'm searching for someone to do public relations."

Catherine forced a smile. "Thank you, Ms. Mayor. I'll consider it."

Carson blew out her breath and rubbed her small hands together. "All right, then, first thing tomorrow we start looking at ways to beef up city security without letting the guns show. And while we're doing that, we keep all lines of communication open between Humans and Zentraedi—including malcontents."

"Shut your mouths and let him speak!" Clozan bellowed to the sixty-two Zentraedi attendees of the Cairo parley, whose loud grumblings and separate discussions had overwhelmed the envoy of Khyron's Fist. Many, following the Quandolmo's example, wore galabas and headcloths. "The least we can do is keep from squabbling among ourselves." Six feet tall and bullishly built, Clozan was the leader of the Quandolma band, which had organized the summit. The name meant "resurrected ones," and the band's glyph was a laughing skull.

Standing atop an inlaid table with megaphone in hand, Nello, the Khyron's Fist envoy, had been trying to put the best spin possible on the rout at the Southern Grand Cannon. "It was not a defeat, but a calculated sacrifice. Captain Bagzent and two others escaped with computer documents that will be invaluable to our efforts."

"Who made this Bagzent 'captain'?" someone shouted from the rear of the room. "That's a Human rank."

"What good are documents when it's weapons we need?" yelled another.

Nello waved his colorless arms in a pacifying gesture. "These are identity documents that will help us get aboard the factory—"

"Why go up the well in search of targets when we have plenty of them right here?"

Nello swung to the source of the question. "The factory isn't a target but a source of needed parts for weapons—"

"*We* are weapons enough," the same speaker interrupted.

"As long as we have hands and feet and teeth, we have weapons!"

Clozan shot to his feet once more, banging his huge fists on the table. "Shut up, shut up, all of you! I will kill the next one who speaks out of turn!"

That the representatives had to be threatened was proof of the damage done to the Imperative in three short Earth years. Once, Clozan's every word would have been obeyed without question: a flagship commander in Dolza's personal fleet, he had enjoyed more authority than Breetai and Reno combined. Now all he had was the Quandolma, and all the Quandolma had was Northern Africa, from sea coast to tropics, which amounted to little more than an expanse of uninhabited desert, oddly reminiscent of the dun-colored wastes of Fantoma.

Excepting Antarctica, Africa had taken fewer annihilation bolts than any other landmass. Ravaged by disease and drought in the decades preceding the Global Civil War and by tribal warfare afterward, it had scarcely enough Human survivors to attract the notice of the warships' bioscanners. In light of the earlier indignities, many Africans thought of Dolza's anni bolts as a kind of coup de grace.

Cairo hadn't sustained a direct hit, but nearby Alexandria had, and what with the radiation born there and the slow eastern drift of clouds raised by the plasmic brutalizing of the Mediterranean, from Spain all the way round to Israel, slow death had come to Cairo's fourteen million. The city was hot, and would remain hot for a score more years.

Dammed at its delta by Alexandria's debris, the Nile had overflowed its banks to the south, leaving some of Cairo underwater. The bazaars were deserted and there were no songs in the desert air, calling the faithful to prayer. Looters had moved in once the Nile crocodiles had sated themselves on the dead. But the place was almost as unchanged as Buenos Aires. Many of the mosques and minarets and obelisks were still standing, as were the pyramids at Giza and Saggara, and the Sphinx. Clozan's crashed flagship contributed a new geometrical relic to the area.

Clozan had chosen the Al Azhar Mosque, just inside the walls of the Old City, as headquarters for the Quandolma, and the mosque's renowned library of 250,000 ancient books as the site of the summit. But it wasn't Islamic architecture or handwritten manuscripts that had drawn Zentraedi envoys from around the world, but Clozan himself. And come they had, from as near as the Congo and as distant as Australia, representatives from the Paranka, the Lyktauro, the Iron Ravens, the Shroud, the Crimson Ghosts, the all-female Claimers and the Senburu, arriving in military and passenger planes borrowed from ruined airports, jury-rigged trucks and all-terrain vehicles, recovery craft and theater scout recon pods salvaged from crashed warships, all to pay tribute to Dolza's once-great battle-group commander . . .

And now they wouldn't even listen to him.

A full minute of pounding his fists on the table and the grousing and muttering still hadn't subsided, so he reached for the closest envoy—who happened to be from the Burrowers—and heaved him through the window into the courtyard below. That seemed to get everyone's attention.

"Now, allow the envoy from Khyron's Fist to make his point before you ask your questions." Clozan nodded to Nello. "Proceed—but be succinct, or you're the next one to leave the room."

Nello thumped his chest in salute. "*T'sen* Clozan. The identity documents won in the raid on the Cannon can be used to infiltrate a group of our Human allies into the factory. Several have already volunteered. The Humans will establish contact with our full-size comrades aboard the factory and determine the best means for smuggling supplies to our mecha production teams on the surface."

The room fell silent for a long moment. Clozan stared hard at Nello. "Explain yourself."

"A new form of mecha will soon be made available to us—a variation of Female Power Armor that is said to be the equivalent of the Veritech."

"Said by whom?"

Nello blanched. "I can't say, because I myself haven't been told."

"Is secrecy now part of the Zentraedi way?" the Paranka envoy asked. Everyone looked to Clozan for the answer.

"Yes," he said, after a moment of deliberation. "And other Human strategies as well. Covert operations, abductions, ransom demands, terror tactics—these are all part of the Human arsenal, and it's crucial that we learn to incorporate them into our campaign. We must go where Khyron's honor forbid him to go, and fight the Humans on a fully integrated battlefield.

"Look how subtle the RDF has become: they make a pretense of answering to the United Earth Government as a means of deflecting the criticism of Humans sympathetic to our cause; they refuse food to the wretched Zentraedi of the Southlands, hoping they'll respond by rioting; they encircle the Arkansas Protectorate with rapid-deployment forces; they steal control of Monument City out from under the Zentraedi who founded it; they entice our full-size comrades to undergo Micronization . . . The RDF is not only waging a psychological war against *us*, but against all our people. And we must be willing to embrace any strategy that enables us to endure and conquer."

Throughout the library, envoys traded impassioned looks. This was the old Clozan speaking.

"We can triumph, but we must be judicious. We must operate on a need-to-know basis and take care to ferret out Human or Zentraedi spies among our ranks. We have something the Humans lack, and that is the unrelenting might of the Imperative. We need only to *un*learn what the Humans have—"

Clozan's deep voice was overpowered by a rumbling sound that shook the room.

"It's coming from outside," Nello said.

Burnoosed heads swung to the window the Burrowers' envoy had been through. Filling the western sky was a flotilla of dirigiblelike warships, slung with command gondolas and bristling with weapons. Someone in the library recognized the eagle emblems emblazoned on the ships' noses as belonging to Anatole Leonard's Army of the Southern Cross.

Clozan whirled on the assembly, rage in his narrowed eyes. "We've been betrayed!" he screamed as the first volley of missiles came streaking toward the mosque.

CHAPTER TWELVE

Poor Zand: one step behind Lang in arriving on Macross Island, overlooked by Russo for inclusion on the first team sent in to survey the Visitor, off-island on Lang's personal business when the Zentraedi attacked and the SDF-1 jumped across the Solar system, one day late (because of inclement weather) in reaching the SDF-1 after the UEDC had ordered it back into the skies, forced by circumstance to remain on the surface while Lang got to design a starship inside the factory satellite, ignored by Hunter after petitioning for a slot with the REF . . . Poor, poor Zand. No wonder he was competitive, driven, obsessed. And no wonder Earth got to reap the results of his madness.

Major Alice Harper Argus (ret.), *Fulcrum: Commentaries on the Second Robotech War*

AT HIS DESK IN MONUMENT CITY'S ROBOTECH RESEARCH Center, Lazlo Zand, wand-writer in hand, made stream-of-consciousness entries in an electronic notebook. In a loopy code of his own devising, he wrote: *Dana . . . Dana Parino . . . Dana Parino Sterling . . . Parino, Dana . . . Sterling, Dana . . . Sterling DNA . . .* His writing hand halted and he leaned back from the screen, grinning maniacally at what his subconscious mind had conjured. Yes, yes, he thought. Sterling DNA: now *there* was a grail worth pursuing.

What had happened these past few months, he asked himself, that his life should suddenly seem rife with wondrous possibilities? First had come the promotion to chief of Protoculture studies, resulting from Lang's appointment to the UEG. Next, a visit from Thomas Edwards, inquiring if he might be interested in doing some special research—developing a food additive capable of bonding to Protoculture at a molecular level, so that "persons" whose systems contained both the additive and Protoculture could be identified, perhaps even monitored, from a distance.

The purpose of such a chemical was immediately obvious to Zand: the UEG—whose interests Edwards was plainly representing—wanted Earth's Zentraedi biochemically tagged. An acceptable response, given the upswing in acts of malcontentism. But Zand didn't concern himself with the ethics of the UEG's decision; what mattered was that the government had come to *him*. Not Lang or Penn or Bronson or Blake, but to Lazlo Archimedes Zand.

Then, most recently, who should come looking for him but Miriya Parino Sterling, wondering if he'd be willing to talk to little half-breed Dana about world events as they applied to the aliens. Mom was concerned about the effect the news might have on her daughter, and she wanted him to serve as a sort of therapist—though *shaman* seemed the more appropriate term, in that Parino had hinted at investigating the feasibility of somehow *extracting* the Zentraedi in Dana and banishing it. As if she expected him to fashion a psycho-centrifuge for the kid; strap Dana into a seat, spin her into a beneficial schizophrenia, and separate out her Human and alien character traits, like plasma from blood.

Again, he left the ethical questions unanswered. If Miriya Parino wanted to deliver her daughter into his hands, who was he to dissuade her? But what had happened to bring on such a fortuitous series of developments—without his having had to indulge in any of the usual counterfeit groveling? He was still the same sleazy amoralist he had always been. Did it, then, have something to do with the ongoing experiments with Protoculture? Had Protoculture "gotten into him," as Lang had promised it would, and were the visits from Edwards and Parino manifestations of the so-called "Shapings"?

Dana Sterling was the reason he had remained in Monument an extra week instead of returning to the Tokyo center. He wanted a crack at her before Parino's anxiety had a chance to abate, and was even now waiting for mom and daughter to show up. When the office intercom chimed, he nearly jumped out of his skin.

"Professor Zand," some research assistant said, "Dana Sterling is here."

"Good, good. And the mother?"

"No, Doctor, she's here with her . . . godfathers—"

"Not—"

"Rico, Konda, and Bron."

Zand buried his face in his hands and shook his head back and forth. Those three! He'd had dealings with them in the past when Lang's Age Determination Project was up and running, and they'd been next to useless; speaking in clichés they'd lifted from films and television, always joking around, like they were the Three Alien Stooges. Zand made up his mind to be civil to them, nevertheless, and on rendezvousing with them in the neurology lab said how splendid it was to see them again.

"Ah, I bet you say that to all the aliens," said the stout one, Bron, who was sporting a PWF gimme-cap.

"No, really, it's a—"

"Hey, Doc, you hear the one about the woman who takes her husband to the doctor because he thinks he's a chicken?" This, from the tall one with purple hair, Konda.

"I'm sorry, but I've no time for—"

Rico, wiry and mercurial, high-fived him. " 'T'sup, Zandman."

Little green-blond Dana was standing among them, regarding Zand warily. "Dana," he said, approaching her with a big smile, "I've heard so much about you." As he was squatting, making himself her size, she punched him square in the nose—hard enough to smart if not draw blood. His eyes began to water and he pinched his nostrils shut. "Bell, dat basn't berry nice, was it?"

"I don't wanna talk to you," she told him.

"I'm sorry to hear you say that, because your mommy wants us to talk."

"My mommy's always making me do stuff I don't wanna do."

"But I promise it won't be so bad. I just want to ask you some questions about your house, and what you do when you're at home."

Dana looked to her godfathers for counsel, and the three

of them nodded. "Go ahead, Dana," Bron said, "talk to the skinny doctor with the funny hair."

She was beyond precocious, he told himself as he was leading her back to his office. Mature enough to field word associations, perhaps even a multiphasic personality evaluation or a thematic apperception test. Zand's imagination swirled at the thought of the family portrait Dana would draw. And, of course, he would have to order CAT, PET, CT, and nuclear scans, ultrasounds, EEGs, computed tomography studies, a full physical workup . . .

"So, tell me, Dana," he said when they were seated next to each other in his office, "do you ever get angry?"

"Sure, I do."

"And what makes you angry?"

"Doing what I don't wanna do."

"And what do you do when you get angry?"

She picked up his favorite paperweight—a fossilized chunk of amber he had purchased in Mexico twenty years earlier—and threw it against the wall, where it shattered. Zand made a concerted effort to keep from grimacing—or crying. He swallowed hard and found his voice. "And does the anger seem to come from any place special in your body—your head, your tummy, your—"

"Here," she said, pointing to her right fist, which she suddenly hurled at him, striking his jaw a glancing blow.

Zand shook the stars from his vision. "What are your feelings toward your daddy?"

"He's neat."

"Yes, he is neat. But anything else?"

"He cooks and cleans and washes the clothes."

"Very interesting, Dana. And do you love him very much?"

"Sure."

"More than you love your mommy?"

"Only when my mommy leaves me in the snow for too long."

Zand looked puzzled. "She leaves you—"

"But I don't get mad—just *wet*. And I always know when she's going to do it."

"Do you mean that you sometimes know what's going to happen before it happens?"

"Yep."

"Do you think you could teach me how to do that?"

"Maybe. If I can poke you in the eye first."

Zand ignored the remark. "Do you know what 'Zentraedi' means?"

"Adopted."

Zand sat back in his swivel chair. "Are you Zentraedi?"

"Half of me is."

"And which half is that?"

"The half that's gonna die."

"We've been betrayed," Niles Obstat said to the inner-circle members of the Special Operations Group—Dimitri Motokoff, T. R. Edwards, and the officers of the South-lands, India, Southeast Asia, and Australia desks. A week had passed since Anatole Leonard's Cairo attack, and the intel group was meeting in its nondescript though heavily secured building in suburban Monument City. "There's a double agent loose in the RDF or the UEG."

"No other explanation," Edwards commented.

"Intelligence about the summit was withheld from Leonard for fear of just such action."

Edwards nodded gravely. "He superseded his authority."

"His authority?" Obstat said. "He superseded his own mandate not to deploy his forces unless asked. And since when does North Africa fall within Brasília's jurisdiction?"

General Motokoff read from a situation report. "The Army of the Southern Cross defends its actions, stating that the raid was retaliatory, in response to the assassination attempt. The group that planned and funded the attack was allegedly based in Cairo."

"That's a total fabrication," Obstat said. "Why would some group thousands of miles from Brasília involve itself in the affairs of the Southlands? And it still doesn't explain how Leonard was apprised of the summit to begin with."

Motokof had anticipated the question. "The ASC claims that they got it out of the woman—the sympath—who survived the Brasília bombing. This can't be substantiated, because she finally succumbed to her injuries."

"Very convenient," Obstat said.

"Definitely a mole in the house," Edwards remarked.

Obstat turned to him. "Who in the UEG and the RDF had access to our intel on Cairo?"

"The bigot list was pretty extensive. Senator Milburn and the six members of the UEG's Ways and Means Committee, Senator Longchamps and the five members of the Intelligence Oversight Group, most of the RDF general staff, including Reinhardt, Hunter, Aldershot, Herzog, Maistroff, Caruthers, and a couple of others." Edwards fell silent for a moment, stroking the flesh side of his face. "It's possible . . ."

"Say it," Obstat barked. "We're only at the theorizing stage."

Edwards shrugged. "I'd have to check on this, but Max Sterling might have been told about Cairo."

"Cairo was supposed to be strictly need-to-know," Dimitri Motokoff said. "How did our bigot list get so long? And who the hell would have included Sterling on this?"

"Sterling has the necessary security clearance," Edwards was quick to respond. "Reinhardt or Hunter could have dropped something about Cairo as part of the Grand Cannon premission briefing. In the event he was obliged to conduct a field interrogation of an injured enemy, let's say."

Obstat considered it and shook his head. "Sterling wouldn't betray the RDF to Leonard. He was the one who broke the story on the Brasília riot."

"Suppose he let something slip to his wife," Edwards said.

Motokoff eyed Edwards with blatant disdain. "You're suggesting that Miriya Parino would sell out her own people?"

"Perhaps not 'sell.' Anyway, the ones in Cairo weren't 'her people'—they were malcontents." Edwards gave the distinction a moment to sink in. "Look at it this way: the UEG expects her to be a model Zentraedi, right? And the malcontents are making it difficult for all the Zentraedi. So what better way for Parino to demonstrate her complete acculturation than to spill what she knew about Cairo. Sterling would have told her that the RDF wasn't going to interfere with the summit, making Leonard the logical choice."

Obstat snorted in ridicule. "This isn't worth pursuing."

Once more, Edwards shrugged. "As you say, we're only theorizing. I don't put much stock in it myself, but it's apparent that *someone* approached Leonard or one of his officers."

Obstat muttered something under his breath.

"It won't happen again," Edwards said with assurance. "Give me a few weeks and I'll root out our double agent."

Obstat nodded and looked to Motokoff. "What's the latest on Cairo?"

"Blowback galore. The media are calling it 'St. Valentine's Massacre Two.' Over fifty Zentraedi killed by Prowler and Mongoose missiles, including, I'm sorry to report, the operative we placed among the Shroud. The Al Azhar Mosque was completely destroyed. A few newspapers are comparing it to the burning of the Alexandria library back in Greek times or whenever it was. But running side by side with every piece condemning the wanton destruction is a piece praising Leonard for the preemptive strike. Everyone's asking how the ASC knew about the summit when the RDF didn't. Or why—if the RDF did know—the summit was permitted to take place. Either way, the RDF emerges the loser. At the same time, Leonard's popularity has taken a quantum leap in the Northlands.

"The Aliens Civil Liberties Union is using Cairo to back up what they've been saying about restrictions on Zentraedi rights. But, the truth be told, a lot of people secretly respect the fact that Leonard is decisive and ruthless; they're sick of the RDF's equivocating. Most of all, the idea of an organized Zentraedi terrorist machine has people between here and Sydney taking to the streets, demanding that something be done to nip malcontentism in the bud. And the demonstrations are directed as much against the Zentraedi as they are the RDF. There've been some angry confrontations between Leonard's supporters and advocacy groups."

Obstat hung his head and exhaled wearily. "Wait'll they get wind of this upside."

"I thought you might like to see how things are progressing," Dr. Bronson told Lisa as she emerged from an elevator on level five of Breetai's flagship. The elevator was a recent installation, and the broad corridor it opened on had been partitioned from the original 90-foot-wide catwalk that ran around the perimeter of the bridge, 150 feet above the deck.

Lang had issued orders that the ship be referred to as the SDF-3, but to Lisa the leviathan still belonged to Breetai, and it was going to take more than a shiny new elevator to make her think otherwise. *Nupetiet-Vernitzs* was the Zentraedi term for "flagship," and this one was more than three miles long and could accommodate upward of 100,000 crewpersons, not including space for an additional 28,900 Micronized in the stasis chamber. Though anchored in the zero-g heart of the factory satellite, the ship manufactured its own gravity.

"I think you'll be very impressed," Bronson said as he was leading her down the corridor in the direction of the command bubble—the so-called unblinking eye of the bridge. "It's turning out to be a labor of love for many of those involved."

Wherever Lisa looked, helmeted workcrews and techs were busy at tasks. The corridor was noisy with construction sounds: the sibilant roar of servowelders, the explosive thud of riveters, the whine of screwguns. Men and women consulted scrolls of blueprints or data screens filled with dizzying calculations. Waste bins overflowed with empty coffee containers and sandwich wrappings. Along the starboard bulkhead was a bank of perhaps twenty portable toilets.

Bronson halted at the hatch to the command bubble and motioned to the mushroom-shaped button that controlled it. "Admiral, if you would do the honors."

Lisa pressed her right palm against the button. The hatch divided, and the two halves pocketed themselves swiftly

and silently in the bulkhead. Her first look at the interior of
the bubble was enlivened by an immediate sense of déjà vu.

"Of course, it's a long way from completion," Bronson
said. "But, as per your request, we've endeavored to dupli-
cate the layout of the SDF-1's bridge down to the smallest
details. Well, I should say 'whenever possible.' Changes in
technology these past twenty years dictated that we make
certain adjustments. But I hope you'll agree that we've at
least succeeded in capturing the *feel* of the old ship. After
all, this wasn't meant to be a simulation—some movie
set—but a fully functioning command center."

Lisa's eyes roamed the oblong room. She turned through
a full circle. "I'm amazed he let you get away with this
much."

Lang, she meant, who had argued vehemently against
replicating even the look of the fortress's bridge, citing the
unnecessary redundancies that had been incorporated into
the SDF-1, the physical limitations, the innovations his
systems-design teams had made since the remodeling and
"Human-sizing" of the Visitor. But in the end, thanks in
large part to steadfast support from Reinhardt, Forsythe,
and several others, Lisa had gotten her way.

Bronson, now standing akimbo in the center of the room,
was beaming. For his benefit, Lisa kept her smile frozen in
place, appreciative of his efforts to cheer her. But she found
it difficult to summon much enthusiasm for any aspect of
the SDF-3 in the wake of news from the surface about Leonard's preemptive strike on Cairo. Demonstrations, protests, riots . . . most of them directed against the RDF for
failing to act. It was a classic no-win situation. Max Sterling was branded a murderer for killing fourteen Zentraedi
in the raid against the Southern Grand Cannon, and Anatole
Leonard was praised for leading one that ended in four
times as many deaths. Spearheaded by Senator Wyatt
Moran, Brasília was threatening to secede from the UEG
unless the Army of the Southern Cross received the funding
and recognition it was seeking.

"The Expeditionary mission could be scrubbed if public
opinion shifts another notch," Lang had said only that
morning. "The cost of retrofitting the flagship alone could

finance the rebuilding of both ALUCE and Sara Bases, and the construction and deployment of a dozen ARMOR-series defense platforms."

There was nothing new in what Lang said, but hearing the words had made her feel selfish and narrow-minded about wanting to fulfill Henry Gloval's dream. And now, as her eyes took in the alterations done to Breetai's command bubble, she realized that the mystifying sensation of déjà vu wasn't always a positive experience.

Glancing at the laser communication and scanner console that took up half the starboard bulkhead, she couldn't help but picture elfin-faced Kim Young and the ever-fearless Sammie Porter; in the same way, she saw Vanessa Leeds strapped into an acceleration seat below the twin four-by-four astrogation screens, and Claudia Grant at the starboard duty station below the wraparound forward viewport . . .

If death was a joke God had played on Human beings, sudden death must have been God's idea of torture. For instead of numbing the hurt, swiftness encapsulated it. Shared experiences fled into memory like eclipsed light. Sudden death left you feeling that your own life was a mere dream. That someone could be alive one moment, then lost to this world forever, was sleight of hand of the cruelest sort.

Her first love, Carl Riber, killed in action on Mars; her father, killed in action at Alaska Base; Claudia, Sammie, Kim, and Vanessa, killed in action in Macross City . . . War had made players of everyone in the world, and given that Lisa had been in the fighting for three years longer than most, she would have thought she had a leg up on the business of dying. But it wasn't so. She grieved daily, sometimes hourly, for those taken from her. Carl's pacifism had lent a particularly tragic element to his death, whereas her father's death at the site of the Grand Cannon seemed somehow fitting for a minister of war. Shortly before Rick had flown in to rescue her, she had seen her father literally derezz on screen . . . leaving her to deal with all the usual unresolved issues between fathers and daughters.

But there were no unresolved issues between her and Claudia; none that the two of them hadn't discussed and processed endlessly after Roy Fokker's death. Especially in the weeks before Khyron's attack on Macross. Claudia had become withdrawn after Roy died, not any less a friend, but more inclined to solitude. When she ventured out, it was usually to one of Roy's old haunts, where she would sit alone with her memories. But it was Claudia who had helped Lisa admit to herself that she was in love with Rick, and indeed find the strength to tell him. Lisa had lost count of the many glasses of Whaler and Lovely Yoshie she had lifted to Claudia during the past year. And still she wondered if she could ever forgive Claudia for saving her life that fateful day in Macross—for helping Henry wrestle her into the ejection module, under the pretense that she had more to live for than they did.

Lisa walked to the facsimiles of the duty stations she and Claudia had manned for almost twelve years. Where the SDF-1's viewport had opened on stars and sky, the command bubble's overlooked a mile-long, 350-foot-high hold carpeted with complex arrays of alien and Human technology.

Lisa swung away from the view to regard the raised platform that would soon support the padded captain's chair, and she thought about Henry Gloval, her long-limbed, soot-black-mustachioed Russian commander and second-best friend. She imagined him sitting there, with his white cap tilted forward over his dark eyes and his unlit briar clamped between his teeth, and she tried hard to envision herself sitting in that chair, with Captain Forsythe occupying her place and strangers at all the other stations, and she fought back tears of anguish and vague foreboding.

Was this what Rick felt every time he watched a VT take to the skies? Lisa asked herself. Wait till he got a load of the stadium-size situation room Bronson and Lang were building for him.

"If there's anything you don't like, Admiral, or anything you'd like to see added," Bronson was saying, "now's the time to let us know."

Lisa cleared her throat and straightened somewhat. "Two small items, Doctor. I want a sign posted above the hatch that reads Watch Your Head, and I want the seatback of the command chair outfitted with a slashed-circle no-smoking symbol."

The passenger list for shuttle flight 18–1787, departing Albuquerque Base for the factory satellite on March 23, 2016, gave the name of the occupant of seat 14 as Jeng Chiang. His occupation was listed as food service technician and his security rating was 6, which restricted him to upper levels three through six of the main body of the factory. Ratings of less than seven were denied access to the SDF-3 and its immediate environs, or to any of the secondary pods, including the numerous transfer corridors that connected them to the central body. Additional information on Chiang—available on request from the RDF's Bureau of Investigation—showed that he was born in Hong Kong in 1990 and had lived and worked in New York City until 2010. He moved to Caracas, Venezuela, in 2011, and had been visiting Angel Falls when the Rain of Death occurred. Since then, he had worked in food preparation at the Southern Grand Cannon from May 2014 through October 2015. An interview and background check had been done in Albuquerque, where his security contract was on file.

Tall, lean, and brooding, Chiang wore round, wire-rimmed glasses and parted his blond-brown hair on the right. Strapped into his seat, he had his face turned to the porthole, as had been the case since lift-off. He had endured the flight without complaint and, beyond a brief exchange of pleasantries, had said little to his seatmate.

The factory filled the view out the small window, but between it and the approaching shuttle were some twenty Zentraedi warships and the tugs that had towed them from lunar orbit to their Lagrange anchorages, attended to by reclamation crews of full-size Zentraedi. Chiang identified the dreadnoughts the shuttle passed en route to the factory docking bay: landing ship, cruiser, destroyer, command ship, reconnaissance pod, recovery pod . . . There was nothing extraordinary about the talent; indeed, enemy warship identification had been a hobby of many of those who'd lived in inboard Macross City. The difference was that Chiang was able to supply the Zentraedi names: *Quiltra*

*Queleual, Thiev Salan, Thuveral Salan, Queadol-
Magdomilla* . . .

The background prepared in Albuquerque made no mention of Chiang's two years inboard the SDF-1, or of his facility with Zentraedi—though those facts were undoubtedly on file in some electronically dazzled Macross City databank.

Under the name Lynn-Kyle.

Kyle had come a long way since Macross, in any case. An advocate of peaceful solutions in those days, he was now a dissident. His contempt for the RDF had stood the test of time, but had been overridden by his abhorrence for Anatole Leonard's Army of the Southern Cross. *Leonard's Army* . . . like a film director insisting that his or her name be appended to the title of the work.

His dislike for Leonard had begun the previous year in Cuiabá and blossomed into full hatred after the massacre in Brasília. Kyle had arrived in Cuiabá with a group of disabused Zentraedi he had first met in Detroit. Back when he had had one foot in political activism and one in show business, managing the career of his cousin and onetime lover, Lynn-Minmei. The two interests had merged in the "People Helping People Tour," which Kyle had organized in the hope that music would bring Humans and aliens together. But Minmei was exhausted from the demands placed on her during the early reconstruction years, when her celebrity had reached absurd heights and people had clamored for personal appearances. The reasons were simple: Hollywood and New York had been destroyed, and few of those celebrities who'd survived the Rain—in Montana or Wyoming—had ever been big names to begin with. Kyle had been feeling the strain as well, though he hadn't recognized it at the time. Drinking too much, losing control, disregarding all that he'd learned from years of physical and spiritual training in the martial arts. For over a year, Minmei put up with his verbal abuse, until she became so emotionally drained that she couldn't sing.

The night he had walked out of her life was etched in his memory. He could place himself on that littered, moonlit beach in Monument, hear the mournful foghorns of the ferries, recall the words of his melodramatic harangue. He had convinced himself that he was speaking his mind when all he'd actually been doing was concocting a theatrical exit for himself, one he wanted Minmei to remember all her life. It was paramount that she experience some of the pain he was feeling.

He worshiped her that much.

Meanwhile, he hadn't had a clue what to do next; but chance had delivered him to a saloon frequented by Zentraedi, and he had hooked up with them and hit the road south—thus missing by weeks the annihilation of Macross, the dimensional fortresses, and the dream of abandoning Earth for the stars. He remembered thinking, *Now there can be no option but to live together as one race.* He had no residual anger for Khyron or Azonia and the crushing he had almost sustained at their hands. They had done what they had needed to do.

He had renewed hope, and money enough to support himself and his fellow travelers on the long trip to the Southlands. They'd spent time in Mexico and Nicaragua, shipped for Venezuela, and journeyed by truck and riverboat to Cuiabá.

Then came the backlash to Khyron's attack on Macross: the resurgence of discrimination, the alleged food shortages, the Zentraedi bashing . . . And once more he had found himself an advocate for their civil rights—a "sympath," as those of his ilk were defined by the military. Taking their lead from Wyatt Moran and Anatole Leonard, the petty pols and bureaucrats the Bureau of Reconstruction Management had installed in the Southlands had turned a deaf ear to him, and the result was the Brasília massacre.

Kyle had been there, one of those pressed against the barricades when the VTs had opened fire and the Centaur tanks had rolled in. He still didn't know how he'd managed to survive. But with survival had been born a sense of militantism: he wanted to see the Zentraedi avenge themselves on Leonard.

The problem was that they lacked the leadership to accomplish that. The groups at the Xingu River camp couldn't be convinced to take the long view; instead of raiding strategic targets, they wanted to attack symbols: first Leonard, then the useless Grand Cannon. But Kyle had ultimately fallen in with a group of Zentraedi females who believed, as he did, in planning a carefully reasoned defensive. At first Xan Norri, Vivik Bross, and the rest of the Senburu had refused to listen to a Human male. But when they understood that he wasn't out to get into their pants, as were most of the jungle scum and riffraff they dealt with, they began to take him into their confidence—more so when they realized that he knew quite a bit about the inner workings of the Human military machine.

He was long past using his real name, though some Humans and aliens from the old Detroit days knew who he was, who he had been. His face had appeared larger than life in *Little White Dragon*, and shown up so often on the news during the reconstruction years that people would still ask where they had met him before. But he had now altered his appearance to the extent that no one remarked that he resembled Lynn-Kyle, the actor.

He had been present at the inaugural flight of the Senburu group's weapon—their much-improved version of Female Power Armor. And he had carried news of that weapon back to the Xingu camp, arriving simultaneously with the three survivors of the Grand Cannon debacle, who had returned with the spoils of their action—what they had taken for "documents."

But what Khyron's Fist had in fact procured were computer codes that rendered hackable the factory satellite's security system databank. Security had always been the RDF's weak link—a lapse in security twenty years earlier on Macross Island had permitted Conrad Wilbur's anti-Robotech movement, the Faithful, to take shape right under the noses of Emil Lang, Henry Gloval, and the rest, and nothing had changed since. Security leaks were an almost everyday occurrence on the factory, where some 10,000 technicians, soldiers, mechanics, service personnel, and researchers were permanently stationed, with hundreds more arriving and departing daily on shuttles and transport ships. And as for running background checks and issuing security ratings, interviewers had little more to go on than an applicant's word, along with perhaps a few verifiable details covering the previous two years. Personal histories had been erased in the Rain: birth, marriage, military, employment, and tax records; social security and passport numbers; banking statements, criminal records, on-file fingerprints or retinal-scan images . . . Only a relative few had emerged with traceable pasts. The rest were free to reinvent themselves without fear of being outed by friends or loved ones, or contradicted by documentation. Twenty-first-century Earth had been forced by circumstance to operate under the honor system, which frequently meant that people did pretty much as they pleased. And it was that much easier when one's inventions could be given electronic weight in a hacked database.

"Jeng Chiang" had never been interviewed in Alburquerque. Nor had any of Kyle's seven Human cohorts aboard the shuttle. The RDF's computer only *said* that they had been cleared for travel to the factory.

As the shuttle was entering the docking bay, Kyle could feel the slow return of gravity, vaguely oppressive, but comforting nonetheless. The debarking and contagion control procedures were tedious, but within ninety minutes of docking all forty aboard had been cycled out of the airlock into a brightly lit room where factory personnel were on hand to escort them to their postings. None of the eight co-conspirators made eye contact.

"Seylos?" a low voice off to Kyle's left asked. He turned and found himself eye to eye with a muscular Zentraedi with oily hair and a contorted mouth.

"I'm afraid you're mistaken," Kyle told him. "My name is Jeng Chiang."

The Zentraedi eyed him up and down. "You resemble a close friend of mine."

"I hope you find him. Close friends are hard to come by."

The alien relaxed somewhat, satisfied that his instincts had been correct. The code phrases, commencing with *Seylos*—Zentraedi for "loyal"—had been supplied to Kyle on the surface. He hadn't asked how long the alliance had been in existence, and no one had volunteered that information.

"My name is Theofre Elmikk," the alien said after a moment.

Kyle nodded. "You understand why I'm here?"

Elmikk narrowed his eyes in scorn. "I do, but I'm against it. Why waste time smuggling parts to the surface when there are already enough comrades aboard to take control of this factory?"

"And do what?" Kyle inquired in a harsh whisper. "This thing isn't going anywhere."

"Perhaps not. But we could train its working weapons on Earth and finish what Dolza began."

Kyle snorted. "I know you don't care about killing your comrades on the surface, but what good is revenge if you don't live to bask in the praise of the Masters? You'll die here, avenged but sentenced."

"So be it."

"Do you speak for everyone aboard?"

Elmikk hesitated, then thumped his chest. "I speak for myself."

Kyle smiled wryly. "Until you speak for all, you'll follow orders—is that understood?"

Elmikk stepped into Kyle's space. "I won't take orders from a Human."

Kyle held his ground, immovable. "You're not. I'm only here to relay them and to help establish a pipeline for the supplies. Can you live with that. *Elmikk.*"

The Zentraedi fell silent for a long moment before offering a tight-lipped nod.

"Good," Kyle said. "Now take me to a secure place where we can go over the shopping list."

CHAPTER THIRTEEN

Regardless that it wasn't entirely his invention, the Lorelei Network would be Milburn's downfall. However, the Lorelei Scandal notwithstanding, there seems to have been a certain inevitability to Milburn's rapid fall from grace. By 2017—largely through circumstances beyond his control—he had become the odd man out in the very apparat he had created. Maistroff and Caruthers had come aboard as a team; Stinson and Longchamps, rivals initially, paired off, as did Moran and Edwards. But in the end—after the deaths of Moran, Maistroff, and Caruthers, and of Edwards on Optera, and the worldwide obloquy to which Stinson and Longchamps were subjected after the long-overdue return of the SDF-3—it was Milburn who prevailed, reentering the public arena and rising to a position of political prominence.

Sara Lemule, *Improper Council: An Analysis of the Plenipotentiary Council*

"**C**ALL ME JONATHAN," WOLFF SAID WHEN RON Bartley saluted and addressed him as captain. "I know it goes against protocol, but I've never been comfortable with honorifics—especially among team members." Wolff had sparkling eyes and a leading man's smile. "What do you say to being on a first-name basis?"

Bartley wasn't sure how he felt about it—or, at that moment, about Wolff. "With all due respect, sir, what might be good for morale might not be good for adherence to the chain of command."

Wolff put his hands on his hips and directed a laugh toward the rest of the team, as if including them in on the joke. "I figure Mr. Bartley deserves an A-plus for that answer. What do you guys think?"

No one knew whether to take him seriously or not, though Malone and Guttierez offered courtesy grins. Wolff cut his eyes to Bartley. "Don't concern yourself with who's in command, Mr. Bartley. I'll be calling the shots, but only when I've heard from everyone involved. As for calling me Jonathan, try telling yourself you're actually saying 'Captain.' "

Bartley stiffened. "I'll give it a try—Jonathan."

Wolff's smile bloomed again. "You'll get used to it, I promise. You might even come to enjoy it. But until then how do you want me to address you—as Mr. Bartley, Lieutenant Bartley, or just plain Bartley?"

Bartley felt himself redden in embarrassment. Was Wolff trying to get his goat, or what? "Ron," he said after a moment.

"Ron. Okay then, Ron. Let's shake on it."

At six feet two, Bartley was as tall as Wolff but put together differently. Where Wolff was lean and wiry, Bartley was thick and solid. He was clean-shaven and wholesome looking, with hazel eyes and coarse hair the color of tomato sauce. His teeth were crooked, and he sometimes had to wear reading glasses. Wolff's tinted aviators seemed nothing more than fashion accessories to go with the tailored uniform and spit-shined boots. A poser, Bartley had thought on watching him stride into the armory only moments earlier. The slicked-back black hair and that swashbuckler's mustache . . . What was Wolff going to do if Cavern City ever ran short of hair gel?

"What's it going to be with you guys?" Wolff was asking the rest of Cavern City's ragtag contingent of RDF regulars. "First names or honorifics?"

Everyone exchanged looks, then one by one they stepped forward to introduce themselves: Paul Ruegger, Roger Malone, Martin Guttierez, Billy Quist, Sonya Ortiz, Gary Jacobs, Paolo Macbride, Jimmy Boomer . . .

"Most of us were relocated here from up north," Bartley thought to point out. "As I guess you could tell from the names. But Martin and Paolo are Venezuelan, and Sonya's from Surinam."

Wolff nodded, appraising everyone. "Where's the rest of the outfit—out on patrol?"

Bartley snorted. "We're it—since the raid on the Cannon, anyway. We lost six there, and another twenty were transferred to the Argentine two weeks ago."

The seemingly unflappable Wolff frowned. "No wonder Mayor Carson appealed directly to Monument City for help." He fell silent for a moment, then shook off whatever disquiet he may have been feeling. "Where are you from, Ron?"

"California, originally. Near Santa Cruz. But Geena's family helped settle Cavern—my wife, I mean."

"Any kids?"

"A two-month-old daughter. Rook."

"Named after the chess piece or the European crow?"

"The chess piece. Geena's an amateur champion."

"Really. Well, Geena and I will have to match wits someday." Wolff took a long look around the cavernous room. "In the meantime, I suggest we get started indexing what you've got in the way of weapons and materiel."

Talk about a crow, Bartley thought, as he was leading Wolff across the room to the supply lockers. The captain had done nothing but try to impress them from the moment he'd arrived, flashing that smile of his. Real Robotech Boy Wonder. There were words to describe guys like Wolff: braggarts—or was it swaggarts? Whatever. Guys that got through life on their good looks and charm. Privileged guys. And Wolff was like the walking definition of charm—the personification. Absolutely. Real high opinion of himself. But just how much of him was on the level remained to be seen.

Wolff spent a few minutes cataloging Cavern City's limited inventory of defensive weapons and entering TO&E assessments in a cheap electronic notebook. "Not much in the way of small arms and munitions. What about heavy equipment?"

"Three first-generation Falcons at the airport," Malone told him. "One LVT Adventurer One, but it's waiting for parts—and missiles. Coupla Howard choppers and a Sea Sergeant, but that's got a bad Jesus nut. We had a Commanchero, but that went south with our other half."

Wolff entered more notes. "How many VTs?" he said without lifting his eyes from the display screen.

"None."

Wolff looked back and forth between Malone and Bartley.

"Excalibers?"

"None," Bartley said.

"Raiders? MACs? Spartans? Gladiators?"

Bartley kept shaking his head, astonished to find that he could derive amusement from underscoring how vulnerable the garrison was. But there was something about the effect his head shaking was having on Wolff . . .

"Son of a bitch," the captain said, "we're regular sitting ducks, aren't we?"

Grudgingly, Bartley stopped smiling to himself. Wolff spoke as if he were already one of them, taking on their fight, when he could have gone on playing the patronizing VIP from Albuquerque.

The captain switched off the notebook and perched himself on the edge of a packing-oil-stained crate of Wolverine rifles. "There's no question that RDF Command wants to help Mayor Carson turn Cavern City into some kind of model municipality, or else they wouldn't have sent me down here. But I want to be perfectly straight with you guys about what we're up against. Zee-town or no Zee-town, this place is an ideal malcontent target, precisely because of what Carson's trying to do. The malcontents are going to see it as a symbol, just like they did the Cannon."

Bartley eyed his teammates, who were all exchanging secret tell-us-something-we-don't-know glances.

"I know what you're thinking," Wolff went on. "That I'm wasting my breath stating the obvious. What I'm getting at, is that no matter what Command's intentions, we shouldn't count on Monument or Albuquerque to provide what we need. Oh, sure, I'll file my TO&E report, and in it I'll ask for twice the number of Destroids we decide on, but any mecha released are going to be slow in arriving. The Argentine has priority in the Southlands, and up north it's the Arkansas Protectorate, which has already siphoned off half of Detroit's and Denver's civil defense mecha."

"Why is Arkansas being fortified?" Malone asked. "To keep intruders out, or to keep the Zentraedi in?"

Wolff shook his head. "You're not the only one asking,

Rog. And, to be honest, it scares the piss out of me. But getting back to our own special mess, all I'm suggesting is that we keep our options open and improvise when we have to. We do whatever's necessary to protect Cavern City. Can we agree on that much?"

Heads nodded. With some eagerness, Bartley noted. Damn Wolff, he was charming them. A guy who had had it all, figuring there was nothing he couldn't accomplish.

"What's in those?" Wolff asked suddenly, gesturing across the room to a series of bays curtained by roll-down iron gates.

"Just some useless pre-War stuff," Bartley answered.

Wolff inclined his head to one side. "What sort of useless stuff?"

"Centaur tanks. Somebody moved them here from their mothball site at the Cannon. By *truck*," Bartley was quick to add.

"They're not worth a damn, sir," Malone said, not bothering to correct himself. "Most of 'em don't even run."

But Wolff was already on his way. "Let's have a look, shall we?"

Ruegger hurried past the captain, punching buttons recessed into the wall alongside each bay. With a grating sound, the gates began to rise. Someone else hit the lights, and in swirling storms of suspended dust were revealed twelve archaic metal monsters, some with missing treads, some with missing cannon turrets. All were shot up, dented, and rusting.

Wolff, however, was grinning, ear to ear. He laid a hand on tank four's battered left headlamp. "I'll be damned if this doesn't put a new spin on the situation."

"How so?" Malone wanted to know.

"We're not as defenseless as I thought."

Malone and Bartley traded bemused looks. "But these things haven't seen action since the Global Civil War," Malone said for both of them. "And like I said, most of them don't even run."

Wolff waved a hand. "No big deal. We can recommission them."

"Who can?" Bartley said. "Samartino was our only mechanic, and he died at the Cannon."

"So, we'll requisition a replacement." Wolff adopted a sly look. "The base commander in the Argentine is a personal friend of mine. I'll ask him to temporary-duty a team of old-school techs to show us the ropes. Once we've seen them rebuild one tank, we can do the rest."

"Hope they'll be able to teach us how to drive them, too," Billy Quist muttered to Guttierez.

"We don't need *them* for that," Wolff said. "I studied these babies back in Albuquerque."

"Studying's one thing . . ." Quist said.

Wolff laughed, nodding his head to Quist while looking at everyone else. "Billy Worry-Wart."

Everyone laughed. "That's Billy," Guttierez said. "Our Grumpy."

"Yeah, well, know-how's good for nothing without replacement parts," Quist argued. "We'll end up cannibalizing eight tanks to get four that run, and four won't mean shit against a couple of Tactical 'Pods."

Wolff only laughed harder. "Parts are the least of it. Anyway, there won't be any cannibalizing." He fingered his mustache like a movie knave. "Of course, we might have to borrow against the city council's appropriation for civil defense and make a quick trip to Freetown . . . But that's improvisation for you: it takes you places you never expect to go."

Bartley allowed a slow grin, Malone and the rest way ahead of him.

"I always wanted to see Mexico," Malone said.

"Then you're with me?" Wolff said, looking around. "We're a team?"

"A pack's more like it," Quist mumbled.

"Right," Guttierez said. "The Wolff Pack."

Wolff nodded in gleeful surprise. "Now *that* has a ring to it."

If there was poetic justice to Brasília's ascending to world prominence after the Rain, the survival of Mexico City was nothing short of perverse irony. In the eco-

enthusiastic years preceding the Global Civil War, common
wisdom had it that Mexico wouldn't weather the millen-
nium, let alone anything beyond. Bloated, polluted, subject
to health-threatening inversions and devastating tectonic up-
heavals, the city had been dismissed as a casualty of the
modern age long before the coming of the Visitor or the
Zentraedi. And yet somehow Mexico City had been overlooked by Dolza—though the west coast, from Mazatlán to
Huatulco, had been obliterated—and five years later, people
were still offering theories as to why: the thick smog had
concealed the city from the bioscanners; those same scanners had been dazzled by electromagnetic disturbances
whose source was nearby Popocatépetl; Aztec magic; the
place had already appeared dead.

Whatever the cause, Mexico of 2016 was alive, as was
much of the country south and east of the capital. Alive, if
not exactly thriving. Even in the absence of fossil-fueled
cars, smog alerts were a daily event; and there were the
power failures, the periodic food shortages, the epidemics
of cholera and dengue fever, nowhere more evident than in
the trash-barren barrios surrounding the fortified core of the
distrito federal, on the infernal side of the periphery highway. Southward, Mexico had spread itself halfway to
Cuernavaca; and north to the ancient ruins at San Juan
Teotihuacán. And it was from that squalid, disease-ridden,
near-waterless sprawl of crumbling pyramids and garishly
painted cinder-block that Freetown was born.

It had begun as Zee-town, a ghetto for aliens, many of
whom, nostalgic for their former gianthood, found solace in
Teotihuacán's massive earthwork structures. Then the Mexican mafia had moved in, mingling easily with the impov-
erished population and organized gambling and prostitution
rackets and drug, arms, and contraband operations. In the
beginning, the *federales* had tried to purge the area of crime
by means of daylight raids and death-squad disappearances,
but the military government soon abandoned the effort. It
allowed Freetown to fester, contenting itself with the kick-
backs it received in exchange for supplying electric power
and, when available, potable water. A police force of spo-
radically paid mercenaries maintained peace of a sort,

though it never interfered with gang business or warfare. As a result, Freetown had more crime bosses than it had criminal organizations, but the names of three individuals stood out: Antonio Ramos, kingpin of the narcocartels; Brian Cassidy, supplier of everything from counterfeit scrip to mecha parts; and Neela Saam, a Zentraedi female who provided alien enforcers to Ramos and Cassidy and women to Freetown's numerous brothels, in addition to middling in black market goods and information.

And by the end of her first week in Freetown, Seloy Deparra had had dealings with all three of them. Too, she was by now the leader of a Zentraedi band that included Xan Norri, Marla Stenik, Vivik Bross, and seven other original members of the all-female Senburu group. The rest had decamped on meeting Neela and being introduced to the easy life. Neither Seloy nor Xan had tried to talk them out of it. Let them work as bodyguards or prostitutes; the new Senburu wanted nothing less than the unflinching loyalty any Zentraedi would have shown for her commander. However, Seloy had taken an instant dislike to Neela, who claimed to have been a lieutenant under Azonia, though neither Seloy nor Vivik could remember her. Was Neela inventing a past, as many Humans had done after the Rain? Had she been so corrupted by *Human* beings that she believed a Quadrono legacy afforded her cachet?

Seloy couldn't decide. But on this, the third meeting with Neela, she found herself in the grips of a murderous impulse. It was just the four of them this time, Neela, Xan, Seloy, and the infant, seated around a filthy table in a bar on Avenida Feo. Neela hadn't asked about Hirano, but in fact it was Hirano that was keeping Seloy from acting on her impulse; the presence of the child and the realization that the murder of a Zentraedi by a Zentraedi was conduct as corrupt and unbecoming as the pursuit of cachet among Micronians.

"The parts you requested will be available tomorrow," Neela was saying. "Though I must admit, it seems an odd assortment."

"Odd how?" Seloy asked contentiously.

Neela showed a twisted smile. "*Queadlunn-Rau* inertia-vector control system shunts, faceplate focusing sights, plasmic restraint chambers, power gauntlets . . . Nothing out of the ordinary there; you're obviously in possession of Female Power Armor. But these other items: Phalanx SDR-zero four-MK Twelve missile drums, along with shoulder joints, chest plastrons, MT eight-twenty-eight fusion turbines, pylons for a Decamissile array . . . Could it be that you've gotten your hands on an RDF Spartan as well?"

A small and shapely woman with short hair, violet eyes, and plump lips, she looked as if she had patterned herself after Azonia. Marla speculated that Neela had used sex to solidify her position in Freetown. The preliminary meetings had established that she could probably lay her hands on what Xan needed to transform the Power Armor the Senburu had left in the care of confederates in the Southlands. For an additional charge she could also arrange for the supplies to be airlifted south. The provenance of some of the parts was an abandoned military base near Tula; the rest had come from crashed warships looted by itinerant Human and Zentraedi foragers. Neela had confessed that she was merely acting as a go-between; Brian Cassidy was the actual provider. In exchange, Xan was offering the money she'd received from the sale of a Tactical Battlepod to a group known as the Paranka, based in the Argentine. The amount was more than adequate, but instead of being happy with the deal, Neela kept pressing to learn how the parts were going to be used.

"In other words, why would you want Defense Force missiles unless you had access to Defense Force mecha?" Neela continued. "The other thing that interests me is that you haven't asked about Protoculture. Which means either that you plan to rely on fusion, or you have enough cells to satisfy your purposes."

Not wanting to reveal anything about the smuggling operation under way on the factory, Xan told Neela that she had guessed correctly about their trusting to fusion. The MT-828 reactors had only been included in the first place to mislead her.

"I see," Neela said, not entirely convinced. "I suppose

we all do what we can. But if you should happen to get a line on 'culture cells, I hope you'll come back and see me."

"Count on it," Seloy told her.

Neela glanced back and forth between Seloy and Xan. "Will you be remaining in Freetown for a while? I only ask because there's money to made here—especially for women as attractive as you two."

Xan spit on the floor at Neela's feet. "We have more important concerns than money."

"Lorelei alpha is scheduled for insertion into orbit on May one," T. R. Edwards reported to the members of Senator Milburn's political cabal: Stinson, Longchamps, Maistroff, Caruthers, and Moran. "Lorelei beta launches in July, gamma in October, delta in January. Expectations are for the network to be fully operational by no later than June 2017. As an added bonus, it looks certain that Lynn-Minmei will be hosting a call-in show."

Milburn's face lit up with amused disbelief. "How did this happy coincidence come about?"

"Nothing coincidental about it, Senator. When I heard she was shopping around for a new agent, I made sure one of them got wind of the project."

"Wonderful," Milburn said, leaning back in his swivel chair.

Maistroff scowled at the senator's patent admiration for Edwards. "Can't we rush Lorelei some? You're talking about more than a year."

"Can't be done," Edwards said. "It'll take at least that long for Zand to cook up a traceable food additive. Then, if systematic tagging is the goal, we'll have to see to it that the additive-laced food is made available to Zentraedi worldwide." He shook his head. "This sort of operation requires a great deal of time—and patience."

"Edwards is right," Milburn told the general. "Just stay on it, Edwards. Now, tell us about Zand. How did he strike you?"

Edwards touched his faceplate, stroking it lightly. "Hungry, ambitious, easily influenced. Not as brilliant as Lang or Bronson, but depraved enough to suit your purposes better than either of them would. In fact, I'd like your permission to introduce Zand to Anatole Leonard."

"What's the point of that?" Stinson asked.

"To give Zand hope, for one thing. He won't admit it, but he's pathologically jealous of Lang—he has been for years. And no matter what Zand accomplishes on his own in terms of research, the RDF is always going to remain Lang's turf. But if Zand suddenly felt that he had a defense force of his own . . ."

"You mean the Army of the Southern Cross," Caruthers said.

Edwards nodded.

"What use would Anatole have for Zand?" Moran cut in, obviously irked by the proposal. "He's against anything associated with the RDF—and that includes most aspects of Robotechnology."

"Yes, that's the reborn Faithful in him." Edwards glanced quickly at Moran. "Excuse my bluntness, Senator. I know you were also a member of the Faithful."

Judging from the facial expressions, Edwards realized that Moran's former affiliation with the religious cult was news to everyone at the table—a fact that delighted him. What Moran didn't know was that Edwards had facilitated the disbanding of the Faithful on Macross Island. At the time, he had been in the employ of Senator Russo, a man he had never liked in spite of the operational latitude Russo had given him. Russo's disappearance following the Rain remained one of the War's many unsolved mysteries— though Edwards could certainly understand why the head of the United Earth Defense Council would opt to go missing rather than run the risk of being recognized by some mob of survivors and strung up by his bootheels.

Senator Moran was beet red when he finally responded to Edwards's assertion. "Gentlemen, my flirtation with the Faithful arose out of a conviction that reconstruction of the Visitor would bankrupt us, not out of some superstitious belief that the ship had been sent by God or the devil to tempt Humankind."

"Of course, Wyatt," Longchamps said, managing not to sound patronizing.

"Finish your thought," Milburn told Edwards. "How do you propose to get Leonard interested in Zand?"

"Through Leonard's aide, Joseph Petrie—the hacker's hacker. Given a choice, Petrie would rather be a machine than a Human, and I think he and Zand would hit it off. As for Leonard, he'll gladly accept who or whatever you send him. He was extremely grateful for the intel we provided on Cairo, and he's eager to reciprocate. I recommend you continue to throw him scraps—so long as it's in your interests to do so, and providing he doesn't decide to bite the hand that's feeding him."

Moran showed Edwards a disgusted look. "You underestimate him."

Edwards narrowed his good eye. "I doubt it, Senator. But you're entitled to your opinion." The half cowl he wore felt like a cool hand clamped to the side of his face; with the cowl removed, the tortured flesh it hid felt like a lumpy growth. Some people questioned the keenness of his depth perception, but Edwards knew he could see deeper with one eye than most could see with two. And he likewise knew that he would never surrender the faceplate or have the flesh repaired—as Zand, among others, had offered to do when they'd met the previous month. A souvenir from Alaska Base, the scars had become a kind of talisman.

"How are things proceeding with Operation Tiger?" Stinson threw out to no one in particular. "Are we still sterile?"

"No leaks," Edwards assured him. "But I have to tell you, we've had a bitch of time obtaining trustworthy guards willing to staff the Protectorate. On the whole, RDFers tend to be a tolerant bunch." He gestured to Maistroff. "But the general has managed to winnow a couple of dozen xenophobes from the Detroit and Denver civil defense contingents. They're being transferred to the Protectorate border to make them available when needed."

"Now all we need is a plausible excuse for moving all full-size Zentraedi in this sector to Arkansas," Stinson said.

Longchamps showed the palms of his hands. "Can't we simply say that such a move is in the interest of their safety?"

Caruthers scoffed. "They're safest right where they are."

Milburn mulled it over for a moment. "What about spreading reports of a disease that's killing only aliens?"

"Movie thinking," Maistroff said dismissively.

"We could say that we've intercepted intelligence about raids by Human-supremist groups."

Edwards kept his mouth shut until, ultimately, everyone was looking to him for suggestions. "You're not going to scare three hundred full-size aliens out of Monument, Denver, Portland, and Detroit with rumors about diseases or incursions. You have to engineer it so that they're leaving of their own free will, or else you've already got a security nightmare just getting them to the Protectorate."

"What's your plan?" Moran asked antagonistically.

"It's twofold. First, we make it uncomfortable for the full-size by turning public opinion against them. We're already working on this by arranging for a series of firebombings to occur at RDF bases throughout the sector, in which the Zentraedi will be implicated." Edwards paused for a moment. "I understand that UEG sanction of Operation Tiger requires a majority vote, and I know you're close to having that, but it couldn't hurt to add a few Human fatalities to the firebombings. Short of some truly savage action by the malcontents, you may need fatalities to secure the support of the RDF."

Milburn made his lips a thin line, then allowed a grim nod.

"The second part requires that voluntary relocation to the Protectorate be made to seem an appealing option. The answer is obvious when you consider why the Protectorate's twelve hundred full-size have elected to live there, as opposed to Monument, Denver, or the factory satellite."

"Because of the training they're receiving in design and construction," Stinson said, with transparent impatience.

"Precisely. So I suggest you promote Operation Tiger as a plan to turn the Protectorate into a surface counterpart of the factory. A place where all full-size aliens will not only be able to escape discrimination, but to learn vital skills and offset the negative propaganda of malcontentism by making a contribution to the Expeditionary mission. Then it just becomes a matter of transporting three hundred giants to Arkansas aboard cargo plans and trucks and whatnot."

The room fell silent while Edwards's idea was considered; then, one by one, Milburn and the rest sat back in their chairs, smug and satisfied.

Six silly dilettantes who thought they had their sights set on power, Edwards told himself. Six fatuous politicians, indulging in card tricks. Not one of them understood that power wasn't something to be coddled, or cajoled, or won; it existed unto itself and answered to no one. Real power was a force to be tapped, then wielded like a blunt instrument. It wasn't something you exercised, but an energy that could be borrowed and brought to bear against whatever obstacles stood in your way.

At some point it was going to be necessary to prune the cabal of its dead wood: Milburn, Stinson, and Longchamps. Access to the RDF made Maistroff and Caruthers useful, as access to Leonard made Moran useful. But by then, Edwards would have put Zand and Petrie together and would be playing one duo against the other. The time required could be equal to that of the construction of the SDF-3, but things would eventually come together. Someone would probably have to go along on that damned mission in the event the REF returned from Tirol better equipped than when they left. Maybe Stinson and Longchamps could be persuaded, or maybe Edwards would be forced to go himself. How long could the mission require, after all? A year at the most? And during that time, Moran could assist the Army of the Southern Cross in doing away with the RDF once and for all.

But could Edwards stand being cooped up in the SDF-3 with Lang, Hayes, Reinhardt, Hunter, and the others for as long as a year? *Admirals* Hayes and Hunter—now, there was a bit of comic relief. Exactly what had their promotions been based on—not dying aboard the SDF-1 with that idiot Gloval? And wouldn't the two of them be surprised when T. R. Edwards suddenly emerged from Leonard's army as a general.

He had had limited dealings with Hayes or Hunter, though occasionally when he saw Hunter some of the old hatreds would rise to the surface. Hunter was the one who'd come soaring into Alaska Base to rescue Hayes, of course. But how much weight could Edwards give that? How could Hunter have known that someone else had survived and had been trying to call out to him as he and Hayes were lifting off—someone with half his skull blown away and already vomiting from radiation sickness?

Then again, Hunter had ties to Roy Fokker, and Edwards's only regret about not having been aboard the SDF-1 was that he hadn't been around to see Fokker crash and burn. He remembered hearing about it, but no glasses had been raised to Fokker's memory. Their rivalry during the Global Civil War lacked the mutual respect rival World War I dogfighters had for their opponents. Plain and simple, Edwards and Fokker had loathed one another. And he loathed Fokker all the more for dying prematurely.

The thing was, hatred wanted a victim, and Humankind seemed too broad a target. During the coming years, while he was plotting the fall of the RDF and the rise of the ASC, he would have to try to narrow the focus of his personal goals.

CHAPTER
FOURTEEN

By early spring of that year [2016]—and after considerable effort—a second Earth-tech-capable docking bay had been opened in the factory satellite, on this occasion in the underbelly of the so-named three-o'clock pod. Lang's technicians had been faced with the problem of opening a portal in a triple reinforced ceramic-composite hull that immediately wanted to repair and re-seal itself—a Protoculture-driven design feature shared by many Zentraedi facilities and warships. With Breetai's flagship already parked inside the factory, there was no ship available for use in conjuring open one of the coded bays, but Lang overcame the problem by using a disabled Zentraedi destroyer the reclamation crews had located in lunar orbit. Tugs steered the destroyer through a series of approach vectors until at last one of the factory's concealed gates opened. The ship was left in the breech while teams of EVA specialists labored frantically to disconnect the gate from all Robotech systemry; then, ultimately, an Earth-tech iris-portal was installed in the hull. . . . May of 2016 saw two significant launches from the three-o'clock pod's retrofitted gate: on May one, the launch of a Ghost QF-3000 EC, whose payload was the first (alpha) telecom satellite of what would eventually become the Lorelei Network. Then, on May 17th, the launch of the unmanned though highly controversial "Hades Mission," the goal of which was the retrieval from Plutospace of objects lost from Macross Island's original Robotech Research Center.

Ahmed Rashona, That Pass in the Night: The SDF-3 and the Mission to Tirol

"I CAN'T BELIEVE YOU'RE ACTUALLY GOING THROUGH with this," Catherine Wolff told her husband as he was stuffing his duffel with clothes selected seemingly at random from the bedroom closet.

"You've seen the reply from RDF Command," Wolff said. "What choice do I have?" The response to his report had been a month coming and contained just what he had expected to hear.

"Oh, I see: since the RDF has ignored your requisitions, you have no choice but to supply this place with the mecha it needs."

Catherine was pacing the tiled floor at the foot of the double bed, and Jonathan's black canvas duffel was propped against the night table. Johnny was in the adjoining room, immobile in front of the interactive TV the Wolffs had purchased in Albuquerque before leaving for Venezuela—a transition-easing surprise for their son. The four-room, sparsely furnished apartment was in a new building at the western terminus of Cavern City's soon-to-be-completed monorail line. Because the canyon was somewhat wider there, the claustrophobic feel of downtown was tempered; and what with the trees, the neat houses, the churches and shopping centers, the area had an almost suburban air.

"Monument isn't dismissing the requisitions. But it might take months for any mecha to arrive, and we'll be defenseless until then."

"So is that your fault? You were sent here to evaluate the situation, not to fortify the city."

"Cavern's our *home*, Cath. This trip to Mexico's no more than I'd do for any place we lived."

She smirked. "The town hero. What are you going to do for your second act—run for mayor?"

He glowered at her, then let go of the anger. "There are twelve Centaur tanks sitting in the armory that only need a few parts to get them running. I'm certain those parts are available in Mexico because Mexico's old Volkswagen factories were turning out their own version of Centaurs at the end of the century. And since I'm the only one whose studied the things, it makes sense for me to go."

Catherine folded her arms under her breasts. "Who, may I ask, is paying for this little shopping spree?"

"The city council is paying for most of it."

"Most?"

"We might be required to cover some of the travel expenses—but I'm sure we'll be reimbursed."

She rolled her eyes. "You're unbelievable sometimes."

"You want me to go overland, Cath? Fine. I'll be back in a month instead of a week."

She didn't respond immediately, and when she did her tone had softened. "Is it dangerous?"

"No more than dealing with black marketeers anywhere. But instead of looking for ration coupons or luxury goods, I'll be looking for tank parts."

"Then take us with you."

Wolff showed her an imploring look. "Come on, Cath. There's always a chance something could go wrong. Having to think about your safety would be a distraction."

"As distracting as thinking about my happiness, I'll bet."

Wolff pretended not to have heard the comment. "Anyway," he said, "I've already got company for the trip."

"Who?"

"Malone. The one you said looks like he should be fronting a rock band."

"Good choice, Jon. And be sure you check out the nightclubs while you're there."

"Cath—"

"But then, you've always been good at making friends, haven't you? I mean, we've been in Cavern for less than two months and you've already formed a clique. What was it Geena Bartley called it—a pack? Now you can just leave me to rot here."

Wolff's eyes flashed anger. "If you rot here, it'll be by your own choice." Remembering that Johnny was in the next room, he lowered his voice. "I know you had your heart set on a transfer to Portland or Monument, but that didn't happen, so I suggest we both make the best of it. Johnny's adapting, and you'd get used to the climate if you didn't try to fight it. Besides, this place is wide open with possibilities—for jobs, for friends, whatever."

"Friends like Geena Bartley and the other wives of Cavern City's noble garrison of Robotech defenders? Gee, maybe I should join a parent/teachers group while I'm at it, or swear allegiance to the Church of Recurrent Tragedies?"

"You knew this was my life," Wolff seethed.

She nodded. "That's true, Jon. I'm just wondering what happened to my life. You weren't the only one with plans."

"So make them happen here. You could start by taking the job Mayor Carson offered you."

She smiled wanly.

Wolff tightened the drawstrings of the duffel. "I promise, when I get back from this mission we'll sit down and figure out a plan."

"What kind of plan?"

Wolff shrugged. "If you're not happy here in two years, I'll agree to apply for a transfer."

"Wrong," she said. "I'll give it one year; then I'm gone."

"Down there," Narumi said, pointing to a clearing in the forest far below them. "Two hours to be there."

Bagzent exhaled slowly and ran the back of his wrist over his sweat-beaded brow. Two more hours—he could surely endure that much. But for the past ten days, it had been torture keeping pace with the aborigine who had led him through hundreds of miles of forest to the meeting place specified by the Senburu females. Now, standing on the limestone rim of the basin that hid the Senburu camp, Bagzent allowed himself a relieved exhale for the first time since departing the Xingu.

"We go," Narumi said, setting off at a brisk clip on sturdy brown legs that carried him effortlessly through the thickest vegetation. Bagzent nodded to his comrades—the two other remaining members of Khyron's Fist—and hurried after the Indian, down into the bush, down into the tangled biomass that was the green heart of the Southlands.

For all the adversities—heat, rain, swollen streams, stinging insects, barbed trees—Bagzent had come through the journey with an unanticipated appreciation for the planet on which he and so many Zentraedi were marooned. An appreciation and something more, something his mind had been striving to define these past few days. Early on he thought that perhaps the sameness of the forest had left his mind hungry for visual information in the same way his body hungered for nourishment. But slowly he began to realize that what he had taken for sameness was in fact the opposite: living diversity raised to an unfathomable magnitude. Each plant and tree and airborne or crawling insect fitting into the whole like the interconnected parts of some grand machine. Birds eating fruits, then shitting the seeds which would grow new trees, yielding more fruit for those same birds . . . Animals feeding on the flesh of other animals . . . Flora that exhaled gases necessary for the survival of the fauna . . . Snakes living out their infancy in earthen tunnels excavated by armies of leaf-cutting ants . . . Other ants nesting inside the thorns of trees . . . Vines that provided drinking water, trees that provided nourishment . . . It was impossible for him to conceive that Amazonia hadn't been fashioned by Masters like those on Tirol, and yet Narumi insisted time and again that *Earth had no Masters*; that even the Micronians that inhabited the planet had had nothing to do with its fashioning, but were themselves only part of the whole, and were, like Earth's other living things, at the mercy of foul weather, earthquakes, volcanic activity, and the impacts of meteors. More, that the jungle had *evolved*—shaped itself over eons—guided only by the thoughts of a rarely seen, intangible being Narumi called Wondrous Spirit.

All this was incomprehensible to the Zentraedi, and especially baffling to one who had known only the insides of Battlepods and warships and rarely the surface of worlds. And coming as it did, on the heels of the Fist's Pyrrhic victory at the Grand Cannon, the experience of interconnectedness had begun to erode his convictions about warfare—to undermine the destructive fervor hardwired into him by the Imperative.

If order was inherent to the world of Wondrous Spirit, whose bidding did the Zentraedi do by fomenting disorder?

Whatever the answer, Bagzent had found himself asking continual questions of Narumi and the other Indian guides, eager to know the taste of each fruit, to learn which trees supplied timber for construction and which supplied leaves for medicine, to identify the forest's animals by their deposited scat. His respect for the aboriginals was unbounded, for like the Zentraedi, they existed in the moment and they lived their lives with a sense of fierce determination. Unlike the Zentraedi, however, Narumi's people were not without personal and collective histories, nor did they answer to an embedded Imperative. At all times they seemed to know their place in the physical world; without them, Bagzent and his comrades would be lost to the forest . . .

Entering the Senburu camp two hours later, Bagzent saw that several other malcontent bands had accepted the females' invitation. Already present were representatives from the Steel Wind, the Shroud, and the Crimson Ghosts, all of whom had been guided to the basin by either aborigines or rough-and-tumble Humans who made the jungle their refuge.

Bagzent recognized most of the male warriors, but only a few of the Senburu females. Xan Norri he had met years ago in Macross, when she was working for—and perhaps providing sex to—the Robotech scientist Harry Penn. The petite and combative Marla Stenik had spent time at the Xingu camp. Vivik Bross and Seloy Deparra—Senburu's apparent leader—he knew by reputation as Quadrono aces under Azonia.

The camp was much more elaborate than the one Khyron's Fist and others had hacked from the northeastern jungle bordering the Xingu River. The women had taken over an abandoned gold-dredging operation and had refurbished the processing plant and some of the heavy equipment. Employing bulldozers and cranes, they had erected several tall buildings and cleared a landing strip suitable for small planes. The accomplishments were both daunting and humiliating to the men—none less so than the centerpiece of the camp: a deliberately modified *Queadlunn-Rau* battle suit, accoutered with three times the usual number of autocannons and twice the pulse lasers. The 55-foot-tall weapon retained its humanoid appearance, though the twin-lobed top-mounted booster pack and suggestion of gun-turreted head made it look like the offspring of Power Armor mated with Robotech Destroid.

Bagzent kept one eye on the thing through the rest of the day and throughout the long night, getting little sleep as a result. The following morning he managed nonetheless to summon enough energy to drag himself to the briefing the Senburu had scheduled.

"We've decided on the name Stinger," Seloy Deparra announced, once everyone had been fed and gathered round the alloy-clad, cloven feet of the hybrid mecha. "The reason we haven't afforded it a Zentraedi name should be obvious to all of you who understand the nature of terrorism: we want the Humans to be on speaking terms with this weapon"— she gestured to the Stinger—"because we plan to introduce it as a recurring feature in their lives."

Deparra explained that the battle suit itself had been salvaged from a crashed destroyer, of which there were many studding the forest in the vicinity of the Senburu camp. Bagzent had noted several on his way in, though he doubted he could make his way to them again without Narumi's help. The RDF-mecha parts welded and riveted to the battle suit had been supplied and delivered by Zentraedi operating in Freetown.

"And certain parts have come to us indirectly from the factory satellite," the Senburu leader continued, "by means that are better left undisclosed. Our goal, in any case, is to make these available to your groups so that you can conduct your raids with more resources to tap than the boldness of the Imperative."

Deparra motioned everyone away from the mecha; then, on her signal, the Stinger launched from the clearing and jinked through a series of lightning-quick maneuvers.

"Six autocannons, a quartet of high-speed triple-barreled pulse lasers, flight speed equivalent to that of the Veritech, limb strength equivalent to that of the Gladiator, missile capacity greater than that of the Spartan and Excaliber combined . . ."

Bagzent tried to follow the Stinger's aerial gyrations, but the attempt left him dizzy and even more disheartened.

"Modifications to the inertia-vector control system make it unmatched in maneuverability by current Robotech mecha," Deparra added.

The Stinger performed a low-level flyby and landed.

"What do we have to do to get one?" a member of the Shroud asked with suspicion.

Deparra's sloping eyes found him in the crowd. "For now, all we're asking from the male groups is assistance in locating parts—any Destroid, intact or disabled, will suffice—and financing to pay for what can't be procured by salvaging. This means that some of you may have to engage in commonplace robberies in place of unadulterated mayhem. Just remember: the goal is to render our enemy terror-stricken. Once we've accomplished that, we can begin to formulate our demands."

Deparra lifted her face to the mecha. "Each of our prototypes has outperformed its predecessor." Lowering her head, she scanned the audience, fixing briefly on Bagzent. "The time has come to test one on a live target."

Take Manhattan as it was before the Rain, and roof the whole island over at the height of the Empire State Building. Next, extend the walls of most of the buildings up to the ceiling and obliterate all the windows and doorways and architectural adornments. Efface all setbacks so that the building walls become sheer and featureless. Now remove the cars, the parks, the people and their pets, dim the lighting to a phosphorescent glow, and raise the gravity slightly above Earth normal. The result would approximate the chase shaft that bisected the ovoid central body of the factory satellite between the ceiling of level seven and the systems-clad floor of the bridge, a five-mile-long technodungeon of dendritelike relays, arterial-like conduit, and ligamentlike cable, serviced and policed by an array of bipedal and airborne robots. Not the sort of place a rational person would choose to visit, let alone solo, but Lynn-Kyle had never considered himself rational, and he functioned best when alone. Granted that the vastness of the space could send even the most intrepid of explorers to the edge of agoraphobic panic, but Kyle had immunized himself to all unreasonable fears by learning to think of the thousand-foot-high chase as a kind of crawlspace—for someone Godzilla-sized, to be sure, but a crawlspace nonetheless.

It was fourteen hundred hours factory time and Kyle was on his lunch break. The cafeteria for service providers was two levels down, but he had stopped there only long enough to be observed by several coworkers before riding an empty cargo elevator up to level six. His rating didn't permit him to ascend beyond six, but a Human member of the alliance who worked security on seven had been waiting for him at the elevator and had stayed with him all the way to the retrofitted ladder and hatch that accessed the chase. The climb alone had taken five minutes.

Kyle had a battery-operated miner's lamp strapped around his head and a large bucket-style pack on his back. Shown the route by Elmikk a week earlier, he moved quickly, fingertips in constant contact with the towering walls at his left side.

Under normal conditions the outer walls would have run straight from one end of the shaft to the other. But the same glitches that had shut down mecha production the previous year had somehow deluded the factory's central computer into believing that the chase had been penetrated by non-Zentraedi interlopers, and as a consequence security partitions had risen from the floor, dropped from the ceiling, and slid from the walls, turning the chase into a veritable maze. Huge reservoirs of drinking water or lubricants had been drained dry, smaller basins had been filled; conduit systems had reconfigured; some areas had been misted with acid or flooded with toxic fumes. There were places where the temperature was subzero, other places hot with radiation. The route Elmikk and his cohorts had explored and mapped avoided the worst of the danger zones, though Kyle understood that the configuration of the bulkheads would surely change if the main computer went back online. And the factory's robot defense units, quiescent the past year, would mobilize.

The route took Kyle past examples of some of those units: a 42-foot-tall Destroyer, whose reverse-articulated legs had walked it into a corner; four crashed, silent assassin "Buzz-Bot" airborne robots; and several multi-armed precision engineer drones—also grounded—which featured optic and sensor arrays for locating and tracking intruders by heat, motion, and sound.

As things stood, Kyle had two roles in the smuggling operation he had helped organize: he was the first to see the "shopping list" carried up the well by Humans who interfaced on the surface with the Senburu group, and he was the one who made the pickup of Protoculture microcells and passed them on to carriers who smuggled them down the well. Theofre Elmikk was tasked with filling the list, but the actual procurement was done by a team of vacuum-deployed aliens under Elmikk's command—giants who worked outside the factory, dismantling derelict Zentraedi ships. Once the smuggled parts made planetfall—at Denver, Albuquerque, Monument, or other ports of entry—they were muled to the Senburu's Southlands mecha facility by Humans or alien members of the alliance.

For one trained in the arts of stealth, purposeful swiftness, and fearless concentration, the labyrinthal trip from the ladder-fed hatch to the drop point—a distance of just over one mile—required ten minutes. Having already logged eight round trips that week alone, Kyle made it in nine minutes. He glanced at the luminescent dial of his watch: 14:38. He had to be back at his food-processor station in the kitchen by no later than 15:15. He would be late if the drop wasn't made in the next five minutes.

But even as he was thinking it, he heard, just ahead of him, the pneumatic sound of a hatch being raised. And a moment later, highlighted by the stark illumination of a level seven corridor, a hairy fist the size of a passenger car appeared in the opening, quickly and efficiently ridding itself of its palmed parcel of purloined Protoculture.

In the center of the flatscreen, against a viscous, transparent background, a faintly blue and vaguely circular object was being buffeted on all sides by smaller, oval-shaped objects, a few of which had managed to attach themselves to the circle by means of slender stalks.

"The large object is the Protoculture molecule," Lazlo Zand was explaining to T. R. Edwards. "Surrounding it are molecules of the protein I've developed. Notice how the Protoculture resists all attempts at bonding." Zand intensified the magnifying power of the electron microscope, zeroing in on an arc of cell wall. "What's mystifying is how such an impermeable substance can be so utterly responsive." Zand recalled the earlier screen; by now some half-dozen ovals were firmly stalked to the Protoculture molecule. "Luckily, my protein seems to be getting through to it."

"Looks a little like the factory satellite," Edwards commented, narrowing his eye somewhat.

Zand regarded the screen in pleasant surprise. "So it does."

Edwards had flown to Tokyo immediately on learning of Zand's success, and just now the two men were in the professor's office at the Robotech Research Center. A disorderly rectangle tucked away in subbasement three, the office reeked of mildew and Zand's rather pungent body odor. A few plants, including a bonsai, were dying, and the wastebaskets overflowed with fast-food wrappings.

Edwards clapped his hands on his thighs. "I'm very pleased, Professor, as I'm certain my employers will be."

Zand's eyes bulged when he grinned. He switched off the computer feed to the screen, called on a bank of overhead lights, and planted himself behind his desk.

"In fact," Edwards continued, "something interesting came up while I was submitting my last progress report. My employers have asked me to arrange a meeting between you and a young man named Joseph Petrie, a very talented hacker. Either here, or in Monument, or—if you're not adverse to travel—in Brasília."

"This Petrie is a Southlander?"

"He's chief aide to Field Marshal Anatole Leonard."

Zand's expression went from confusion to consternation.

"No reason for concern," Edwards said. "Petrie has a strong interest in machine intelligence and my employers feel that he could profit from meeting you."

Zand's fears weren't entirely allayed. "Do you represent the Army of the Southern Cross, Mr. Edwards?"

Edwards ridiculed the idea. "I have no military affiliations, Professor. I assure you, this meeting is strictly in the interest of science. Though I have to admit, it wouldn't hurt to count someone like Leonard as a friend."

"Why is that?"

"Because the Army of the Southern Cross is basically a fledgling operation, compared to the RDF. And who knows, Leonard might have need for a researcher such as yourself."

"Yes, but—"

"Don't get me wrong, I know you're loyal to the RDF. But I also know how hard it can be to get funding for research, and right now Leonard is hungry to achieve parity with the RDF in terms of state-of-the-art technology." Edwards trained his eye on Zand. "Don't tell me you don't have your pet projects, just as Lang has his."

Zand swallowed audibly. Pushpinned to a cork bulletin board were photos of a dozen Zentraedi, including Rico, Konda, Bron, Miriya Parino, and an infant that could only be Dana.

"I have a few ideas—"

"Of course you do. But it's damned hard getting anyone to listen when Lang's busy sucking up every available research dollar. I mean, can you believe the RDF agreed to fund that robot mission to Pluto?"

Zand's look hardened. "He always gets what he wants."

Edwards nodded in sympathy. "The pecking order. Just like in the military." He leaned forward conspiratorially. "Between you and me, you should have heard some of the comments about Hayes and Hunter when word got out about their promotions. You don't think people felt overlooked?"

Now Zand nodded. "They have it so easy, designing their ship and filling it with mecha while the rest of us have to scrape by on allocations from the UEG. You begin to feel useless."

"The Japanese used to have a slang word for it—*chindogu*, I think it was. An object of questionable value, like an umbrella with a remote control, or a toilet seat that adjusts to the dimensions of your ass."

"Exactly, exactly."

"That's why I mention Leonard: as a potential funder, nothing more than that."

Zand took a breath. "Yes, thank you, Mr. Edwards. And please tell your employers that I'd be delighted to meet Mr. Petrie, where and whenever it's convenient."

"They'll be pleased to hear it." Edwards fell silent for a moment, then said, "Seems unfair that Lang should get everything he wants just because he happened to get his brain boosted."

Zand stared across the desk without saying anything.

"I was with him when it happened, Zand. Inside the Visitor. One minute he's touching things on the console in Zor's cabin; the next, he's out like a light. But when he woke up, his neural circuits had been rearranged—just like what happened to one of the recon robots we sent into the ship."

Zand wore a faraway look. "I would give anything . . ."

"To take the jolt?" Edwards asked. "So what's stopping you?"

Zand cleared his head with a shake. "For one thing, Mr. Edwards, that console no longer exists."

Edwards snorted, then smiled affably. "There was nothing special about that console. It was just a matter of Lang's sticking his finger where it had no place being. Making contact with that impermeable Protoculture of yours. Lang wasn't going for broke, Professor—it was an accident. But don't tell me there isn't something you guys salvaged from the SDF-1, maybe something right here in the Center, that couldn't produce the same effect."

CHAPTER FIFTEEN

Numerous versions exist of Jonathan Wolff's "shopping trip" to Freetown, including those reported by Wolff's companion, Roger Malone (in Strange Days: Fighting Men and Women Talk About the Malcontent Uprisings*) and Brian Cassidy (in Mizner's* Rakes and Rogues: The True Story of the SDF-3 Expeditionary Mission*). Attempts at arriving at an authentic version—mostly by members of the "Wolff Cult"—have repeatedly failed. However, all are in agreement that the Wolff legend has its true beginning in Mexico.*
Zeus Bellow, The Road to Reflex Point

AROUND THEM LAY TORSOS AND BODY PARTS: smooth, hairless heads, unadorned limbs at odd angles, a forest of upraised arms, all racial types and skin shades represented, bloodless and fashionably thin, reflecting the outré, "deepspace" trend of 2009—before the arrival of the aliens that would usher in a whole new look.

The mannequin morgue occupied the rear of a garage in what had been a Wal-Mart department store in the northern suburbs of Mexico City, looted during the race riots of 2012, burned and abandoned the following year, and now engulfed by the sprawl of the Freetown barrio. Hidden among the mannequins, Jonathan Wolff and Roger Malone had an unobstructed view of the doorless shipping and receiving entrance. They had been sitting like that, hunkered down among the plastic heads and bodies, for well over an hour.

"Is this going to happen without gunplay, Captain?" Malone asked, using the honorific the way one would a so-briquet. He was a twenty-two-year-old with pleasing features and a thick mane of blond hair that fell below his broad shoulders. Even in Cavern City, he favored bandannas and brand name tees like the ones he was wearing now. "You think this Cassidy's for real?"

"Is anybody for real in Freetown?" Wolff answered. "Are we for real?"

Malone shook his head in dismay. "Mexico sure ain't what I thought it would be."

Their handguns were enabled and within easy reach; it had been that kind of week.

On first arriving in town they had made the usual mistakes: taking a pricy room in a spy-ridden hotel, inquiring indiscreetly about people who might have a line on tank parts, showing way too much of the two thousand World Dollars liberated from Mayor Carson's slush fund. Wolff quickly realized he had been wrong to assure Catherine that black marketeers were of a kind no matter where you went or what you went looking for. Sure, even in Albuquerque you could get scammed out of a few dollars by money changers with a knack for prestidigitation, but at least there you didn't get shot at. Whereas by day four in Freetown, Wolff and Malone had been shot at twice, most recently by three gangsters in the employ of a teenager who'd approached them on the street with an offer of ubertech computer chips—chips Malone later identified as having come from a ten-year-old Petite Cola robovendor. Then, the following day, there'd been the four would-be muggers and the ensuing brawl which accounted for Wolff's still-bruised knuckles and Malone's fading shiner.

It was the fight that had convinced them to forsake their swank suite for a flea-infested hotel room on Reforma Nueva, where they'd slept in shifts and ordered in meals of McTacos while reformulating their plans. Through it all, though, Wolff had remained confident, reasoning that it was only a matter of time before word on them reached the ears of someone who could actually do the deal: procure the tank parts and orchestrate their transport to Venezuela.

And ultimately that someone had turned up, in the form of a pigeon-chested black Irish named Brian Cassidy, who happened to be Freetown's most celebrated fence.

"I've only come out of curiosity, you understand," Cassidy had told Wolff at their first meeting. "Two guys with World Dollars to spend, asking about tank hardware . . . You have to be military, don't you, now."

Wolff saw some benefit in being honest with Cassidy and had admitted that he and Malone were RDFers.

"And why's the Defense Force coming to Brian Cassidy all of a sudden?"

"Because the RDF won't have anything to do with Centaurs."

"Centaurs," Cassidy had exclaimed, grinning. "Well, now you've handed me a regular challenge, haven't you?"

That had been five days ago. Then, only that morning, Cassidy had sent word that the purchases had been made, and that the deal would go down at noon in Wal-Mart's receiving bay number one.

"It's gotta be close to noon now," Malone was saying. His watch had been slipped from his wrist even before they'd exited Mexico's airport.

"Five minutes," Wolff told him.

But another forty-five minutes would pass before they heard the six-note horn signal Cassidy's runner had told them to expect. The blasts were followed by high-beam flashes against the back wall of the garage; then a boxy, petropig truck nosed slowly into view through the gaping, fire-blackened entrance. Before the truck came to a halt, two Zentraedi armed with Wolverines leapt from the rear. After a moment, Cassidy climbed out of the front passenger seat and asked in a loud voice if anyone was there.

Wolff and Malone picked their way out of the morgue and approached, their handguns visible but nonthreatening. The Wolverines tracked them until Cassidy told the Zentraedi to lower them. Wolff and the Irishman shook hands, street fashion.

"Did you get everything we wanted?" Wolff asked.

"More than you wanted. You won't be disappointed."

"Where are the parts from?"

Cassidy shook his head. "That information wasn't included in the deal."

"Let's have a look."

Wolff started toward the truck, but Cassidy blocked his

path. "Sure thing, soldier. But first I'd appreciate having a look at the balance of payment."

Wolff cut his eyes to Malone, who lifted his T-shirt to reveal the bundles strapped to his abdomen.

Satisfied, Cassidy gestured gallantly toward the rear of the truck. He, Wolff, and Malone were halfway there when shots rang out from behind the concrete that pillared the entrance. Hit in the shoulder, Cassidy fell, while his enforcers returned fire and Wolff and Malone dove for cover behind an overturned dumpster.

Within moments, the two Zentraedi were cut down, as well as Cassidy's Human driver, who tried to make a break from the cab of the truck. The Irishman, meanwhile, had dragged himself to safety.

A hail of rounds forced Wolff and Malone to the grimy floor, unable to respond; but Wolff lifted his head in time to see a Zentraedi female dash through the entrance and clamber into the unoccupied driver's seat. When she had backed the truck out, three more alien females, firing handguns over their shoulders, vaulted into the rear of the truck.

"Cursed women," Cassidy moaned as the truck was speeding from the scene.

Wolff and Malone ran to him. Malone folded his bandanna into a square and pressed it against Cassidy's shoulder wound, then went to check on the three others. Wolff knew without looking that they were dead.

"Neela set us up," Cassidy said in a pained voice.

Wolff had heard the name. Neela Saam was a Zentraedi female, who had made a name for herself in Freetown. "Want to talk about it?"

Cassidy shut his eyes and nodded his head. "The Centaur parts came from a malcontent group called the Crimson Ghosts. Their headquarters is one of the old arms factories down near Tula. But Neela helped put the deal together."

"So were those Ghosts that took the truck?" Wolff asked.

"The Ghosts are an all-male band. But there've been rumors about an all-female band operating in Freetown. The Senburo or Senburu, something like that. Neela must have told them about the sale, figuring she was striking a blow for malcontentism."

"Have someone watch your back next time you make a delivery," Wolff said.

Cassidy looked peeved, in spite of the pain. "This is my town, soldier. No one does this to Brian Cassidy. I'll have the heads of those four Zents on my desk before the sun goes down."

The paved but seriously deteriorated highway between Cuiabá and Brasília was routinely swept for mines, but recent reports of malcontent activity in the area required that all vehicles travel in convoys under RDF escort. So it was that Edmundo Ortiz found himself at the tail end of a line of two hundred and six tractor-trailers, pickups, passenger cars, and RDF armored personnel carriers.

It was a cloudless June morning and Mundo was behind the wheel of a vintage right-drive Mercedes truck loaded down with several tons of rice and coffee from the fincas of the Planalto de Mato Grosso. Outside the curving sweep of the wiper blades the Mercedes's windshield was red with road dust, as was every horizontal surface and nook and cranny of the cab, from the duct-taped vinyl seat cover to the plastic statue of the Virgin of Guadalupe that sat on the dashboard. A swarthy man of sixty years, Mundo had his right arm out the window and the radio tuned to a station that played Mexican ranchero and pre-War country-western from the United States.

Mundo had been a professional driver for more than forty years, and was no stranger to the 500-mile Cuiabá-to-Brasília run. In the late seventies, he'd been one of the first to drive the Trans-Amazon from the coast clear to the Peruvian border, back when everything west of Porto Velho was *pura selva*—pure jungle, as it was once more, though no longer virgin forest but scrubby secondary growth that had reclaimed the frontier settlements abandoned after the Rain. Gone, too, were the indigenous peoples, the gold and diamond prospectors, and the once-productive cattle ranches. Now Cuiabá, the geographic center of the continent, was itself the frontier, vulnerable north and west to raids by the aliens who controlled the river systems of the interior.

At the head of the line, and largely responsible for the tedious pace—the convoy had left Cuiabá at midnight and had not yet reached the bridge over the River Araguaia—was some newfangled RDF vehicle said to be capable of detecting and disarming land mines, including enemy knockoffs of the ceramic-encased AM-2s. Two Veritechs providing aerial escort had thus far kept to the skies for the entire trip. Mundo could see both of them up ahead, flying tandem in Guardian mode, a few degrees south of the highway.

Mundo was smoking his tenth cigarette of the morning and dreaming lazily about the platter of grilled meat he would have for lunch at Pito Aceso in Goias Velho when some kind of craft flashed over the cab of the truck, streaking toward the front of the convoy. Just as the roar of the thing's engines was catching up with Mundo, one of the Veritechs vanished in a fiery explosion that blossomed in the southern skies.

Mundo's feet sent the brake and clutch pedals to the floor, and he leaned forward in the seat, with eyes wide and mouth open. Then, all at once, what had been the windshield was a thousand pebble-size pieces of glass and the top of his right thigh was on fire. He looked down to find his lap filled with windshield and a small fire spreading from the perimeter of a neat hole that had been punched through his khaki trousers. Reacting without thinking, he began to beat at the flames, becoming more and more aware of the shrapnel lodged in his flesh.

A second deafening explosion rocked the truck. Mundo's right hand flailed at the door lever, and he rolled out of the cab and onto the sun-blistered surface of the highway. The sky was filled with fire; he could feel the searing heat on his face and the back of his hands. The roar he had heard only moments earlier returned, and he looked up to see some sort of patched-together Battloid hovering like an outsize bumblebee a couple of hundred feet above the midpoint of the convoy. Then the mecha was suddenly at the epicenter of a fireworks display of corkscrewing trails of smoke, and a split second later explosions began to mushroom, head to tail, down the length of the convoy.

* * *

Much to Malone's grudging admiration, the captain refused to call it a bad deal and return home. "We're out a grand, but Cassidy's out a lot more than that," Wolff had said. "He'll come through. And if he doesn't, I'll personally replace the thousand we lost and we'll start from scratch."

But it never came to that. The Irish fence contacted them at the hotel on Reforma Nueva: the shipment had been retrieved and there was something he wanted them to hear. They were to leave at once for an address on Victoria.

The address corresponded to a theater out by the pyramids. Teotihuacan's Temple of the Sun—partially stripped for building materials—loomed over everything in the area. At the theater entrance, Wolff and Malone were frisked by two armed Zentraedi sporting dark glasses, then escorted inside. A handful of Cassidy henchmen seated in the front rows were applauding and whistling in a mocking fashion.

On stage were Cassidy himself—left arm in a sling—and two others: an aged, dark-complected man in a bloodstained surgical gown, and the obvious source of that blood, a Zentraedi woman gagged and tied to an armchair. Just now her head was bent forward, and her long brown hair was touching her bare knees. The hair concealed much of her torso, and for that—and arriving late—Wolff was grateful. If she wasn't already dead, she would be soon.

"Ah, and it's a fine day in Freetown," Cassidy said in a theatrical voice. He gestured to the torturer. "Soldiers, meet Antonio Ramos . . . interpreter."

Like Neela Saam, Ramos was a notorious name in Freetown. A noted heart surgeon before the War, he now controlled the trade in narcotics throughout Central America and was rumored to dabble in ritual black magic.

"I told you we'd find them, and so we have," Cassidy continued. "Three were killed defending the truck they stole from me, but we've learned a good deal from this one."

He walked to the chair and lifted the woman's head by the hair; she was certainly dead. Malone clamped a hand over his mouth and angled his head away from the stage.

"The four were members of a group that calls itself the

Senburu, though I've no proof that Neela set them on us. This one claimed they've been watching the Crimson Ghosts for some time, knowing the Ghosts are providing weapons and parts to any and all buyers—even those whose aims aren't always in synch with the malcontents."

Wolff was appalled by Cassidy's sadism, but forced himself to ask the man what else the Zentraedi had revealed about the Senburu.

"Only that they're not operating in Mexico, as I was led to believe, but in the Southlands."

"Where in the Southlands?" Wolff pressed.

"She was mute on that point. But she did confess that her group needed the tank parts."

Wolff's brow furrowed. "Did she say why?"

"For something she called a 'stinger.' "

The first reports to reach Monument City were sketchy: all anyone knew was that a convoy under RDF escort had been attacked near the city of Goias, in the Southlands, and there were civilian casualties and extensive destruction. Then, as an accurate picture of the malcontent raid began to emerge, the UEG's Select Committee on Military Policy convened in extraordinary session in the hardened subbasement of the Capitol Building. The government was represented by senators Milburn, Stinson, and Huxley; the RDF by Reinhardt and Hunter. Also in attendance were intelligence chief Niles Obstat and weapons specialist Dr. R. Burke. Burke had just arrived from the factory satellite and had yet to get his surface legs; Reinhardt and Hunter had just arrived from fly fishing in the Rockies and were still in their civvies.

"The most recent update lists 205 dead," Huxley was saying, reading from a fax sheet. "That total includes two RDF pilots, a tank commander, and three enlisted-ratings attached to the construction battalion. Teams from Cuiabá Base are still picking through the wreckage, and Field Marshal Leonard is demanding to know what we intend to do about the attack. The Army of the Southern Cross has moved two companies into Mato Grosso, where they're awaiting word from Leonard."

Rick listened to Huxley's report with growing alarm. If the RDF didn't act decisively, Leonard would have the excuse he needed to assert control over the whole of the southern Amazonia. The showdown that could result carried the potential for military confrontation. The pattern that had led to the Global Civil War was being woven again.

"Do you have the names of the VT pilots?" he asked after a moment.

"First lieutenants Dieter Baumann and Liu Houze."

Rick nodded gravely. "I know them. And I can't accept that either of them would allow the enemy to get that close to the convoy." His voice betrayed his bewilderment. "The rebels don't have any mecha sophisticated enough to subvert our scanners or employ countermeasures. Exactly how many vehicles were hit?"

"One hundred and ninety," Huxley said grimly. "Almost the entire convoy. It was a massacre."

Rick wrote the number on a notepad. "Do we have reliable intel on the number of enemy mecha involved?"

Huxley cut her eyes to Obstat.

"One," Obstat said.

Rick stared at him. "I don't understand."

Obstat cleared his throat. "Eyewitness reports state that one craft was responsible for all the destruction."

"Impossible," Reinhardt told him. "Even a fully laden Officer's Pod isn't capable of delivering that much destructive power. Cuiabá's eyewitnesses are obviously in shock."

Obstat's expression confirmed that he had expected skepticism. "Cuiabá found no evidence of atomics, plasmics, or pulse lasers used against the vehicles. Detonation footprints point to the exclusive use of multiple independently targeted warheads—probably Decas and Mongooses. Descriptions supplied by the ten survivors who could talk were assembled and handed over to a computer for evaluation." Obstat struck a key on his terminal that lit the wallscreen. "Here's what the machine came up with."

Approximately the size of a Gladiator, the headless mecha that appeared onscreen had armored limbs and carried a bulbous, twin-lobed thruster array on its shoulders. Everyone regarded the thing in bafflement.

"Any thoughts, Dr. Burke?" Senator Stinson asked.

The Robotechnician plucked nervously at his chin. "I've seen something like this before, but I'll need to consult my files before I can say where or when. My inclination, however, is to suggest that it's a variation of Zentraedi Female Power Armor."

The most maneuverable of the aliens' self-propelled exoskeletons, Female Power Armor—also known as the *Queadlunn-Rau* battle suit—was a deadly combination of missile launchers, autocannons, and triple-barreled pulse lasers, enhanced by a high-speed focusing sight built into the faceplate and an inertia-vector control system that regulated acceleration and fuel efficiency in the absence of Protoculture cells. Unlike the Battlepod, Power Armor had mechanically operated legs and arms, and was capable of speeds in excess of Mach four; and unlike Male Power Armor, which was essentially a deepspace labor mecha, it was designed to meet the rigors of intra-atmospheric flight.

Rick did some quick calculations on his notepad. "The total payload of Female Power Armor is only, what, about one hundred and twenty short-range missiles."

"One hundred and twenty-six," Burke corrected.

"Still, allowing for targeting errors and such, we'd have to be talking about at least *two* battle suits, possibly three."

"Unless this one has undergone substantial modification, as is indeed suggested by the computer's rendering."

Rick looked to Obstat. "Have you had any advance intelligence on this weapon?"

"I think we have. From a Captain Jonathan Wolff, squadron commander in Cavern City."

Rick nodded. "I know Wolff. What about him?"

"Seems he recently took it upon himself to visit Freetown to buy parts for some Centaur tanks he's overhauling. In any case, his little shopping foray was almost thwarted by members of an all-female Zentraedi group called the Senburu. They apparently tried to hijack his tank parts to use for a mecha they're assembling—something they referred to as a 'stinger.'"

Rick glanced at the wallscreen. "Is that what we're looking at—a Stinger?"

"They didn't build this machine out of twenty-year-old Centaur tank parts," Burke said. "Destroid hardware, certainly. Along with an abundance of Protoculture circuitboards. There's no other way to account for its operation by one or two pilots."

Huxley glanced around the table. "Are Protoculture cells suddenly available on the black market?"

Obstat shook his head. "Not in quantity."

"What about the Senburu?" Rick asked the intelligence chief. "If they're headquartered in Mexico, why would they attack a convoy thousands of miles away?"

"We don't know that they are headquartered in Mexico." Obstat struck another terminal key, calling a map of the world onscreen. "This is our latest breakdown of malcontent bands and territories. All we show for Mexico and Central America are the Crimson Ghosts, an all-male group led by a Zentraedi named Jeram Salamik. The Southlands have three known groups: a band known as the Shroud, based in the north; the Paranka, or Burrowers, in the Argentine; and however many remain of Khyron's Fist. Africa has the Iron Ravens and perhaps a splinter group from the Quandolma, and India's seen some malcontentism by the Lyktauro. But the only all-female band we've heard about is the Claimers, whose actions so far have been restricted to Australia and New Zealand."

Senator Milburn scarcely let Obstat finish. "It appears to me that the malcontents have continued to organize, despite Field Marshal Leonard's move in Cairo."

"The number and the talent pool of their Human allies must be increasing as well," Burke said. "I can assure you, this Stinger's control and management operating systems were not engineered without Human assistance. Or without someone with hands-on experience in mecha engineering."

Milburn gave his head a mournful shake. "I'm sure I don't have to tell anyone here how news of this attack is going to be received in Monument and other cities. People are going to demand reprisals, and if we falter, they're going to be looking to Anatole Leonard."

Rick shot Milburn a look. "We can only take reprisals

against the group responsible, and we can't do that until we've located them."

"I disagree, Admiral," Stinson rejoined. "While the Senburu may have been directly responsible, they are obviously being funded and supplied by other Zentraedi— perhaps from the Arkansas Protectorate."

"Arkansas's aliens are friendlies," Rick objected. "You can't punish them for the violent actions of others."

Milburn answered him. "But that's precisely the point: we can't tell the friendlies from the enemies. Besides, any action taken in Arkansas would be prophylactic, not retaliatory. What we're really battling is the Imperative, and we simply want to assure those we've been empowered to protect that their safety comes first. Or would the RDF prefer to defer to the Army of the Southern Cross?"

Rick gritted his teeth. "I want it on record that I'm opposed to taking any action in Arkansas until proof of complicity can be established."

"So recorded," Milburn said. "The UEG will have to vote on any proposed action. In the meantime, I strongly suggest that the Expeditionary force reevaluate the security of its operations aboard the factory satellite."

In the same way that self-images of obesity could live on in newly thin people, recollections of gianthood persevered in Micronized Zentraedi. Though self-image didn't count for much when you found yourself at the receiving end of a tongue-lashing by someone the size of Breetai.

"The Protoculture cells used to power the Stinger could only have originated here," the commander was telling his lieutenants, Jevna Parl and Theofre Elmikk, "and I want the flow of smuggled technology stopped immediately."

Standing side-by-side on a Human-size catwalk on level seven of the factory satellite, Parl and Elmikk were no more than ten feet from Breetai's huge, flesh-and-metal face—his eye filled with anger, his breath like malodorous gusts of wind, spittle flying like bucketfuls of water. Exedore was also on the catwalk, silent and observing, and somewhat out of the harm's way.

"M'lord, the inventories have been checked and rechecked," Parl replied, "and all Protoculture cells and circuitboards are accounted for."

Breetai's lip curled. "If all are accounted for, it's clear that the contraband was never inventoried. The source is surely the warships our EVA teams are disassembling. What is the procedure for monitoring the workers?"

Parl relaxed somewhat as Breetai's eye focused on Elmikk, who supervised the labor crews. It was only right that Elmikk bear the brunt of the castigation, Parl thought. As liaison to Lang's technical crews, Parl rarely saw cells or boards until they were already installed in devices transported to the in-progress SDF-3.

"On reentering the factory," Elmikk was saying, "both Human and Zentraedi workers leave their suits and gear in the airlock, where everything is scanned for Protoculture. Then the workers themselves are searched."

"And the heavy work drones?" Sometimes referred to as "Mr. Arms," the 220-foot-long, multi-armed robots were factory-programmed for hauling cargo and attending to all facets of spaceship maintenance and repair.

"They are thoroughly searched after each operation."

"Detail how the workers are searched," Breetai ordered.

"They are made to show their hands, spread their toes, lift their arms, open their mouths . . ."

"Are they scanned for Protoculture?"

"Your Excellency," Exedore cut in. "Because of Protoculture present in the genetic composition of the Zentraedi, X-ray or magnetic scanning is considered unreliable."

"Exedore, there are aspects to this operation that make it something more than mining ore from Fantoma. What if chips are being ingested and excreted?"

Elmikk hesitated. "I don't know that anyone has addressed that possibility."

Breetai smirked, and looked at Exedore. "It strikes me that cells might present a problem for the Human digestive system."

"You are correct, my lord. Only a Zentraedi could carry and pass a Protoculture cell without harm to himself or the device itself. I will confer with Dr. Lang about developing a scanner capable of identifying the presence of other-than-systemic Protoculture."

"That's a beginning, but it may not be enough, Exedore. Since you are the sole Zentraedi allowed to travel routinely between the surface and factory, it can be deduced that Human coconspirators are responsible for smuggling the cells down the well."

Exedore bowed his head slightly. "An astute deduction, m'lord."

"Then this shouldn't be our concern," Elmikk said. "The Humans have their own security procedures for determining which are allowed access to the factory. Let them investigate this matter."

Breetai regarded Elmikk for a long moment. "Smugglers require product, Elmikk, and that product is being supplied by Zentraedi laborers. Their actions imperil the lives of Human civilians as well as those of our comrades on Earth. So see to it that the work crews understand that Breetai wants the traitors found, and he vows to assume a personal hand in their punishment."

CHAPTER SIXTEEN

> *Chief among the RDF's many failures during this period [the Reconstruction years, 2012–2017] was its tacit approval and participation in Operation Tiger. If Reinhardt and the command staff had been merely hoodwinked by the Milburn-Moran apparat, their actions could be excused as unfortunate; but since evidence abounds that Reinhardt was fully aware of what he was doing by authorizing the operation, the RDF's participation appears all the more reprehensible. Reinhardt was not entirely to blame, however. Pressured by UEG on one side and by the REF on the other, he constantly ran the risk of alienating one by placating the other. Such were the circumstances forged by the Army of the Southern Cross and the Expeditionary mission. And caught in the middle were the Zentraedi, of all persuasions. . . . Given the conditions in the Protectorate, it is remarkable that only 32 of the 1396 detainees died.*
> Jill Boyce, *Death Under Canvas*

WITH THE DESTRUCTION OF DOLZA'S FORTRESS BY the SDF-1, the ships of the Zentraedi Grand Fleet—deprived of any hope of Protoculture replenishment—were suddenly abandoned to the gravitational urgings of the small planet they had come halfway across the galaxy to obliterate. For reasons unknown, Wuer Maatai, commander of the Jiabao Battalion, had opted to steer for Earth's daylight side; but of the 10,700 Jiabao warships that had survived the nuclear outpowering of the Grand Cannon, only 8,550 were successful in reaching Earth's envelope, and of those, some 7,000 were soon reduced to little more than glowing meteors whose ballistic descents terminated in impact craters. 1,554 ships, bearing an estimated 1,860,000 animated and torpedoed alien warriors, struck the surface intact. Less than 100,000 survived. What with ensuing deaths from injuries, illness, and starvation, in addition to the diaspora to Macross and other cities of the Northlands, scarcely 4,000 remained in 2013, roughly a third of whom were full-size.

Because Wuer Maatai did not survive, it was never ascertained whether fate or the commander himself had delivered the Jiabao to south-central North America. The end result was fortuitous, in any case, in that the mountainous, oak, hickory, and maple-forested northwest corner of the former state of Arkansas comprised the calm center of a swirling firestorm that ultimately incinerated St. Louis, Atlanta, Dallas, and Oklahoma City.

Simultaneous with the fiery arrival of the Jiabao, the bulk of Arkansas's Human population abandoned their homes and businesses and fled the area, only to die of radiation poisoning at the edges of their safe haven. The few that remained forged a wary truce with the Zentraedi, but one that grew stronger as illness and the traumatizing effects of defeat settled over the bereft aliens; and within months the two groups of survivors were working hand in hand—the Humans assisting in repairing the XTs' nutrient synthesizers; the giants helping to rebuild what their warships had atomized or crushed.

By late 2014, the Macross Council had granted autonomy to the Arkansas Protectorate—so-called despite its occupying only a quarter of the district—and the RDF had established a base for the engineer corps, with an eye toward the formation of a reconstruction battalion capable of tolerating the perilous radiation of Earth's remaining hot spots.

Though not a member of original Jiabao settlement, Ranoc Nomarre had been a resident of the Protectorate for almost two years. Short and muscular, he had an angular face, jaggedly scarred along the right cheek, and a crew cut that made his head appear more blockish than it actually was. Early on, the training in construction techniques struck him as antithetical to his warrior nature, but he had gradually grown to appreciate what it meant to raise a structure rather than raze one. He especially enjoyed the daily routines of study and hands-on labor, the scenic beauty of the Ozark Mountains and the Buffalo River, and the fact that he had a roofed-over space to himself in the enormous facility built by RDF CeeBees.

Lately, however, the routines had changed. As a response

to increasing incidents of malcontentism, security had been tightened and inspections had become no-notice searches. Then the Protectorate's borders had been closed and fortified by platoons of civil defense Destroids. And just as suddenly Ranoc Nomarre had acquired two roommates. Similar surprises were rumored to be occurring throughout the facility.

At the moment, the new arrival named Utema was emptying the meager contents of a duffel onto a parcel of soft ground he apparently proposed to claim as a bed.

"You say you're from Detroit?" Nomarre inquired mildly.

"And Macross before that." Curly-haired and unremarkable looking, Utema had a gravelly voice and a rotten disposition. "Had a factory job, but I quit it to wander. A year later I was sick of the wastes and wound up in Portland, working at a fish hatchery." He spat and jerked a thick thumb at the other newcomer. "He's from Monument."

The narrow-shouldered and somewhat retiring Rilpa nodded. "Macross and Monument." He was without a duffel, and his Zentraedi uniform was filthy, frayed, and crudely patched.

Nomarre had never seen the Twin Cities, though he knew Detroit and Denver well enough. A former Botoru, he had taken part in Khyron's hostage raid on the latter city, though his foolish protest at the rough treatment Lynn-Minmei was receiving had earned him a kick in the gut from the Backstabber himself, and subsequent ostracism from the Earthbound battalion. Fifteen days of walking had carried him to the Protectorate, where he'd been ever since.

"How are things in Monument?" Nomarre asked Rilpa.

"Not good. It's another Macross now. Our kind have no say in what goes on. The Humans that stand with us are outnumbered by the ones who see a dissident in every Zentraedi. They detonate firebombs and blame us for the deaths and destruction. I'm glad to be gone."

"The same for me," Utema said.

"So you enlisted to work here?"

Rilpa smiled in amusement. "There was no enlisting. We were conscripted—all the full-size."

"All of you?"

"Same in Detroit," Utema said before Rilpa could respond. "The RDF announced that all full-size were needed at the factory satellite to help disassemble warships. We're supposed to get our training here, then be lofted offworld."

"But surely some of you declined?" Nomarre said.

Ripla shrugged. "Why would anyone? We're trying to show that we can make a contribution to the future. Besides, who'd pass up an opportunity to go upside and escape the conditions here?"

Nomarre mulled it over for a moment. "I still don't understand about the RDF's plans to send you to the factory. The Protectorate doesn't have a launch facility. The closest base is in Denver."

"So, they'll ship us to Denver after the training," Utema said.

"But we've had close to two hundred new arrivals in the past three days. Wouldn't it have been easier to train you in Monument instead of sending you here?"

"Who can say what Humans call 'easier'?" Rilpa said.

Nomarre stared at him. "It doesn't seem strange to you that all full-size are now either on the Protectorate or at the factory?"

"Strange, how?" Rilpa answered, sounding annoyed. "If there was a problem, the RDF would have gathered everyone up, full-size and Micronized."

Utema snorted nastily. "It's because of the dissidents. The REF wants to see its dimensional fortress completed before anything more happens on the surface. They must be thinking that the sooner they meet with the Masters, the sooner they'll be rid of us."

Nomarre fingered his scar in silence, then asked, "Is there any news from the Southlands?"

"An attack on a civilian convoy," Rilpa told him.

Nomarre hadn't heard. "Did the Army of the Southern Cross retaliate?"

"Leonard's threatening to."

"That's the one thing I'm not going to like about being here," Utema said. "We have to rely on the RDF to defend us against a Southern Cross attack."

Nomarre told him not to worry. "That's one of the reasons why there are CD Destroids on the border."

"They were a lot closer than the border when I came through," Rilpa said.

Nomarre cut his eyes to him. "How much closer?"

"I'd guess within two hours of right where we're standing."

Nomarre was about to point out that any incursion of battle mecha was in violation of Protectorate provisions, but he never got the chance—the walls and corrugated roof of his living space had begun to vibrate in sympathy with the distant rumble of heavy machinery. The three Zentraedi hurried outside to find the hills surrounding the facility alive with moving pinpoints of light.

Nomarre spun through a full circle. "Running lights."

"Excalibers and Gladiators," Rilpa said. "A couple of Spartans, too."

No one said anything for several minutes as the Destroids continued their slow march on the facility. Rilpa's assessment had been accurate; Nomarre put the total number of mecha at better than three hundred. And he recognized something in the mix besides Destroids: four bell jar-shaped towers, rising up from mecha-pulled flatbeds 100 feet wide.

Resizing chambers.

Katherine Hyson's career had been on the upswing ever since she'd nailed the interview with Lynn-Minmei. A year after the interview aired, she had—in addition to the weekly celebrity-driven show—a reality-based crime drama in production, and the coveted position as anchor of the MBS evening news. Just now, sitting composed at the anchor's desk, hair and face done to perfection, Hyson waited out the producer's countdown, then looked straight into camera one and announced, "Good evening, I'm Katherine Hyson, and this is World News for July 28, 2016."

On the TelePrompTer, copy began a slow scroll.

"Seven days have passed since a battalion of civil defense mecha rolled across the borders of the Arkansas Protectorate, turning what had been an autonomous area into an internment camp. And yet despite persistent rumors of armed rebellion, involuntary downsizing, and a retaliatory raid by Army of the Southern Cross commandos, the government-imposed media blackout remains in effect."

Hyson adopted an earnest expression and turned over a sheet of hardcopy. "Mitigating against the rumor of rebellion comes word tonight that only days prior to what has been termed 'Operation Tiger,' more than two hundred fullsize Zentraedi were relocated to the Protectorate from Denver, Monument, Detroit, Portland, and other Northland cities, ostensibly to receive specialized training in demolition, in preparation for transfer to the factory satellite." Stock footage of the Protectorate and the factory ran under the commentary; then Hyson was onscreen once more.

"Crowds of advocates and Micronized Zentraedi have assembled at RDF checkpoints leading into the Protectorate to protest the government's actions. And now, for an update on the tense situation along the border, here is MBS correspondent Rebecca Hollister."

"Thank you, Katherine," the youthful, brown-haired woman whose face appeared onscreen said. "Though 'tense' doesn't begin to describe the scene here, as more and more people arrive hourly, demanding answers from the United Earth Government and the RDF."

Hollister had a wireless microphone in hand and a pearl-like audiobead in her left ear. Behind her stood a tight press of grim-faced Humans and a scattering of Zentraedi, some wearing sloganed smartshirts, others displaying LED portascreens.

"The Arkansas Protectorate remains fenced in on all sides by Excaliber and Gladiator units from as distant as Albuquerque. The roads are barred to traffic, and we've been warned to maintain a safe distance or risk being fired on. What's more, MBS has learned that in the first hours of Operation Tiger, perhaps as many as six sizing chambers were trucked into the control zone, and speculation runs high that a policy of enforced downsizing has already been put into effect. If this is true, it marks the first occasion of government-imposed Micronization since October 2014, when the process was used on six members of Khyron's forces, captured and sentenced after the theft of a sizing chamber from Fort Breetai, in Detroit.

"An anonymous though highly placed source in the UEG has stated—and I quote—that 'any downsizing under way in Arkansas is not being meted out as punishment, but in an effort to shortcut the violent lusts of the Imperative, which are stronger in the full-size than in the Micronized.' "

Hollister raised her eyes from the hardcopy she'd consulted. "But to many of those who have kept a week-long vigil here, the UEG's tactics smack of fascism—no matter what the justification." She paused, giving weight to her words; then said, "Back to you, Katherine."

Hyson, when she swiveled away from the blue screen, was visibly flustered by the mediagenic intensity of the young woman's delivery. But her professional composure returned swiftly as she promised herself that Rebecca Hollister would never again upstage her.

"While tensions mount in Arkansas," she began, "related developments continue to unfold around the world. Here in Monument, several arrests have been made in connection with the firebombings that have plagued the city for the past six months, leaving more than fifteen dead. Those arrested are said to be known sympathizers, who, in addition to carrying out a campaign of terror, may have been involved in a smuggling operation that was supplying Southlands malcontents with state-of-the-art weapons."

Hyson turned a page. "When we return: Protests turn to riots in Calcutta, Sydney, and Tokyo ... A look back at the Japanese internment camps of the past century ... And a malcontent band identified as the Crimson Ghosts takes credit for Wednesday's attack on the Panama Canal, in which as many as one hundred people were killed and three ships were sunk. Also: Reaction from Brasília to the RDF's actions in Arkansas. And the 'official' explanation for Admiral Hunter's secret talks aboard the factory satellite.

"Stay tuned."

The factory satellite was sometimes affectionately referred to as "Little Luna." But as anyone who had been stationed on Moon Base Aluce before the war would tell you, the comparison began and ended with the name. The factory's size, near-Earth-normal gravity, and plethora of retrofitted rec and entertainment rooms made it feel like a world apart, a place where you could speak your mind without fear of censure.

Rick had never fully grasped the distinction until the visit he paid the factory after Operation Tiger was set in motion. Even in the docking bay he felt as if a great weight had been lifted from his shoulders; that he was temporarily free to be himself, unfettered by economic considerations or, worse, politics. Here there were no hidden agendas, only the camaraderie that developed naturally from teamwork. If this was a foretaste of what the Expeditionary mission would be like, it couldn't launch soon enough.

With him had arrived Gunther Reinhardt, Rolf Emerson, and Max Sterling—who hadn't been aloft in some time. They'd come to deliver a personal explanation of Operation Tiger to Breetai, and to apprise him of the RDF's plans to make amends.

The only secure place suitable for a meeting between Humans and giants was the factory bridge. But instead of using the command bubble, Rick chose to hold the meeting in the bridge area itself, with all Human company seated on folding chairs set up on one of the catwalks. Breetai stood level with them, and Exedore sat in the commander's right hand. There were no computer consoles, wallscreens, or recording devices. Rick saw it as a gathering of allies.

"I wanted you to hear it from me before you heard it from any one else, Breetai," he was saying. "The UEG's decision to invade Arkansas was done without provocation. There've been no threats of a raid by the Army of the Southern Cross, and there's no evidence that weapons are being smuggled out of Arkansas to the Southlands. The government is answering terror with terror, hoping to beat the dissidents at their own game."

"I see," Breetai said in a booming voice. "But the UEG should be made to understand that the Zentraedi are not subject to the same fears that rule Humans. The Imperative is nourished by acts of terrorism."

"Tell me, Admiral," Exedore said, "is it true that all full-size in the Protectorate are to be Micronized?"

"Yes," Rick said, swallowing hard. "The RDF surrendered control of such decisions to the UEG, and now we're paying the price. But I want you to know that both Lang and Zand refused to supervise the Micronizations. The sizing chambers are being operated by Zentraedi."

"But it's a wise decision," Exedore said, betraying no more emotion than Breetai had shown on hearing of the enforced downsizing. "It's far better that everyone on the surface is of one size. Of course, there's no truth to the remark I've heard that the Imperative runs stronger in full-size; but, even so, I think it's for the best that size is eliminated as an issue. We Zentraedi understand your race's natural fear of giants."

"You'll find that most Zentraedi will be unmoved by the events," Breetai said.

Rick nodded. "I know that, Breetai. But I wanted you to understand that the RDF is opposed to the decision. If we could, we'd allow some dissident group to retake the Protectorate. As for the protests, they're coming mainly from our own people. Many of the same people who fear you would fight to protect your civil rights."

Exedore stroked his chin in thought. "This is something I have yet to comprehend about your race, Admiral. You do all but arm your enemies."

"It's no more than each of us would expect," Reinhardt said. "There can be no basis for civilization without the guarantee of civil rights for all."

Exedore's smile was patronizing. "The Masters circumvented that by creating their own race. And it seems to me that, given enough generations, Humans could do the same on Earth."

Rick shook his head. "We value individuality too much to allow that to happen."

"Then, you, too, place yourselves first," Breetai said.

"We do," Reinhardt said tentatively, "but we make concessions for the collective good."

Breetai snarled. "The Zentraedi understand sacrifice. But what concessions can be made for those Humans and

Zentraedi that are offended by the invasion of the Protectorate?"

"An effortless solution presents itself, m'lord," Exedore said. "The detainees could simply be returned to full size."

Rick glanced at Reinhardt before responding. "I hope it will come to that, Exedore. But until then, what we'd like to do is establish a Zentraedi mecha squadron within the RDF."

Sterling's and Emerson's mouths dropped.

Breetai put his free hand on his hip and laughed. "You actually mean to arm us."

Rick got up from his chair to stand at the catwalk's handrail. "I want to be clear about this, Breetai. General Reinhardt and I thought by making the RDF subordinate to the UEG, we could deflect any pressure on the Expeditionary mission. That turns out to have been wrongheaded. Now, when what we want most is unified commitment to the mission, we have dissension. The RDF is condemned for combating malcontentism and for failing to combat it. But we just might be able to accommodate everyone if we can assign Zentraedi to deal with problems in the Southlands."

"An excellent idea," Breetai said. "Let me be the first to volunteer."

Rick made a face. "We'd have to turn you down. You're too important to the Expeditionary mission. Anyway, it would mean you'd have to submit to downsizing. But I would like you—and Exedore—to supervise the selection of personnel."

"Would our choices be limited to Micronized Zentraedi?" Exedore asked.

Reinhardt told him no. "But as the admiral has pointed out, anyone selected will have to agree to undergo Micronization for the duration of his enlistment."

"Excuse me, General," Sterling cut in, "but won't this be interpreted as just another way of cajoling the Zentraedi into accepting Micronization? Who's the RDF trying to appease—the Zentraedi or the UEG?"

Reinhardt nodded. "I appreciate your point, Captain, but the answer is neither. We're trying to appease the protestors—Zentraedi and Humans. And, to be perfectly blunt about it, we're hoping that distancing ourselves further from the controversy will enable the REF to get on with preparations for the Tirol mission."

"Max," Rick said from the railing, "we're also hoping that you'll volunteer to train the new squadron."

Sterling flashed him a look. "Would training exempt me from combat?"

"It would."

"Then consider me volunteered."

Emerson glanced back and forth between Hunter and Sterling. "Does Field Marshal Leonard know about this yet?"

Reinhardt leaned over in his chair to clap Emerson on the shoulder. "I'm afraid we're going to have to ask you to break the news to him, Major." He paused for a moment. "And when Leonard tells you he won't have armed aliens operating in the Southlands, be sure to remind him that he shouldn't look on them as Zentraedi, but as RDF. Are we clear?"

"Perfectly clear, General," Emerson said with a somewhat worried smile.

On one side of the road stood the protestors; on the other, those who were there to demonstrate against them; and in the middle, meant to assure protection to both sides, a cordon of Robotech CD troops in full riot gear. Recently ushered to the front of the crowd of sympathizers, Miriya Parino Sterling was at once the focus of media attention and the object of jeering from across the highway.

"Hey, Parino," someone shouted. "Sterling should have killed you instead of screwed you!"

"Your husband's killing them down south, and you're up here trying to save them," an irate woman screamed. "Why don't the two of you trade places!"

"When's the divorce, alien?"

She had arrived only that morning, but her unannounced appearance had had a galvanizing effect on the crowd; their vigil would remain a lead story now. Miriya hadn't told Max of her plans to come, though she had already formulated them by the time he and Rick had left for Fokker Aerospace, bound for the factory satellite. There had seemed no purpose in introducing further strife to his sendoff. Dana was in Monument, staying with her godfathers. Some members of the crowd were five days into a hunger strike; that the few Zentraedi among them had joined in meant little, since most could go weeks without food. Miriya had no real aim beyond showing her support, and allowing herself to be photographed doing just that.

"Miriya Parino," someone on her side of the road said, from not too far away. She turned and saw a young brown-haired reporter struggling through the crowd toward her. "Miriya, Rebecca Hollister, with MBS News. Could I ask you a few questions?"

Miriya shrugged. "Why not."

Hollister had circles under her eyes and her hair was in disarray. On a forearm touchpad, she entered instructions for the pencam that was part of her headset array. The camera swung toward Miriya like the barrel of a miniature gun. "What would you like to see happen here, Miriya?"

Miriya gave a toss to her jade-green mane. "I—we—want the UEG to lift the media blackout and the travel restrictions, and to allow an inspection team of Humans and Zentraedi to tour the Protectorate."

"How do you react to claims that Protectorate Zentraedi have been supplying weapons technology to malcontent bands in the Southlands?"

"I want to see proof of that."

"If the UEG offered proof, would you still demand to be allowed inside?"

"Yes. Most of my people are confined to the Zee-towns and ghettos of Human cities, but at least in those they have the freedom to move about and to assemble. Now, just as in Brasília last year, the Zentraedi find themselves stripped of their rights—Zentraedi who have been working selflessly in Humankind's interest, even though the Protectorate was granted autonomy by the Macross Council. Such violations of civil rights threaten the prospect of Humans and Zentraedi becoming equal partners in shaping the future of the planet. Even if those inside are accused of sponsoring terrorism, they should be presumed innocent and afforded fair treatment until their guilt is established."

Hollister entered additional camera commands. "Critics of the policy of granting autonomy—people like Renes Dumjinn—are counseling patience instead of protest. How do you respond to that?"

"We have been patient for more than a week. And if Dumjinn and the rest valued their own civil rights, they would be standing with us now."

"Everyone knows that you have a young daughter. Do you fear for her safety?"

Miriya's eyes narrowed with anger. "I fear for the safety of everyone on Earth if our conflicts are not resolved soon."

"Do you endorse what the malcontents are doing?"

"No more than I would the action of any gang of criminals, Zentraedi or otherwise. Those responsible for the deaths and destruction must be apprehended and made to stand trial. But it's wrong, it's immoral, to punish an entire people for the violent actions of a few."

"Miriya, looking around this crowd I see only a few Zentraedi. How do you account for the small turnout? And shouldn't this be their fight?"

"Most Zentraedi are not given to displays of caring," Miriya mumbled.

Hollister lifted her round chin. "Then how can we believe they care about Earth's future?"

Miriya held the reporter's smug gaze. "Take it on faith, Rebecca, or eliminate all of us."

CHAPTER
SEVENTEEN

He caught me completely off guard. And I know that he was hurt by my not having a ready answer. But I was simply astonished, and, in fact, I didn't know how I felt about it. The timing was so off; there were just so many projects in the works and so little time to see to them. I wanted to say, "Let me think about it." But I didn't. Ultimately, I said, yes; I accepted. Even though his method couldn't have been more unromantic—questioning me about his question—and even though I sensed we were in for a rocky road, and perhaps one of the longest engagements in history.

Lisa Hayes, *Recollections*

THE LOWERMOST LEVEL OF THE FACTORY SATELLITE REmained an abode for giants. For two miles of its ten-mile length, the 300-foot-wide by 400-foot-high central corridor had been fitted with a catwalk and walkway, but the rest of the corridors and tunnels and the immense holds they linked had been left untampered with by Human hands. If the factory could be said to have a basement, it was level one, especially those areas below the transfer tubes to the six- and eight-o'clock pods: dimly lighted enclosures the size of sports stadiums, containing lakes of stagnant water, mountains of unprocessed monopole ore, mounds of scrapped mecha parts, once the haunt of spiderlike maintenance robots whose lifeless carcasses littered the floor.

It was among all this that Theofre Elmikk convened a clandestine meeting for the full-size and Micronized Zentraedi members of the Seylos contingent of the dissident alliance.

"Hunter and Reinhardt's meeting with Breetai can mean only one thing," Elmikk was saying. "Our smuggling enterprise has been exposed and must be suspended."

More than a few murmurs of relief could be heard. The

security procedures for extravehicular assignments had become so exacting that someone was bound to be caught before long. Still, concerns were voiced about the impact the shutdown would have on the alliance's downside counterparts.

"Our comrades have more than enough Protoculture cells to make a beginning," Elmikk assured everyone. "Enough, at any rate, to keep the RDF occupied while we execute the next phase of the operation."

Throughout the hold, conspirators exchanged questioning glances; this was the first anyone had heard about "phases." All along, the operation had seemed improvised, and suddenly Elmikk was hinting at the existence of a master plan. If so, who had drawn up that plan, and what was Elmikk's position in the hierarchy?

"First, however, we must wait until Breetai's suspicions have been allayed. Then, when security procedures become lax once more, we will begin preparations for commandeering the flagship."

No murmurs met Elmikk's ears; only outright grumbling, which he attempted to quiet with frantic arm gestures. "Yes, it's true that many areas of the flagship are in shambles—including the bridge—but we can't let that stop us. All that counts is that the Reflex and fold systems are operational—which they are. We need only maneuver the ship out of the factory, and we can be gone from this miserable pocket of the galaxy." He was shouting now, trying to be heard over the separate conversations between giants.

"And who is going to pilot it out?" one of the full-size asked. *"You?"*

Elmikk threw his shoulders back. "I have been observing and studying all aspects of the ship. Yes, I can do it."

Those who weren't simply angered by the assertion laughed. Even in those troubled times, a flagship commander had to be someone who could inspire the utmost confidence, and prior to his promotion to liaison officer, Theofre Elmikk had been little more than a servant to Exedore—a kind of researcher, always scurrying after bits of ersatz Zentraedi lore.

"Pilot it, perhaps, Elmikk," a Micronized conspirator

said. "But is it to Tirol you'll fold us, or into the lightless maw of some collapsed star?"

"Tirol," Elmikk snapped, "if that's what you want. But consider this: What exactly awaits us there but a return to enslavement? Whereas there exist worlds in systems other than the Valivarre where we could live like masters. Karbarra, for example, or Garuda. We laid waste to them once; if we must, we'll do it again."

The laughter had died down to sardonic chuckling. "Consider this, Elmikk," someone said. "The Invid."

But he only snorted in derision. "Why should the Regent or Regis concern themselves with Karbarra or Garuda? They're after their precious Flower of Life." He shook his head. "No, comrades, it's *here* the Invid will come. The Masters, too, once they learn that Zor's fortress is interred below."

The grumbling began to taper off. After a long moment, someone asked, "How do you propose we board the flagship, when you're the only one among us with unrestricted access?"

Elmikk smiled lightly, pleased that he'd finally gotten through to them. "By using the heavy work drones to cut a secret tunnel straight through the factory, from hull to null-g heart, where the flagship is anchored. It will be a painstakingly slow process, I know. But when the moment is right, we'll cut through the final few feet, storm the ship and take it. Then, once clear of the factory, we'll execute our fold."

"And our comrades on the surface," a full-size said. "What's to become of them?"

Elmikk allowed a melancholy frown. "Sacrifices must be made."

The separate conversations began again, but this time Elmikk did nothing to stop them; a certain amount of dialogue and compromise was unavoidable. Instead, he fixed his thoughts on the future he had devised, unaware that one of the Micronized conspirators in the hold had come by his Human stature naturally, and was already devising plans of his own.

* * *

"Down boy," Lisa said, trying to back out of an increasingly passionate embrace that had gone on for several minutes and had been working its way ever so slowly toward the twin bed in her quarters.

Rick pursued her, burying his face in the crook of her neck. "Lisa, it's ... been ... six ... months," he said, punctuating each word with a kiss.

"Exactly," she said. "And we have a lot to talk about before you ship back to the surface."

"Talk? That's all we've been doing. And I've got the phone bills to prove it."

She slipped out of his grasp and kissed him once, lightly, on the mouth, before saying, "I want to know everything about what's going on in the Protectorate."

Rick started to say something, but changed his mind, heaving a resigned sigh before going into details about Operation Tiger. Lisa moved away from the bed to perch herself on the arm of the couch, listening without interruption until Rick came to the part about the formation of a Zentraedi squadron, when she asked him almost the same question Max had, about the squadron being seen as a ploy to downsize yet additional Zentraedi. Rick supplied the same answer Reinhardt had given.

"What you're telling me," Lisa said, "is that the RDF is willing to be tried in the court of public opinion."

Rick rocked his head from side to side as he closed on the couch. "I think most people will see it for exactly what it is: our attempt to allow the Zentraedi to police themselves."

"I'm not so sure. I think it's fairly transparent that the RDF is equivocating again. I see it as their saying: 'Don't bother us about the malcontents, we have more important things to do.'"

Rick gestured broadly with both hands. "If you didn't think so, you wouldn't be here, right? You'd be downside with the rest of us, battling it out with Milburn and the UEG on one hand and Leonard and the Army of the Southern Cross on the other."

Lisa bit her lower lip. "I'm not attacking you, Rick. I understand the position we're in. I just wish there was some other solution. Asking the Zentraedi to police themselves is like admitting that we're not a united planet." She regarded him for a long moment. "This just doesn't sound like you."

Rick's expression turned petulant. "How about we trade jobs for the next six months and then have this same conversation." He held her gaze, then softened his look and sat beside her, putting an arm around her waist. "Getting back to where we left off—"

Lisa stood up and walked away from him.

"Now what's wrong?" Rick said, following her with his eyes. "Look, Lisa, I can't control every decision the UEG makes."

Lisa shook her head. "It's not that."

"Then, what is it? You're practically running from me."

She returned to his side and rested her hands on his shoulders. "I don't mean to, Rick. It's just that . . . I don't know exactly. I've been so busy, and it's been so long since I've seen you. I guess it's taking me time to readjust to being together."

Rick looked perplexed. "Yeah, but it's not like we haven't been talking. And I've been just as alone as you have."

"You think? What about Max and Miriya and Jean Grant and everybody? I mean, what friends do I have up here—Breetai? Exedore? Emil?"

Rick loosed a small laugh. "Lisa, this trip's the first I've seen of Max in months. You wouldn't believe how busy I've been."

She blew out her breath and pressed her cheek to his. "Maybe that's what it is: the stress of devoting too much time to work and not enough time to ourselves."

Rick hugged her. "My feelings haven't changed."

She pulled back some to look at him. "Mine haven't, either. If anything, they've grown stronger. I miss you so much."

He held her close and nuzzled her long hair. "I have an idea. But I think I'm afraid to mention it."

"Rick . . ."

"No," he said quickly. "It's probably not what you think."

She showed him a puzzled frown. "What?"

"I, uh . . ." He cleared his throat. "Uh, what would you say to my asking you to marry me?"

"You know what would be great—" Lorelei Network manager Tom Hoos told Minmei. "If you could have special guests drop by from time to time to share their thoughts about current events. Say, someone like Rick Hunter. I'm sure there'd be no shortage of questions from the Zentraedi."

Minmei favored Hoos with a polite smile. She could just imagine those questions: How many Zentraedi do you calculate you killed during the War, Admiral? Or: Did you have sex with Minmei when the two of you were trapped inside the SDF-1 or when you were living together in Macross?

"I'm not interested in turning this into a variety show, Tom. Besides, I don't see why the Zentraedi would want to hear from, or even about, Rick. Or any of my friends, for that matter."

"But that's just the point." Hoos sat back in his desk swivel and spread his arms wide. "They're *your* friends— Lynn-Minmei's friends. Ergo: they're important enough to be heard from."

Hoos was absurdly clean-cut and good looking, but a bit on the overeager side. Lorelei's office complex—on the top floor of Denver's poshest building—also seemed a little too eager to please. More, for a supposedly nonprofit organization, Lorelei certainly hadn't scrimped on the furnishings. Mountains, indistinct in the summer haze, dominated the view from the window wall behind Hoos's desk. From her armchair, Minmei could see clear to the arena dome from which Khyron had literally plucked her.

When ten seconds had gone by and she still hadn't responded to Hoos's half-baked analysis, Sharky O'Toole took up the challenge. In contrast to Minmei's Western outfit of tight-fitting, rhinestone-studded jeans, sim-leather boots, and felt hat, O'Toole had on an ill-tailored lightweight suit that accentuated the bulge of his belly.

"I think what Lynn's saying here—and correct me if I'm

wrong, Lynn—is that her interest in doing this show rests on your being able to target a Zentraedi audience." O'Toole paused, as though monitoring himself on playback. "Well, maybe that's not the best way to put it. What I mean is, that the Zentraedi should be the priority. We all need to put our heads together and figure out what they're going to want to hear."

Tom smiled without showing his teeth. "We're in total agreement that the Zentraedi should come first. But let's face facts: the Zentraedi aren't going to be the only ones tuning in to this show. We expect it to draw a significant, uh, Human following, and I think we should be prepared to give them something as well."

"I don't see why," Minmei said. "If non-Zentraedi want to tune in, fine, let them. But I don't think we should be calculated in trying to cater to them. The best thing that could happen would be for Humans to take an actual interest in what the Zentraedi are thinking."

"So you're saying that special guests are out."

It was obvious that Hoos was struggling to maintain his good humor, but Minmei stood firm. "I wouldn't be opposed to having Zentraedi guests."

O'Toole immediately seized on the idea. "Now, there you go, Tom. Forget your Rick Hunters. Why not go after Breetai, or Exedore, or Miriya Parino? Any of them would fit the call-in format perfectly."

Hoos was suddenly animated. "I like it, I like it a lot. An introductory segment of Minmei's music, some casual chatting about the news, Minmei takes a few phone calls, some more music, a guest segment, a few more calls . . . I wish we could go on the air tomorrow instead of waiting until next year."

O'Toole threw Minmei a covert look. "This has to go worldwide, huh? We couldn't just kick things off in the Northlands and gradually add markets as new satellites are launched?"

Hoos proffered the polished grin. "The thing is, we don't want any of the Zentraedi to feel excluded. Now more than ever, considering what's happening in the Arkansas Protectorate and in the Southlands."

Minmei pressed her fingertips to her mouth. "Do you think the network will help to limit the spread of malcontentism?"

Tom glanced at her and cracked a genuine smile. "Minmei, if Lorelei lives up to expectations, I think it will put an *end* to malcontentism."

In Tokyo, Lazlo Zand's experiment in autoevolution was momentarily foiled by the uncontrollable shaking of his hands. He stared at them in mounting anger and disappointment as the palms broke a stinging sweat. But the physical discomfort was nothing compared to the mental anguish of having his body choose that moment to rebel. Reckoning from T. R. Edwards's visit in May, tonight was the culmination of three months of intense research; but really, the moment was a lifetime in the making.

It was the middle of the night and Zand had the lower levels of the Robotech Research Center to himself, save for a dozen or so maintenance robots busy at their tasks— emptying wastebaskets, cleaning windows, vacuuming floors. He was not in his office, but in the biochemistry lab at the northeast corner of subbasement one, where he'd spent the past few weeks analyzing blood samples he'd coaxed from a host of Zentraedi subjects over the years, including Breetai, Exedore, Jevna Parl, Konda, and others. Analyzing the samples in an effort to determine which, if any, were safely miscible with Human blood.

Alien blood did show typing comparable to that of Human blood, but all attempts at mingling the two had resulted, to varying degrees, in the formation of spontaneous clots—no matter what anticoagulants had been introduced to the mix. Just the same, Zand knew that it was possible on some level, since the mating of a Human and a Zentraedi had generated at least one child. He had, of course, used samples of his own blood in the matching process.

The findings notwithstanding, he had a liter of diluted alien blood hung on an IV rack, with the feed needle already inserted into a vein in his left forearm. Into a vein in the other forearm ran a feed tube from a similarly suspended plastic bag, containing a liter of Ringer's lactate solution to which had been added 50 ccs of what had first been classified as "unknown mecha lubricant," drained from the Invid battle suit Breetai had discovered aboard Khyron's cruiser. Zand's analysis of the fluid had revealed that it was not lubricant, but nutrient of a kind, whose chemical makeup was remarkably similar to that of certain serum constituents of Zentraedi blood. The Protoculture constituents, to be exact.

There was no way to predict the effect the mix of blood and nutrient would have on his body, but he was long past concerning himself with the predictable. Edwards had put his finger on the truth: the only thing that separated Lang from the pack of scientists that had made Robotechnology a life study was Lang's artificially induced understanding of Protoculture—or what he called "the Shapings."

For a time following Edwards's revelatory visit, Zand had concentrated his research on the mother computer removed from the SDF-1, theorizing that its complex neural circuitry might be able to supply a mind-boost equal to the one Lang had received while seated at the comp console in Zor's cabin. But the excised computer was impermeable. Should the Pluto mission ever return with the modules Lang had had removed from the Visitor to Macross Island's Robotech Research Center, perhaps the machine would prove accessible; but until then it was simply a fickle databank that could sometimes be accessed, sometimes not.

Much as the Zentraedi lacked an understanding of the fold or weapons systems they activated aboard their ships, the center's cybertechnicians were largely ignorant about the inner workings of the mother computer. Using receptor-studded helmets comparable to the "thinking caps" worn by mecha pilots, the cybertechs had done experiments in virtual interfacing, but the computer had proved uncooperative; the difference being that VTs and such had been engineered by Humans for Humans, whereas the mother computer had been created by Zor or the Masters for who knew what manner of being or overall design. And since Lang had forbidden anyone to so much as pry open one of the machine's access panels—in the same way he had restrained himself from probing the SDF-1's Reflex furnaces—Zand had ultimately abandoned hopes for a cyber-supplied mind-boost and focused instead on the search for a biochemical booster.

From the start it should have been obvious where the experiment was leading him, but he had somehow missed it— even after recognizing that the Zentraedi blood samples varied slightly in composition. Breetai's blood contained ingredients that were missing in Konda's or Rico's, while Exedore's and Jevna Parl's contained ingredients missing in Breetai's. All samples seemed to pose equal risk to Human beings, except for one—Dana Sterling's.

Regardless of Miriya Parino's contribution of Protoculture-engineered warrior genes, father Maxwell Sterling had bequeathed her his own type O-negative, which made her the perfect donor.

It had come time to move beyond the theoretical to the experiential.

The shaking in his hands was finally subsiding. He inhaled deeply; exhaled slowly through pursed lips. With his right hand he adjusted the flow valve on the blood-drip tube; then, with his left, he did the same to the tube draining the ur-Protoculture/lactate solution. Gravity fed the fluids into him.

At first he felt only an increase in his pulse rate, no more than might be attributable to the byproducts of his anxiety.

But then it was if someone had drawn a translucent veil over his eyes. His consciousness underwent a sudden and frightening shift. Colors intensified; the slightest sounds were amplified. He glanced at the digital display of the clock on the workstation countertop.

"Three-eleven, forty-six," he directed to a voice-activated disk recorder. "Onset of effects, somewhat like those of a psychotropic or hallucinogen, but accompanied by a sense of deep-seated dread." He cut his eyes to the monitor, whose leads were attached to his chest and wrists. "Pulse, ninety-eight; blood pressure, one-sixty over ninety-two and climbing . . . Tightness in chest and top of head, as though someone was tightening a wide band around my temples—"

Zand paused.

"Three-thirteen: almost lost consciousness. Synesthesia occurring. Parade of geometric shapes in front of my eyes. Hearing colors, seeing sounds. Bitter taste in my mouth, tongue feels swollen to twice its normal size. Difficulty talking and breathing. Fear. Terror. Have I killed myself?"

No sooner had he asked the question then he felt a searing heat inside his skull. Only the tape would tell if he had screamed before the darkness overtook him.

CHAPTER EIGHTEEN

The Zentraedi were designed with Micronization in mind. Activation of their Protoculture-encoded proportional system requires anywhere from one to three hours of exposure to specifically directed protonucleaic radiation in a "sizing chamber" (T'sentr Nuvinz Uamtam). Micronization can be reversed through a more complex, lengthy, and physically taxing process. Few report experiencing pain, but lassitude and nausea are not uncommon. Frequent transformations performed within a short time (i.e., two within twenty-four Earth-standard hours) can result in severe metabolic disturbances, respiratory failure, and coma. Hastily performed procedures have been known to cause death.

Ziembeda, as quoted in Zeitgeist's *Alien Psychology*

BAGZENT HAD DUG A HOLE FOR HIMSELF——LITERALLY and figuratively. The literal hole, measuring some 26-by-50 feet, was just large enough to conceal a Tactical Battlepod, from foot thrusters to top-mounted AA lasers. Roofed with cuttings from broad-leafed shrubs, the hole was situated on the eastern slope of a narrow valley, along whose rivered floor ran the Manaus–Cavern City Highway. The minesweepers that now rode point for most Southlands convoys were capable of detecting buried metal objects, but only when their scanners had been specifically tasked and when those buried objects lay within a quarter-mile of either side of their paths. Bagzent was confident that the sweeper winding its way through the valley was unaware of his presence. The RDF soldiers at the controls—indeed, everyone in the 134-vehicle northbound convoy—were no doubt relying on their escort of Veritechs to root out trouble before it appeared.

Four of the five holes dug into the opposing, steeper slope of the valley also housed Tactical Battlepods—pods of the newly formed Shroud and Fist contingent, each crewed by a pilot and a copilot/gunner. As on the Grand Cannon raid, Bagzent's second was Narumi, the Amazonian. The western face's fifth and somewhat grander hole contained a Stinger. Technically superior to the prototype Bagzent had flown in the attack on the Cuiabá convoy, this one was unmanned and answered only to the prompts of a computer program.

Imperatived, it was truly a Zentraedi machine.

The dimensions and purpose of the figurative hole were less clear, though Bagzent could trace the onset of its excavation to feelings stirred by the arduous hike into the Senburu camp and the surprises that awaited him there. He had been profoundly moved by the sight of the Stinger in flight; not because a powerful weapon had been added to the Zentraedi arsenal, but because Seloy Deparra and her comrades had actually *created* something. The excitement he'd experienced sprang from hopes for a new beginning, perhaps a new direction for the Zentraedi race. Deparra, though, must have read those hopes in his eyes and seen them as a threat to the rebel cause. Her method of invalidating them had been to award him the honor of being the first to fly a Stinger in combat. But for Bagzent, still in the throes of a kind of rebirth, the assignment had seemed a chastisement. Even worse, the initial stage of the Senburu's terror campaign had called for an attack on civilian targets.

Narumi, for all his jungle lore and unrestricted access to Wondrous Spirit, had had no reservations about killing civilians. The Amazonian had recounted tales of vengeful, bloodthirsty raids on rival villages, and tribal warfare in which innocent families were routinely slaughtered. But even now, weeks after the Cuiabá massacre, Bagzent was filled with self-loathing, resulting from the 200 murders he had carried out in the name of insurrection. And for once his remorse and confusion had nothing whatever to do with the sound of Minmei's voice or the sight of two Humans in a loving embrace.

News of the RDF's invasion of the defenseless Arkansas Protectorate had alleviated his guilt, but only for a short time. The RDF was only answering terror with terror, just as the Invid had after the defoliation of Optera. Animals didn't seek to avenge themselves on a predator for the loss of one of their flock. It was true that living beings fed on one another, but not out of cruelty. Bagzent could find no counterpart in the natural world to the vicious cycle of Zentraedi- and Human-made violence.

And yet, there he was, concealed in a hole, lending his support to that perpetuating cycle of terror and counterterror. If only there was someone he could talk to about his feelings, someone who would at least hear him out without incarcerating him—as any Human would do—or executing him outright—as any Zentraedi would. But no friendly ear existed in either camp. So, principally out of fear of being tried for war crimes or treason, he would continue to participate in the Senburu's campaign. Until such time as he could discover some way out of the hole.

"Appearing from the ground" was a commonplace Zentraedi terror tactic—one they had employed on countless worlds, though never on Earth. The goal in using it against the convoy was simply to make it appear that the Zentraedi were *everywhere*: omnipresent in the blue skies, the blue-green seas and lush forests, beneath the very ground the convoys traversed. And just now the tactic was reinforced by a weapon that could deliver unassisted on the commitment to terror.

It was possible, in fact, that Bagzent wouldn't even have to fire a round.

A reconnaissance pod concealed ten miles to the south had reported that the convoy was escorted by six Veritechs—three times the usual number, which in itself was confirmation of the effectiveness of the terror campaign. The present plan called for the pods to maintain radio silence until the VTs were well within range; then, one by one, to emerge from their pits and draw fire, leaving the Stinger free to execute its commands.

Static crackled from the radio in Bagzent's pod, followed by a raspy voice. "Five, report." The voice belonged to Rudai, coleader of the Shroud and Fist.

"Five, online," Bagzent said.

"Four targets have entered the valley. One, Two, Three,

and Four pods will launch to engage. Stand fast, Five, until the Stinger is away, then throw yourself at any VTs guarding the convoy."

"Agreed."

"And remember, Five: this time leave us something to loot for supplies."

"Copy, One," Bagzent answered. "Five, standing fast."

"Kill or be killed, *T'sen* Bagzent."

"Kill or be killed, *T'sen* Rudai. Five, out."

Bagzent hit the radio kill switch and glanced at Narumi, who occupied the pod's lower seat. "Periscope video. Wide field."

A wide-angle view of the valley appeared onscreen a moment later. One and Two pods were already in the air and Three was halfway out of its hole, limbs and leaves lodged in every body seam and joint. The minesweeper and lead vehicles of the convoy were just nosing into view on the right-hand side of the screen. In pursuit of the four Battlepods, three Veritechs streaked into view, all in fighter mode and flying nap-of-the-earth.

Atmospheric engagement between Zentraedi and RDF crafts was still a relatively new game. At the start of the War, Breetai's troops had engaged in limited air and ground fighting on Macross Island, and again, two years into the War, when the SDF-1 had returned to Earth. Then, much later, members of Khyron's Seventh Mechanized Division had skirmished with the RDF in the Northlands. But for the most part, pilots on both sides were still feeling each other out. It had been Bagzent's experience that most Veritech pilots played a cautious game, jinking and juking, always angling for the leg shot that could instantly cripple a pod. Very few braved in-close combat, or had faith enough in their skills with the autocannon to mechamorphize in-flight to Guardian or Battloid mode. Aggressive technique was, in fact, what had made Max Sterling a legend.

And from the look of things, Sterling himself had to have trained the pilots of the escort team. Before the Zentraedi of the Shroud and Fist had even had time to position themselves on the steep slope, the VTs were swarming all over them, reconfiguring from fighter to Guardian to

Battloid for near-point-blank exchanges of autocannon fire. In an instant, Three had its legs blown out from under it and Two was holed and on fire. Steps ahead of missile explosions, One and Four were making desperate hops for higher ground, firing blindly at their pursuers. Even when the Stinger finally launched from its pit, spewing plasma bolts and heat-seekers, it was quickly set upon from all sides. Two fighter-configured Veritechs sustained direct hits and came apart in midair. Elsewhere, however, two dauntless Battloids were raining armor-piercing rounds into the Stinger's shoulders and torso.

Flames and thick black smoke were pouring from gaps in the convoy where missiles had found their targets. But far more of the Stinger's projectiles had missed and done little more than crater the slopes.

"Five! Five!" Rudai yelled over the radio. "Laun—"

Onscreen, directed energy loosed from the undercarriages of two VTs obliterated Rudai's pod. A second later, Four—almost at the ridgeline—lost a leg and tumbled down the slope, uprooting trees and gouging the soft earth. Then the Stinger itself was spun around by autocannon fire, and, billowing smoke, began to plummet.

"Bagzent," Narumi said from below. "Launch?"

Bagzent stared at him for a long moment without responding. "Closeup of one of the Veritechs," he said at last.

Narumi narrowed the field of the video camera and tracked one of the mecha.

"Lock on the taileron insignia," Bagzent said, eyes riveted to the instrument panel's display screen.

Slowly the insignia came into focus: the standard RDF fighting kite. Save that centered inside it was the *Cizion*—the V-like sigil of the Zentraedi.

A Zentraedi squadron? Bagzent thought in disbelief.

"Launch?" Narumi asked.

Bagzent shook his head. "Hide."

Full-size, their bodies required substantial portions of nutrient, taken in conjunction with daily doses of Protoculture-based supplements. Micronized, however, the need for sustenance was greatly diminished, which made it all the easier to refuse the foul-tasting gruel their captors had the audacity to call food.

In what had become the training facility's "dining hall"—a workspace that had once accommodated a mere one hundred full-size and could now house the entire population of the Protectorate—Ranoc Nomarre pushed his meal away and drew his hands down his face in a gesture of acute distress. A month of fasting had weakened his body, but he worried less about weight loss than the loss of his sanity.

Three months to the day had passed since the occupation of the Protectorate. Initially there had been no explanation from the UEG or the RDF; then the Zentraedi were informed that the Protectorate had been identified as the source of mecha parts that were ending up in the hands of dissident bands. The Gladiators and Excalibers that encircled the facility were there to prevent any additional supplies from reaching the Southlands.

Once the sizing chambers were erected, however, the official explanation changed: While there was no *proof* to support the charge of complicity, the Army of the Southern Cross was convinced of the Protectorate's guilt and had threatened to invade unless the UEG and the RDF agreed to shut down the giants' construction facility. To minimize any chance of going to war with its analog in the Southern Hemisphere, the RDF had further agreed to oversee the immediate downsizing of all Protectorate residents.

General Maistroff, head of the occupying forces, had given his word that everyone would be returned to full size once the Protectorate's innocence was established. But until then all full-size were expected to comply with the RDF by submitting to voluntary Micronization.

Protests would not be tolerated.

But there were protests, regardless. Why was a news blackout in effect in the Protectorate? the Zentraedi had wanted to know. And why were civilians and the media being kept from entering and reporting on the proceedings?

On two occasions, Destroids had opened fire on "noncompliants," killing twenty, including Utema, Ranoc's roommate for less than a week. And all these weeks later, the smell of rotting flesh still permeated the air, despite the fact that the corpses had been moved miles from the facility and interred in a mass grave.

After that, the RDF achieved full compliance, even from those for whom the Micronization process was a guarantee of malady or premature death. With Zentraedi supervising the process, the sizing chambers ran continuously for five days, and during that time twelve more died as the result of suicide or sloppy technique and in botched escape attempts.

The events had effectively eclipsed Ranoc's earlier sense of fulfillment and confidence in the future. At least once a day he was assured that Micronization didn't necessarily mean the end of his career in construction; that the training in materials and techniques would continue, and that everyone would eventually be taught to operate heavy machinery and to work with Human crews. But Ranoc didn't believe for a moment that he would ever be returned to full size, and his anger grew until it had hardened into hatred for his jailers. He regretted having spoken up for Minmei years earlier, and he wished that he could have died a warrior's death with Khyron in the skies over Macross.

With Micronization completed, the number of Destroids had been reduced to 50, though some 600 Defense Force and civil defense troops remained in the Protectorate. And one of those soldiers was looking Ranoc's way just now, a bulky, square-jawed corporal named Shaw who seemed to delight in taunting everyone.

"What's the matter, Nomarre," the corporal asked from his post by the dining hall door, "you got a problem with the food?"

Ranoc sent him a baleful look. "Since you call it food, why don't you come over here and eat it?"

Shaw nodded knowingly to one of his comrades. "But, Nomarre, if you don't eat, you won't grow up to be a big, strong Zentraedi."

Ranoc waited until the laughter died down. "If and when I do," he said at last, "I promise you'll hear from me, Micronian."

Shaw and his buddy apparently didn't see any humor in

the remark, and were headed Ranoc's way when sirens began to blare in the distance.

Shaw pointed a thick finger at Ranoc. "More of you trying to escape. Which only means more of you dead."

Ranoc might have concurred, but for the fact that beneath the shrill wailing of the sirens whomped the unmistakable sound of cannon fire. Heads swung south to the source of the barrage, and a moment later, nearly everyone in the hall was making for the exits to see for themselves what the commotion was about. Ranoc wondered suddenly if the RDF had been telling the truth about a threatened attack by the Army of the Southern Cross.

The next exchange of fire erased any chance of that: the opening roar was certainly the product of Excaliber forearm cannons. But the answering salvo came from no Humanmade weapon.

"Battlepods," someone in the crowd of Zentraedi jamming the doorway said.

The oak forest south of the facility was crisscrossed with energy bolts and ablaze. The sky was crazed with lightninglike discharges, and the reports of explosions echoed in the surrounding hills and rumbled underfoot. Ranoc saw two Battlepods launch themselves above the flaming treetops, lasers and particle-beam cannons flaring. One was immediately atomized by Raidar X fire; the other dodged a flashing fusillade of bolts and dropped back into the trees.

"This is madness," Ranoc said to no one in particular. "Unless there are hundreds of them, they'll be wiped out."

From all directions, Excalibers, Guardians, and Spartans were converging on the kill zone.

"Maybe now is the time to escape," someone suggested.

"You'll be cut down," Ranoc admonished him.

Just then something metallic shot high into the sky from amid the torched trees, something that could almost have been mistaken for Female Power Armor. At the apex of its flight, nearly indistinguishable in a upward storm of tracer rounds and antiaircraft fire, the object became the epicenter of a veritable fireworks display of missile launches.

Ranoc threw himself to the ground as the projectiles fell indiscriminately on the construction facility.

"Good evening, I'm Katherine Hyson . . ."

"And I'm Rebecca Hollister . . ."

"And this is World News for November tenth, Twenty-sixteen."

Hyson, looking paler and not quite as perfect as she had the previous summer, wore a fixed smile. In response to a slight sag in the ratings, the honchos at MBS had installed Hollister as co-anchor of the evening news—Hollister, who had become the network darling since her live coverage of the Protectorate occupation.

Hollister's TelePrompTer had come alive, though the mousy brunette scarcely glanced at the screen—or at any of the crib sheets on the desk—having been blessed with a near photographic memory.

"The question everyone is still asking six weeks after the attack on the occupied Zentraedi Protectorate," she began, "is how the malcontent band, now identified as the Steel Wind, managed to infiltrate the RDF's perimeter of Destroids. There is some concern that information about the deliberate—and unexplained—withdrawal of troops from the southern perimeter may have been leaked to the malcontents. But leaked by whom? MBS put the question to Admiral Richard Hunter only this afternoon as he was leaving a meeting of top RDF brass."

The footage of Hunter ran without comment from Hollister or Hyson: Hunter, surrounded by aides and reporters, walked briskly from RDF headquarters in Monument City toward a waiting limousine. "I have no comment at this time," he said.

"Which seemed to be the refrain from everyone we tried to speak with," Hollister resumed. "Except, that is, for Major Joseph Petrie of the Army of the Southern Cross, who spoke to us via satellite from Brasília."

Petrie's youthful face came onscreen, with his name and rank subtitled. "We're not saying that the RDF would purposely apprise the malcontents of a defensive weakness at the Protectorate. But in terms of public relations, it was certainly in their best interests to enlist Zentraedi to liberate the facility, since their own hands were tied by the UEG. The RDF had the foresight to downsize over a thousand potential insurgents, and now they're bowing to the pressure of a couple of outraged and outspoken sympaths. As applies to the formation of the so-called Twenty-third Veritech Squadron, this is simply another indication of the RDF's ceding of police powers to the aliens themselves. Something that will not occur in the Southlands."

Hollister returned to the screen. "Sanctioned or not, the Steel Wind's attempt at liberating the facility must now be deemed a victory, with news today that the RDF is withdrawing all its troops from the Protectorate. Unfortunately, this comes a little late for the forty-six members of the Steel Wind who were killed during and after the attack, and the thirty-two Protectorate Zentraedi who have died over the past six months.

"And what of the survivors and the enormous facility itself? UEG spokespersons maintain that former detainees who wish to be returned to full size can apply for factory satellite positions, and all others will be able to find construction work on Human crews."

Hollister paused and turned to Hyson. "Katherine."

Hyson's fixed smile returned as she accepted the handoff and shifted her eyes ever so slightly to the TelePrompTer.

"Today, the public and the media got their first look at an example of the malcontent weapon used in the Cuiabá Massacre in June, and in the September attacks on a convoy in the Venezuela Sector and on the Protectorate."

A grounded Stinger appeared onscreen, on display in a well-guarded enclosure at RDF headquarters. Members of the media were seated on folding chairs in neat rows, and at the podium stood a smartly uniformed, blond-haired RDF information officer identified as Lieutenant Eileen Summers.

Summers's briefing covered all the salient points. The craft everyone was looking at—a modified version of a Zentraedi battle suit—was known by the malcontents as a Stinger. The one on display was not the one that had been used by the Steel Wind, but had been captured in Venezuela by the Zentraedi Twenty-third Veritech Squadron. An as-yet-undetermined number of Stingers had been built by an all-female band of technicians at a hidden base in the jungles of the central Southlands.

"Can you provide any details on how the RDF came by this information?" one reporter asked the lieutenant.

Summers's expression remained solemnly thoughtful. "We can provide that our intelligence derives from ongoing investigations into various smuggling operations in Freetown, Mexico."

"Can you name names?" someone else asked.

"One of the individuals under arrest in Mexico is a Zentraedi female named Neela Saam; another is an arms merchant named Brian Cassidy."

"Does this all-female malcontent band have a name?" asked a reporter from MBS, known for having a nose for good stories.

"Neela Saam used the term *zopilote* when she referred to the group. The word is Spanish for 'vulture,' but the RDF is calling them the Scavengers."

A woman's hand went up. "Since many Zentraedi are known to be techno-illiterate, how and where did these Scavengers learn to design and build mecha?"

Summers cleared her throat. "We're still looking into that. But it's possible that some of them may have received their training in Macross or Monument."

Hyson was fuming when she reappeared onscreen; she calculated that she'd had less than two minutes of actual on-air time. She did, however, have a long segment after the commercial break, enough at least to put her even with Hollister. She was ready with the lead-in when the director's voice barked through her earbead.

"Katherine, ignore the intro to your piece. We've got a newsbreaker."

Hyson glanced expectantly at her TelePrompTer.

"Katherine," the director said, "give it back to Rebecca."

Hyson tensed from head to toe, but managed to turn to her co-anchor and say, "Rebecca."

"Thanks, Katherine. This just in from the Argentine: The Paranka, also known as the Burrowers, have launched an attack on the city of Zagerstown, approximately one hundred miles northeast of Buenos Aires. The death toll now stands at one hundred forty-seven, but is expected to exceed two hundred and fifty. We'll have more on this and other stories when we return."

2017

CHAPTER
NINETEEN

Malcontentism notwithstanding, cities worldwide continued to prosper [during the period of Reconstruction], and fewer and fewer among them wanted any involvement with the UEG, the RDF, or the Bureau of Reconstruction Management. The events of 2012 [the Zentraedi Rain of Death] had made everyone wary of groups that purported to speak for all Humankind—groups like the then-defunct United Earth Defense Council. Separatism was the order of the day. Except in the Southlands, where Anatole Leonard was beginning to emerge as a kind of King Arthur, promising to rid the land of evil, unify its numerous city-states, and usher in a Golden Age. But, as the Southern Cross dergue would come to learn, Round Tables seldom endure. Feudalism would eventually return to the Southlands, setting the stage for the chaos that attended the Invid invasion.

S. J. Fischer, Legions of Light: A History of the Army of the Southern Cross

A STRANGER TO THE RIOTOUSLY LUSH, RIVER-FED heartland of the continent he hoped someday to make his domain, Anatole Leonard gazed down at the treetops from his throne in the superhauler gondola, astonished to discover just how impact-cratered and strewn with crashed alien warships was his fantasy realm. Small wonder that the malcontents had access to so much weaponry and supplies, or that they had been able to construct terror machines like the Stingers—missiles from which had killed 271 in Zagerstown only a month earlier.

Quick glances out the port and starboard windows reaffirmed that the three other ultratech, dirigiblelike behemoths that comprised Leonard's flotilla were keeping pace with their leader. Somewhere in the undulating terrain below lay their objective: the forested basin that sheltered the Scavenger's mecha installation.

"Sir, the on-board comp has established a features match

with satellite recon's topo map," the air commander reported. "GPS readings are also in synch. Target is twenty-
five clicks north-northeast." He pointed out the windscreen
to the horizon. "Beyond that ridgeline, there. Do we announce ourselves or go in cold?"

"Announce ourselves how?" Leonard asked.

Muscular and curly-bearded, the captain chuckled to
himself. "Sir, I was thinking about an old movie where a
helicopter assault was conducted to the strains of Wagner's
'Ride of the Valkyres.'"

Leonard didn't return the captain's over-the-shoulder
grin. When, one hundred miles out, the fleet hadn't met resistance, concern increased that the Scavengers were purposely holding back, luring them in the way Khyron had
the RDF in 2013, as part of his plan to abduct Minmei and
Lynn-Kyle.

"This isn't the movies, Captain. Either we've been expected for over an hour now, or we've somehow caught
them napping. If it's the former, they will announce to us
soon enough; and if it's the latter, we should take full advantage of their sloppiness. No announcement. And no
quarter once you have the fire command."

"Aye, sir."

"No quarter?" Professor Zand asked in a loud voice from
his seat in the rear of the gondola. "Is that prudent, given
what we might be able to learn from the captives? Perhaps
you're unaware that I've had extensive experience interrogating the Zentraedi. Not in the field, it's true, but some of
the same laboratory techniques can be applied. In any case,
who knows what the Scavengers may have in the way of
usable mecha or Protoculture. And we don't want that destroyed, do we?"

Leonard glanced at Zand, his broad, hairless brow deeply
furrowed. "Don't mention that infernal word to me, Professor. I find it as offensive as taking God's name in vain. It
has long been my wish that the hardware of the Southern
Cross could be fueled by something other than that alien
evil." He nodded his chin at Zand. "Maybe you could brew
something up for us—something Human-grown."

Zand smiled stiffly. He was sweating profusely in his

rumpled suit, and had his bony hands clamped on the seat's padded armrests. "I am up to the challenge, sir."

Leonard faced front once more, concealing a long-suffering look. He had never had much use for scientists, least of all academics like Zand, who was as creepy as they came. Behind the wraparound dark glasses, Zand had the same all-iris eyes as that other one, Emil Lang, whom Leonard had never met. Had pupilless eyes become a fashion thing among academic types? he wondered. Zand was aboard as a favor to Joseph Petrie, who was obviously in awe of the professor's knowledge of cybernetics and Robotechnology; more, however, as a favor to T. R. Edwards. It was the half-faced double agent who had provided satellite intelligence on the suspected location of the Scavengers' camp and foreknowledge of the RDF's plans for an assault.

Leonard's principal reason for insisting on a no-quarter assault was to ensure that it be seen as more than a simple exercise in beat-them-to-the-punch competition. His only misgiving was that Seloy Deparra and the child might be among those at the facility. It would be just like Seloy to join the Scavengers. But he couldn't permit her possible presence to influence his decision. The assault would illustrate to the world the difference between RDF and Southern Cross policy on terrorism. In reprisal for the Cuiabá Massacre, the RDF had Micronized the population of the Protectorate; the Army of the Southern Cross would have executed them. The RDF gave lip service to civil rights by holding public trials; the Southern Cross considered itself sole judge and jury. And now, with Zagerstown still making headlines, everyone would see what Anatole Leonard meant by retaliation.

"Sir, we have visual contact with the target," the captain announced, indicating a large clearing bordering a meandering, café-au-lait river. "No signs of enemy activity. No scanner locks on any of our craft."

"Onscreen," Leonard commanded.

The superhauler's video cameras conveyed shaky images of warehouses, huts, and heavy machinery—cranes, bulldozers, and backhoes.

"Looks like an old gold-dredging operation," the captain commented.

Leonard nodded. "You have the fire command, Captain—let's see if we can't wake them up."

Shortly, a flock of missiles ripped into the clearing, punching gaping holes in the warehouses and destroying many of the outbuildings. Muddy water fountained from the river, a crane toppled, and thick-trunked trees were flattened. But there was no return fire, no Zentraedi anywhere to be seen, even when Leonard called a halt to the attack.

The clearing wasn't large enough to permit a landing. Instead, while Leonard and his officers remained aloft, Southern Cross commandos in carbon-fiber body armor rappeled down on nylon ropes and conducted a building-to-building search. Live video brought the action to the gondola screens.

Some minutes later, the camera operator was ordered to one of the warehouses, where a colonel—a lean, crisp-uniformed black wearing a tan beret—was pacing in front of the doorless entrance. "Sir, all buildings have been secured," she began. She made a quarter-turn to the right to indicate the interior of the warehouse. "There are twenty-two Stingers inside, in various states of assembly."

Leonard arranged himself for the camera inside the gondola. "Where the hell is everyone, Colonel?"

The colonel pointed to an outbuilding at the edge of the clearing, a tangle of bare trees towering over it. "There, sir."

Leonard threw Zand a glance. "I guess you'll get a chance at interrogating them, after all, Professor."

"Not this bunch, sir," the colonel interrupted. "All seventeen have committed ritual suicide."

Leonard was quiet for a moment, then he put his hands on his ample midriff and laughed. "Well, good for them. They've saved us the trouble of killing them."

Rick came through the door to Gunther Reinhardt's cabin brushing snow from the shoulders of a down-filled jacket and stomping it from knee-high boots. His nose was red and running and bits of ice were stuck in his hair. Reinhardt approached with a cup of coffee, which Rick eagerly accepted.

"There must be five feet out there," Rick said between sips. "Only the main roads are plowed. I almost didn't make it."

"Motokoff's stuck, so he won't be coming," Reinhardt told him. "But Lang and Obstat are here."

"Caruthers and Maistroff?"

"No word from either of them. They don't know a thing."

"Good. Let's see if we can keep it that way."

Built of logs and fieldstone, the cabin sat high in Monument City's only wooded valley. Rick followed the balding general through several closed doorways to a sunken den, where Lang and Obstat were warming themselves in front of an inviting fire. Ostensibly, everyone had come to play poker.

"Look on the bright side, Rick," Lang said, "even reporters stay home on nights like tonight."

Lang was right: Rick couldn't remember the last time he'd been able to leave his house without confronting a bevy of media people, all demanding to know his reaction to this accusation or that development. The debacle surrounding the Protectorate had become the story that wouldn't go away. Then came Zagerstown, and now Leonard's attack on the Scavengers' base in Amazonia.

Obstat rose from his chair and extended a hand. "I understand that congratulations are in order, Admiral."

"Thanks," Rick said, shaking hands.

"Is it official yet?" Lang asked.

"As of Christmas. Even though I had to send the ring upside by courier."

Obstat laughed. "My best to Admiral Hayes."

"I'll tell her next time I see her—whenever that is."

"Any date set?" Lang asked.

"The way things are going, we might have to wait till Tirol."

"You two should consider getting married aboard the SDF-3," Reinhardt said. "Make it a kind of christening."

Obstat laughed again. "Wouldn't the media eat that up!"

"The price of fame," Reinhardt said. He went to the bookshelf, unlocked the door to a cleverly concealed compartment, and spent a moment studying the display screen of a device inside. "We're still bug free, gentlemen. Not that we have to move on immediately . . ."

"No, we should get started," Rick said. "The personal stuff can wait for later."

"Where do we start?" Obstat said.

"With the Protectorate," Rick told him. "Is there any word on how the Steel Wind knew to strike from the south?"

Obstat shook his head. "To the best of our knowledge, it was blind luck. Maistroff denies he had any specific reason for withdrawing Destroids from that part of the perimeter. I don't see how he would stand to gain from undermining his own defenses, in any case."

"Assuming Maistroff was deliberately affording Steel Wind an opening," Reinhardt said, "he was probably counting on a full-scale riot by the detainees. A riot would have justified giving free reign to his Excaliber troops."

"He should never have been placed in command," Rick said.

Reinhardt looked at him. "That was Milburn's doing."

"Yeah, they're quite the cozy couple, aren't they." Rick looked at Obstat. "Were Milburn and Maistroff briefed on the location of the Scavenger base?"

"Yes. Along with Moran, Stinson, Caruthers, Edwards, and probably as many as twenty others."

"T. R. Edwards?" Lang asked. Then, when Obstat had confirmed it, "I don't know if it's relevant, but I had several run-ins with Edwards on Macross Island when he was an intelligence agent for the World Unification Alliance."

Rick was nodding his head. "Roy Fokker used to tell me stories about Edwards."

Reinhardt stoked his beard and turned to Obstat. "Can Edwards and Moran be removed from the intel loop without arousing suspicion?"

"It would be easier to feed them false intel and wait to see if it gets to Leonard," Rick said.

"With Moran, possibly," Lang answered. "But Edwards

wouldn't be fooled by a maneuver like that. It would be safer to simply remove him from the loop."

"Done," Obstat said. "And Milburn?"

"Milburn, too," Reinhardt said. "And Maistroff and Caruthers, if we can swing it."

Rick shook his head in puzzlement. "What would motivate any of them to go to Leonard with top-secret information?"

"Perhaps no one did," Lang said. "Perhaps *Leonard* got lucky. Forgive me for mentioning it, but I believe it was an RDF information officer who blithely announced to the world that the Scavengers were based in Amazonia."

"There's another issue we need to discuss," Reinhardt said. "Disciplinary action for Lieutenant Summers."

Rick snorted a laugh. "Summers's media briefing didn't provide Leonard with a missing clue. All she said was 'Amazonia.' And how many millions of square miles is that?"

"You're right," Reinhardt was willing to admit. "Which only reinforces that someone in the loop went to him with our satellite intelligence."

"Was it really mass suicide, or did Leonard execute the Zentraedi?" Lang asked.

Reinhardt shrugged. "No one's come forward with evidence of an execution. But one thing's certain: they missed out on capturing the Scavengers. Only five of the victims were females."

"That means the Scavengers are still at large," Lang said, "and another Zagerstown could occur at any time."

"So long as it happens south of the Venezuela Sector," Reinhardt muttered.

Lang stared at Reinhardt while Reinhardt and Rick were trading glances. "We're phasing out all RDF operations in the Southlands," Rick explained. "Cuiabá, the Argentine, every base except Cavern City, where Captain Wolff has somehow managed to score repeatedly against the dissidents. The Twenty-third's success against the Shroud and Fist was chiefly Wolff's doing."

Lang adopted a defeated look. "In other words, the RDF

is surrendering control of the Southlands to Anatole Leonard."

No one spoke for a long moment. Wind howled at the cabin's insulated windows and infiltrated the stone chimney to rouse the fire.

"Perhaps we should concentrate on discussing Rick and Lisa's wedding plans," Lang said. "Before those get sabotaged as well."

When word had reached her of Neela's undoing in Freetown, Seloy Deparra knew that it was time to abandon the mecha base. Later she would hear on television that the "Scavengers," as the RDF had branded them, were believed to be operating from a secret installation in Amazonia. But before that, she had received warning directly from the dispirited remnants of Neela's organization—some of them former Senburu, more recently into prostitution and enforcement—who had carried south the news that those arrested by the RDF had informed on the "*zopilotes.*"

Seloy was neither surprised nor unduly alarmed; after all, the Scavengers had already enjoyed a good run. And she liked that the name selected for her band of female techs referred to a beast that fed on carrion, which was exactly how she had come to think of the Human race—as decaying flesh. But knowing Anatole Leonard as well as she did, she understood that he would scour every square mile of jungle until he found them—scorching the forest if necessary—and she couldn't allow that to happen. Not when so much remained to be done.

As for Neela's employees, they hadn't traveled south to escape the long arm of the RDF, but to beg Seloy's forgiveness for doubly dishonoring the Imperative: first, by failing to protect Neela; and, second, by not having somehow arranged for the death of their weak-willed comrades. Seloy had granted them permission to amend their disgrace through an act of mass suicide. It was nothing more than coincidence that the seventeen had done so on the morning of Leonard's attack, only a day short of the camp's abandonment by the last of the Scavengers.

The new base was high in the foothills of the mountain

range that ran the length of the Southland's western coast. Nourished by the clouds themselves, the jungle here was even more lush and varied than that of the lowlands. From the crude balcony of her quarters, Seloy could look down on treetops, pairs of brightly colored birds in flight, the white-water rapids of a river. In the mornings, mist lingered on the valley floor, evanescing as Earth tipped toward its star. Even Hirano, learning to talk in sentences these past few months, was stirred by the balcony view. In fact, all the Scavengers were becoming increasingly enamored of the forest and its profusion of animal and insect life. Xan Norri was especially fond of wasps and spiders. The Amazonian indigines who had guided the Scavengers to the site called that area of the mountains "the eyebrow of the forest."

Seloy had no regrets about having abandoned the partially completed Stingers. The Shroud and Fist had already made the Stinger obsolete by allowing theirs to fall into RDF hands. How long could it be now before Penn or Bronson or some other mecha engineer discovered a way to thwart the Stingers by encoding every Destroid and Veritech with an IFF signature that would render them easy targets, despite their innate maneuverability and enhanced firepower? More importantly, the flow of Protoculture cells from the factory satellite had ceased; Theofre Elmikk was apparently more cautious with his operation than Neela had been. Not that Seloy trusted Elmikk for a moment. Like all male Zentraedi, he was incapable of thinking like a Human, and was therefore bound to fail at whatever plan he set himself to. The Shroud and Fist, the Steel Wind, the Burrowers ... all of them blind with rage, consistently subverting themselves.

The latest entry in the field, for example. The so-called New Unity, made up of the ten former members of the Steel Wind who had escaped Arkansas with their lives and some forty former detainees from the Protectorate itself. Detainees: another word Seloy liked. Ranoc Nomarre, the New Unity's leader, was a small, facially scarred male, unsure of himself, untested in battle, still seething about having been downsized—operating on pure hatred for anything Human. He had visited the lowland camp in its final days, all but begging Seloy, Marla, and the others for a Stinger. Hostility oozed from him when he had described his three-month ordeal in the Protectorate, and the difficulties he'd endured in reaching the camp—shipping across the Gulf of Mexico and the open ocean on the same freighter that had carried the Steel Wind north a month earlier, hacking his way through the forest, fording swollen rivers ... Once a member of Khyron's Seventh Mechanized, Nomarre was a guaranteed threat to the cause, but Seloy had bestowed a Stinger on the New Unity nonetheless. Terror was terror, whatever form it took.

With only fifteen Stingers remaining—not counting those scattered about the Southlands, the property of one male group or another—Seloy understood that she was going to have to be more circumspect about who got what. No easy task, what with representatives of outlaw bands turning up every week petitioning for mecha. Excepting the one that had gone to the New Unity, the Scavengers' most recent donation of a Stinger was to an all-female group known as the Claimers. Founded in Australia by ex-Quadrono lieutenant Tomina Jepp, the group had plagued Southeast Asia with successful raids. But what had interested Seloy and persuaded her to part with a Stinger was Jepp's disclosure that the scientist Lazlo Zand, stationed at Tokyo's Robotech Research Center, had been making discreet inquiries about the possibility of procuring "alien artifacts."

Besides, what was one less Stinger? If the terror was to continue, the Scavengers were going to have to come up with something new and daring to spring on the Human race—something not necessarily limited to inflicting damage on cities and convoys.

Seloy was forever trying to will herself to think like a Human. When she looked at Hirano, she thought about Miriya and her daughter, Dana. Miriya had appeared on television frequently during the Protectorate occupation, proclaiming how her first cause was Zentraedi rights, even though she was married to a Human. But how might Miriya feel if she knew the truth about her best friend? Would it matter any if Miriya learned the truth about who had fathered Hirano? Indeed, would the fact that Seloy was alive mean anything, or had Miriya Parino been more corrupted by Human ways than she herself realized? Sufficiently changed to consider Seloy one of the enemy?

Human thinking was difficult. Taxing. Humans had been through scores of wars, almost as many as the Zentraedi, so in some ways the idea of terrorizing them with weapons seemed naive. What were their most deeply seated fears, and how could they be unleashed? If only there was a way to use the Stingers to truly *sting* the Humans. To somehow infect everyone of them with terror.

Terror as a kind of contagious disease.

An epidemic of terror.

"Where did you get a tan this time of year?" Lang asked Zand the moment he saw him.

"Sunlamps," Zand said, ignoring Lang's offer of a chair in favor of adopting a guarded position against the far wall.

The two were in Lang's office in the Robotech Research Center. With the UEG in recess and the factory projects on schedule, Lang had decided to spend a week or so in Tokyo, catching up with everyone. Zand was at the top of the list of people he wanted to meet with. Suddenly, now, the vague unease Lang had felt in recent phone conversations with Zand was blossoming into full-fledged concern.

"Sunlamps?" Lang said skeptically.

"All right, all right, if you have to know, I took some time off and went to the beach."

"What beach? There isn't a sun-drenched beach within a thousand miles."

Zand made a minor adjustment to his dark glasses. "I don't remember the name of the place. Somewhere in Thailand."

Lang sat back in his chair. "Let me be sure I have this straight: you decided you needed some time off, so you, what?—you jetted down to *Thailand* to a beach you can't remember the name of, and you soaked up some color."

"Exactly. You have it straight."

"You traveled alone?"

"I happen to enjoy traveling alone."

Lang stood up and walked across the room. Without announcing his intentions, he swept the sunglasses from Zand's face and looked into his eyes. It was like looking into a mirror.

Lang staggered back, supporting himself on the edge of his desk. "Good God, you've done it. You found a way to take the mind-boost."

Zand whipped the glasses out of Lang's hand and put them on. "What are you babbling about? You know as well as I that Zor's console was destroyed."

Lang stared at him, wide-eyed. "You found a way. Tell me what you did, Lazlo. Don't shut me out."

Zand hesitated, then grimaced sinisterly. "You're right, Doctor, I did find a way. You want the details? I injected myself with a mixture of Zentraedi blood and a couple of ccs of fluid from that Invid craft we found. I was unconscious for three hours. I'm sure I almost died. But believe me, Doctor, my IQ is right up there with yours now, and it's increasing—every day, every *hour*. And soon I'll have an understanding of the Shapings. I'll have powers you never dreamed of."

Lang lowered himself to the desk like one deflated. "Lazlo, listen to me. You don't realize what you've done. You think this is all some competition, but it isn't, and you're going to begin to understand the downside of the boost. The hunger that surpasses any known addiction. The moments of madness—" Lang paused to catch his breath. "Why couldn't you have talked to me first?"

"Talked to you? Talked to you? When exactly was I supposed to do that? The great and all-powerful Lang, always addressing the UEG, or receiving one honor or another. Designing mecha, designing starships, traveling up and down the gravity well like a superhero . . . Tell me, Doctor, when was I supposed to talk to you?"

"Lazlo," Lang said softly, "I never realized—"

"That's right, you never did, and that's been the problem all along. But no more. Because I don't need you anymore. I have people who accept me for what I am, not as just some pale alternative to the great Lang. I have funding, I have projects. I have my own mission, my own destiny to *shape*. And perhaps it's not as bound up with yours as you'd like it to be, but I can't help that the lowly disciple has grown up to found his own movement, Doctor. And we'll just have to wait and see which of us turns out to be the more influential."

Zand spun on his heel and hurried out of the room. Lang followed him out into the corridor but soon gave up the chase, stopping to lean on a water cooler and collect his thoughts.

Was Zand—even Zand the perennial risktaker—strong enough to navigate the razor's edge of madness and survive? The objective and curious half of Lang's mind belonged not to the world of Human emotions but to Protoculture and the Shapings. But the Lang that cared for Lazlo Zand was the more powerful one, and already he mourned the loss of a friend and brilliant colleague. Zand—after Milburn and Moran—had joined the list of people he could no longer count on. When was it going to stop?

His thoughts were interrupted by a mellifluous soprano voice singing a rendition of one of his favorite pre-War songs, "A Day in the Life." He followed the voice down the corridor and through several turns until it led him to the cybertechnology lab. By now several of the center's machine intelligence specialists—short-haired men and women sporting baggy, retro fashions—had joined in the song, but the soprano's was the only voice on key. Lang had guessed from the start that it was the android, JANUS M, though he hadn't been told anything about its learning the Beatles classic.

The cybertechs grinned when they saw him enter the room.

"We thought this might get your attention," one of them said.

The android stopped singing to stare at Lang. In its jumpsuit and real-hair wig, it couldn't have looked more lifelike. "That was lovely singing, JANUS," Lang told it.

The living machine smiled. "I'm glad you enjoyed it, Doctor Lang."

"I liked it very much."

"That's good, because next time you'll have to pay to hear me sing."

The techs laughed as Lang's smile collapsed; then Lang began to laugh with them. He approached the android and stood facing it. "JANUS," he said, "retinal scan." And the android's eyes immediately became lifeless.

"Yes, Doctor Lang. Your request?"

A dermal plug in the back of JANUS's neck concealed an access port for high-speed data transfer. Lang inserted a remote transmitter into the port and studied the readout on a nearby screen.

"I see that someone has added a batch of new coding," Lang said to the cybertechs.

"Lui just wanted to try out his snappy-response program," a young woman supplied sheepishly.

Lang swung to her, smiling. "I like it." He removed the remote from the android's neck port, then dug into his pocket for some NuYen and handed it to JANUS. "I'd like to hear you finish the song."

JANUS bowed from the waist, Japanese fashion, and picked up "A Day in the Life" at the up-tempo bridge.

As Lang listened, he began to recall a conversation he and Zand had had years earlier, concerning the prospect of inserting an operative into the Milburn-Moran clique to gather covert intelligence. Zand had suggested using Lynn-Minmei, and Lang had countered that Minmei was too guileless; that a spy of the sort they had in mind would have to be created.

Lang continued to watch the android sing for a moment more, then moved to one side of the room and commanded his lapel communicator to page his research secretary.

A minute later, Haruke's voice issued from the communicator speaker. "Yes, Doctor Lang?"

"Haruke, I want you to do two things for me. First, I need someone to compile a complete software précis on Lynn-Minmei—and I mean complete. Cull from every available source—including my journals, beginning with January 2010. Then, see if you can locate the telefax or cyberbox number for a Sharky—no, make that *Samson* O'Toole." Lang spelled out the name. "He's a talent agent, so I'm certain he has an agency listing in either Monument City or Denver."

"I'll attend to it immediately, Doctor Lang."

"One last thing, Haruke: If you find O'Toole's number, contact him and say that I'd like to extend an invitation to him and Minmei to visit our Tokyo installation. I'll call to give him the details. But say for now that there's someone here I think Minmei should meet."

CHAPTER
TWENTY

There is some speculation that the sting that netted the RDF's Neela Saam and Brian Cassidy actually involved the procurement of the nuclear bomb detonated by the Iron Ravens. However, Obstat's Special Operations Group was so fixated on arresting Saam and Cassidy and obtaining information about the Scavengers that it ignored early leads which could have prevented the tragedy in Oasis. The nuclear device inflicted more death and destruction in five minutes than all the Malcontent groups combined would inflict in five years of marauding.

Weverka T'su, *Aftermath: Geopolitical and Religious Movements in the Southlands*

DESPITE ITS HAVING INCURRED THE MORAL OPPRObrium of the RDF and any number of Zentraedi advocacy groups, Anatole Leonard's preemptive strike against the attendees of the Cairo summit had been secretly praised for neutralizing the malcontent threat in Africa. As a result of the Southern Cross's action, Clozan and the sixty members of the Quandolma were dead and all but one of the continent's lesser-known groups had disbanded. The exception was the Iron Ravens, forty-four strong, under the leadership of a former infantry commander named Jinas Treng. Made up of Zentraedi crash survivors from throughout sub-Saharan Africa, the Ravens were nomadic and rarely a problem to anyone but farmers and ranchers, most of whom had opted to provide the Ravens with whatever food or livestock they needed rather than take them on.

The band was armed, but not nearly as well as its counterparts in the American Southlands. In lieu of Battlepods and Stingers, it made do with turn-of-the-century gasoline-guzzling trucks and buses, which, while certainly as ingeniously modified as anything in a post-apocalyptic film fantasy, were short on firepower. Consequently, Jinas Treng's threats to destroy Oasis—a city from which the Ravens had been repeatedly repulsed—went largely ignored. Treng's threats had become so routine, in fact, that the commander of Oasis's small garrison of Destroids had stopped reporting them to RDF headquarters in Monument City.

The former Lualaba River port of Kisangani, Oasis was a city of approximately 65,000, renamed in 2012 after emerging as the only city south of Cairo to have escaped the Rain. Located in the heart of Africa, more than one thousand miles from either coast, it had become a mecca for displaced peoples from more than a dozen neighboring nations—the continent's one radiation- and AIDS-free city where water and food were in relatively good supply.

The 1-megaton nuclear device detonated by the Iron Ravens on March 15, 2017, killed 53,431, and put an abrupt end to thoughts of Africa rejoining the modern world anytime soon. The source of the device would never be known, though evidence pointed to a band of mercenary Humans once linked to the regime of Daddy Omaa of the Central African Union, a notorious distributor of Chinese-made atomics and biological warfare weapons during the Global Civil War.

Treng's justification for committing the most heinous act since Khyron's destruction of Macross was that, on learning of Anatole Leonard's raid on the Scavengers' camp, he had felt compelled to demonstrate to the world *his* meaning of retaliation. Captured less than a week after the bombing, Treng was overheard to snicker to the first reporter that got close enough to him, *"The Imperative made me do it."*

"Oasis will remain hot for ten years," Max Sterling was telling his guest, Rolf Emerson, a week after the capture of Jinas Treng. "That's why the Twenty-third was assigned the Ravens to begin with. Defense Force Command couldn't risk subjecting Human pilots to such intense radiation. It's bad enough that two members of the Nuclear Emergency Search Team died." He shook his head in disgust. "Of course, the Twenty-third would have insisted on going, even if they hadn't drawn the mission."

"You've trained them well, Max," Emerson said. "Their sense of dedication is inspiring."

"They're not so much dedicated to the RDF as they are to a Zentraedi ethic." Max looked at Miriya for confirmation.

Miriya nodded without saying anything. The three of them were in the small living room of the Sterlings' highrise apartment. Dana was playing at Emerson's feet, tying his shoelaces into knots.

"What's going to happen to Treng?" Emerson asked.

"He'll stand trial for war crimes."

"A waste of time," Miriya said suddenly. "Treng has already admitted his guilt. The thing to do now is to let him run." She used the Zentraedi term *Kara-Thun*, which referred to a trial-by-combat ritual, wherein a traitor to the Imperative could be absolved of a wrongdoing by defeating an appointed opponent. "I'd gladly volunteer as the chase."

Max looked at her askance. "Not exactly a fitting role for the model of acculturation."

"What does that mean, anymore? The factory satellite is supposed to be acculturation headquarters, and it was from among the Zentraedi there that Breetai and Exedore chose the members of the Twenty-third. Besides, Max, since the RDF has turned the policing over to the Zentraedi, why not the punishment as well? It was the Twenty-third that captured the Iron Ravens, so it should be the Twenty-third that is granted the honor of dispatching them."

Emerson cut his soulful eyes to Max. "I think Ilan would have agreed with Miriya."

"I was sorry to hear about Ilan, Rolf."

Emerson took a long breath. "It's strange. She never visited Zagerstown until the day of the Paranka's Stinger attack." He studied his hands. "But after the attack, she called to say that she'd seen the light, and had to take part in the uprising."

"And Ilan Tinari would have understood the need to let Treng run," Miriya told him. "Unlike Humans, we Zentraedi do not distinguish between friendly and unfriendly fire. Death comes wherever one finds it. So much the better when it comes in battle."

"Do you miss Buenos Aires?" Max asked, hoping to change the conversation.

"I sure miss the food."

Max made a gesture of dismissal. "Montana's beef is every bit as good as the Argentine's."

Emerson shrugged noncommittally. "There are some people I miss, too. But I'll be going back and forth for a while—until the base is fully phased."

"What are your duties in Monument, Rolf?" Miriya asked.

"Same as my old duties, only more so. If Senator Moran is elected president of a unified Southlands, his resignation from the UEG will open the door for establishing a Southlands embassy here in Monument."

"Makes the Southlands seem like a separate nation," Max said, disgruntled.

"It *is* a separate nation. Let's face it, we've blown our chance at becoming one world by allowing politics to take precedence over the needs of the people. With Moran and Leonard ruling the Southlands, and comparable separatist movements going on in Europe and Asia, we're returning to turn-of-the-century factionalism."

"There's a pleasant thought," Max said, then smiled lightly. "But I'll confess, Rolf, I'm glad to have you up here."

"And Rolf's lucky to have arrived just in time for the thaw," Miriya said sarcastically. "I want to hear what you have to say about Monument when you're up to your knees in mud."

"Mud-*dah*," Dana mimicked.

Emerson looked down at her and grinned. "Do you like to play in the mud, Dana?"

Dana glanced briefly at Miriya. "Mommie yells at me. But I do it anyway."

Max laughed. Rolf and Dana had really hit it off. That he had the energy for a three-year-old was commendable; but that he had the patience for a three-year-old like Dana was exemplary. Not even Dana's Zentraedi godfathers were as tolerant of her shenanigans. Not even Professor Zand—though his patience with her seemed more a product of scientific interest than anything else.

"Too bad Admiral Hunter had to cancel," Emerson said. "I was looking forward to meeting him."

"Rick's not as available as he used to be," Max told him. "Although he did find the time to get engaged."

Miriya adopted a dubious look. "Now let's see if he can find the time to get married."

Only Emerson laughed. Max asked about Anatole Leonard's reaction to Oasis.

"For a change, he's leaving it to the media to point out that Oasis was the RDF's responsibility, and that such an act could never have occurred in the Southlands. The Army of the Southern Cross grows stronger without having to retaliate this time."

Miriya's green eyes narrowed. "In five years there won't be an RDF. The REF will return from Tirol to an Earth governed by Anatole Leonard."

Rolf regarded her for a long moment. "Will you be among them—the REF, I mean?"

Miriya looked at Dana. "I don't think so. No matter what happens between the RDF and the Southern Cross, I think Dana's better off on Earth than she would be locked inside that horrible factory for her entire childhood."

Lynn-Kyle and Theofre Elmikk met openly in the factory's level-six cafeteria. Kyle wore his service-personnel whites, a bar-code identity-information badge woven into the fabric of the unisuit's shirt collar and left sleeve. Elmikk wore his typical look of misanthropy.

"If I could have a minute of your time, *T'sen* Elmikk," Kyle said. "I have a few questions about food allocations for your work crews."

"We have nothing to discuss," Elmikk said, with a wary glance around the cafeteria. "My work crews have all they need just now."

"I'm talking about the crews operating *downside, T'sen* Elmikk."

The Zentraedi's expression hardened. "Those crews are no longer my concern."

"As long as the upside crews are well fed, is that the idea?"

Elmikk lowered his voice. "As I explained, I'm responsible to those directly in my command. The others should understand how difficult it has become to meet everyone's needs just now."

"I'm sure they do understand. Nevertheless, without adequate supplies they could starve. It's been six months since they received anything from you. As it is, they've been harassed by hostile forces in their environment. And now that the pressure on you has eased some—"

"They deserve harassment for the sloppiness of their work," Elmikk sneered. "That sloppiness reflects on *all* of us."

"Then I should inform them not to rely on you for further aid?"

"Tell them whatever you like."

Kyle laughed shortly. "Perhaps Jevna Parl would be more interested in the plight of those lower down in the food chain."

Elmikk met Kyle's openly hostile gaze. "Parl cares only about his relationship to Breetai. He would never jeopardize that by reaching out to others."

"I think you misjudge Jevna Parl's loyalty to the overall cause, *T'sen* Elmikk. He believes, as most of us do, that everyone should be equally provided for so that none go hungry."

The Zentraedi mulled it over for a long moment. "Listen to me, Cheng, or whatever your real name is—"

"Jeng Chiang," Kyle said calmly.

"Of course," Elmikk said. "My advice to you is that you begin to think of your own future, rather than expend your energies on lost causes. If and when the *hungry* realize their goal, where do you imagine you'll be? I'll tell you, Chiang: you'll be dead. They will have no further use for you, just as I have no use for you. So why not simply go down the well and find something better to do with the time that remains?"

Kyle stared at Elmikk's back as the brawny alien lumbered off. Their plan for hijacking the SDF-3 had to be nearing completion, he told himself, or Elmikk wouldn't have been so brazenly confident. He looked up at the cafeteria's forty-foot-high ceiling and contemplated the two heavily secured levels that separated him from Lisa Hayes and Breetai. They might as well be on the dark side of the moon.

Routinely, every evening, Breetai watched *Little White Dragon* in the privacy of his quarters aboard the transformed flagship he had once commanded. He would sit crosslegged on the deck, sometimes with several pounds of Human food, and the video—transmitted from an entertainment center on level three of the satellite—would run on the twenty-by-thirty-five-foot screen affixed to the bulkhead. Occasionally he would fall asleep before the video finished, or his attention would be distracted by thoughts of the refurbishing of the ship or the mission to Tirol and what it might hold for all of them. There were so many variables: an attack by the Invid, an attack by some other race the Zentraedi had crushed, an attack by Zentraedi ships that had somehow escaped the final disgrace of the War. How, in any event, might the Masters react to the Earthers' sudden appearance in Fantomaspace? Would they befriend them, or seek to enslave them as they had so many other races? And what, then, would be the fate of the Zentraedi? Not repatriation but execution, Breetai imagined. Swift and expedient, without prelude.

Lately, his thoughts had centered on the injustices Zor and the Zentraedi had conspired to deliver to Earth. Now, as if the Rain hadn't been enough, the survivors had to contend with scattered bands of programmed killers. The so-called malcontents had to be eradicated because they were a threat, just as Khyron had been, to the greater mission.

With Exedore's help, Breetai had come to understand the malcontents' hunger for vengeance, the loss of lives, the reprisals, the escalating violence. Most Zentraedi had instigated and lived through much worse. But he could neither condone the actions of his comrades nor demonstrate much respect for the RDF's attempt to find solutions to the malcontent dilemma. There were no solutions. It wasn't a matter of awarding them half the planet, or of supplying them with food, jobs, or civil rights. The Zentraedi rage came from a place no Human could visit—except perhaps those unfortunate few Breetai had encountered whose upbringing had instilled in them the equivalent of an Imperative, a pervasive lust to destroy. Though they were loath to admit it, Humans did have masters; they took the form of "parents," or sometimes the conditions of the Human society itself, with its complex laws meant to safeguard Humans from reverting to the violent ways of their ancestors in the animal kingdom.

What Breetai couldn't understand was how he had allowed himself to become so distanced from the concerns of his Earthbound comrades. In reference to some Human legend, Exedore often called the factory satellite their "ivory tower." And if Breetai didn't grasp the full meaning of the reference, he at least grasped the implication.

Little White Dragon was onscreen just now, at the point in the plot where the long-haired hero, played by Minmei's cousin, Lynn-Kyle, was dodging arrows loosed by a bearded giant wearing a black eye-patch and a plumed helmet. As often as Breetai had watched the film, he was forever discovering new things in each scene: background details, foreshadowings, or what were called "nuances" of characterization.

All at once, however, he knew that he was watching a scene he'd never seen before. Had the techs in the factory satellite sent him the "director's cut" or some such thing as a surprise? Onscreen, in any case, was the Lynn-Kyle character, in his standard belted robe and black slippers, in the midst of a monologue.

"The giant doesn't understand that I need not so much as strike out with fist or foot to defeat him; that I could simply stand aside and allow him to be undermined by his own troops," the character was saying.

The added scene had a different visual quality from the rest of the film—an almost live quality—and must have been shot long before or long after the major action, because Kyle's black hair, while long, was not as long as it should have been, nor did the strangely unfamiliar robe fit as well as it should. More, the backdrop was nothing more than the bare bulkhead of a starship—the SDF-1, certainly—awaiting special effects.

"For they covet what he has and they scheme to take that from him and flee this place for distant shores. They toil in secret, inching in on his safe domain. But I cannot stand aside; I will rob them of the honor of defeating him, even though I risk all that I have. That is as it must be, for the giant and I are linked by destiny."

With that, the film returned to a familiar scene. But Breetai was left with the nagging feeling that the Lynn-Kyle character had been talking directly to him.

"I'm so glad you could come, Lynn," Emil Lang told Minmei in the reception area of the Tokyo Research Center, taking her hand and kissing her on both cheeks. Minmei had a silk kerchief tied around her head, and was wearing a polka-dot sleeveless dress that was a bit lightweight for April.

"How could I say no to you, Dr. Lang? After everything you've done for me."

Lang smiled and shook hands with Minmei's manager, who wore an expensive knit suit and abundant gold jewelry. "Mr. O'Toole."

"Call me Sam, Doc."

"We had to be in Tokyo anyway," Minmei said. "The Lorelei Network is launching next month, and they want me to do my first show from here."

"The Zentraedi network," Lang said, nodding. "I'd heard that they'd signed you to do an interview show or something."

"More a talk show, Doc. But we're working on a guest list, too. Zentraedi guests, that is."

Lang looked at Minmei. "I hope this doesn't mean that you're giving up on touring."

"Not on your life," O'Toole answered for her. "That's our second—well, okay, our third reason for being in Asia. We're in the final stages of setting up a world tour to co-

incide with Minmei's inaugural appearance on Lorelei."
O'Toole grinned at Minmei. "We figure she can do the talk
show on live-remote from whatever city she's playing at the
time."

"Will you be the sole act, Lynn?"

"Aside from the usual warmup bands. Unless you've
found a partner for me, Dr. Lang."

Lang stared at her, then laughed. "Lynn, it's funny you
should say that . . ."

He began to lead the two of them on a tour of the main
floor of the center. When Lang wasn't describing the
goings-on in various labs, he and Minmei talked about old
friends from the SDF-1 and Macross City, and the upcoming trial of Jinas Treng. She asked after Lazlo Zand, and
Lang simply told her that he was busy with research, when
in fact he had no idea where Zand was. Lang noted that
Minmei avoided mentioning Rick or Lisa; he assumed that
their engagement was the reason. She did, however, wonder
if it would be possible for her to visit the factory satellite,
and Lang promised to make the necessary arrangements.

As they approached the staff room at the building's
northeast corner, Lang placed his right hand in the deep
pocket of his white jacket and depressed the button switch
on a coded transmitter. Seconds later a soprano voice was
lilting from behind the closed door to the staff room.

"Who is that singing?" Minmei asked.

"The person I asked you here to meet," Lang said. "My
niece. She's been working as a research assistant, but everyone here thinks she has a wonderful voice, and I was
wondering if you couldn't give her some advice on how to
get started as a professional."

"Is she related to the Bernards?"

"No, uh, the other side of the family."

Lang ushered Minmei and O'Toole into the staff room,
where his alleged niece was sitting at an electronic keyboard, improvising melodies for several of the techs from
cybernetics. O'Toole took one look at the center of attention and said, "Somebody pinch me, I think I'm dreaming."

"Uncle Emil," the singer said.

"I don't mean to disturb you, Janice, but I know you'd never forgive me if I didn't introduce you to—"

"Lynn-Minmei!" the android said, shooting to its feet. "Oh, my God!" The techs had outfitted JANUS M in jeans and a top that made the most of its custom proportions. Just now, though, the techs were torn between who to watch: Minmei or their creation.

"Lynn and Sam," Lang said, "I'd like you to meet Janice Em."

"You have a terrific voice," Minmei said.

"Terrific," O'Toole parroted, eyeing Janice blatantly. Five six, she weighed 110 pounds, and projected a kind of wan beauty, offset by large, deep-blue eyes.

Janice adopted a demure pose. "I was just toying with some vocal lines."

"Sing them again," Minmei said, walking over to the keyboard.

Janice seated herself; her perfectly formed fingers played over the keys and she began to sing. Minmei gradually joined in, harmonizing with Janice's melody. Lang and the cybertechs were the picture of restrained exaltation. O'Toole stood openmouthed in disbelief.

"Do you have an agent?" O'Toole asked when Minmei and Janice were finished.

Janice's eyes edged ever so slightly toward Lang. "At the moment, Mr. O'Toole, I answer only to my Uncle Emil."

The woman introduced herself as Tan. Athletically built, she had thousands of facial freckles, lackluster red hair, and the furtive look of a sympath—an advocate.

"How did you know where to contact me?" Zand asked her.

Tan laughed. "Word travels, Professor. Let's just say I heard about you from a guy who heard about you from a guy who heard you wanted to establish contact with the rebels."

"I never specified rebels."

"Maybe not. But you did say 'unaligned alien groups,' didn't you?"

Zand nodded. "What band do you represent?"

Tan held up her hands. "You're jumping the gun, Professor. You haven't even told me what you're after."

"I understand. It's just that a man of my position . . ."

"Sure, Professor. You don't want to risk exposure. But stop worrying—from now on you'll only be dealing with me. If I don't have what you need, I'll find the people that do. You won't have to be personally involved in any of it."

Zand relaxed somewhat. After a glance around the small park that surrounded the shrine, he sat down beside Tan on the bench she had chosen as their point of rendezvous. They were only a few miles from the research center, but Zand felt as if he were hundreds of miles from Tokyo.

"Now," Tan said suddenly, "exactly what did you have in mind when you said you were interested in 'alien artifacts'?"

Zand reseated his dark glasses. "I'm looking for examples of Invid battlecrafts—any that may have been captured and taken aboard by the Zentraedi, and have since ended up on Earth."

Tan made an exaggerated show of surprise. "No wonder you couldn't say over the phone. Here I was thinking you meant Zentraedi artifacts when you were talking about Invid stuff." She shook her head. "But I'm afraid you've got me, Professor. I wouldn't even know where to begin looking."

"But you'll ask around? Spread the word?"

"Sure, but—"

"What about Flower of Life?"

Tan laughed in astonishment. "You've got to be kidding. Why not ask me for Khyron's brain? Trust me, whatever Flowers there were died with him."

"Yes, but I've heard rumors about the Flower growing on Earth, and I know that some of Khyron's troops still operate in the Southlands."

"You mean the Fist."

"Yes, yes, the Fist."

"I don't know, you'll have to give me a little time—"

"What about a couple of liters of blood from a full-size Zentraedi?"

Tan regarded him in wary puzzlement. "Giants' blood?

You should have thought of that before you had everyone in the Protectorate Micronized."

Anger contorted Zand's features. "I didn't have anything to do with that. It was those UEG fools."

Tan shrugged. "Maybe so, but the only full-size are on the factory, and you'd certainly have an easier time getting onboard than I would."

Zand worked his jaw. "All right. But you will remember to inquire about Invid craft and the Flower?"

"I'll remember. Give me a couple of weeks."

"Two."

Tan shook her head in amusement. "Okay, two weeks."

Zand pulled a piece of paper from his jacket pocket, scribbled a phone number, and handed it to her. "Call me day or night when you have something."

Tan glanced at the paper and pocketed it. "You can be sure of it, Professor."

CHAPTER
TWENTY-ONE

It has been remarked that old habits die hard. How else to explain the re-emergence of the corrupt fin-de-siècle World Unification Alliance as the equally corrupt Reconstruction Era United Earth Government, or the resurrection of the technophobic Faithful as the Church of Recurrent Tragedies? Rebirth would attend even the sinisterly wrought Lorelei Network when, in 2026, it reappeared as the EVE Network.

Zachary Fox, Jr., *Men, Women, Mecha:*
The Changed Landscape of the Second Robotech War

"**H**ELLO, CALLER, YOU'RE ON THE LORELEI NETwork."

"Minmei?"

"Yes, this is Minmei, and you're on the air."

The WorldPhone connection was interrupted by brief static. Then: ". . . name is Karita, and I just wanted to say that I'm a big fan."

"I'm glad you enjoy my songs, Karita. And I'm glad for the chance to talk personally with you and all Zentraedi who have learned to appreciate the joys of music."

It was her first call and she was nervous, but the cameras didn't seem to be capturing her inner agitation. On the monitor screen she appeared calm, confident, warm, accessible—all that the network chiefs were expecting of her. "Remember that the Zentraedi aren't so much fans as worshipers," one executive had thought to point out. "They're going to be satisfied just seeing you and talking to you. So in a sense, it won't so much matter what you say to them, as how you look when you say it."

Which explained why wardrobe had selected such a short shirt, and why the hair stylist had insisted on making the most of her bangs.

"I've been a follower of yours since the War, Minmei," the caller was saying. "In fact, I was a charter member of the fan club that Rico and Konda started on Commander Breetai's flagship. I held a position onboard as sizing-chamber operator. I know Rico, Bron, and Konda personally. Well, I knew them, anyway."

"You haven't seen them for a while?"

Some of the excitement left Karita's voice. "Not in a long while. We can't all be lucky enough to be living like celebrities in Monument City."

"I'm sure you have a fine life just where you are."

"You think so, Minmei? You think I have a fine life? Maybe you want to hear about my life since I left Monument."

"I'd be very interest—"

"I could see that Monument wasn't going to be worth a damn once everyone from Macross started relocating. I'll never understand why they couldn't have just built another city for themselves and left Monument to the Zentraedi. But I suppose we should be grateful for the year of autonomy we enjoyed. After all, we're the defeated ones. We're fortunate even to be alive, isn't that so?"

Minmei tried not to sound flustered, but she wasn't comfortable with the turn the conversation had taken. "I think that all of us are fortunate to be alive."

"Yes, of course that's true. And a lot of Humans have had to suffer the rigors of deprivation in the aftermath of the Rain. But I wonder how many of them have ever been denied food or been chased by an angry mob. I wonder how many of them know what it's like to lack the skills necessary for survival, to be a needful thing wherever one goes, just another mouth to feed—another *alien* mouth to feed. To be blamed for every strike the malcontents have launched against the Human race—"

"My guest today is going to be addressing just those issues, Karita," Minmei cut in, her voice quivering with urgency. "He was the head of a construction battalion in the Protectorate, and he has a lot of interesting things to say about the plight of the jobless and the homeless, and about the malcontents—"

"More *talking*," Karita said, full of invective. "Another voice to spew the UEG party line that civil rights for the Zentraedi will be reinstated as soon as the uprisings are put down. How easy for your guest, or for Rico or Exedore or Miriya to talk from their cozy homes in Monument or on the factory satellite about the plight of their comrades. Well, I think it's just a pack of lies, Minmei, it's just a pack of Human lies—"

In the studio control booth, the show's producer drew a finger across his throat and opened the microphone that fed into Minmei's earbead. "I had to dump that one, Lynn. But pretend he's still on the line. Fake an upbeat good-bye, and we'll go to a song."

Minmei looked into the camera. "Uh, thank you for being so forthright, Karita. We certainly do have a lot of work cut out for us if we're to solve these problems. And solve them, we will. Uh, please feel free to call us again sometime soon." She smiled and forced a sigh. "I think we're off to a good start. And we'll return right after this song."

A live version of "To Be In Love" played behind concert footage filmed in Portland in 2013. Momentarily free of the camera's scrutiny, Minmei threw a panicked look at the control booth. "Are they *all* going to be like that?"

Behind the glass partition, the producer made a calming gesture. "Don't worry, we'll screen the next few callers."

Minmei took a moment to collect herself. When the music video ended, she faced the camera, awaiting the producer's on-air signal. "Welcome back to the Love Line. That was the first song I wrote, and it's still one of my favorites. Now, I see we have another caller waiting. Bagzent," she read from an off-camera computer display screen, "you're on the Lorelei Network."

"Yeah, Minmei. I just wanted to respond to some of the things said by your first caller."

Minmei gulped, but managed to say, "Go ahead, Bagzent."

"I just wanted to tell him—what was his name? Karita? I just wanted to tell him that if he's after inner peace and freedom, he's looking in the wrong direction. Freedom isn't about where you live, or how well you live, or even how you're treated by your fellow creatures. You find freedom by surrendering yourself to Wondrous Spirit and accepting that you're a part of something bigger than Earth or the Sol system or the Fourth Quadrant of the galaxy.

"Wondrous Spirit knows that I've done shameful things in my lifetime. During the War, I destroyed a lot of Veritechs, in space and on the surface of the planet you know as Mars. And after the Rain, I aligned myself with Khyron and participated in his raids on Detroit. Just these past two years I've taken part in the capture of the Grand Cannon, and I've led Stinger attacks on convoys everywhere from the Venezuela Sector to Mato Grosso.

"I've taken hundreds of Human lives, Minmei. But I recently made a choice that's made all the difference in my life: I denied the Imperative. I chose life over what most Zentraedi would consider an honorable death. And when I did that, Wondrous Spirit took me in and forgave me for all my past crimes. Now, each day I rejoice in the sights and sounds and smells of the world Wondrous Spirit brought into being. This is what Karita has to learn if he wants to be free. This is what all Zentraedi need to learn, whether they're on the factory, or Micronized residents of the Protectorate, or armed hostiles aligned with one of the malcontent bands, such as I was. Love life. Love the world for what it is. Love Wondrous Spirit."

Bagzent hung up, and Minmei gave her head a slight shake, as if snapping to. "Um, thank you, Bagzent, for those . . . uplifting words." She glanced briefly at the control booth to find the producer beaming and nodding his head. "Now let's go to . . . Tomina, from Australia. You're on the Lorelei Network."

"You silly creature," a raspy feminine voice began. "You've got no more intellect than one of those squeeze toys fashioned in your image during the War. Many a male Zentraedi fell prey to your big eyes and your child's voice, but the Quadrono knew an imposter when they saw one. And as for 'Bagzent' and his 'Wondrous Spirit,' let me say that he's typical of the brainless clones and Flower addicts that comprised Khyron Kravshera's Seventh Mechanized Division."

Minmei struggled for something to say. "Miriya Parino was a Quadrono, wasn't she? Maybe you know—"

"I didn't call to talk about Miriya Parino or any other *hajoca* Zentraedi. And I definitely didn't call to waste my time talking to you." Tomina paused for a moment. "But I do have a message for Doctor Lang or any RDF officers who might be listening. They should be advised that the Claimers have recently come into possession of something that belongs to them, and we're going to keep this thing until satisfactory terms of exchange can be arranged."

"Please, Tomina," Minmei said, "not another nuclear bomb."

The woman laughed. "No, Minmei, not a bomb. Something even more powerful: a Professor Lazlo Zand."

Minmei stared into the camera, slack-jawed. "I don't understand—"

"We've abducted him, you pathetic excuse for a female! And we're going to kill him if the RDF won't meet our demands." Tomina forced a laugh. "Zand won't be as lucky as you and Kyle were when the Backstabber grabbed you. The Claimers have no such weaknesses. We'll be in touch soon."

Minmei stared openly at the control booth. "Go to a song, go to a song!" the producer was yelling into her ear.

"Put that away!" Seloy ordered the brown-haired Scavenger holding the WorldPhone. She gestured to the TV monitor on which a music video of Minmei's "Stagefright" was running. "And zero that thing before I smash it to pieces."

The six Scavengers inside the thatch-roofed hut hurried to comply. Outside, a sonorous rain was drenching the cloud forest camp, and the air inside the hut was superheated.

"You don't see what they're doing with this satellite network?" Seloy told them. "They're tracing the calls to their point of origin. Operatives of the RDF or the Southern Cross are probably already moving on Bagzent and Tomina Jepp. Idiots!"

She stormed from the hut, out into torrential rain, and

across the clearing to Xan Norri's personal quarters in a longhouse the aborigines had built. Inside, the mecha designer, Vivik Bross, and Marla Stenik were all on their haunches around a fire whose smoke was slowly exiting through the sodden thatch.

"I'll wager they switched the television back on as soon as you left," Xan said after Seloy had explained what she had witnessed in the hut. "Nearly everyone in camp is watching the show. They might not be enslaved to her in the same way the males are, but they're fascinated that one female—one tiny, seemingly guileless female at that—could wield such power over so many males."

"Fascinated enough to willingly risk detection by the RDF," Seloy said in disgust, squeezing water from her red hair. She walked in a circle. "I thought we were smarter than that. But, then, I never thought I'd see the day the RDF would create a Zentraedi Veritech squadron, either."

"We are smarter," Marla said. "But we're not without faults and shortcomings."

Seloy shot her a glance. "Don't you dare rank us with them, Marla. They envy the powerful. All I want is revenge."

"Power in another guise," Marla countered.

Seloy maintained her gimlet stare. "A Zentraedi guise, at least. We'll never succeed if we conduct ourselves like Humans. We might as well surrender to Anatole Leonard, or seek honorable death here and now. *Kara-brek.*"

Xan rose and went to Seloy, placing her hands on Deparra's wet shoulders. "You contradict yourself, *T'sen* Deparra. There can be no honor in death until Humankind has been repaid in full for the humiliation it has heaped on our people." She cracked a smile. "And rest assured, *T'sen,* I've discovered a way of doing that without having to rely on any of our comrades—male or female."

"How?" Seloy asked. "Tell me."

Xan's smile blossomed sinisterly. "I've been studying Earth's endless array of spiders, and they've given me an idea. In place of terror, we're going to vector *madness.*"

* * *

In a mecha bay, forward in the much-altered flagship, Theofre Elmikk raised the audio gain on his headset earphones, impatient for word from his confederates that the inner hull of the factory satellite was breached and that the assault on the weightless ship had begun.

Elsewhere in the compartment, scattered among construction teams of Humans and Micronized Zentraedi, additional members of Elmikk's rebel brigade were engaged in retrofit work. The bay—indeed the entire ship—was less populated than normal, owing to the premiere of Lynn-Minmei's call-in show on the newly launched Lorelei Network. Excused from duty, hundreds of Zentraedi were gathered in front of giant TV screens or vying for use of the phones that could put them in direct communication with their idol. Even Exedore, Jevna Parl, and Breetai himself had announced that they would be attending a special screening of the show on level eight of the factory. As a result, the flagship was relatively deserted.

And ripe for seizing.

Elmikk's mind and body were flooded with stimulants only the aroused Imperative could supply. Working in utmost secrecy, in stolen moments when they should have been dismantling derelict ships, his confederates had spent nearly a year cutting and boring a meandering passageway into the heart of the factory satellite. Heavy work drones—the 112-ton so-called "Mr. Arms" models—had helped open a portal in the outer hull, midships, between the three- and six-o'clock pods. From there, under the very eyes of hundreds of slumbering computer-controlled security robots, the passageway had been punched straight into the immense service chase that separated the satellite's seventh and eighth levels. There, after passing through some partitions and bulkheads and zigzagging around others, it shot ship's upward—close to where the drops of Protoculture cells had been made when Elmikk's smuggling operation was up and running—to the edge of the null-g zone where the former flagship of Breetai's battle group was being transformed into a crass replica of Zor's fortress.

All along, Elmikk had been vigilant in his search for the proper moment to commandeer the ship. When he had learned about the inauguration of Lorelei Network, he took it as a good omen.

Just now, four Mr. Arms and two skeleton-crewed EVA vehicles were lasering a 200-by-200-foot-wide opening through the last remaining inch of the satellite's inner membrane. Because the completed opening would immediately seal itself, there would be no turning back for the full-size Zentraedi tasked with storming the ship. While their EVA vehicles were attacking from the outside, Elmikk's contingent would advance on the bridge, disabling the ship's internal security en route. Just as their earlier efforts had been eased somewhat by the factory's still-glitched central computer, the successful conclusion of the plan would owe something to the formation of the Twenty-third Squadron—most of the squadron's pilots had been drawn from SDF-3 security, leaving trainees to fill in for hardened soldiers.

"*Ferret team to control*," a familiar voice said through the earphones. "*We're committed.*"

Elmikk employed a coded communications frequency to pass the word to his cohorts in the bay, and the effect was instantaneous: kicks from giant legs undermined scaffolding, sending scores of Humans plummeting to the deck; sweeps of giant arms and flicks from giant fingers sent scores more tumbling and sprawling; claps from giant hands flattened entire teams. At the same time, one full-size hurried across the bay to Elmikk and gently plucked him from the floor. Joined by three others, Elmikk's runner raced for the levitation tube that accessed the bridge.

Before they had made it halfway, two of the four were brought down by SDF-3 security guards—the factory's only armed Zentraedi. Nevertheless, Elmikk's carrier and another managed to reach the tube unharmed. Elmikk knew from his years aboard the satellite that the guards at the upper-level stations were unarmed; more importantly, most of them had taken the day off. Success was assured, he told himself, hoping that luck was riding with the assault team outside the ship as well. The EVA vehicles were at least equipped with industrial lasers that could be used against any resistance.

When the levitation tube had deposited them at the forward end of the bridge, Elmikk instructed his carrier to set him on the elevated catwalk that ran aft to the command bubble. He then ordered his two full-size comrades to wait by the tube egress to intercept anyone in pursuit.

Only two tasks remained; maneuvering the flagship out of the factory and folding it to freedom. Once free of the satellite, the ship would slow only long enough to collect members of the brigade, along with any others who wanted in on the mutiny. As for the fold, Elmikk was confident he could execute the commands in correct sequence. Correct enough to steer them clear of stellar interiors, at any rate, if not jump them directly to Tirol. His confederates were ignorant of the fact that fail-safes hardwired into the fold systemry of all flagships ensured against hyperspace mishaps. Their ignorance served him well, however, since a properly executed fold would accord him with enough cachet to assume unchallenged command of the ship.

And wouldn't Breetai and the rest be in for a surprise. Vilify Theofre Elmikk though they would, the Zentraedi would have to respect the brilliance and daring of his action.

Behind him, Elmikk heard the clamorous sounds of a struggle; then rapid bootsteps, which he assumed to be those of his full-size comrades. He had just begun to turn his head when he was snatched from the catwalk deck by the tall collar of his jacket and pressed to the transparent convexity of the eyelike command bubble. It was only then that he took note of Exedore and Jevna Parl, standing side by side in the now-Human-sized control center. When he finally managed to look behind him, Elmikk found Breetai's one good eye glowering at him.

"Had you actually convinced yourself that you would succeed at this?" Exedore asked, advancing a step toward the transparency.

"You're dead, Formo," Elmikk snarled. "All of you—dead. The ship is ours. You'll be sorry you're not off listening to Minmei."

Exedore looked past Elmikk to Breetai and fingered a switch on a console that replicated one on the SDF-1. "Listen closely," he advised.

Elmikk listened, but didn't hear a thing.

Exedore cleared his throat. "Allow me to describe what you would be hearing if vacuum didn't prevent the transmission of sonic waves: the sounds of your heavy work drones and EVA vehicles exploding. The agonized sounds of your confederates in the moments before death. The sounds of your dreams being torn asunder."

Elmikk went slack in Breetai's fingertip hold.

"Your apparent self-deception notwithstanding," Exedore continued, "what made you think you possessed sufficient vigor to command a flagship?"

Elmikk's mouth twisted out of shape. "I know all about the fold fail-safes, Forma. Vigor resides in the ship, not in the ship's commander."

Exedore cupped his chin with his right hand. "Again, you seem to have been misinformed. Command of a flagship is awarded only after one has demonstrated the ability to execute a fold in the absence of fail-safes. This ship has no such backup systemry, Elmikk. You and your brigade of mutineers would have ended your lives in the nuclear core of a star."

Elmikk shut his eyes and kept them shut for a long moment; then, using his hands to angle himself away from the curved transparency, he risked a turn toward Breetai. "How did you know, *T'sen* Breetai? Who among my people betrayed me? Grant me that much peace of mind to see me to my doom."

Breetai growled lightly. "I'll grant this, Elmikk: Your treachery came to me in a scene."

No sooner had Tomina Jepp announced the abduction of Lazlo Zand than her location was pinpointed and an encrypted call was placed from Lorelei headquarters in Tokyo to T. R. Edwards in Monument City. Once in receipt of all relevant data, Edwards placed three calls: one to the Special Operations Group's chief-of-station in Sydney, Australia, the city closest to Jepp's location; the second to the director of intelligence for the Army of the Southern Cross, in Brasília; and the third, placed some fifteen minutes later, to

Niles Obstat, who immediately relayed the data to RDF Command.

Though tuned to Minmei's show from the beginning, Rick Hunter didn't receive confirmation on the source of Jepp's call for almost two hours, and even then he was not apprised of how the call had been traced or which agency had traced it. Rick's first action was to call Cavern City, where the Twenty-third Squadron was based, and place Jonathan Wolff in charge of liaison between RDF Command and the Zentraedi Veritech team.

While all this was occurring, a crack Southern Cross squadron of reactor-driven LVT Adventurer II jet fighters was already airborne. Diplomatic protocols had already been seen to, and the squadron commander was in constant communication with Field Marshal Leonard and T. R. Edwards, who was receiving hourly updates from SOG's COS in Sydney.

Having placed a second call to the Lorelei Network, during which she had issued the Claimers' demands—the immediate release of Jinas Treng and Neela Saam—Jepp had been positively identified in the town of Alice Springs, in Australia's Outback, and was under surveillance by operatives there. Confidence was high that Jepp would unknowingly guide the follow team to the Claimers' base, and, presumably, to the spot where Lazlo Zand was being held.

The base was discovered to be a series of large caves in a feldspar-rich sandstone formation southeast of Ayer's Rock, where the thirty-six members of the Zentraedi outlaw band were living in feral conditions. Scans by FLIR and an IFF device similar to the one employed by Destroids to discriminate between Zentraedi and Earth mecha revealed that Professor Zand, guarded by two Zentraedi females armed with pre-War assault rifles, was chained to the floor of a small cave more than a mile from the Claimers' warren.

Under orders from Leonard, the fighter squadron struck at their target on arrival, loosing a dozen Decamissiles straight into the caves. It was doubtful the Claimers even knew what hit them. Zand was not so much rescued as saved by the faulty firing mechanism of the rifle one of his female captors had shoved down his throat shortly before she and her companion in the cave were shot to death by SOG operatives.

Ash was all that was left of the Claimers by the time the Twenty-third Squadron arrived on the scene. Tomina Jepp had been found on a dirt roadway ten miles west of Ayer's Rock. The story went that, faced with captivity, she had committed suicide by setting fire to her vehicle and herself.

"None of the *Little White Dragon* videos and laser disks aboard the factory contain the scene you describe," Lisa assured Breetai. "Every one of them was examined for signs of tampering, and the results were negative."

"I know what I saw," Breetai said.

"And no one is doubting you, Commander," Exedore said quickly. "We simply have no explanation to offer."

It was the day after the attempted skyjacking of the SDF-3, and the three of them, along with Jevna Parl, Harry Penn, R. Burke, and assorted security officers, were in the factory's command center. Breetai was standing on the bridge, so positioned that his face was level with the command bubble.

"You're certain the actor in the scene was Lynn-Kyle?" Burke asked.

"I have no doubt that it was Lynn-Kyle."

Lisa shook her head in puzzlement, then turned to the chief of security for the factory. "Post photos of Kyle at all checkpoints, and conduct a compartment-by-compartment search of all levels of the factory. Also, I want a review of all background checks done on factory service personnel. And until further notice, no one is to go down the well without full authorization from station control, REF and RDF control, contagion control, and security control. Is that understood?"

The woman saluted. "But permit me to point out that the video Breetai watched ran over a month ago. The person responsible has had almost that long to arrange for departure. He or she might already be downside, Admiral."

"Then find out if anyone has failed to report for duty, Captain," Lisa said more harshly than she meant to.

"Sir!"

Lisa looked to a second officer. "Do we have casualty figures?"

"Six Human technicians and eight Micronized Zentraedi died as a result of injuries sustained in the mecha bay; eight Humans and four Zentraedi are in guarded condition in sick bay. Five Humans and three Zentraedi died in attacks on their tugs in the work zone. In addition, three full-size security personnel died inboard the SDF-3, and two others are in critical condition."

"How many of Elmikk's people were killed?"

"Our initial total was twenty-one—all but two in the work zone."

"How many do we have in custody?"

The officer glanced at Breetai. "Until this morning we had fifty-six. That figure includes the twenty members of Elmikk's labor crew who were outside the factory when the raid occurred."

"Have the numbers changed since this morning?"

Again the officer looked at Breetai.

"I had all but Elmikk executed," Breetai announced.

Everyone stared at him in mute horror until Jevna Parl said, "Commander, I must protest. You vowed there would be no executions without a consensus."

Breetai was stone-faced. "As commander, it was my prerogative, Jevna. Elmikk's confederates could not have been rehabilitated. We would certainly have had to deal with them in the future—perhaps with disastrous results."

"But, Breetai," Lisa managed. "The courts might have sentenced them to Micronization."

Breetai sneered. "Need I remind you that the malcontent bands are made up of Micronized Zentraedi?"

"Of course not, but . . . All of this could have been avoided if you'd told me or any REF officer about Elmikk's plan *before* he had the chance to carry it out. There still would have been a trial—and sentencing for the guilty."

Exedore answered for Breetai. "With all due respect, Admiral Hayes, you miss the point. We Zentraedi do not comprehend the concept of punishment before the fact. Any plan, scheme, or strategy, no matter how pernicious, is only that until its execution. In other words, there is no crime in the planning. How, otherwise, would the Zentraedi have tolerated the likes of Khyron? Micronization, or some other form of corporal punishment, for a 'thought crime' would have been a greater cruelty than honorable death, and substantially more dangerous, ultimately. Consider the inordinate number of former Protectorate residents that have turned to suicide or acts of malcontentism. In the absence of any demonstrable wrongdoing, they have no understanding of what was forcibly done to them."

Jevna Parl broke in. "You justify an outmoded barbarism, Exedore. The Zentraedi have changed; we are more than what we once were."

"That had better be the case for every Zentraedi aboard this factory," Breetai said balefully. "I confess that Elmikk fooled me. But I vow that I will not be dishonored a second time."

CHAPTER
TWENTY-TWO

It was during her brief hospitalization for stress-related depression that [Katherine] Hyson met Crystal Simmenz, the woman who would become her lover and companion. A close cousin of Leonard's adjutant, Joseph Petrie, Simmenz, living then in Brasília and flirting with the fledgling Zentraedi-rights movement, is now known to have been the person who "recruited" Seloy Deparra for Leonard. The story goes that Leonard, months into the affair, had ordered Simmenz disappeared, along with those who had assisted in Deparra's artificial insemination. But Petrie intervened, and Simmenz was instead sentenced to spend the next several years on the locked wards of a variety of mental health facilities. How she reached Monument City Hospital, where she encountered Hyson in the spring of 2018, is unknown. Hyson wrote an e-book about Simmenz's allegations that did not find a publisher until 2050, when Anatole Leonard's relationship with Deparra was corroborated by the discovery of the Supreme Commander's private journals, and Miriya Parino Sterling finally revealed what she knew about Deparra and the hybrid child, Hirano.

footnote in Marco Gala's
Halflife: Monument City Between the Wars

"WHEN THE EVENING NEWS RETURNS," Rebecca Hollister said from the anchor's chair, "we continue with our follow-up of some of the year's major stories." No sooner did the show go to commercials than the squabbling began all over again.

"I developed that feature and I should be the one to present it!" Katherine Hyson yelled from the side of the set, where she was being gently restrained by two strapping MBS security guards. "It's mine, Hollister, it's mine!"

Rebecca looked imploringly at the director. "Phil, you've got to get her out of here. Promise her anything, just get her the hell away from me until we wrap. I refuse to have a scene on camera."

The director was already angling for Hyson. "I'll take care of everything. You just concentrate on what you're doing. Remember, tonight's the key to sweeps week."

Rebecca vented her exasperation while two men from makeup refreshed her face and hair. "Really, Phil, I don't even know why you allow her inside the building. Don't force me to seek a restraining order."

The director showed the palms of his hands as he closed on Hyson and the guards. "No problem," he mouthed in a whisper. The assistant director assumed the task of counting the show back on the air.

"In Monument City, the long-awaited trials of Jinas Treng and Theofre Elmikk were postponed indefinitely in response to violent riots by Zentraedi advocacy groups around the world. Chief Justice Justine Huxley has stated that a special war crimes tribunal will be created to handle the trials at some future date. Until then, Treng—accused of detonating the nuclear device that destroyed Oasis—and Elmikk—accused of attempted skyjacking of the SDF-3— remain in custody at an undisclosed location.

"In related stories, both the RDF and the Army of the Southern Cross scored victories in their increasingly competitive struggles not only to rout the Malcontents but to win the confidence and support of the Human and alien public. In India, an RDF Veritech team sank the Russian-made destroyed *Biko*, which the Lyktauro Malcontents have been using to launch raids on coastal settlements throughout Southeast Asia; while in Eastern Europe, the ASC carried out surgical strikes against rebel bases in the New Marxist Republic, which have been supplying arms to Malcontents in the Southlands.

"In the Argentine, meanwhile, Field Marshal Leonard's troops have captured the last of the Paranka, also known as the Burrowers, whose Stinger attack on Zagerstown in November 2016 left 271 dead. And in Venezuela, Catherine Wolff, spokesperson for Governor Carson of Cavern City, reports that the Zentraedi Twenty-third Squadron has dealt a devastating blow to the Shroud and Fist in the Upper Orinoco region.

"But nowhere is the rivalry between the RDF and the

ASC more pronounced than in central Mexico, where special forces troops from the two armies have been engaged in the search for a sizing chamber believed to have fallen into Malcontent hands. The Zentraedi have inflicted heavy damages on both sides, and several specialists in alien terror tactics are now beginning to question whether the chamber even exists. Says one unnamed source, 'The rumor bears the signature of the Scavengers.'

"And it's expected that later this week the various member city-states of the Southlands will ratify unification and secede from the United Earth Government. Wyatt Moran, who resigned his position in the UEG last month, will be instated as President of the Southlands, with Anatole Leonard serving as both minister of war and commander-in-chief of the armed forces. Moran has promised that he will press the UEG to divert funds from the Expeditionary mission to the rebuilding of forward observation bases on the Moon and Mars. Two outspoken critics of the REF mission, Bishop Nboto and Joanna Ricter-Fields, have already pledged to support Moran's plan.

"In other news, controversy continues over the efficacy and the ethics of the Lorelei Network. Does the music network have the interests of the Zentraedi in mind, or are its owners engaging in mind control aimed at pacification? Lynn-Minmei, host of the popular call-in show *Love Line*, was unavailable for comment. But her new singing partner, Janice Em, told MBS News that Minmei plans to continue doing her show while on tour. In an attempt to avert some of the allegations, the Lorelei Network has begun distributing free food to Zentraedi throughout the Southlands.

"In Denver, epidemiologists at the Center for Disease Control have no explanation for the virus that has killed five in Mexico and in outlying areas of the Venezuela Sector."

Rebecca lifted a thin stack of hardcopy pages, stood them on end, and tapped them on the top of the desk. "When we come back, video transmissions from the edge of the Solar system, where robots are salvaging pieces of ice-bound Macross Island ... The Nicaragua Canal nears completion ... The timely electronic publication of Kermit

Busganglion's *The Hand That's Dealt You* . . . And the REF releases photos of its latest creations—the Alpha Veritech, the Hovertank, and the gargantuan Ground Mobile Unit— and of its new, and some say 'sexy,' uniforms.

"All after these words."

2018

CHAPTER TWENTY-THREE

I like Janice, and her range is absolutely astounding, but I feel like she's being forced on me. I've never had a partner because I've never wanted one. But the way Emil and Sharky make it sound, the partnership is more about patriotism than show business. "Your voices are the perfect complement to one another," Emil told me the last time he phoned. "Together, you and Janice will be a force to be reckoned with should there be a second Zentraedi invasion while the SDF-3 is absent." I don't know what to do. I'd hoped I'd outgrown being a weapon. I haven't even asked Janice how she feels about it—she's such a robot sometimes, the idea of being a machine probably doesn't bother her in the least. But I guess I'll have to give it a try. I know I'll never forgive myself if there is another invasion and my voice alone fails. So here I go being used again.

from the diaries of Lynn-Minmei

RICK AND LISA HAD MANAGED TO SPEND CHRISTMAS of 2017 together on the satellite, and Lisa made a surprise visit to the surface for the vernal equinox. But they hadn't seen each other in almost five months when Rick and his adjutant, Vince Grant, traveled up the well in August of 2018 to inspect the GMU and to tour the completed sections of the SDF-3. The years on the factory had turned Lisa hard and lean, and the tight fit of the new REF torso harness enhanced her figure. Rick couldn't keep his hands off her, and had taken several playful slaps as a result. They were in the factory hold where the 245-foot-long Ground Mobile Unit—also known as the MTA-Titan, for Military All-Terrain Mecha Transport and Assault Vehicle—was under construction when Rick finally got around to posing the question that had been on his mind since leaving Monument City.

"Can we get married right now—while I'm here, I mean? Before another year goes by."

Lisa seemed stunned, though flattered. "Rick, you know that's impossible. First of all, who would perform the ceremony?"

"Lisa, you've got chaplains from every denomination on-board. We could even get *Breetai* to perform the ceremony."

"Is that your idea of a conventional wedding? As admirals, maybe we should perform it ourselves, huh?"

Rick tugged her away from a host of eavesdroppers. "What's your real reason for saying no?"

"Rick, I want this as much as you do. But I want our wedding to be something special, not just some rushed affair. Besides, we both have so much—"

"Don't even say it. You were saying it a year ago, and you'll be saying it a year from now. And that's exactly why I'm saying we do something for *us* for a change."

"Now's a really bad time, Rick." She lowered her voice somewhat. "Things haven't been the same here since the skyjack attempt. Breetai's been blaming himself for what happened, and he and Jevna Parl have had a falling out over the execution of Elmikk's troops. And that's only half the story. I haven't even seen Emil in weeks."

"He's angry about the UEG's decision to fund the rebuilding of Sara and ALUCE bases." The acronym stood for Advanced Lunar Chemical Engineering.

"That decision is going to delay our mission by years."

"Right, again. But why do we have to delay *our* mission?"

Lisa almost weakened, but shook her head instead. "A delay is going to mean *more* work for us, not less."

"But it's beginning to feel like we're slipping apart, Lisa."

She stroked his arm. "We're not. We're getting stronger. It only feels that way because of the time between visits."

"And I think the separation would be easier to take if we were married."

"How would it be easier?"

"Because I'd know we're a team."

She laughed lightly. "We're already a team. I love you, and nothing's going to change that."

"I love you, too. It's driving me crazy how much I love you."

Lisa was about to step into his arms, protocol or not, when Vince Grant approached, obviously uneasy about something. "Sorry to have to interrupt—especially with bad news. But it can't wait: Max Sterling was shot down in the Congo."

"Oh, no," Lisa said weakly.

"He's okay," Grant said. "He escaped from the malcontent group that brought him down and was picked up in good shape by a member of the Twenty-third. The Argentine was the closest place where he could be evaluated for radiation-related illnesses, so Reinhardt ordered him brought to what used to be the base hospital."

"That's a relief," Rick said.

But Grant wasn't finished. "Miriya Sterling is missing," he announced. "The same day Max went down, she disappeared from Monument."

Lisa's eyes widened in concern. "Where's Dana?"

"She's fine. She's with Jean and Bowie right now," Vince said, referring to his wife and child. He cut his eyes to Rick once more. "Also, there's been a Stinger attack on a cargo plane en route to Cavern City."

Rick looked at the floor, then up at Vince. "How many killed?"

"That isn't known, because the plane hasn't been found." He paused. "General Reinhardt requests your presence downside ASAP."

Purposely silent, Rick looked at Lisa.

She adopted a brave smile. "The hand that's dealt you, Rick."

It was his own fault. He had had no business tagging along with the Twenty-third on their assignment to capture whomever remained of Jinas Treng's Iron Ravens. But he'd wanted a close look at the radioactive ruins of Oasis. And in the end it was the Ravens who had found him.

It should have been obvious that a band that had once possessed a nuclear device might also have ground-to-air missiles. Something capable of knocking a carelessly piloted VT out of the sky. And Max had been nothing if not careless—embarrassingly so. He was lucky he hadn't died on impact; even luckier that a member of the Twenty-third had been able to home in on Skull One's locator. But not before Max had gotten to enjoy the hospitality of the five Zentraedi malcontents that had downed him.

Their leader, Chodar, powerfully built and ponytailed, was disappointed that their missile had found a Human-piloted plane; he'd had his heart set on destroying one of the Zentraedi-piloted mecha. But Chodar's disappointment had changed to delight when he learned that he had captured none other than the ace of the RDF and the husband of the noted *hajoca*, Miriya Parino. Unaware that Max understood Zentraedi, one of Chodar's comrades—a bando-liered malcontent named Hossek—had suggested bringing Max to an upcoming meeting of the bands.

Max's chance for escape had come when they had asked him to sort through the circuitboards and junk they'd ripped from Skull One's cockpit console. They wanted usable parts—gifts, no doubt, for the Scavengers, who were hosting the meeting. Max had tricked his captors into thinking that Skull One had something extra special; and while the Ravens were busy puzzling over the useless device, Max had grabbed a Zentraedi assault rifle and shot his way out of their vermin-ridden headquarters, killing Hossek in the process.

Outside in the leveled city, he'd killed a second, the bald one named Zekku and then another, using a rock to crush the alien's skull. And then finally Chodar and the last Raven, bringing a wall down on them by using the over-loaded Zentraedi weapon as a bomb. Much later, when he analyzed the bloodlust that had driven him, he would attribute it to the feelings that had welled up inside him on first seeing Oasis from the air and thinking about the 50,000 innocents that had been murdered in an instant. Even so, it had been horrible to find himself in combat once more, back in the business of killing.

Now, here he was in a soft bed in the Argentine, pampered, fussed over, and feeling well enough in body if not in spirit. The view out the window of his private room encompassed part of the airstrip he'd looked across from the veranda of Rolf Emerson's on-base residence. The doctors had given him a clean bill of health—he had indeed been rad-dosed in Oasis, but not dangerously so—though they were insisting on keeping him under observation for a couple of days. He was for some reason prohibited from making calls, but he assumed that Miriya had been notified of his status.

He would know soon enough, in any case, because Rick had flown down to speak with him personally—Rick, who rarely left Monument other than to visit the factory satellite now and again. Max was certain he was in store for a major reaming-out, first for having gone to the Congo, then for allowing Skull One to get shot out from under him.

A nurse entered the room, smiled, and went to the window to adjust the horizontal blinds. "Captain Sterling, Admiral Hunter is on his way up. Is there anything I can get you before he arrives?"

"How about earplugs," Max said dourly.

Rick strolled in a few minutes later, looking fit, even distinguished in his REF uniform. His hair was long, and his face bore a few lines. He was starting to look like an admiral. Max had a memory of the young hotshot he had served under on-board the SDF-1. A lifetime ago.

"So you had to see Oasis, huh?" Rick began.

"You know how hungry you get for devastation when you haven't seen any in a while."

Rick nodded, narrow-eyed, then snorted a laugh. "How are you feeling, Max?"

"Okay. Amazingly."

"I heard you spent some time with the Iron Ravens."

Max nodded and glanced out the window. Two jets belonging to the Army of the Southern Cross were taxiing down the runway. "Did you come all this way to ask after my health and debrief me?"

Rick walked to the foot of the bed and folded his arms across his chest. "Max, Miriya has disappeared. She . . . borrowed a VT-1D from Fokker. We traced her to the Venezuela Sector, then lost her. It's obvious she didn't want to be found, because she disabled the trainer's locator. We had nothing to go on until we learned that shortly before arriving at Fokker she was visited at your apartment by a woman—a Human—identified as a malcontent operative. A mal gal, as intel puts it."

Max was dumbfounded. "I've been waiting years for the malcontents to show up and try to use her in some way. But this—stealing a VT—" He cut himself off in naked alarm. "Where's Dana, Rick?"

"She's fine. She's with the Grants. Also, Rolf Emerson wants you to know that he's at your disposal if you need help with Dana or anything."

"When will I be able to talk to her?"

"Whenever you want. We just didn't want you upset while you were recuperating."

Miriya, gone, Max told himself again and again, unable to fathom it. "Get me out of here, Rick. I have to find her."

Rick walked from the bed to the window, then turned around. "Hear me out before you say anything. I understand your wanting to find her. But it might be better to let Obstat's intelligence people handle this."

"Why, Rick?"

"Because of Anatole Leonard. And Wyatt Moran. We've been trying to keep the story contained, but Moran's threatening to give it to the press unless we agree to issue an order for Miriya's apprehension."

"On what grounds?"

"Sedition."

"That's crazy. Miriya's not a malcontent."

"You and I know that, but Moran has a way of getting people to take his view, and, between you and me, Max, the RDF doesn't have the veto power it once had. Moran was quick to remind everyone of where you and Miriya stood on the Brasília riot."

"For all the goddamned good it did," Max said.

"The point is that Leonard has hated you both since you blew the whistle on him, and it's no safer for you to be nosing around in the Southlands than it is for Miriya to be. The RDF has no jurisdiction south of Venezuela. Even my coming here had to be cleared with the Army of the Southern Cross."

Max stared at Rick. "Listen to what you're telling me! Miriya's in jeopardy down here, so I should go home and let intelligence handle it?"

Rick made his lips a thin line. "Officially, that's what I'm telling you. Because I can't afford to demonstrate any favoritism and risk giving Moran more support in the UEG."

"How did this happen, Rick? How the hell did we let things come to this?"

"We made mistakes."

"So what's your 'unofficial' advice?"

Rick sat down on the bed. "Two days ago, a cargo plane en route to Cavern City was raided by Stingers and sky-jacked."

"For parts?"

"Unlikely. The plane was carrying food, mostly. I know it's a stretch, but maybe there's a connection between the skyjacking and Miriya's disappearance. Anyway, we've assigned Wolff to head the retrieval operation."

"He's still in Cavern City?"

"Command offered him a promotion and transfer back to Albuquerque, but he declined."

"Guts-and-glory Wolff."

"Should I tell him I've assigned you temporary duty to his Pack?"

Max grinned. "But, uh, I'm going to need a commercial ticket to get there."

"Oh, that's right. You lost your VT, didn't you?"

"Thanks, pal," Max said, "for rubbing it in."

Rick clapped him on the knee. "Guess you'll just have to use the one I flew down here." He nodded toward the window. "It's waiting for you on the strip, whenever you want it."

Lazlo Zand sat alone in the dark in his office in the Tokyo Research Center, staring at the telephone and contemplating how to approach the task at hand. In the months since his abduction by the Claimers, he had noticed a gradual strengthening of some of his powers, regardless of his being denied the elements he felt were needed for a full transformation to occur. His reconfigured eyes allowed him to see in the dark with a cat's clarity; and, like Lang, he was subsisting on substantially fewer calories, and on a mere three hours of sleep per day. More importantly, when working with Protoculture he was sometimes able to perceive ghostly images hovering at the periphery of his vision. Were these what Lang had been referring to years earlier in the engine room of the ravaged SDF-1? Was he getting a glimpse of the Shapings themselves, or were these wraithlike figures merely the guardians of some greater mystery?

Zand grasped the necessity of pushing the boundaries of the psychic envelope if he was ever going to supersede Lang. And in the absence of Flower of Life and/or ur-Protoculture derived from Invid mecha, his only hope for transformative evolution, his only key to accessing the future was via Dana Sterling. She was a nexus of some sort, a meeting place of events, and he needed to tap into her and somehow divert the flow of energies into himself. He needed to posses her as she was possessed by the Shapings.

And now that Mommy had suddenly disappeared, he thought he had a chance of doing just that. For the past year or more, Daddy Max had been growing a bit wary of little Dana's sessions with "the eccentric professor," and Dana's three self-appointed Zentraedi Guardians had grown positively *protective*. But with Daddy off combing the forests of Amazonia for Mommy, Rico and company on the factory satellite, and the comely five-year-old being shuffled between the Grants and some nobody named Rolf Emerson, who was around to interfere? Especially when he would only be trying to help Dana through a difficult period. Mommyless, Daddyless ... poor little thing. Come and tell Uncle Lazlo all about it. And don't worry about these devices you're hooked up to; they're only so Uncle Laz can get a clear picture of what's going on *inside you*.

The plan would entail relocating to Monument City temporarily, but that was a small price to pay for continual access to the key to the Shapings.

But what to say to Jean Grant, Zand thought, staring at the telephone. He had never been good at small talk. Best come directly to the point. Maybe he'd be lucky enough to reach the Grants' answering machine.

But if not: *Mrs. Grant, I was just calling to express my concern for Dana, and to let you know that I'll soon be spending some time in Monument and that if there is anything I can do for the child—perhaps simply talk to her, as her mother has had me do in the past—please feel free to contact me at any hour. Should your busy schedule forbid it—I know how it can be for medical doctors—rest assured that I will be checking with you from time to time until this crisis has passed.*

The approach to Cavern City's runway, at the eastern terminus of the narrow, steep-sided canyon that cradled the city, was tricky at the best of times and downright challenging when you were facing headwinds, had a lot on your mind, and were crafted to a Veritech you had just been introduced to. Max executed a perfect landing, nonetheless. Two VTs from the Skull and one from the Twenty-third were already on the ground when Max touched down. The three pilots were waiting in the hangar, along with a red-haired Wolff Pack lieutenant named Ron Bartley.

"I haven't been here since we retook the Grand Cannon," Max said, much aware of Venezuela's humid heat, as he shook hands with Bartley.

"I wish I'd gotten to meet you then, sir."

Max blushed. "We were in and out. Only a day of R&R in Cavern." He glanced around. "By the looks of things, this place has changed a lot."

"Wait'll you see the city," Bartley told him.

Wolff's man led the four pilots to a battered jeep and settled himself behind an outsize steering wheel. The RDF base was only a few miles from the airfield, but Bartley took the long way around to give Max a glimpse of the expanded city center. Max was grateful for the breeze.

Cavern's linear sprawl of glass and adobe buildings now stretched for six miles along both sides of the natural chasm that bisected the city. Simple bridges spanned the chasm; an elevated monorail paralleled it on the north side.

"The city keeps growing higher because it has nowhere

else to go," Bartley commented. "Mayor Carson has tried to restrict immigration, but Zent refugees keep arriving every day." He looked over his shoulder at the dark-complected pilot from the Twenty-third, Boru Hesh. "No disrespect intended."

Hesh shrugged. "We refer to one another as Zent. No reason you shouldn't."

"Where are all the building materials coming from?" Max asked, wiping sweat from his upper lip.

"From the Cannon. You can recognize pieces of the thing in everything that's been built in the past two years."

"At least it's finally being put to good use."

Bartley cut his eyes to Max. "Think it would've made a difference if they'd finished it on time?"

"Against the fleet?" Max shrugged. "Ask Boru."

"There would have been fewer ships to fall to Earth," Boru opined. "Otherwise, conditions would be much as they are now."

When they finally arrived on the RDF base, Bartley again took the long route, wheeling the jeep past the mecha hangars before heading for Wolff's office.

"Centaur tanks," Max said in exaggerated disbelief. "This has got to be the museum, right?"

"You're not the first one to use that line, sir," Bartley said.

"Is it true Wolff went to Freetown for parts?"

Bartley nodded. "I can introduce you to the guy who went with him—Roger Malone."

"No wonder people refer to your unit as a 'pack.' "

"We gave ourselves that name, sir," Bartley amended. "But it's true, we're like a family. Even though I would have been the last person to say that when I first met the captain."

Max thought about his own family. He had spoken with Dana and she was fine. And he had managed to convince himself that he was doing all he could to locate Miriya. "Is Wolff married?"

"Uh, yeah, he's married. Has a son, too. Mrs. Wolff works for Mayor Carson's office. But I think she'd rather be living in Monument or somewhere *happening*."

Max recalled Rick's statement about the promotion Wolff had turned down. "It's not always easy doing equal service to a marriage and the military."

Bartley rocked his head from side to side. "I've got a wife and kid myself, but all of us understand the priorities. I figure there'll be time enough for family life after we get the planet cooking again." Bartley made an abrupt stop in front of Wolff's tile-roofed office, and everyone piled out into the glare of the midday sun. The captain himself—with his signature shades and pencil-thin mustache—hastened outside to greet them. His khaki shirt was mottled from perspiration.

"A real honor, Captain Sterling," Wolff said, pumping Max's hand.

"You're no stranger, either," Max told him.

"Yeah, but believe only the good stuff."

Max introduced Wolff to his Skull teammates and to Boru Hesh. Wolff asked after some of the Twenty-third pilots who had flown raids from Cavern City against the Shroud and Fist. Then, after directing Bartley to show Max and the others to their quarters, he spun on his heel and hurried back into his office.

Two hours later, ten men were grouped around a long table in a briefing room that was stiflingly hot, despite a large fan that was lazing overhead. Wolff, wearing wraparound sunglasses and a clean shirt, stood at the head of the table. "At six-thirty local time four days ago," he began, "four Stingers attacked a cargo plane en route to Cavern from Monument." He aimed a laser pointer at a wall map studded with colored pushpins. "The last commo from the flight crew was at grid reference MM-seven-two. Now, we're reasonably sure we've found the plane—it was ID'ed by satellite look-down—but the question of why it was skyjacked remains unanswered. The skyjacking of a lone cargo plane crewed by five civilians doesn't fit the malcontents' standard MO."

"What was the cargo?" a member of the Wolff Pack asked.

"Food and medicine." Wolff held up his hands to silence conversation. "I know what you're thinking, but it doesn't hold up. All reports indicate that the malcontents aren't going hungry, thanks to the Human trash that have thrown in with them. And we don't know of one case where they've gone after medicine or medical supplies."

"Maybe their *modus operandi* is changing," someone suggested.

Wolff nodded. "Okay, maybe it is. But what else?"

Max gestured to the map. "Which band controls the area where the plane was located?"

"The Shroud and Fist—an all-male group armed with a couple of Tactical 'Pods and second-generation Stingers. We've been mixing it up with them on and off for two years now." Wolff motioned with his chin to Boru Hesh. "So has the Twenty-third. The surveillance satellite diverted over the area shot opticals of six longhouses, four Stingers, and our missing plane, concealed under a scrambler tarp."

"They're hiding the thing?" someone asked in puzzled amazement.

"It's bait," the Skull's Bill Mammoth said.

"Of course it is," Wolff told him. "But I put it to you again: Why? What are we being set up to encounter?"

CHAPTER TWENTY-FOUR

On the occasion of our second meeting [with Tan Fose], I real-
ized that I was being set up—that I had been targeted for abduc-
tion by some malcontent group. But what did that matter, if in the
end I would have access to what I needed to complete the trans-
formation: access to Protoculture, Zentraedi blood, artifacts, and
who knew what else the aliens were harboring. Even as I lay
chained to the dank floor of that cave in Australia, I was thinking of
how to make the most of my predicament. Reasoning that sexual
congress might result in a transfer of bodily fluids, I asked one of my
female captors if she wished to have her way with me while we were
awaiting a reply to the demands Tomina Jepp had issued the RDF.
    Lazlo Zand, *Event Horizon: Perspectives on Dana Sterling and*
                                        the Second Robotech War

THE FORESTS OF SOUTHERN VENEZUELA WERE NOT UN-
like those of Singken, a planet the Zentraedi had conquered
early in the Masters' campaign to rule the Local Group.
Tasked with the conquest, Azonia's Quadrono had been re-
lentless in their attacks on Singken's techless populace.
Even now Miriya could recall the sight of an entire continent aflame, millions of acres of trees and grassland torched
by the directed energy of Female Power Armor. To be
walking in such a forest now, alone and weaponless, filled
her with a disturbing sense of irony.

It had been five days earlier that a malcontent operative
had paid a late-night visit to the high-rise apartment in
Monument. The woman had the unkempt look of a
sympath, only rougher around the edges. Miriya recalled
her wary, haunted eyes. She said she had a message from
an old friend, but when Miriya asked who, she received not
a name but a one-time-only diskette. "Know this much,
T'sen Parino," the woman told her. "Many T'sentradi have
died to see this delivered to you."

Miriya had played the disk and listened, intuiting that it was from Seloy Deparra long before her friend spoke. *Yes, it's me, Miriya Parino. Alive, and in urgent need of your help* ... Seloy had said nothing about what she'd been doing since the Brasília riot; only that Miriya needed to travel to the Southlands immediately—*if their friendship still mattered to her*. Coordinates were furnished, along with instructions to take along survival gear and food.

"Activate this when you reach the designated place," the messenger had added, pressing a locator device into Miriya's left hand. "Walk west, keeping the river on your right. You will be found."

"But how am I expected to get to this place?" Miriya asked.

"That much is up to you. Surely a Quadrono can find a way."

Miriya had been tempted to let Dana sleep, but her heart forced her to say good-bye, to cradle the half-asleep child in her arms and explain as best as she could.

"You know how you and Bowie are best friends?" she had whispered in the dark. "Well, I, too, have a good friend whom I haven't seen in many years. I knew her even before I met and married your father. And now this friend needs my help very badly, so I have to go to where she is. Right away, darling, tonight. So Mommy has to ask you to be brave while she's gone, and to be good for Jean and Vince, who are going to take care of you until I come home. Jean will be here soon to get you. Do you understand?"

Dana nodded, asking, "Does Daddy know?"

"He'll find out."

"Is this about the angry Zentraedi?"

Clever, clever, child, Miriya had thought. "I don't know, Dana. But you're not to tell anyone, okay? And always remember that you have the best of Human and Zentraedi inside you, and that there's no one else like you in the entire universe. You're special, you'll always be special, and your Daddy and I love you very, very much."

"I know," Dana said. "And I won't tell what you said. But please, Mommy, don't do anything bad."

The words were still echoing inside her. How simple it was for children, their world of black and white, good and bad.

She had been walking for three days, keeping the meandering river on her right as instructed, and had probably put close to forty miles between herself and the Veritech trainer she had commandeered from Fokker Base and abandoned to the forest. How easy it had been for the well-known *Mrs. Sterling* to infiltrate Fokker. Rank really did have its privileges.

Initially, she had raged against the forest's heat and insects, but had since resigned herself to the discomforts and had actually managed a few hours' sleep the previous night. Her thorn-torn clothes, the backpack and sleeping bag, even the dehydrated meals, had all come from Max's closet at home. On landing, she had disabled one locator only to activate another, but as yet there had been no sign of Seloy. For the past half hour, however, she had been closing on the odors of a cook fire, and she thought she could distinguish distant voices amid the cacophony of insect sounds.

Another fifteen minutes of stealthful walking brought her to the edge of a small clearing. Peering through tangled brush, she counted eight Zentraedi males, busy at camp chores. A few mules were grazing on leaves, and two of the men had their heads buried in the engine compartment of a much-abused canvas-topped truck. Just inside the treeline north of the clearing stood a captured Veritech, Battloid-configured and repainted in camouflaging colors. Miriya was debating the wisdom of showing herself when someone laid the barrel of a handgun against her hair-plastered right cheek.

"Raise your arms above your head and stand up slowly," a man said quietly in broken Spanglish. He was shirtless and toned, with youthful features and spiked, light-brown hair.

"Par dessu, T'sen," Miriya said.

Surprise wrinkled the Zentraedi's face. "Are you with the Scavengers?" he asked in their language.

Miriya shook her head. "I'm unaligned. But I'm ready to fight the fight; to kill or be killed—"

"Save your enthusiasm for the captain," the man interrupted. He prodded her in the small of the back, motioning her into the clearing. "*T'sen* Nomarre," he shouted, "*kyy teezel.*"

While the rest of the band were gathering round, a small, scar-faced man with thick brows and a high forehead emerged from a thatch-roofed lean-to and began to saunter toward her, dark eyes widening with each approaching step. "Am I to believe what I'm seeing?" He stopped to glance at his comrades. "Don't any of you recognize her? This is Miriya Parino!"

The quizzical stares and sinister smiles became gapes of confoundment.

"You're wrong, *T'sen*," Miriya said quickly. "But your mistake is easily explained. Parino and I are members of the same clone queue. I know her, of course, but appearance is all I share with her. My name is Jiwei Coor."

Nomarre looked skeptical. "You're lying."

"It's the hair," Miriya said, fingering her damp green strands. "I've tried to recolor it to lessen the similarity, but it doesn't seem to accept Human-made dyes."

Nomarre regarded her in silence for a long moment. "What you doing out here, 'Jiwei Coor'?"

Miriya glanced around. "Looking for you."

"For us?"

"Any band that will have me, I mean. I've grown sick of my life among our acculturated breathren in Cavern City. I wish to put my warrior skills to work for the cause."

Nomarre signaled the shirtless malcontent to holster his weapon and told Miriya she could lower her hands. "So, Jiwei Coor perhaps shares Parino's fighting spirit as well as her features." He motioned her to a log that served as a bench. "I am Ranoc Nomarre, and we are the New Unity."

"I've heard of you," Miriya said. "Is this your permanent camp?"

Nomarre made up his mind about something, then shook his blockish head. "We're on our way to a meeting hosted by the Scavengers."

Miriya pretended to be impressed. "Will you take me?"

Nomarre grinned. "We certainly will, *T'sen*." He walked over to her and grabbed hold of her chin. "They will tell us who you really are. And if you're lying, I will personally gut you."

Miriya was careful not to resist. "You'd gut one who has been the most vocal supporter of equal rights for our race? Who told the truth about the Brasília Riot, and pressured the UEG to end the occupation of the Protectorate—"

"Who married a *Human*," Nomarre countered. "Who birthed a *Human* child. Whose alleged concern for her people makes her the ideal RDF spy ... And what do you know of the Protectorate, female. I was *there*. One of the detainees, one of the many forcibly Micronized. Parino— ever the media celebrity—did *nothing* to prevent it." Nomarre swung to his men. "Cuff her."

Miriya allowed her hands to be shackled behind her back, but she kept her eyes riveted on Nomarre. Sympathy notwithstanding, she couldn't permit him to interfere with her mission.

While he was shoving her toward the truck, where he apparently meant to store her, she tried to make him understand that she wasn't his enemy. When all appeals to reason failed, she simply skull-butted him in the face, fracturing his nose.

As he fell back, she leapt straight up, bringing her knees to her chest and her arms out in front of her where they belonged. No sooner did Nomarre recover from the skull-butting than she uppercut him with the backs of her shackled hands. His pained moans brought his comrades running, but by then she had hold of Nomarre's handgun, a few blasts from which sent everyone diving for cover.

Projectiles and energy beams tried to find her as she scrambled to the far side of the truck and jinked across the clearing for the safety of the forest. She paused to aim one blast at the Battloid's optic sensor, then disappeared into the trees, leaves and branches falling around her as if pruned by a volley of lethal fire from the camp.

Night was falling, but not fast enough to conspire in her escape. Breathless, she squatted on her haunches, set

Nomarre's handgun on timed release, and gripped the thing tightly between her knees. Then she laid the chain of the cuffs over the muzzle and leaned the rest of herself as far from the discharge as possible. The blast slagged the chain and drove bits of molten metal into her exposed flesh. She screamed through gritted teeth, picked herself up off the ground, and plunged deeper into the woods.

Miriya was down there somewhere, Max told himself as he soared over the jungled escarpment that formed the western boundary of the Venezuela Sector. He had wanted to visit the spot where she'd set the trainer down, but Rick had urged him not to. Specialists from SOG's Technical Services Division had literally dismantled the mecha component by component, searching for anything that could be construed as a message or a clue to Miriya's disappearance. The extrapolated timing of her vertical landing coincided with that of his crash in the Congo.

Dana had confessed that Miriya had gone to help a good friend—one she'd known longer than Max. Was it Seloy Deparra, Max wondered, alive after all these years? If so, what did Seloy want from Miriya now? And why did it entail such secrecy? Unless Seloy had joined a malcontent band . . .

Flanking his VT now were those of Willy Mammoth and Nick Fowler, with Boru Hesh flying rear guard. They were fifteen miles southwest of their objective when their IFF scanners began screaming; ten when they encountered the first Stinger.

The technohybrid had launched from the canopy like a rocket, spinning and spewing missiles in a 180-degree arc. The RDF pilots broke formation and spent five minutes shaking heat-seekers before they could even think about offensive maneuvers. When they did, a second Stinger appeared, vectoring in from the northeast and seeding the sky with a whole new crop of red-tipped pursuers.

Max powered straight up out of the fray and went to Battloid mode to rain downward bolts on the bulky shoulders of this latest arrival, holing and crippling it. At the same time, Fowler, Mammoth, and Hesh were all giving chase to the first Stinger, dodging a flock of corkscrewing missiles while pouring everything they had at the Stinger's eminently targetable hindquarters.

Max's hands clutched reflexively when he saw Mammoth take two Decas in the belly and roll over, leaking white smoke. Even so, his own missiles had found their mark and the Stinger was falling as well.

"Skull Two to Skull Leader," Willy said calmly. "Looks like I'll be sitting out the next dance."

"Let go of it, Willy," Max told him over the tactical net. "It's only a piece of hardware."

"I'll make sure to mention that when Command sends me the bill. Enabling autoeject."

"Watch your ass on the way down," Fowler said. "Those branches are gonna want a chunk of you."

"Maybe I'll just go in headfirst."

"Evac'll be on the way," Max said.

"I'll be partying with the Stinger pilots in the meantime," Willy said. "Over and out."

Max switched to the command frequency. "Captain Wolff, Skull Two is going to be dropping into your area, south-southwest of the main logging road. If you'll handle recovery, the three of us will proceed to the objective and make arrangements for your arrival."

"You're not out to steal our thunder, are you, Captain?" Wolff asked.

"Just trying to hold onto whatever surprise we have left, Jon. Although even the Wolff Pack deserves a break once in a while."

"Only on my say-so," Wolff said. "But good hunting until then, guys."

Max zeroed the VT's autopilot and executed a low flyby over the objective, expecting ground fire but receiving none. Through the treetops he could make out the crude huts, the scrambler tarp, and two upright mecha. The onboard computer identified the mecha as Stingers; infrared confirmed the presence of at least three Humans in two separate huts.

Reconfiguring the VT to Guardian mode, Max ordered Fowler and Hesh to remain airborne while he went in for a closer look. The malcontent camp was uncomfortably quiet. He landed, autocannon in gauntleted hand, walked the Guardian to the scrambler tarp, and tore it loose from its stakes. The skyjacked cargo plane looked as though it had been looted; during the attack, the Stingers had ripped several gaping holes in the fuselage.

The VT's external mikes picked up the distressed sounds of one of the survivors, and in a moment Max saw a man stagger from one of the huts, clawing at his back.

"Help me, somebody help me!" the man was screaming. "Take 'em away, they're crawling all over me!"

Max raised the canopy and climbed out of his craft. "Easy does it, fellow. You're going to be all right."

He hadn't even gotten the words out when the man whirled on him—face beaded with sweat—and attacked, knocking Max aside and disappearing around the corner of a hut. "They're going to kill us, they're going to kill us all!" Max heard him screaming.

Shaken, Max returned to the VT and told Fowler to land at the opposite end of the camp and begin a hut-by-hut search. "But for God's sake, be careful."

Max drew his sidearm and cautiously entered the hut the man had exited. Facedown on the floor was a dead crewmember. Rodents were brazenly gnawing at the corpse. Max tasted bile in his mouth, and made a slow turn to the right. Standing with his back to the wall was the plane's pilot—Captain Blake, Max recalled. Blake, panting and gripping a survival knife in both hands, wore the same crazed look as the man Max had confronted outside.

"No one's going to hurt you," Max said in the most soothing voice he could manage under the circumstances. "I'm Captain Sterling, from—"

Blake leapt at him, slicing the air with the knife. Max slid to the ground, extending a leg into Blake's midriff, knocking the wind out of him. "I don't want to have to hurt you, Cap—"

Blake rallied and came at him with the knife raised in both hands. Max saw the futility of trying to talk the man down and took charge, slipping to the side of the blow, backhanding Blake across the jaw, spinning him around, and sending him headfirst into the mud wall. Two more jaw-jarring punches were required to send Blake to the ground and keep him there.

Fowler was calling to Max over the radio. "Captain, I've found the woman, Ramirez, but she seems to be in shock. The one with her wasn't as lucky. Looks like he was rat food."

"I've got the same situation," Max said, frightened and breathing hard.

"What happened here, sir?" Fowler asked.

"I don't know." Max heard a noise and started, but it was only one of the rodents. His heart was racing. "Any word from Wolff?"

"The Pack's just arrived. They extracted Willy, he's okay."

"Did they find the Zentraedi pilots?"

"They have them, too. Three women."

"I thought you said the Shroud and Fist was an all-male group," Max said when he and Wolff had rendezvoused in a longhouse at the eastern extreme of the malcontent camp.

Wolff scratched at his head. "Maybe they've decided to go coed?"

Hands cuffed behind them, the three alien women wore utility jumpsuits emblazoned with the Zentraedi sigil. The tallest of the three had long honey-blond hair and an up-turned nose. Another was petite but fierce looking. The third was powerfully built and had a shaved head.

"You feel like talking to us?" Max asked them in Zentraedi.

They were taken aback, but only momentarily. "Don't mistake us for *hajoca*, Human," the hairless one said. "We have nothing to say to you."

Max translated for Wolff's benefit, then turned to the women again. "You may not be traitors, but right now you are something equally deplorable—prisoners."

The tall one's face flushed with rage. "Filthy Micronian! You think you can defeat us? The Scavengers will wipe this planet clean—"

"*Alinnen*—enough!" the bald one said, cutting her off. "*Sesannu!*"

Max grinned at Wolff. "I think we might be able to get somewhere with these three if we separate them."

"Good thinking," Wolff started to say when the radio clipped to his belt chirped.

"Wolff, this is Rosen."

Wolff depressed the radio's talk button. "Go ahead, Rosen."

"We've got a situation developing out here. The two Stingers have self-activated. They're making all kinds of—*shit!*"

Cannon reports from outside shook the longhouse. Over the radio came a squabble of voices and a loud hissing sound, followed by a single *whump!* from the Centaur's main gun and a deafening explosion.

Reflexively, Wolff had ducked under a crudely built table. "We better get out there," he told Max.

Max glanced at the three Zentraedi. None of the three had moved a muscle, and just now the bald one was grinning. "*Kara-brek,*" she said softly, as if to Max. "*Kara-brek, kara-brek ...*" One at a time, her comrades took up the chant, gradually upping the volume and the tempo.

"*Kara-brek, kara-brek, karabrek, karabrek ...*"

At the same time, the ground under their feet had begun to quake from the rhythmic fall of heavy footsteps.

Max and Wolff exchanged sudden, knowing looks and broke for the doorway—not a moment before the arms of a Stinger burst through the sidewall and the entire longhouse blew to pieces.

It took several minutes for the dust to settle, and for Max and Wolff to dig themselves out from under the mud-and-wattle rubble and to pick the thatch from their hair.

"The Stinger was programmed to make sure those women wouldn't be taken alive," Max said. "They knew all along they were going to die."

"Us with them," Wolff said. "If things had gone according to plan."

Max forced an exhale. "I should have taken the Stingers out as soon as I arrived. When I didn't meet any resistance,

I kept thinking about Leonard's raid on the Scavenger base, and assumed we were home free."

Several members of the Pack had showed up to check on Wolff and Max. "How are your men?" Wolff asked Ron Bartley.

"They seem all right. The Stinger emitted some kind of particle cloud before Rosen took it out, but no one's any the worse for wear so far."

"Was that the hissing sound we heard?" Max wanted to know.

Bartley nodded. "No evidence of radioactivity or known chemical agents."

Wolff threw him a look. "Not good enough. I want Rosen's Centaur wrapped and sealed for decontamination, and everyone in the Pack into antihazard suits. On the double."

"The battle for possession of the surface is almost over," Breetai told Jevna Parl on the bridge of the factory satellite. "The flow of Protoculture cells from this facility has stopped, the Protectorate is a failed experiment, the few dissident groups that remain are squeezed into an inhospitable area of the Southlands."

"I'm aware of all these things," the gnomish Parl said.

"And still you will not be dissuaded?"

"What is the alternative? If I am no longer with you, I am against you. Would you have me attempt to undermine you here, as Theofre Elmikk did? Would you dishonor us both by imprisoning me aboard the factory?"

Breetai growled. "All because I executed the traitors."

Parl shook his head. "Because you chose to define them as traitors, Breetai. You claim that our new allegiance must be to the REF, but why must we swear allegiance to any group? Why must the Zentraedi serve any masters?"

"Not everyone can rule, Jevna."

"Perhaps not. But everyone should have the right to pursue freedom. Elmikk and his comrades were not traitors to our cause—to the *Zentraedi* cause—only the Human one. You were not hearing the voice of the Imperative in their attempted mutiny. Their actions were those of free beings, and you had no right to condemn them."

Breetai sneered. "So Jevna Parl has discovered himself to be a malcontent."

"A Human word."

"A freedom fighter, then."

"Since you're compelled to define me, yes, consider me a freedom fighter."

"And should I choose to grant permission for you to go down the well?"

"I will join the ranks of the disaffected."

"And attempt to undermine me from afar."

"Not you, nor any aboard this artificial world. Only the uncharitable below, stingy with the freedoms they hold so dear. I will do all I can to undermine them." Parl paused for a moment. "You command the power to prevent that; you could withhold permission. But if that is your choice, I would rather you kill me."

Breetai folded his arms across his massive chest. "I will honor your request."

Parl blanched.

"No, not to kill you, Jevna. On the contrary, I want to see you live to regret your decision."

CHAPTER
TWENTY-FIVE

JANUS M proved to be a better spy than any of us (at the Robotech Research Center) would have imagined, in part, I believe, because of the countless volumes on espionage "tradecraft" we downloaded into her. . . . When I learned that Minmei and "Janice" had been asked to accompany Moran and Milburn to the fete celebrating Southlands unification, I tasked the android's programmers with transforming her into an ambulatory voice-stress analysis device for the event. The cybertechnician team went me one better by programming her to probe for data when the conversation turned to certain, key topics, such as the malcontents, Anatole Leonard, and the Lorelei Network. Upon uploading JANUS days after the fete, I realized at once that Moran had deliberately outed Milburn, perhaps in the hope that, as my "niece," Janice would relate what had transpired over dinner. But I have always suspected that Moran recognized Janice for what she/it was; and though their close relationship would continue until the launch of the SDF-3, I wonder if JANUS wasn't so much an agent provocateur as an unwitting agent of disinformation for the Army of the Southern Cross.

Emil Lang as quoted in Justine Huxley's
I've Been to a Fabulous Party

THE POSSIBLY CONTAMINATED CENTAUR SAT IN A controlled-environment mecha bay on the RDF's base in Cavern City. Inside the tank waited Wolff Packers Rosen and Kimball, who'd taken the brunt of the Stinger's seemingly harmless particle-cloud release prior to its self-activated attack. Elsewhere on the base, in isolation and under constant surveillance, were the three surviving crewmembers of the cargo plane. Sterling and Wolff, along with a mecha specialist named Gillespie, stood on an observation balcony that overlooked the glassed-in decontamination area. Gillespie, formerly of the Argentine Base, was one of the techs who'd helped recommission the

Centaurs two years earlier and had stayed on as chief engineer.

"What exactly are we looking for, Jon?" Gillespie was asking Wolff.

"I don't know that we're looking for anything. I just want the thing fully checked out."

"It's quite possible the cloud your men claim to have seen was nothing more than escaped mecha coolant of some sort."

"I'll buy that. Just show me there's nothing unusual about the tank and I'll be on my way."

Gillespie bent to a radio tuned to the Pack's tactical frequency. "How are you two doing?"

"Peachy," Kimball said in piqued voice. "Just get on with your tests so we can get out of here."

Sterling and Wolff traded worried looks.

It had been a long, overnight haul back to Cavern City, everyone on edge—spooked—and griping about having to wear the antihazard suits. The cargo-plane crewman Max had first encountered had been found, unconscious but alive, and he, Blake, and Ramirez, along with the bodies of the two dead crewmen, had been placed inside a personnel carrier normally used to carry malcontent captives. Then the camp had been razed. Max's team had remained with the Pack for the trip, hanging above the logging roads; Willy Mammoth, suddenly VT-less, had ridden in Wolff's Centaur.

"You know, it's getting damned hot in here," Kimball said over the net. "What's taking so long?" Max could hear the sound of Kimball's hand slamming against the tank's topside hatch.

"Try to relax, son," Gillespie said. "We're working as fast as we can."

"You better be. I don't know about my pal Rosen, here, but I can't take too much more of this *heat*."

All at once, just as two medics in bubble-helmeted antibiohazard suits were approaching the tank, the top hatch flew open and Kimball scampered out onto the turret.

Wolff grabbed the radio handset. "Kimball, get your ass back inside—"

"Get me out of here!" Kimball bellowed in an inhuman voice. Then he threw himself onto the closest medic, driving him to the concrete floor. The other medic was quick to react, and he and Kimbell tumbled in a thrashing tangle of limbs.

On the balcony, Wolff keyed the public-address system. "Security to decontamination. Code red."

"Let me go!" Kimball was screaming, frothing at the mouth. "I'm burning up! What's wrong with you people? How can you stand it? How can you—"

The Packer suddenly went limp in the medic's arms. The medic placed a device against Kimball's neck, then quickly straddled him and began to pound on his chest. Rosen poked his head from the hatch but stayed put.

"We better get down there," Wolff said.

"Not without suits," Gillespie told him.

An emergency medical team and four fully suited hulks from security hurried into the bay through an airlock. Max and Wolff watched them work on Kimball for five minutes. Finally one of the medics glanced up at the balcony and shook his head.

Wolff looked grim. "Let's see if Dr. Lopez learned anything from the crew," he said, tapping Max into motion. Lopez, another Argentine transplant, was the base physician. "Looks like Kimball caught something from that particle cloud."

"Maybe not," Max said. "The ride in was rough going. And everybody was stressed out to begin with."

Wolff eyed him askance. "It's coincidence that the one guy who flips out also happens to be the guy who took the brunt of the cloud?"

"One of the guys. Rosen seemed all right."

"I knew Kimball pretty well, Max, and he wasn't the type to stress out. It was something the Stinger released. The malcontents probably tried it out on the crew, then decided to bait us with the cargo plane. They put up just enough resistance to make us think it wasn't a trap and to get us down on the ground. Dollars to donuts, the Scavengers are experimenting with a biochemical weapon."

Max offered a reluctant nod. "They've had Human help

in growing food, locating crashed ships, and securing nuclear weapons. So why not some strain of biological left over from the Global Civil War."

"If that's true, Lopez or someone should be able to identify it."

"Let's hope. But what bothers me is that the group that downed me in the Congo mentioned something about attending a Scavenger meeting. They could be planning to distribute this stuff to other bands."

Wolff gave his head a mournful shake. "Sorry you got yourself dragged into this, Max. I'm sure you'd rather be in Monument with your family."

Max was quiet for a moment; then he filled Wolff in on Miriya's disappearance. Wolff listened without comment, until Max mentioned that she had gone to ground in the southwest of the Venezuela Sector.

"You think there's a connection between Miriya's landing here and this biological or whatever it is?"

"Do you know the name Seloy Deparra?"

"Should I?"

"No reason to, I guess. She was a Quadrono, like Miriya. Miriya and I thought she was dead, but I'm beginning to think she's alive, and that's why Miriya's in the Southlands."

"And maybe this Deparra is tied up with the Scavengers, is that the idea?"

Max nodded.

Wolff didn't respond immediately. "You know, it's funny," he said at last. "My wife's disappeared, too. Not that she's gone missing or anything, but she moved out on me a month ago when I turned down a promotion and a transfer."

"Admiral Hunter told me about that," Max said. "Between you and me, I think he'd like to enlist you in the REF."

Wolff grinned. "I'd go to Tirol at the drop of a thinking cap. But I don't feature spending the next couple of years locked up in that factory. I'd rather wait till the SDF-3's completed, *then* sign on."

"Would your wife . . ."

"Catherine."

"Would she be willing to go along?"

"No way—even though 'down to earth' isn't a term I'd use to describe her. But space, forget it." Wolff studied Max. "What about you and Miriya?"

"We have a daughter to think of."

"Yeah. I have a son. Hell, I don't even know how I'm going to handle being away from him if Catherine decides to return north, let alone if I'm upside."

Both men were silent for the rest of the walk to Lopez's laboratory. The doctor, a small man with shoulder-length black hair, had been trying to contact Wolff. He had identified the biochemical agent that had felled the crew, and possibly Kimball as well.

"It's a virus," Lopez said. "The etiology seems consistent with recent cases reported in Mexico: fever, rage, madness ... Sometimes there's a rash, such as I found on Captain Blake's back; sometimes not."

"Biological warfare," Wolff said.

Lopez nodded. "Apparently so."

"Is there a vaccine or anything?" Max asked.

"We don't understand it well enough. I've sent my findings to the Center for Disease Control in Denver. They've been grappling for months trying to identify this thing. So much electronic data and paper documentation was lost during the Rain, there's no way of telling if the virus is new or something that's been around for a decade."

"Could it have been a weapon used during the Global Civil War?" Max asked.

"Possibly. But, again, it's a tedious process trying to identify it. Not everyone appears to be susceptible, and not everyone who contracts it dies. Witness the difference in Captain Blake and his copilot, Ms. Ramirez. And you two and Kimball."

"That's encouraging," Wolff commented.

"Perhaps. But just the same, I'll want blood samples from everyone who took part in the raid on the malcontent camp. The virus has an extremely rapid incubation period—sometimes a matter of a few hours—so the sooner we have everyone tested the better. I'd also like your permission to quarantine the entire base until we know what we're dealing with."

Wolff shook his head. "I can't make that call. It's up to Mayor Carson."

Lopez's broad nostrils flared. "Then I'll just have to deal with her."

In the private dining room of Monument City's most elegant restaurant, Southlands President Wyatt Moran and UEG Senator Braxton Milburn sat with Lynn-Minmei and her new partner, Janice Em. Well into the main course, the two politicians were drinking with abandon, in celebration of the UEG's as-yet-unannounced decision to ratify the so-called "Moran Plan," which called for the immediate refurbishment of Sara and ALUCE bases and the construction of space-defense platforms similar to those that typified the ARMD series. As head of the Ways and Means Committee, Milburn had been influential in shepherding through the allocations.

"It's time thought was given to something other than the completion of the SDF-3," Janice was saying in her unsettling monotone. "Even though my uncle would die if he heard me say that." She was wearing a strapless lavender gown that Minmei had tried to convince her was too revealing—though Minmei's own was shorter and cut even lower.

"Dr. Lang was certainly our toughest opponent," Milburn told her, tossing back a drink. "But I think he's beginning to understand that the departure of the SDF-3 is going to create a defensive vacuum on Earth. What's more, it's important to have contingency plans in place in the event the ship doesn't return on schedule."

"Which it won't," Janice said, sipping champagne from a long-stemmed glass. "Not with my uncle and Lisa Hayes at the helm."

Moran and Milburn traded stunned glances and laughed. "How refreshing to find a celebrity who isn't wed to political correctness," Moran commented.

Janice stared at him. "Are you referring to my partner?"

"Why, I—" Flustered, Moran cut his eyes to Minmei. "Lynn, I didn't mean to suggest—"

"Just because she hosts the Love Line doesn't make her an enemy of the politically *in*correct."

"Janice, please," Minmei said, showing an imploring look. "Let's not turn this into a debate. Besides, I'm sure that Wyatt was only making conversation."

The android turned to the silver-locked president. "Is that true, Wyatt?"

"Well, I—"

"Because I hate polite conversation. And I really do feel that Minmei's involvement with the Lorelei Network amounts to a political statement."

"That depends on how you view the network," Milburn said, suddenly interested. "The people who have labeled it subversive are the same ones who take offense when anyone talks about young people's music being subversive."

Minmei was quick to speak. "I'm just trying to provide the Zentraedi with some entertainment."

"But they don't hear it as entertainment, Lynn," Janice argued. "You're practically a religious icon to them. So your songs—even the show's phone calls and interviews—constitute a kind of litany. You're a major *political* influence on them, whether you like it or not. Many Zentraedi would be lost without you."

"I'll drink to that," Moran said drunkenly, hoisting his glass. "To found Zentraedi, wherever they are." When Milburn didn't raise his glass in return, Moran raised it for him. "Come on, Brax, we're only having fun. Isn't that right, ladies?"

Minmei forced a smile and reached for her glass.

Moran snorted a laugh in Milburn's direction. "You'd think the man had stock in Lorelei, he's so serious about it."

Over the rim of her glass, Janice trained her eyes on the suddenly fretful senator, analyzing his expression, recording his every move. Dr. Lang would have much to evaluate.

The Cavern City cabbie, a Zentraedi, had the car radio tuned to the Lorelei Network. Minmei's "Sight and Sound" was playing: a minor and seldom heard post-War effort, at once martial and romantic. Max and Wolff were in the back seat.

"You like her songs?" Max asked.

"They're not my taste. But I think she's a fascinating woman. You know her pretty well, don't you?"

"I wouldn't say well, but, yeah, from the SDF-1 and Macross City."

"What does Miriya think of the Lorelei Network?"

"Same as I do: that it's patronizing and manipulative."

"I remember listening to Minmei's first show—when every other call was from a malcontent. I thought for sure she wouldn't be back for a second one."

Max laughed through his nose. "That's the thing about her—her faith in the future never flags."

Wolff's expression turned brooding. "I could use a dose of that. But until they can bottle it, I'll have to settle for scotch."

They were on their way to a downtown bar called The Chasm, an off-base gathering spot for the Pack. Mayor Carson, skeptical of Lopez's theories about the virus and wishing to avoid a panic, had refused to quarantine the base. And since both Max's and Wolff's blood tests had turned out negative, they had decided to make the most of the few remaining hours of what had been a grueling day.

The Chasm was dark, noisy, narrow, and crammed full of RDFers. A couple of enlisted-ratings gave up their table for Max and Wolff, and the two officers sat down and ordered drinks. Conversation entailed yelling into each other's ears. Not six feet from them, an argument was building at the bar.

"Who do you think you are, telling me I can't have another drink?" a scruffy-looking civilian was saying to the bartender. "I'm a regular. What I drink pays your salary. So if I say I want a drink, you give me a drink."

The bartender, a sturdy man with a thin mustache, took it good-naturedly. "Juan, who gave who instructions about cutting you off? I'm only doing what you asked."

Juan glared across the bar. "And why's it so hot in here tonight? You too cheap to turn on the air conditioner?"

"It's on." The bartender leaned his elbows on the bar. "Maybe you should just—"

Before he could get the words out, Juan had shoved him backward into the mirrored wall behind the bar. Glass shattered, shelves collapsed, and bottles of liquor crashed to the floor.

A bodybuilder in shorts and tank top came up behind Juan and took hold of his arm. "All right, amigo, time for you to go."

"More orders!" Juan said, his face beaded with sweat. "I don't have to take orders. I'm not a goddamned soldier."

Juan's sudden, sloppy right cross was easily evaded by the bouncer, but it managed to connect solidly with the jaw of a swarthy, bearded man standing at the bar. More surprised than hurt, the unintended victim returned a powerful left that Juan slipped under, leaving it nowhere to go but straight into the face of the bouncer, who fell back onto Wolff and Max's table.

"You didn't need to stage this for my benefit," Max said, sluicing his spilled drink from his lap as he was backing away from the collapsed table.

"Nothing's too good for a guest," Wolff told him, annoyed but transparently excited by the prospect of an all-out brawl.

Max put a hand on his arm. "Wait a minute. Maybe this isn't run-of-the-mill madness, Jon."

Wolff took a long look around the bar. Vicious fights were breaking out in all corners. "On second thought, we better call for the MPs."

They began to edge their way to the exit, dodging some blows, taking others, and finally stumbled out the door onto Chasm Street. The brawl, too, had spilled outside, though military police vehicles were already on the scene.

"The one sitting at the bar," Max said while gently fingering a split upper lip. "Was he sick or only drunk?"

Wolff didn't respond. He was looking past Max, at something on the opposite side of Cavern's downtown canyon. "Too fast," he said at last. "It'll never make the turn."

Max swung around to follow his gaze. The monorail was speeding toward a station platform at a point where the elevated line jagged slightly to the southwest. And Wolff was right: it was not going to hold the curve.

The mecha that rescued her from a vine-strangled tree she had climbed to escape the New Unity had the torso and arms of a Gladiator, the cockpit module of a Veritech, and the legs and foot thrusters of a Battloid. The buxom pilot was named Kru Guage.

"You were never lost, Miriya Parino," Kru had said over the hybrid's external speakers.

Miriya had lowered herself from a limb slick with dew into a giant, gauntleted hand. "Maybe not, but your timing could have been better. Some of our comrades are in need of hospitality training." She showed Kru the shackles on her wrist and the welts the bits of molten chain had left on her arms and face.

"If you mean the New Unity, I have already informed them that you are our invited guest."

"Did you by any chance tell them my name?"

"I saw no reason not to."

Miriya tried to imagine Ranoc Nomarre's reaction to the news. "Is Seloy Deparra a member of your group?" she asked as she was clambering into the cockpit.

"A member? Seloy Deparra is the leader of the Scavengers."

Miriya had turned it over in her mind for most of the two hours it took to reach the Scavengers' cloud forest camp. That Seloy was alive was one thing; it was quite another that she had allied herself with the most bloodthirsty of the malcontents. But Miriya decided she would reserve judgment until she had heard her friend out. In the rare moments she wasn't preoccupied with Seloy, she thought about Max, who would be searching for her by now, and about Dana. How much more strain could her bond with her daughter endure before it was damaged beyond repair? Miriya trusted that the Grants would do all they could to explain things to Dana. Perhaps they would know enough to seek Zand's help—assuming that the abduction hadn't disabused the professor to all Zentraedi.

Once in camp, Kru Guage purposely refrained from raising the mecha canopy until they had reached a house that was set slightly apart from the rest and commanded a view of the steep-sided river valley. Miriya estimated that there were a hundred women in the camp, many of whom had emerged from huts and lean-tos to observe her arrival. From more than a few came shouts of *"Hajoca!"*

Seloy was waiting inside the house, dressed in jungle fatigues and an olive-drab T-shirt. She was thinner by fifteen pounds, and the humid air had frizzed her red hair; but she had lost none of her statuesque beauty, and her skin had remained white despite years of exposure to Earth's golden sun.

"Par dessu, Miriya Parino," she said, thumping her chest.

Miriya returned the salute, resisting an impulse to embrace Seloy as Human males and females were wont to do. "Why have you waited three years to contact me?" she asked finally. "Max and I thought you were dead."

Seloy almost smiled. "The people who were seeking us in Brasília are seeking us still. For your sake as well as our own, it was better you believed us dead."

"Us? Then Hirano is also alive?"

"Alive, and probably taller than your Dana. Unfortunately, he has his father's looks."

"Who is the father, Seloy?" Miriya chanced the question.

Seloy shook her head. "That must remain my secret."

"If you care about your son, how could you enlist in the Scavengers?"

"Precisely because I care about him—about his future. Brasília taught me that Humans and Zentraedi will never be able to coexist. The differences in our innate composition make us natural enemies, and where two enemies inhabit the same territory, one must be eradicated by the other. My wanderings eventually put me in touch with Zentraedi in whom the Imperative continues to burn, and ultimately with a group of women whom you shall meet in good time. Together we developed the Stingers, which male and female bands have deployed to such advantage all over this world. Eluding Humans has taught us how to think like them, to plan ahead and to employ the terror tactics they have used against us."

Miriya chose her words carefully. "I hope you haven't brought me here to enlist in the fight, Seloy."

Seloy planted her hands on her ample hips. "What if I have?"

"I'll refuse. I've chosen a different path from you."

"Yes, I've monitored you on that path over the years. Speaking to the media, railing against injustices . . ."

Miriya mimicked Seloy's pose. "I'm not a traitor—no matter what you or anyone in this camp thinks. Different paths, Seloy. But to the same end: equal rights."

"Equal rights?" Seloy threw her head back and laughed. "Is that what you think we're after?"

"What are you after?" Miriya asked.

Seloy took her time in responding. "Miriya, I inserted you into Zor's fortress so that you could hunt and kill the Human you had deemed your equal in combat. The Human you later married. That marriage, and your life since, has somehow neutralized the influence of the Imperative. But the bond between Quadrono warriors is not so easily overcome. You know this, or you wouldn't be here now."

"Even so, you owe me an explanation. I won't honor my obligation blindly."

Seloy considered it, then turned and headed for the doorway. "Come, let me show you."

Ignoring the gazes and comments they received—admiring, suspicious, disdainful—Seloy led Miriya on a winding route through the camp, then down along a narrow switchback path that ended at the river. A short stretch upstream was a drainage shaded by exceedingly tall trees, under which stood a dozen or more Stingers.

"You should have seen what we were forced to abandon at our facility in the south," Seloy said. "Even you would have been proud of our achievements."

Miriya had seen photos of the base Anatole Leonard had raided, and in fact she had been impressed, though she kept this to herself.

"At the start of the uprisings, our male comrades preferred to operate in groups of twenty or thirty," Seloy said.

"But maximized mobility came at a price: no attempt was made at coordinating strikes or planning a unified campaign. The Scavengers changed that. Not only did we provide mecha, we armed the males with a new tactic."

"Terror," Miriya said.

Seloy smiled at her friend's disapproving tone. "For a while that was enough to placate our craving for vengeance. But no longer. Now we want nothing less than victory—the death of the Human race." She paused. "Are you aware that the Flower of Life has taken root on Earth?"

"I didn't know."

"But you know what that means, Miriya: the Invid will come. Perhaps not for twenty years. But they will come. And what will the Humans do? They will attempt to sue for peace, just as they plan to do with the Masters."

"It is their way."

"But, ask yourself, is it the Masters' way? Or have you forgotten what they bade us do on Optera and Garuda and Singken? Consider, Miriya, what will happen when the Humans appear in Fantomaspace with their hands extended in *peace*. Think of it. They will be atomized. And what if the Masters arrive here first? How would you rather they find us—marooned and enslaved to a Micronian species, or marooned and victorious, the masters of all we survey?"

Miriya glanced at the Stingers. "It will take more than these to assure victory. Even with ten times as many—"

Seloy was shaking her head. "We now have something more powerful than Stingers. These are merely the delivery systems."

Miriya's face fell. "Nuclear weapons?"

"Even more devastating than those. A disease, Miriya."

Seloy was pleased to see that she had finally shocked her friend into speechlessness. "One of our Human allies—a native Amazonian—led us to a laboratory not far from here, where, in the years before Dolza's Rain, researchers were investigating a strain of virus that had begun to attack monkeys and some Human residents of the jungle. The indigines had known about the disease for a long time, and had their own name for it: 'the Madness.' Infected monkeys or Humans would become violent before they died. There were many stories of hunters or prospectors who had been attacked and killed by crazed monkeys. Two years ago, the researchers died of the virus they were investigating, but their solar-powered facility continued to function and the virus lived on, nurtured by the nutrient cultures the scientists had fashioned. Removed from those cultures, the virus expires rapidly. But when it finds a suitable live host, it thrives and spreads itself through the air to infect others."

Miriya grasped for words. "If the life span is short, how can Stingers deliver it? Won't the virus perish before it can find live hosts?"

From a nacelle in the leg of the nearest mecha, Seloy extracted an alloy carrying case, which she set on the Stinger's foot and opened. Inside were perhaps tens of thousands of black objects smaller than pinheads.

"Microbots," Seloy said. "Protoculture shuttles, actually—the essence of Female Power Armor's self-maintenance systems. But Xan—one of the women I'm eager for you to meet—has discovered a way to modify them to act as vectors for the virus. In place of Protoculture, they now carry the virus, immersed in a drop of the sustaining culture. And they have been tasked for independent flight, Miriya." Seloy touched her nose. "They embed themselves in the nasal passages and throats of their targets."

Miriya stared at Seloy, aghast.

"They're Imperatived, Miriya. Once the Stinger launches them from its missile tubes, they have ten minutes to embed themselves and deliver their payloads. But even if only one in ten thousand succeeds, that one can multiply and disperse itself from Human to Human—by breath, by touch, by sneeze, by *kiss*."

Miriya shook her head in agitation. "It will never work."

"Oh, but it already has. We experimented with the process in Mexico and elsewhere. And only days ago we lured the RDF to a camp in Venezuela and deployed a virus-laden cloud in their midst. Some troops were undoubtedly infected, and by now they have carried the disease back to Cavern City."

"Seloy, there are twenty thousand civilians in Cavern—Humans and Zentraedi!"

Seloy grinned. "Have no fear. We Zentraedi are immune to the disease."

Miriya regarded the near-microscopic shuttles in silence, then said, "You haven't explained why you summoned me here."

Seloy's slanted eyes narrowed perceptibly. "We've asked representatives of all the male bands to attend a meeting here. To each, we will distribute tasked shuttles and a Stinger, with instructions to deploy the virus in their respective territories. The disease, the madness, will spread itself around the world before a vaccine can be developed, and hundreds of thousands will die."

Miriya was steel-eyed. "What is my part in this?"

Seloy locked gazes with her. "I know that the RDF and the Army of the Southern Cross are closing on this camp. I am hopeful that the plan can be executed before they find us, but there is no guarantee. Your part in this is easy, Miriya Parino: I want you to remove Hirano to safety before anything untoward can happen."

CHAPTER TWENTY-SIX

*Cavern City became one of the first cities to suffer in the vio-
lence that succeeded the Southern Cross's abandonment of the
Southlands for Monument City. Petty dictators rose to prominence,
private armies sprang up, and previously allied city-states began to
wage war with one another. A few cities found themselves taken
over by gangs of well-armed marauders. In Cavern's case, the
gang was the Red Snakes, which for years had been terrorizing the
northern Southlands. I was living in New Dublin when I learned
that Raphael Mendoza had died in a drive-by shooting perpetrated
by the Red Snakes. Rho [Mynalo] and I had urged Raphael to
leave, but he considered Cavern, even in the worst of times, his
home. When Rho and I divorced, he applied for a position on the
factory satellite, and opted to remain aboard when Anatole Leonard ordered the satellite removed from the Solar system.*

from the afterward of the Third Edition of Lea Carson's *The Art
of Compromise*

MAX AND WOLFF WERE ASSISTING MEDEVAC TEAMS
at the site of the monorail crash when an officer from
Mayor Carson's office showed up to rush them over to City
Hall. It was three o'clock in the morning when they arrived, but already seated in the briefing room were Carson
and two of her aides, Raphael Mendoza and Rho Mynalo,
along with Cavern City's media secretary, Catherine Wolff,
and Dr. Lopez, from the RDF base hospital.

"The driver of the monorail died," Lopez was reporting,
"but several people have attested to her erratic behavior
prior to the crash. I'm certain an autopsy will reveal the
presence of the virus."

"How many fatalities?" the mayor wanted to know.

"Forty-six confirmed," Mendoza told her.

Carson turned back to Lopez. "And these other incidents?"

"A man armed with a Wolverine opened fire on a restaurant in Lookout Valley. Seventeen dead, including the gunman, fourteen wounded. In addition, there have been three suicides in the past seven hours."

The dreadlocked Mendoza took over. "Emergency rooms at City Hospital and the base hospital are already filled to capacity. Special isolation wards have been set up for victims of the disease—as opposed to victims of the behavior the virus provokes. All police units and fire companies are mobilized, and the Sector Guard is on full alert."

"It's like someone pulled a string and unraveled the whole city. And it's my fault for not listening to Dr. Lopez." Carson looked at him once more. "How many cases of the virus have you verified?"

"Seventeen, including the suicides. But let me clear up one point before we continue: the virus doesn't induce psychoses. Rather, its effect is neurotoxic. It attacks areas of the brain that manage aggression, depriving those infected access to any of the inhibitory devices normally employed in forestalling the commission of acts of violence to oneself or to others. The quick onset and brief duration of the early stage are indications of the potency of the virus itself. Typically, within hours, nerve damage is so complete that the victim becomes comatose and dies."

"And you're certain this disease was carried in by the Wolff Pack?"

Lopez glanced at Wolff and Max. "The members of Captain Wolff's team were obviously unwitting carriers of the virus as a result of their contact with the infected crew of the skyjacked plane and perhaps via direct exposure to a particle cloud emitted by a malcontent weapon. However, we don't know at this time if they were the sole carriers."

Carson scratched at her mop of strawberry-blond hair. "You're saying that someone other than the Wolff Pack could have introduced this virus into the city?"

"It's possible. We don't understand the mechanism of contagion—though it seems to operate much like influenza—nor have we identified the vector, the actual carrier. There is some speculation that the disease is initially transmitted by a tick or a mite, though I think researchers are being misled by the symptoms—the rash, the irritated nasal mucosa, et cetera."

"The Stinger we found didn't launch *ticks*, Doctor," Wolff said. "Besides, we brought the exposed tank in under wraps. So how could the virus get loose?"

Lopez shook his head. "It's likely more than one of you were infected. But as to why some succumbed to the virus while others didn't, I can't say. I should also mention here that there have been no cases reported among Cavern's Zentraedi population."

"Meaning what?" Carson asked suspiciously.

Lopez shrugged. "Meaning only that. The Zentraedi appear to be immune to the virus."

"Rho," Carson said, turning to her director of information, "I want corroboration on that."

The Zentraedi inclined his head in a bow. Max nodded hello from across the table; he and Mynalo had mutual Zentraedi friends in Monument City.

"A team from the Center for Disease Control is on the way," Mendoza told everyone. "In the meantime we've been instructed to seal the city. No one leaves, no one enters."

"That's going to turn this place into a pressure cooker," Wolff said, loud enough to be heard over a flurry of separate conversations. "And what happens when our food supplies run out?"

Carson called for silence. "We can have food trucked in by Disease Emergency Teams. Our biohazard suits will rendezvous with their biohazard suits." She looked at Lopez. "How reliable is the test for this virus?"

"It's reliable only insofar as our being able to single out the infected. We have no test for determining non-infected carriers."

"Does it make any sense to get everyone moved into shelters?"

Lopez shook his head. "One unidentified carrier could infect everyone in the population."

Carson slammed her hand on the table. "*Something* has to be done to protect people from catching this thing."

"We could use one of the hospitals as a quarantine area," Mendoza suggested.

"And if that hospital should fill up?" Lopez said.

"Then we'll use the base hospital as well."

"Why not use the Grand Cannon?" Max said. "It's roomy enough, and it would be relatively easy to isolate."

"The CDC team might want to headquarter itself there," Mendoza said.

Carson was nodding. "Find out if they do. Meanwhile, we'd better start thinking about food and fuel rationing, sanitation, and whatever else comes to mind." She looked at Wolff. "Captain, the RDF will be in charge of policing the shelters and the food distribution points."

Wolff stared at her in stunned incredulity. "That should be the responsibility of the Sector Guard! Unless you plan on using them to protect Cavern from surprise attacks from the malcontents."

"God forbid the Wolff Pack should miss out on any action," Catherine Wolff said, more to herself.

Wolff shot her a look, then cut his eyes to Carson. "This entire scenario—from the skyjacking to our raid on the camp—was calculated. Plainly, the malcontents are launching a new offensive. I strongly recommend that we requisition reinforcements from Monument and—"

"I've already been in touch with Monument," Carson interrupted, "and they've deferred to the Army of the Southern Cross." She allowed everyone a moment to think about it. "Senator Moran and Field Marshal Leonard have apparently demonstrated to the satisfaction of the UEG that this virus threatens not just Cavern City but the whole of the Southlands."

More concessions, Max told himself.

"And assuming you're correct about a malcontent offensive," Carson continued, "the Army of the Southern Cross has every right to be involved."

"How will it work?" Wolff asked angrily. "Who'll be in command of whom?"

"As I said, the RDF will be in charge of distribution of food and essentials within the city. The Army of the Southern Cross will establish a defensive perimeter to safeguard the city against incursions by malcontents or anyone else."

Max could scarcely control himself. "Leonard shouldn't be trusted. Everyone at this table knows he's been looking for an excuse to annex the Venezuela Sector. Now you're giving him a chance to do just that!"

"Lie still or this is never going to work," Lazlo Zand cautioned Dana Sterling.

Still, the unruly five-year-old fought the professor's efforts to fasten an electrode-studded monitor band around her head. "I don't wanna lie still!"

"You don't wanna lie still," Zand parroted. "You won't be happy until you've ruined the experim—the movie."

Dana kicked her legs and twisted her head about, nearly undoing the stays that secured her thin wrists to the arms of the chair. "Aunt Jean didn't say we were going to watch movies. She said I had to talk to you." She screwed up her face and made her lips flap. "More stupid, boring talk."

Zand showed her a death's head grin and spoke through gritted teeth. "That's why we're watching movies. So there won't be any boring talk."

"*Stupid*, boring talk. And I don't wanna watch."

"What's the matter with you?" Zand nearly screamed. *"You don't like movies?!"*

The expression on his face and sudden infernal tone of his voice actually gave her pause. "Not these kind," she answered weakly.

Not five feet in front of her, on a large flatscreen, flying saucers were attacking a city of monumental buildings. Before that—literally seconds before that—floating war machines with snakelike heads had been launching death rays at the machines of a rival army. And immediately following the saucers ran scenes of outsize monster robots marching across a ruined landscape, firing weapons at every living thing in sight.

The whole of Zand's ten-minute, continuous-loop film was comprised of nothing but outtakes from pre-War science-fiction films, along with video footage shot during the Global Civil War and on those few occasions when Humans and Zentraedi had gone at it on Earth: on Macross Island, elsewhere in the South Pacific, in the skies over the Ontario Quadrant. Khyron's cruiser figured in one scene; even Miriya Parino and Max Sterling showed up briefly.

How could their little hybrid urchin not enjoy it? Zand screamed to himself in the same voice Dana's shenanigans had invoked.

The Grants had dropped her off at the Monument City's Robotech Research Center for a therapeutic session, and Zand had been only too happy to oblige. She'd been sullen, withdrawn, hypomanic, and hostile to the Grants' wimp of a son, Bowie. They didn't know what to do with her; they were at their wits' end. Miriya had suggested in her message that they contact Zand if they needed help, and, after all, Zand himself had volunteered . . .

Had there been any word from Mom? Zand had asked the lovely, honey-brown Jean Grant. No, none. And what about Dad, any word from him? None that she could speak of; Sterling was in the Southlands on official RDF business. And what about that precious trio, Rico, Konda, and Bron, where were they? Still on the factory satellite.

Zand wondered if Grant had seen him salivate on realizing that he had Dana to himself, without fear of intrusion by any of her would-be guardians.

He'd had the movie prepared for some time, sitting in a vault in his office, awaiting its premiere. Zand's earlier experiments had established that Dana's brain-wave activity and body chemistry underwent changes when she was subjected to or confronted with violent stimuli. And those same changes were evident when Dana was interacting with her fellow aliens, as opposed to Humans. Blood drawn during those periods showed a marked increase in as-yet-unidentified hormones and enzymes, linked, Zand was certain, to the Zentraedi part of her biophysical makeup. So, all he had to do was activate that part, draw out as much blood as possible without unduly endangering the child, and quickly transfuse that hormone-laden blood into himself.

Easier said than done.

"Show me cartoons!" Dana wailed, flailing her legs.

"Stop wiggling around and watch the screen."

Where Veritechs and Tactical Battlepods were exchanging depleted transuranics and vibrant bolts of energy.

"Now, isn't this much more interesting?"

Dana twisted her head to one side and shut her eyes. "You can't make me watch it."

"Oh, no? *Oh, no?*" He leaned his gangly frame over her, his bony finger attempting to pry her eyes open, only to be kicked solidly in the groin.

"All right, all right, enough of this," Zand said when he could. He disappeared for a moment, returning with a set of eyelid expanders of the sort used in optic surgery. "Can't make you watch it, huh? Just watch this . . ."

Dana began to scream as Zand moved in on her.

He was standing over her, one hand clamped over her mouth, the eyelid apparatus in the other, an especially barbarous sequence running onscreen, when the locked door flew open and a broad-shouldered figure stormed into the office.

Emerson? Zand had time to think before the muscular RDF officer hurled himself at him.

Seloy had insisted that Miriya think carefully before making up her mind about taking Hirano—and raising him should something befall his mother. But Miriya had no time to waste on thinking. No sooner did Seloy sequester her in one of the huts than Miriya was stealing into the camp, searching for someone to ambush. Anything could happen here, especially with embittered Zentraedi like Ranoc Nomarre on the way, and she wanted a weapon. Not even fifty yards from the hut, she located her target: a recent arrival—a lone male—sleeping away the high heat of the afternoon under a shady breadnut tree. A quick chop to the base of the neck was all it took to dispatch him to temporary oblivion. Now, Miriya thought, to work the handgun free of the tight waistband of his filthy pants and conceal it under the untucked tail of Max's hiking shirt . . .

"Are you Miriya Parino?" a child's voice asked in Spanglish.

She turned, hiding the gun, and found herself facing a

sad-eyed child of four, dark-haired and thickly built, dressed in a T-shirt and ragged shorts. "Hirano?"

"You're a friend of my mother, yes?"

"Yes, Hirano. I am her friend."

"She asked me to find you. She wants to know the answer."

Miriya smiled. "Can you take me to her?"

Hirano took hold of her hand and began to lead her through the camp, past groups of Scavengers and others muttering Zentraedi imprecations. "Hirano," Miriya said, "do you know what your mom has asked me to do?"

The child nodded. "She wants you to take me someplace. Then she's going to come and meet us there."

More than a year younger than Dana, Hirano seemed already hardened to life. There was nothing innocent or playful about him. He was serious, focused, sure of himself: a Zentraedi. Ill-suited to a Human world. "Are you frightened about going with me?" she asked.

"Frightened of what?"

"Of leaving your mom. Tell the truth, Hirano."

He looked up at her. "I don't remember you."

"That's because I only met you once, and you were a tiny baby then."

"My mom said you were in the War with her."

"Your mother was a great warrior."

"She still is."

Miriya stopped and knelt down beside him. "Hirano, not all battles are good ones or easy ones to win. The things your mother and her comrades are trying to do here are very dangerous."

"She could get killed."

"That's right, she could be killed."

"Then I would have to live with you and your child, and the three of us could fight the Humans together."

Nothing more was said until they had reached the house on the edge of the mountainside. Seloy wore a white jumpsuit, adorned at the breast with the Zentraedi sigil, and a holstered weapon.

"It is time for *magdomilla*, Miriya—time for strategic talk."

Miriya knelt at Hirano's side once more. "Hirano, I want you to wait outside while your mom and I talk."

Seloy grabbed Hirano by the arm and tugged him to her. "He stays. He has a right to hear your decision and know his fate." She put her hands on her hips. "The meeting will begin soon, Miriya, and after that, there will be much to attend to. But the male groups are careless; any one of them might be traced to this place, and there could be fighting. If your answer is yes, I want you to leave immediately. A Stinger is waiting to carry the two of you to Mexico."

Miriya's thoughts spiraled. Seloy was testing her. Once in Mexico, she could provide the RDF with the location of the camp; but once committed to accepting Hirano, she was honor-bound to silence.

"What is your decision?" Seloy demanded.

Miriya showed her a cheerless smile. "I was so happy to learn you were alive, Seloy. Your friendship means so much to me, I thought nothing could come between us. But I was wrong. You can't expect me to ignore what I've seen here. I want to help you and Hirano, but not if that means allowing you to make Earth unfit for Human life. You ask too much of me."

Seloy smirked. "I feared as much. I shouldn't have asked you to come. You are no longer Zentraedi, Miriya Parino." She drew the weapon. Confused, Hirano made as if to hug her legs, but she pushed him away.

Miriya looked at her friend. "There was a time no Zentraedi would fire on another. Perhaps we've both betrayed the Imperative."

"So smug," Seloy said. "Show your weapon, Miriya— the one you took from the male. I left you unguarded deliberately to test you. Now, at least go to your death honorably."

Miriya reached behind her to draw the weapon from the small of her back. As she did so, Seloy raised hers to fire, but Hirano chose just that moment to lunge for her. The weapon discharged but the projectile meant for Miriya missed its mark and streaked through the roof thatch. By then, Miriya had the borrowed handgun in front of her in a two-handed grip. Seloy kicked Hirano aside and dived to the left. Miriya yelled "No!" and fired.

And struck Hirano.

Twice repelled, the boy had run for his mother and caught the shot in the middle of his back. Miriya and Seloy stood gaping at his crumpled form. Miriya began shaking her head back and forth in anguished disbelief. Seloy was confused, distrustful of her feelings. Did she *love* the boy? Did the agony she felt at his death make a mother of her? When she gazed at Miriya, her face was streaked with tears. Then her features torqued in rage and she charged, screaming *"Hajoca!"* Charged, screaming, squarely into Miriya's gun.

The discharge all but blew her in half. Mother and son lying dead together . . . Miriya's scream seemed to last an eternity. She couldn't recall moving to Seloy's side, crouching beside her, cradling Seloy's head in her arms, rocking and keening. But there she was when the three women appeared in the doorway, weapons in hand, staring aghast at the scene.

"I am not Zentraedi," she moaned. "I am not Zentraedi."

"The Army of the Southern Cross knows all about the legendary exploits of Captain Wolff," Anatole Leonard said on being introduced to Wolff. In the bubble-helmeted, billowy antihazard suit, the field marshal looked twice his normal size, almost too large for the City Hall briefing room. "People refer to your team as a 'pack,' if I'm not mistaken."

"I'm flattered you've heard of us," Wolff told him through a fixed smile.

"Don't be," Leonard said, ignoring the sarcasm.

Leonard's fleet of superhaulers had arrived only that morning, two days after the monorail crash, setting down near the Grand Cannon and at points north, east, and west of Cavern City to establish a defensive perimeter. CDC guidelines required nuclear/biological/chemical suits for everyone entering the city. Leonard was accompanied by his aide-de-camp, Joseph Petrie, and two Southern Cross lieutenants. Waiting for him in the briefing room were Carson,

Mendoza, Mynalo, Lopez, the Wolffs, and two epidemiologists from the CDC.

Given his history with Leonard, Max Sterling had thought it best not to attend.

"I'd like a summary of where things stand," Leonard said, nodding to Petrie, who was recording everything via a fiber-optic rig designed into the face-shielded helmet of his suit.

Raphael Mendoza answered for Carson's team. "The virus is spreading exponentially. Where there were seventeen confirmed cases on August fifteenth, there are at present sixty-five. Twenty-seven have already died of the disease; the rest are in isolation in the east wing of City Hospital. Calamities have increased as well, running the gamut from shootings to firebombings, though not all of these incidents are directly related to contagion and subsequent infection. Panic attacks, copycat crimes, mass hysteria, and personal vendettas all have to be considered as factors contributing to the rise in property destruction and general mayhem."

Leonard mulled it over for a moment, then looked at Wolff. "It seems you returned from your raid on the Shroud and Fist with quite a prize, Captain. Your pack should remember to delouse before returning to civilization."

Carson spoke before Wolff could respond. "Assigning blame is counterproductive, Field Marshal. We have a situation, and that situation needs to be dealt with, regardless of how it arose. And let's not forget that three of Captain Wolff's teammates have been casualties of this virus."

Leonard steepled his gloved fingers and looked long and hard at Rho Mynalo. "As long as we're being blunt, Ms. Mayor, let me state that I'm opposed to having a *Zentraedi* sit in or otherwise participate in this meeting."

Carson reddened with anger. "Rho has been a trusted member of my staff for three years, and I wouldn't think of excluding him. As you well know, Cavern City has a Zentraedi population exceeding five hundred, all of whom are considered full members of the community. Unlike Brasília and Cuiabá, to name only two, Cavern has no Zeetown."

"That may explain why your city alone finds itself victimized by a mysterious plague," Leonard said. "The CDC has yet to demonstrate conclusively that Wolff's team was the only vector for this virus. Now, I'm not saying that Mynalo here is a double agent, but for the time being *all* Zentraedi must be assumed to be security risks."

Carson shook her head. "I simply won't have it."

"In his reports, Captain Wolff refers to the virus as a 'Zentraedi weapon,' " Joseph Petrie thought to point out.

Wolff shot to his feet. "I called it a *malcontent* weapon. Or maybe you fail to see the distinction."

Petrie took it in stride, directing himself to Mendoza. "Do you deny that there have been attacks against Cavern's upstanding Zentraedi citizenry these past two days?"

"No, we won't deny that."

"So it appears that not everyone agrees with the mayor."

"There's an explanation for those attacks," Carson said.

Petrie's grin showed through the helmet faceshield. "And that is that the Zentraedi's apparent immunity to the virus has made them suspect."

Intruding on a sinister silence, Rho Mynalo stood up at his chair. "Mayor Carson, I'm willing to leave if my absence will facilitate an understanding between yourself and the Army of the Southern Cross."

Carson whirled on him. "You're not going anywhere, Rho. If anyone, it's the field marshal who's leaving."

Petrie started to reply, but Leonard silenced him with a gesture. "We seem to have gotten off on the wrong foot here," he said in mock concern. "Why don't we begin again, focusing on the 'situation,' as Mayor Carson puts it. The Army of the Southern Cross is willing and certainly able to lend its services to Cavern City—a Northlands protectorate—but only if we can be assured the freedom to operate as we see fit. We will honor all protocols by keeping the RDF fully apprised of our actions, but we will not take orders from them or anyone else. What this means, essentially, is that we want the authority to control the city's power and telecommunications facilities, and to commandeer any and all housing, food, and vehicles. Strategic decisions made by me cannot be countermanded by the mayor's office, nor by Captain Wolff or any member of the

RDF." He paused to glance at Carson. "Do we understand one another?"

"You must be mad," she told him. "I'm not going to turn this city over to you."

"The decision is yours, of course. But ask yourself this: since Monument has given its blessing to the Southern Cross, will you still have a city to cede a week from now?"

His ultimatum delivered, Anatole Leonard had excused himself from the meeting, leaving it to Carson and Petrie to strike a compromise. The final solution, arrived at after four hours of heated argument, was satisfying only to Leonard's aide.

Frustrated and angered by what he saw as Carson's shortsightedness, Wolff—only steps behind his wife— exited the briefing room while the mayor, Petrie, and the CDC people were still hammering out the details. In the corridor, he hurried after Catherine, catching up with her on the staircase to the lobby.

She recoiled from the light touch of his hand on her shoulder. "Look, Jonathan, I don't have time right now to process our relationship."

"This isn't about you and me. It's about Johnny. Have you had him tested for the virus?"

She rolled her eyes. "No, I was planning to let him get sick so he could miss a few days of school. And perhaps burn the house down at the same time."

Wolff went right on. "How about yourself?"

"Why, Jonathan, all this sudden concern is heartwarming."

"I want you two to move into one of the clear shelters."

"You want." Her eyes narrowed. "Unless I'm mistaken, you don't live with us anymore, which means what *you* want no longer matters as far as we're concerned."

"It's too dangerous to stay in the apartment. There are a lot of Zentraedi living in that neighborhood, and the way things are going you could get caught up in a riot."

"I know the risks. But I'm not about to stick us in some filthy shelter. Anyway, I have a job to do. Lea's counting on me."

Wolff snorted a laugh. "Yeah, forget about the CDC or the Army of the Southern Cross, what this emergency needs is the services of a good spin doctor."

"How dare you belittle me! Maybe I'm not in charge of maintaining law and order like the heroic Jonathan Wolff, but what I do matters. And goddamn you for not remembering that *you* were the one who urged me to take the position in the first place!"

Catherine's tears made a molten mess of him. "I'm only thinking of your safety, Cath. I know I've screwed up—we've screwed up—but we have to think of Johnny—"

"Since when has Johnny ever come first? What have you been to him all these years while I've been mother and father?" She raised a hand as if to slap him, but thought better of it. "If I'm such an unfit protector, why don't you ask Geena Bartley to take care of him. She doesn't work. She's supportive of her husband. She's willing to sacrifice everything for his career."

"Cath, I only meant—"

"I don't care what you meant. If you're not going to be in my life, you have no right to interfere with my decisions. And no, Jonathan, I don't have the virus: whatever hostility I'm projecting is of my own making."

CHAPTER TWENTY-SEVEN

Hollister was never cut out to be an anchor; she was too in love with the field, the image of the lone photojournalist reporting live from the front. That's why she jumped at the chance of an assignment on the factory satellite. There, she would do a series of exclusives, break many a heart, cover the Hunter-Hayes wedding, and be a strong influence on a young reporter named Susan Graham, whose documentary on the SDF-3 mission would earn her a posthumous Pulitzer. How then, you may be wondering, did Hollister ever end up as Supreme Commander Leonard's press secretary?
Altaira Heimel, *Butterflies in Winter*

"AND ON A PERSONAL NOTE, I'D LIKE TO SAY how happy I am to be back on the MBS Evening News, and I'd like to thank everyone for all the kind words and letters of support." Katherine Hyson's smile was strained, and the dullness in her eyes betrayed the effects of the sedatives that had contributed to her inordinately speedy convalescence. "Rebecer Holistin," she went on, unintentionally garbling the name of the woman she blamed for her breakdown, "is currently on assignment on the factory satellite. And now for our top stories.

"Cavern City, beleaguered capital of the Venezuela Sector, remains the focal point of world attention tonight, as experts from the Center for Disease Control continue to seek a vaccine for the deadly virus that has held that city in its grip during the past week. Believed to have been developed by the malcontent group known as the Scavengers, the neurotoxic virus induces episodes of berserk behavior and, in many cases, death. Four hundred and fifteen cases have been confirmed since an RDF unit, returning from a raid on a malcontent camp, unwittingly introduced the virus to the city. Held hostage by the disease, Cavern's thousands remain in virtual quarantine, rocked by sporadic rioting and mob violence directed against the Zentraedi population, who are evidently immune to the disease.

"Along with the presence of the Army of the Southern Cross, the crisis in Cavern has also made the city something of a political hotbed. While reports that Anatole Leonard received the tacit approval of the RDF have yet to be substantiated, spokespersons for the UEG will not disavow rumors that Leonard's occupation of the district constitutes the first step toward the eventual ceding of Venezuela to the Southlands.

"One person who probably won't be heard from regarding the Venezuela controversy is Braxton Milburn, former head of the UEG's Ways and Means Committee, charged today with conspiracy stemming from Milburn's connection to Tom Hoos and the ongoing Lorelei Network Scandal.

"As MBS reported on Thursday, the all-music satellite network was revealed to be a privately funded surveillance system aimed at monitoring the whereabouts of Zentraedi callers, all of whose WorldPhone links were recorded and traced. An analysis of the free food distributed by the network has shown it to contain a chemical agent that binds with Zentraedi blood and served as yet another monitoring device. Based on information released today by the Ministry of Justice, it now appears that Senator Milburn was the mastermind of Lorelei. Lynn-Minmei, who has hosted a talk show since the network's inception, has been unavailable for comment . . ."

It was brutally hot inside the cramped pilot compartment of Pack One, Wolff's tank. The Centaur was parked downtown, at the intersection of Chasm and High Valley Road—a distribution point for drinking water. Max had joined Wolff there to learn what had gone down between Carson and Leonard at the morning meeting. Two minutes inside the old battlewagon and he was bathed in sweat.

"So she gave in to his demands."

"Completely," Wolff said with contempt. "Well, maybe not completely. We're retaining control of power and telecommunications. But otherwise, Leonard pretty much has run of the place. What he says goes, no matter what Carson or Monument think of his decisions. It sucks. And I still can't figure why Command would waive their authority." He looked at Max. "This can't all be because of Miriya's disappearance."

"I'm sure Reinhardt himself would go to the media with the story rather than surrender Venezuela to the Southlands," Max said.

"So what is it, if it isn't blackmail?"

Max unsnapped the collar of his shirt and sat down in the gunner's seat. "It's politics. In order to be guaranteed what it needs to pull off the Expeditionary mission, the RDF is willing to cede territory to the Southern Cross. How much longer could we have overseen Venezuela, anyway? If this virus hadn't happened, Leonard would have manufactured a crisis that allowed him to occupy Cavern."

Wolff exhaled wearily. "Tirol better turn out to be worth the effort." He shook his head. "To save Earth, the RDF has to sacrifice it."

"No less to the likes of Leonard and his gang." Max glanced at Wolff. "That's what they are, you know. Thugs, mercenaries, traitors to one cause or another over the past twenty-five years."

"What the hell are we supposed to do when Leonard's tanks or Destroids decide to handle the next demonstration the way they handled the one you witnessed in Brasília? Do I order the Pack to defend the demonstrators and risk starting an all-out war between the RDF and the Southern Cross?"

Max shook his head. "We intervene, but we don't fire on them. We'd only get our butts kicked in the long run, anyway. And then where would the city be?"

Wolff clenched his fists. "I hate having my hands tied like this. I'm worried Leonard's going to try to provoke me. We have to get to any source of trouble before he does. There've already been four separate mob attacks on Zentraedi neighborhoods. And guess who's gonna come out on top if Leonard shows up at the next one? Not the Zentraedi, that's for damn sure."

"It goes beyond prejudice with him. He has some reason for hating the Zentraedi in a personal way."

"Any idea why?"

Max thought about Rolf Emerson's statement that Leonard had once taken a Zentraedi lover. "Nope."

"Max," Wolff said tentatively, "what would you say to getting out of here?"

"How do you mean?"

"I mean taking Skull Team and the Wolff Pack and all our families out of this place before the shit hits the fan. I know it sounds like desertion, and I know we'll be breaking the quarantine, but I prefer to think of it as saving lives."

"*Our* lives," Max said harshly.

"So what's wrong with that? You said yourself Venezuela's a lost cause. So the RDF is just pulling out a little early."

Max stood up, almost cracking his head open. "First of all, our leaving would give Leonard control over everyone here, which means the Zentraedi won't have a prayer. Second, one of us could be harboring the virus. And finally, the whole lot of us would be court-martialed and probably end up spending the next five years in the brig. Are you willing to risk *that*?"

Wolff ran a hand down his face. "I'm worried about Catherine and Johnny," he said, after a moment. "I tried to convince her to go to one of the shelters, but she wouldn't listen. She figures her job comes first."

Max's expression softened. "Where does that leave Johnny?"

"Geena Bartley was planning to move Rook into a shelter. I'm hoping she took Johnny with her."

A comtone sounded and Wolff reached for the radio. He listened for a long moment, in obvious and ever-increasing alarm, and was ashen-faced when he turned to Max.

"The bastard has done it. There was a riot outside a shelter set up and staffed by Zentraedi. Leonard ordered his troops to put it down with force. They fired on the crowd indiscriminately. At least twenty people are dead; maybe three times that many wounded." He paused for a moment, numbed by his own words. "It was the shelter Geena was taking Rook to."

Anatole Leonard's bullet-shaped, shaved head filled the screen of the vidphone. "Well, Captain Sterling, we meet at last," he said in his humorless baritone. "Not exactly face-to-face, but that's probably for the best."

Max wasted no time setting the tone of the call. "You crazy sonofabitch. Do you know how many people you killed at that shelter?"

"We were merely maintaining the peace."

"Like you were in Brasília?"

"My troops may have been somewhat overeager, it's true. As for the deaths, I'm afraid there wasn't time to sort the innocent from the guilty."

"By guilty, you must mean the Zentraedi, since they accounted for most of the casualties."

"That my troops couldn't distinguish them from Cavern City's Human populace is surely a testament to how well the aliens have blended in."

"Wolff's son was there, Leonard."

Leonard didn't respond immediately. "My sympathies to the captain."

"Lucky for you, he survived the attack. But then I suppose you couldn't imagine Wolff's distress, could you, Field Marshal? You don't have a son, or a family."

Leonard was stone-faced. "Come to the purpose of this call, Sterling. I'm too busy to indulge in games or name-calling."

Max leaned away from the phone's camera. "You're not here out of altruism. Cavern's nothing but a target of opportunity. So much the better if several hundred Zentraedi die in the campaign."

Leonard snorted a laugh. "The Southern Cross will always be indebted to you for the plague you helped bring here. Though I must admit I'm surprised that you weren't more circumspect about procedure after witnessing the deaths of the three Scavengers you captured. The Zentraedi we found at the Stinger base robbed us of the pleasure of observing their mass suicide. But perhaps you thought that biological warfare was beneath the malcontents? I'll wager that your wife could have told you differently." He grinned. "Have you heard from her, by the way? I understand that the Scavengers are always looking for able-bodied recruits."

"Don't expect an easy victory over this city, Leonard. Not while I'm here."

"Yes, and it's a pity you are here, Sterling—in more ways than one. After all, if it wasn't for the quarantine, you could be out tracking down your better half. Or is that alien half? In any case, I'll be sure to let you know if the Southern Cross encounters her while it's out locating and destroying malcontent camps."

She had been placed for safekeeping inside a ramshackle hut, but she was more a prisoner of her thoughts than the hut's walls of sticks and dried mud. She had killed them—killed Seloy, killed Seloy's child. The deaths had drained her of any emotions engendered by the years of living with Max, and of coming to love him and Dana. She was in the hold of the Imperative once more, thinking only of her own survival.

When she heard the crude wooden door open, she thought it might be her jailer—a willowy thing with white hair—or any one of the Scavengers who had hurried to the sounds of gunfire in Seloy's house: Marla Stenik, Vivek Bross, or the scientist, Xan Norri. But instead it turned out to be Ranoc Nomarre, accompanied by a second member of the New Unity, a hulking, bald-headed giant of a man with a patch over one eye. Leida, she recalled, from her short stay in their camp.

Both wore faded T-shirts and baggy pants. The weapon Ranoc was pointing at her fired conventional projectiles—though ones of sufficiently large caliber. Leida's handgun was smaller but equally lethal.

"Miriya Parino," Ranoc said, "you have been found guilty of crimes against the T'sentrati—"

"*Sesannu!*" she said, cutting him off. "I'm aware of my crimes, Ranoc, but you were not appointed my executioner. The Scavengers reserve that right for themselves."

His upper lip curled, revealing rotting teeth. "Don't as-

sume that I care what these females have to say. I've suspected all along that you were a traitor, and now you've
proven it by killing Seloy and the adopted Human child.
Still fearful of your status as a Quadrono, the Scavengers
are afraid to act, but I am not." He leveled the gun. "You
will not escape again."

Impervious to the possible consequences, Miriya hurled
herself at Leida, catching him around his middle and driving him back against the door. As the big man slid down
on his tailbone, she scrambled behind him and locked her
forearms around the front of his neck. His powerful hands
fastened on her arms. The gun slipped from his grasp, but
she was slow in retrieving it. Ranoc fired, grazing the top
of her left shoulder. But by then she had Leida's gun in
hand. Her shots slammed into Ranoc's chest and he died.

"Traitor," Leida hissed, struggling to get to his feet.

She killed him with a shot to the head.

She stood still for a moment, thinking only about what
had to be done, satisfied to be empty of feeling.

She picked up Ranoc's weapon and walked to the door,
expecting to face a charge, but no one was in sight. Off to
one side lay the white-haired guard Ranoc had killed on his
way in. Miriya stepped outside.

"*Deng yar*—don't move!" someone yelled from a nearby
observation tower. A round whistled past her left cheek and
tore through the wall of the hut.

Miriya saw the shooter and returned fire, toppling her
from the platform of the tower.

Bleeding from the shoulder, she headed out, not furtively
but openly, spoiling for confrontations and shooting at anyone who appeared, hitting the majority of her targets. Surrendering to the Imperative and the skills it had afforded
her in a lifetime of combat.

She could see the Stinger from one hundred yards away,
reflective where the sunlight found it, towering over everything in the vicinity except for the trees themselves. That
the mecha was in camp and not secreted in the valley below identified it as the one Seloy had selected to fly Miriya
and Hirano to Mexico.

She moved toward it. The throbbing pain in her shoulder

was superseded by a searing in her left leg; she smelled singed cloth and flesh. *Keep moving, ignore the distress, kill that which impedes your progress, attain your goal, kill that which stands in your way, save yourself . . .* This wasn't something she told herself but something recited to her by the Imperative.

Access to the Stinger's cockpit was via a tall wooden ladder. Miriya began to climb, firing on moving targets below and taking another round in the leg, behind the knee. It pleased her that she had managed to throw the camp into chaos. She dragged herself upward, relying on the strength of her upper body, and tumbled into the cockpit.

A glance at the consoles told her that she could pilot the thing. Anyone who had mastered Female Power Armor could master a Stinger; only the weapons systems were unfamiliar.

The helmet and waldos were a tight fit. She activated an array of controls and the mecha powered up. It lifted off, rounds pinging against the armored exterior.

She was dizzy, but she refused to surrender to the disorientation and pain; if need be, she would push her body to the point of death. The closest RDF base was Cavern City, but Cavern would be busy coping with the virus. It was Mexico or nowhere. But would the RDF blow her out of the sky before she had a chance to identify herself? Was the Stinger even equipped with a radio? And what if the mecha was armed with virused shuttles? Would its destruction vector the disease to a new population?

These were possibly pointless concerns, since two of the Scavengers' Stingers were already in pursuit. She maxed power to the engines, but could neither escape nor evade them. So she took them on.

The pilot of the first was an unworthy adversary. Miriya's tactics were too subtle; she rid herself of the mecha with little effort. The second pilot, however, was adept. She divined Miriya's every move, and at times literally flew circles around her. She placed her missiles with surgical precision, as if she wanted to take Miriya alive.

Miriya's ship was flashing warnings and belching smoke when a voice blared from a concealed speaker.

"*T'sen* Parino, your Stinger is crippled. Will you yield?"

Miriya thought she recognized the woman behind the voice: Seloy's small-boned, pixie-eared lieutenant. "*T'sen* Voss?"

"I am honored to be recognized. I have great respect for you, *T'sen* Parino, as a fighter and as a woman. I always believed that you, more than any, understood and followed the true path of the T'sentrati. I do not know your reasons for killing Seloy and her child, but your actions have not lessened my respect for you. I won't be the one to kill you."

Miriya searched for the radio controls to no avail. Finally, she simply spoke to the air: "You honor yourself, *T'sen* Bross—Vivik. Will you abandon the cause and join me?"

"I cannot."

Miriya felt nauseated. "The Scavengers will know that you allowed me to escape, Vivik. You'll be executed."

"Just the same, I won't kill you."

"Then come with—"

"I salute you, Miriya Parino."

Miriya sensed what was coming. "Vivik, no!"

Bross's Stinger hovered in the air for a moment, then came apart in an expanding sphere of fire and smoke.

Miriya put her face in her hands, grieving for the imminent death of her race.

CHAPTER
TWENTY-EIGHT

The two technicians responsible for orchestrating "Jeng Chiang's" live-video message to Breetai were apprehended during an RDF raid on a malcontent camp located in southern Mexico and charged with acts of conspiracy, sedition, and sabotage. As part of their plea bargain, however, they allowed that they had indeed arranged for the transmission of Chiang's Little White Dragon *"in-take" [sic] to Breetai's quarters. Though long suspected, Chiang was not positively identified as Lynn-Kyle until after the SDF-3 launched for Tirol with Kyle aboard. (See Versace's* Malcontent: Confessions of a Sympathizer.) *A videotape of the intake that thwarted Theofre Elmikk's plan to seize the SDF-3 is rumored to exist.*

footnote in Daluce's *Bridge to an Uncertain Future: Earth Between the Wars*

O N THE PHONE, MINMEI ASKED HIM TO MEET HER AT a scenic overlook located just off the main highway a few miles north of Monument City. Her rental car was already in the small lot when he arrived on a borrowed Marauder motorcycle; otherwise, it appeared they had the place to themselves. Dressed Western, with her long hair ponytailed, Minmei was standing at the railing of a concrete balcony that afforded a panorama of the valley and the mountainous terrain east and north of the city. The day was warm and cloudless, and the view seemed to go on forever.

They embraced, and she thanked him for coming. "I would have suggested a restaurant in town, but the media is still hounding me about the Lorelei Scandal."

"I figured," Rick said, setting the motorcycle helmet down and taking off the leather jacket.

"Why do things like this keep happening to me, Rick? Now I have to look like a jerk for not knowing what was going on. Or— worse—a racist, which you know I'm not.

341

Either way, my voice has been used as a weapon again. Like it's not enough that Lang expects me and Janice to *sing* away the next wave of invaders from space."

"There was no way you could have known what Milburn and the rest were doing. Even we didn't know. And another embarrassment was the last thing the RDF needed right now."

"I guess. But I'm sick of everything going wrong in my life. Every decision I make is jinxed."

"At least you found a partner."

Minmei made a face. "That's probably going to end badly, too. I mean, Janice is the strangest person. And talk about an embarrassment, it's like she doesn't care who she offends with her comments—excuse me, her 'honesty.' "

"That must be the Lang side of her lineage coming out. Look how weird he is."

Minmei laughed, hugged Rick, then swiftly backed out of his embrace and punched him solidly in the arm.

"Hey, what's that for?" he said, massaging his right biceps.

She folded her arms and scowled. "For getting engaged."

"Minmei—"

"Oh, you know I don't mean it. I'm happy for both of you—sort of. I just wish I had someone in my life. I try to look into the future, and all I see are more tours, more clubs, more interviews . . . I announce to the whole world that 'Lynn-Minmei is going to take a new direction,' and here I am, three years later, in exactly the same place: touring, avoiding the press, the center of controversy, Earth's most powerful weapon." She shut her eyes and shook her head. "I'm always getting involved with the wrong people."

"Thanks loads."

"I didn't mean you, silly. I was thinking of Kyle, and now Senator Milburn . . . I still can't believe I had dinner with that man a week before the scandal broke and he never said a word about having an interest in Lorelei. Even though Janice kept talking about the 'politics' of the network."

"Janice did?" Rick said, surprised.

"I distinctly remember her asking for Milburn's views on

the network, and he was just so cool, so casual about everything. Just like Kyle used to be before his drinking got out of hand. You never knew what he was really thinking."

Rick scratched his head. "Where *is* Kyle?"

"I almost wish I knew." She was quiet for a moment, then looked at him earnestly. "Will you promise me one thing? That we can stay friends even after you and Lisa get married?"

"Of course we can."

"Close friends?"

"Best friends."

Minmei linked her arm through his, rested her head on his shoulder, and sighed. "I love the view from here. Remember the view from the park in the SDF-1? Remember how real EVE made the sky look, and how wonderful it was to look at the stars from the observation bay?"

"I sure do."

"You're so lucky to be going back into space. I don't suppose the REF would like to take a singer to Tirol?"

Rick snorted a laugh. "The Expeditionary mission won't be a pleasure cruise. Just ask Breetai or Exedore. We have no idea what we're going to confront."

"So—no singers."

"Not unless we receive some word from the Robotech Masters that they're planning a joyous reception in our honor."

The wind picked up a bit, laden with the scent of pine. "You know what really bothers me, Rick?" Minmei asked. "The image everybody has of me as helpless, or perennially victimized. I'm not. I'm strong, and I want people to understand that."

"Your good friends know that. That's why we always support your choices." Rick grinned. "Even if some of them turn out to be wrong."

She narrowed her eyes, then smiled. "Yeah, just like I support your choices. And let's hope some of *those* don't turn out to be wrong."

They laughed, and began to talk of better days and friends they hadn't seen in a long while. When a family of five drove up in a mufflerless minivan, robbing the moment of its poignancy, they went to sit in her rental.

A moment later, a lone figure began to pick his way out from under the balcony, where he'd been lying amid the beamwork that supported the cantilevered slab of concrete. He had followed Minmei from Monument City, and in fact had been tailing her for the past several weeks. His motorcycle—an older version of the one Hunter rode—was secreted in the bushes below the uppermost switchback in the road that climbed to the parking area.

Minmei was deluding herself, Kyle thought. She wasn't strong, she wasn't independent. She would continue to be victimized. She needed someone to watch over her, to spot the bad choices before they happened, or to effect the course corrections that would keep them from going bad. In short, she needed him. The Zentraedi rebels had undermined themselves and were finished. She would become his new cause; Kyle, her invisible guardian. Even if that meant returning to the stars.

Zand's nose was broken, his eyes were blackened, and his right arm was in a sling. Lang stood staring at him from the doorway to Zand's office in the Tokyo Research Center, to which the professor had fled following the regrettable incident in Monument City.

"Tell me exactly what happened, Lazlo," Lang said, closing the door behind him and pulling a chair up to Zand's hopelessly cluttered desk.

"What happened? I was assaulted by a brainless RDF major named Rolf Emerson, that's what happened. I've a good mind to sue him for all he's worth—which is probably next to nothing."

Lang forced a breath. What was he going to do with Zand, the colleague he had selected to assume the mantle of chief of Special Protoculture Observations and Operations during his absence? Thanks to Janice, Lang—via allies in the UEG—had managed to bring about the downfall of Milburn and the Lorelei Network. Would he now have to arrange for Zand, a friend and fellow scientist, to be similarly exposed to governmental and media scrutiny?

"I've met Emerson," Lang said after a moment. "He hardly seems the type to assault someone without provocation."

"Then you're not as good a judge of character as you'd like to think you are."

"You could be right," Lang said, holding Zand's gaze. "But from what I've heard, he discovered you subjecting Dana Sterling to certain tests?"

"Yes, he did. And what of it? You've done the same in the past. How else are we to understand the nature of Protoculture without investigating Sterling?"

"You make it sound like the child is the key to the Shapings."

"She *is*," Zand whispered conspiratorially. "She is the focal point! I was trying to activate the Zentraedi side of her when Emerson burst in and ruined everything. He charged at me. I couldn't stop him; he seemed immune to my strength."

"Your strength?"

"He said he would kill me with his bare hands if I ever touched her again. The fool accused me of being *pruriently* fixated on her! He's not intelligent enough to grasp the truth—that I'm fixated on her *soul*!"

Two sets of pupilless eyes locked across the desk.

"Lazlo, you're beginning to sound like a vampire."

Zand threw up his still-functioning arm. "You're a fine one to talk! Don't we both feed off Protoculture? Aren't we both obsessed with the limits of the mind and immortality?"

Lang collected himself before responding. "Listen to me carefully, Lazlo. The mind-boost I received at Zor's console happened *to* me. No matter what you may have heard or what you choose to believe, I wasn't seeking it. It was different for you—you conjured it—and your willfulness seems to have factored into the results. As a scientist, I'm intrigued; but I'm also concerned for you. Stay away from Dana Sterling. Do nothing to harm her. If she is a nexus of energies, a focal point, as you say, then you are courting disaster by preying on her. Once tipped, the scales of Protoculture will balance themselves by any means possible, and ill-intent is always paid back in kind.

"What's more, parents are a fearsome breed, and little Dana's are certainly as fearsome as they come. If the Shapings operate through Dana, they operate through Max and Miriya as well, and their progeny must not be tampered with. Don't make the mistake of assuming that there aren't even greater powers at work in the universe than what we've discovered in Protoculture. So refrain from rousing them, Lazlo. Whatever you do, don't anger them."

Max hadn't slept since learning of Miriya's sudden reappearance two days earlier. At the time, all Rick would say was that she had turned up in Mexico, and had been taken into custody by the RDF. In bits and pieces—while Rolf Emerson was using his influence with Leonard to get Max released from Cavern City—Max had learned of Miriya's wounds, the stolen Stinger, and how she had nearly been shot down by the Veritech teams that had intercepted her south of Mexico. The obvious damage done to the Stinger was all that had saved her. When the RDFers finally established radio contact with her, Miriya was the one who had suggested a thorough inspection of the mecha by biowarfare experts, and isolation for herself.

Max was hurrying down a corridor in the Mexico base hospital now, fully suited in protective garb, as were the staffers on the ward. Leonard hadn't liked releasing him from Venezuela, but Emerson had couched it as a personal favor rather than an official request. On landing his VT in Mexico, Max learned that shortly after his departure from Cavern City the Wolff Pack and the Army of the Southern Cross had finally traded shots. Cavern seemed a lost cause. The disease was continuing to spread, there had been further outbreaks among Wolff's crew, and everyone along the trench wanted out. Max wondered if Cavern would wind up buried like Macross, or merely abandoned like Oasis in the Congo Sector.

His eagerness notwithstanding, he was apprehensive about seeing Miriya. He felt as if he were going to be better off *not* knowing the reasons for her disappearance. Rolf had brought Dana to Mexico, but Max thought it best that he first visit with Miriya alone. Rolf had said something about wanting to talk to him about Lazlo Zand and Dana, but that what he had to say could wait until some other time.

Miriya was being treated less like a prisoner than a patient, though two armed guards in antihazard suits were stationed outside her door. Her wounds were fairly serious, but her condition had stabilized during the previous twenty-four hours. Blood and fluid replacement had been a major concern, but what with the Freetown's large Zentraedi population, Miriya couldn't have picked a better place to put down.

Max's first look at her was unnerving; it was difficult to tell when a Zentraedi was wan, but Miriya certainly looked weak, and she was swathed in dressings. He went to her side and gently hugged her, wishing he could rid himself of the NBC suit. "I thought I'd never hold you again," he said through the faceplate. She was wooden in his arms. Distant.

"Is Dana all right?" she asked without emotion.

"She's downstairs with Rolf. We can call for her whenever you want."

"Yes, I want to see her." Miriya turned to stare out the double-thickness window glass at the arid mountains. The sky was gray and turbulent with storm clouds.

"Do you want to talk about it?" Max asked after a moment.

"Do you?"

"I think I need to, but I'm not sure."

Miriya took a starting breath. "I heard from Seloy Deparra. That's why I had to leave Monument."

Max nodded. "I thought so, from what Dana told me."

"Seloy and her son left Brasília after the riot and fell in with the Scavengers. Her reputation as a warrior made her the ideal person to lead them. She also had the requisite desire for vengeance."

"What did she want from you?"

"She wanted me to take Hirano to safety. She was expecting an attack by the RDF or the Southern Cross, and she didn't want him caught up in the violence."

"I haven't heard anything about a raid," Max said.

"Seloy called a meeting of representatives from the other bands. They're about to implement a new offensive."

"We know about the meeting. Does it have to do with the virus?"

Miriya looked at him. "You know about that?"

"I've been stuck in Cavern City for most of the time you've been missing."

Miriya frowned in sudden concern. "Are you all right?"

"I am, but Cavern isn't. Jonathan Wolff and I were the ones who carried the virus in, though we're still not sure how." He began to fill her in on his brief imprisonment in Oasis, his convalescence in the Argentine, Rick's visit, and the Wolff Pack's raid on the Shroud and Fist's camp in Venezuela.

Miriya said nothing.

"Have you been debriefed?" Max asked.

She nodded. "By Niles Obstat."

"Can you tell me anything about the Scavenger's plan for the virus?"

"Cavern City is only the beginning," Miriya said flatly. "They have access to enough of the virus to contaminate the entire Southlands—perhaps the world. It comes from a research laboratory some Amazonian indigines led them to. They plan to use tiny robots to spread the disease—almost-microscopic things called 'shuttles,' that have been retasked to embed themselves in the nose and throat. That's the reason for the meeting: to distribute the shuttles to the other malcontent bands. Seloy hoped to infect a few people in as many places as possible; that way the disease would soon spread itself around the world."

"How did you manage to escape the Scavengers camp?" Max asked.

"The Imperative provided all that I needed." She paused, then added, "I can lead the RDF to the base. But my loyalty is now suspect. You have to convince Rick that I'm telling the truth—and quickly. There isn't much time left."

Max was nodding. "Rick won't need convincing, but I can't make any promises about the others." Max regarded her through the permaplas plate. "Seloy must realize you'd come to us."

"Seloy's dead, Max."

He was startled. "I'm sorry—"

"Don't be. It was the risk she took when she summoned me. But her death will only delay the onset of their plan, not prevent it." She reached for Max's gloved hand. "I killed her."

Max felt a shudder of dread and horror pass through him. The cause of Miriya's flat tone and distant stare was revealed. "Where's Hirano?"

"At the camp." Miriya's gaze was unfocused. "Max," she said, with sudden anger. "I want to take part in the attack."

He had his mouth open to respond but she cut him off. "And don't tell me you understand, because you *don't*."

"My respect for the Robotech Masters continues to grow," Lang was saying, studying the magnified and enhanced image of a shuttle-bot onscreen. "A remarkable piece of work. Simple, elegant, artistic . . ."

"Let's not leave out 'deadly,' " Gunther Reinhardt thought to point out.

Lang turned to the briefing room table, gathered at which were the brigadier general, Rick Hunter, a half-dozen staff officers in their customary places, and Rolf Emerson and Max Sterling.

"It's the virus that's deadly, General," Lang said. "The shuttles, in seeking Human flesh, are merely executing their program." He laughed to himself. "I'm sure Harry Penn will be amazed to learn just how well he trained his former Zentraedi student, Xan Norri."

"Miriya also supplied us the name of Seloy Deparra's second-in-command—Marla Stenik," Reinhardt said. "I think it's safe to assume that Stenik is now the leader of the Scavengers."

"We don't have any information on Stenik," Rick added, "except that she was a Quadrono, like Deparra."

Colonel Motokoff spoke from the foot of the table. "The hell with the Scavengers, I'd like to know what we have on the virus."

Lang answered. "The reason it wasn't identified by computer search is that all records of it were deleted during the Rain of Death. The Indians of northwestern Brazil have known about 'Crazed Monkey Disease' for generations, and there are references to it in a number of works by ethnographers, explorers, and specialists in tropical medicine. This research lab Miriya mentioned operated on solar-generated power, and those generators are apparently still in operation, or the virus samples would certainly have died by now."

"Is there a treatment?" Rick asked.

"None that we know of. But the CDC and the Institute of Health assure me that a vaccine shouldn't be long in coming now that we know what we're dealing with. The RDF's first order of business should be to take out that lab."

"Thank you, Doctor," Reinhardt said with patent sarcasm, "but we don't know where to look for it. Miriya's after-mission report indicates that Deparra told her the lab was close to the Scavengers' present base in the eastern foothills of the Andes, but that doesn't give us much to go on. The lab was set up as a joint undertaking by Brazil and Peru, and records of its location probably exist in what remains of Lima or Rio. The problem is, neither Moran nor Leonard will come forward with information until we include them on what we've learned."

Rick looked at Reinhardt. "What are their demands?"

"To be made partners in any attack we launch on the base. Naturally, they want their share of the glory."

"What happened to Leonard's idea that Miriya is working with the Scavengers by trying to lead us into a trap?" Max asked.

"He can't risk standing by that," Emerson told him. "He knows that the Army of the Southern Cross has to be included in the attack no matter how things play out in the end."

"I vote we leave him out of it," Max said. "If the Scavengers are routed, the location of the laboratory won't matter."

Lang shook his head. "It's not that simple. We can't be sure some other malcontent band hasn't already been equipped with Stingers and shuttles, and the know-how to work with the virus."

"Are you telling me Leonard has us over the barrel *again?*"

No one spoke for a moment; then Reinhardt said, "The decision isn't the RDF's, in any case. All we can do is present what we have to the UEG and wait for them to decide how to proceed."

"Then it's a foregone conclusion," Max muttered. "Moran will argue that the Southlands are imperiled, and that the Southern Cross should be involved." He glanced at Reinhardt, then Rick. "Just try to make it work so that we're not answering to Leonard like we were in Cavern City. Otherwise, the Scavengers will have nothing to worry about. They'll be able to sit back and watch units from the RDF and the Southern Cross go at it. Christ, they won't even need to deploy the remaining virus. It'll be pure insanity by then."

Max might have gone on had not Niles Obstat entered the room at just that moment, saying, "We have the location of the laboratory."

"How?" Reinhardt asked.

"Through Thomas Edwards's sources in the Southlands."

"Now, there's a switch," Lang muttered, mostly to Rick and Reinhardt.

"Then we don't need anything from Leonard or the Southern Cross," Max said.

Reinhardt nodded. "We should have enough to convince the UEG that this is our baby. Those bastards owe us at least that much for dropping Venezuela into Moran's lap."

CHAPTER
TWENTY-NINE

Emerson never had his talk with Sterling about the occasion he discovered Zand and Dana at the Monument City Robotech Research Center. From his journals, it is clear that Emerson planned to tell Sterling on the return of the SDF-3 from Tirol. Until then—what with Dana in his care—he would see to it personally that Zand didn't come anywhere near the child. The Sterlings would only learn of Zand's experiments—indeed, of Zand's grotesque end and Emerson's heroic death—from Dana herself, on her arrival on Tirol.

Selig Kahler, *The Tirolian Campaign*

EIGHT STINGERS HAD BEEN MOVED FROM THE CAMP IN the valley to the site of the research laboratory in the denuded highlands. Eight mecha, one to sting every major city in Earth's western hemisphere: Portland, Detroit, Monument, Denver, Albuquerque, Mexico, Brasília, and Cuiabá.

Each craft would be piloted by two Scavengers who had volunteered for their mission—indeed, who had vied for the honor of suiciding for the cause. Khyron's name wasn't mentioned when the final choices had been made. The Backstabber may have been the first Zentraedi on Earth to surrender his life and the lives of his crew to ease the psychic burden of the disaffected, but the Scavengers owed him no tribute. The Stingers would fly for the glory of the Quadrono.

Marla Stenik was one of the twenty-five who had made the trip to the lab. The rest of the Scavengers, along with some fifty males representing half-a-dozen bands, had remained in camp to engage the RDF and buy time for the highland contingent. When Kru Guage and Vivek Bross had failed to return from her pursuit of Miriya Parino, Marla knew that the last days were upon them. Parino would reach Mexico or some other city, and soon enough the assembled might of the Robotech Defense Force would descend on the Scavengers' cloud forest camp.

Weeks earlier Marla had tried to dissuade Seloy from summoning Parino, sensing even then that the tide was about to turn for the rebellion. Parino had fought against her Quadrono comrades during the War's final battle, and there was no reason to believe she would act differently this time—certainly not as a result of what had happened in Brasília or Cairo or Arkansas. If Parino had been at all sympathetic to the cause, she would have come unbidden long ago. Marla recognized, however, that Seloy had felt compelled to contact Parino because of Hirano—even if Marla had no real grasp of what it was to be so devoted to another person that one would risk everything for that person. Seloy wanted her son to live, no matter what became of her; and who better to guarantee the boy's survival than Parino, who herself harbored a hybrid in the Human world?

Motherhood obviously had its own Imperative.

The highland laboratory was a windowless, three-level rectangle of aluminum and concrete that ran on solar power and converted energy gleaned from a nearby waterfall. On a rise behind the main building was a small graveyard where the research staff had buried some of their dead after Dolza's Rain, bolts from which had struck near enough to irradiate the entire area but leave the structure intact.

Xan Norri was in charge of overseeing the impregnation of the shuttles with the Human-harmful virus sustained by the lab's climate-control devices. Each Stinger would be armed with as many shuttle-stocked missiles as could be spared. In the event that the Stingers were engaged before they reached their target cities, the missiles were tasked to launch and disperse their payloads over population-rich areas, in the hope that infection of even a few Humans would lead to eventual systemwide contagion and mass death.

Xan was too important a resource to squander on the mission, but default leaders such as Marla were easily pro-curable, and so she had volunteered to fly—to sting Brasília, in sweet revenge for the injustices Leonard and the

Army of the Southern Cross had committed against Zentraedi throughout the Southlands.

Standing just now at the cloven feet of her Stinger, watching as the mecha's missile nacelles were loaded, Marla heard rumbling sounds to the east. The thin mountain air was saturated with water, impatient for stormy release, but she knew that it wasn't thunder she was hearing but the echoing report of weapons.

Jonathan Wolff was suddenly back to being a student. Because Centaurs were useless in the rugged terrain surrounding the Scavengers' camp, RDF command had assigned Wolff, along with Packers Bartley, Malone, and Ruegger, to *observe* in four prototype Hovertanks piloted by members of a special mecha detachment out of Albuquerque Base. Ugly and cumbersome, with rounded, downsloping deflection prows, the reconfigurable ground-effect vehicles were fashioned of heavy-gauge armor in angular, flattened shapes and acute edges. In standard mode, they rode on a powerful cushion of self-generated lift. Mechamorphosed, they became squat, two-legged, waddling particle-beam cannons the size of houses.

Even so, Wolff would have preferred his antiquated Centaur. Not only had he forgotten how to be an attentive student, but the Hovertank unit had been assigned a subordinate role in the mission, safeguarding the lower valley while Max Sterling and the Skull Team attacked the camp itself.

Though only days removed from the events in Cavern City, Wolff was like someone fresh from a nightmare. The epidemic had been contained, but the city was not likely to recover. When word had arrived from Max Sterling of Miriya's reappearance and RDF Command's plans for an offensive, the Pack had been shipped north to Mexico for a briefing. Catherine and Johnny were there now. Monument City looked to be the next stop for Wolff, providing he didn't seriously fuck up in the meantime.

In the end, the Pack had only been allowed to breach the quarantine because Cavern had effectively become the property of the Southlands. More importantly, in the wake of the internecine exchanges between the Pack and the Southern Cross, Anatole Leonard was especially eager to see Wolff leave. It was of some consolation, then, that the field marshal had been denied the chance to participate in the offensive against the Scavengers.

There was some furious fighting going on upvalley, but it might as well have been a video game for all the impact it had on the Hovertank unit. Wolff was surprised to see so few Stingers in the sky; mostly what the Hover's cameras found were Tactical Battlepods. Conventional wisdom would have dictated pounding the hell out of the camp and attacking by land, but Command's principal concern was the virus, and they didn't want anyone going to ground until the place was secured, or in the unlikely event of a fullscale surrender by the malcontents.

Wolff had his eyes glued to the video screen when the Hover's scanner console issued a chorus of beeping sounds, and the pilot—a thick-necked former VT jock named W. T. Super—swiveled his backless seat to face the threat-assessment display.

"Major paint, bearing two-niner-zero, south-southeast," he said for Wolff's benefit.

Wolff left his seat to study the screen over Super's shoulder. "Don't tell me we're finally going to get to put this thing through the paces."

"Sorry to dash your hopes, Captain, but whatever's headed this way is too big to be a Stinger or a Battlepod."

"Cyclops recovery ship?"

"Bigger."

Wolff stared at the radar signature for a moment and cursed. "That's a goddamned superhauler. It's *Leonard*."

"Position us in the thick of the fray," Leonard ordered the air cav commander of the superhauler from his seat in the gondola. "See to it the Skull are forced to take the fight elsewhere, even if it means taking flack from the pods. And make certain those Hovertanks remain where they are. Pin them down with fire if you have to."

Leonard paused, then looked expectantly at the leader of the commando unit.

"Rappel lines readied," the woman said without having to be asked.

Leonard nodded. "I want us down on the ground before these RDF idiots can do any more damage."

The view from the gondola encompassed the entire precipitous eastern face of valley, on which the Scavengers' camp was perched like an eagle's nest. Several of their thatch-roofed huts were in flames, as were sections of outlying wild forest where RDF mecha had crashed.

"Computer projections based on available data indicate approximately one hundred and sixty enemy forces," a tech reported from his duty station. "Most of them are bunkered east of the camp."

"Child's play." Leonard snorted in satisfaction. He could well imagine how surprised Sterling and his VT wingmen were to see him there. Even now, the command net was noisy with the pilots' confused squawkings.

"Acknowledge them, but offer no replies or explanations," Leonard told the communications chief.

Again, he owed T. R. Edwards for the advance intel on the RDF's strategy. But rather than allow Edwards to risk compromising himself, Leonard had instructed him to furnish General Reinhardt with the location of the research lab the RDF was so desperate to obliterate. If giving up the place would increase his chances of extracting what he wanted from the camp itself, they were welcome to it. He had no designs on the lab, in any case.

In exchange for agreeing to Rolf Emerson's request that Sterling be released from Cavern City, Leonard had been promised access to portions of Miriya Parino's top-secret debriefing. As anticipated, Emerson had declined to apprise him of the location of the Scavengers' camp, but he had divulged certain things about Parino's escape, including the fact that malcontent leader Seloy Deparra was dead.

On learning of her death, Leonard had been torn between delight and sorrow. As much as he'd wanted to, he hadn't asked about the child; to do so might have tipped his hand. He took it as a good sign, however, that Parino hadn't mentioned a child. Hirano was alive, in the custody of some other Zentraedi, to be sure, but alive nonetheless.

The boy was centermost in his thoughts when he rappeled into the jungle camp, amid the clamor of the superhauler's batteries as they punished the surrounding area. Had Seloy told Hirano who his father was? Had the boy told anyone? If not, would he come to accept Leonard as his parent? Could the Zentraedi in him be expunged by love or by punishment?

Leonard hit the muddy ground awkwardly, encircled by ten of the best the Army of the Southern Cross had to offer. No antihazard suits, no gloves or rebreathers now; what the Southern Cross had for the malcontents—or any other alien pretenders to Earth's crown—was far more deadly than anything the Scavengers had for them.

"I want a captive," Leonard yelled above the roar and clatter of the guns, the ear-smarting detonations of air-to-ground missiles.

Half the team scattered to carry out his command. Much of the camp was in flames, the immediate area strewn with alien corpses shot or burned beyond recognition. East of where Leonard had dropped, two Skull VTs had set down as Battloids and were wading through the wreckage, taking fire and answering it with glowing, superheated autocannons.

The malcontent Leonard's commandos returned with five minutes later had pallid skin and shaggy black hair. Smeared with mud and blood, she had empty bandoliers strapped across a flat chest. Leonard grabbed her by the front of her filthy sweatshirt and snarled into her face: "The child. The male child that was with Deparra."

The Zentraedi met his minatory gaze with defeated eyes and gave her head a mournful shake. "Dead. Dead with Deparra."

Leonard trembled. "You're lying. Where is the boy?"

"Killed by Parino. Dead."

Leonard felt faint. "Show me," he said. "I want to see the bodies."

The woman pointed to the platform of a tall, wooden structure—an observation tower. "Up there."

He stepped behind her and shoved her toward the tower. They walked between smoldering huts and worked their way around the burning trunk of a fallen tree. Leonard ordered her to ascend the tower's ladder ahead of him.

"In the tradition of those who live in these forests, we left the bodies for the carrion birds to pick clean," the Zentraedi explained as she climbed. "On the ships of the Grand Fleet, the bodies of warriors were recycled. Is this not the same thing?"

"Climb," Leonard told her.

But she refused to go any higher, and made room for him to pass her on the ladder. "Look for yourself."

Stepping onto the platform, he saw that she had told him the truth. He screamed, then fell to his knees. "Damn you, Seloy! You had no right. You had no right to bring my son into this!"

Then he unclenched his fists long enough to unholster his weapon and shoot the alien off the ladder.

As she had requested, Miriya was on loan to the Twenty-third Squadron for the attack on the research laboratory. No matter the outcome, the final battle had to pit Zentraedi against Zentraedi. Not only because of the danger the virus posed to Humans, but because of what the battle would signify to the world. If there was ever to be a chance for a lasting peace between the planetary races, the Zentraedi had to prove that they could police themselves.

The laboratory was a white-and-terracotta speck on a vast, mostly treeless plateau. And they were there—the Scavengers with their Stingers—just as Miriya knew they would be. At the briefing in Mexico, much had been made of the Twenty-third's role in the overall attack plan, and of how the squadron should comport itself. The RDF, ordinarily bent on adhering to the rules of civilized warfare, wanted the Scavengers stopped at all costs. Assuming the Stingers were already loaded with the virus, it was vital that they be destroyed there, close to the jungle from which the virus had sprung, rather than in proximity to any inhabited areas. And if that meant striking by surprise—preemptively, as the Southern Cross had done time and again—than so be it, and the media be damned.

The Scavengers had been caught unawares by the Twenty-third's dawn raid. Early on, though, the Stingers—serving as hulking bipedal antiaircraft arrays—had mustered an effective defense, preventing the VTs from getting close enough to the facility to do much damage. Now, however, the mecha were fast depleting themselves of warheads, and a few had lifted off, not to engage but to escape, or perhaps to make for remote targets. Each one that managed to avoid the aerial melee quickly found itself pursued by two or sometimes three Veritechs.

Miriya's undisclosed personal strategy didn't include her becoming part of a chase team. She landed her VT west of the laboratory complex and immediately scrambled out of the ship. Fearful that the main building would soon be targeted, the nonpilots among the Scavengers were beginning to scatter across the barren landscape, but three Stingers were still on the ground, their pilots hurrying to complete prelaunch procedures. It was toward this group that Miriya raced, weapon in hand, eluding fire and generating plenty of her own in return. She was no longer in the grips of the bloodlust that had secured her escape from Seloy's camp; her purpose now was not merely to survive but to *conclude*. Victory by itself would not be enough for Earth's Human population. Unfettered by an Imperative, Humans required catharsis and resolution, a sense that wrongs had been righted, that the scales of justice had been balanced. The situation wanted a prisoner who could be brought to trial.

And Miriya knew she had found that prisoner when she spied Marla Stenik.

There was nothing dramatic or especially heroic about the capture. Miriya shot Stenik's copilot as she was ascending the ladder to the Stinger cockpit; then she simply trained her handgun on the weaponless leader of the Scavengers.

Stenik almost appeared to have expected it. "At least permit me the honor of a warrior's death, *T'sen* Parino."

"You will have that honor," Miriya told her. "But not here."

The answer puzzled Stenik. "Where, then?"

"Where your death can be a public spectacle. And where I can be your public executioner."

CHAPTER THIRTY

> *That the [Malcontent] Uprisings ended with a whimper instead of a bang was in keeping with the overwhelming sadness of those years. Was there a positive side? Yes, I say, in that the Zentraedi survived as a race. Those that died on Earth were pawns in a much greater battle. For, in fact, the Uprisings were the last stand of the Imperative.*
>
> Lisa Hayes, *Recollections*

IN EARLY NOVEMBER 2018, EXASPERATED BY YEARS OF HAVing had to cater to the fragile egos of on-air celebrities, the executives of the Monument Broadcasting System announced that the Evening News co-anchor team of Hollister and Hyson would be replaced by a computer construct, designed and programmed—in line with MBS specifications—by cybertechnicians of the Tokyo Robotech Research Center. The brown-haired, blue-eyed, somewhat-androgynous-looking computer-generated hologram, known simply as "the Anchor," made its network debut on November 21 that same year, garnering the biggest ratings and largest audience share the show had received in more than five years.

"In what is generally agreed to have been the decisive moment of the Malcontent Uprisings, a joint force of RDF and Southern Cross personnel swooped down on the Andean stronghold of the group known as the Scavengers and dealt the rebellion a death blow, capturing its leadership and thwarting a diabolical plan to infect the world with a deadly virus.

"Now, three months later, the reverberations of that un-qualified win are finally being felt. Today, in the clear skies over New Mexico, Scavenger leader Marla Stenik, and the so-called 'Butcher of Oasis,' Jinas Treng, were—in the parlance of the Zentraedi—'allowed to run' against RDF captains Miriya Parino and Breetai Tul. Found guilty last month of insurrection, terrorism, and thirty-four separate violations of the Reconstruction Powers Act, Stenik and Treng were removed from solitary confinement on Albuquerque Base to an undisclosed location elsewhere in New Mexico, where—as dictated by the *Kara-Thun* ritual—each was returned to full size and given a fully armed and operational Tactical Battlepod.

"Breetai Tul, on his first downside visit since 2015, chose a Battlepod as his weapon, while Miriya Parino, in a symbolic gesture, elected to remain Micronized and to pilot a Veritech.

"The *Kara-Thun*, or 'Death Dance,' is a form of trial by combat, in which convicted Zentraedi have an opportunity to avoid sentencing by besting their opponents in one-on-one challenges. Such was not the case today, however, as Parino and Tul assumed quick control of the lethal contest and defeated the renegades. MBS will broadcast footage of the aerial 'death dance' as soon as it is made available by the RDF.

"And so, at long last, Stenik and Treng have been executed, ending the fervent debate that attended their captures and trials. In a statement issued only hours ago, Miriya Parino expressed her hope that the *Kara-Thun* would demonstrate the Zentraedi's thorough repudiation of the actions of the Malcontents, and mark the beginning of a healing process that would ultimately reunite Earth's two races.

"Today also marked the UEG's official recognition of the Army of the Southern Cross as a full partner in the newly created Earth Defense Force. The aging armament of the Southern Cross will be replaced by a new generation of Protoculture-driven reconfigurable mecha, and it will be entitled to equal say in the construction of the Mars and Lunar bases and the deployment of Space Station Liberty and a network of defense platforms. As of January first, Anatole

Leonard's new rank will be Commander-in-Chief of the Southern Armed Forces, and there is some talk of Leonard's opening a secondary headquarters in Monument City.

"As stipulated by the accord—and in spite of passionate pre-accord lobbying by President Wyatt Moran and others—the Robotech Expeditionary Force, under the command of Brigadier General Gunther Reinhardt and Admiral Richard Hunter, will retain full possession of the factory satellite and the starship, SDF-3. Moran has indicated, however, that he will continue to fight for the creation of a bipartisan plenipotentiary council to oversee the Tirol mission itself, and to ensure Southern Cross participation in the events. Leonard has already named former intelligence officer T. R. Edwards, now a colonel in the Earth Defense Force, as his personal choice to represent the military interests of the Southlands and the nonaligned territories . . ."

"Turn that damned thing off," Leonard said, gesturing to the hotel suite's flatscreen television. "Who the hell wants to hear some electronic phantom deliver the news— especially one that only knows half the story."

Leonard's leg was in a cast from a wound he had sustained at the Scavenger's camp. Closest to the TV, Joseph Petrie told the screen to zero itself. Leonard was right, of course. The MBS had no inkling of the subtext of the accord that partnered the RDF and the Southern Cross. All things considered, the media's misapprehension of the facts benefited Leonard, since his strategy called for feigning ignorance of the covert machinations of the RDF. Petrie had been concerned about the commander's recent bouts with depression—episodes that had commenced about the time of the attack on the Scavengers' camp—but Leonard seemed reborn since arriving in Monument City for the recognition ceremonies.

"The RDF thinks that they've played us for fools," Leonard told his three guests—Patty Moran, T. R. Edwards, and Lazlo Zand. "They think everything's falling neatly into place for them. They assume they've appeased us by accepting us as partners and affording us full participation in the reconstruction of Gloval and ALUCE bases. Anything to keep us occupied while they transfer more and more of their surface operations to the factory satellite. And a year from now, when the SDF-3 folds to Tirol with eighty percent of Earth's mechanized defenses aboard, guess who's supposed to be left holding the bag? *Us*, that's who." Leonard stormed around the room for a moment, then stopped and whirled on his audience.

"But wait till they get a whiff of the stink we're going to raise when that starship is declared mission-ready. We'll let the entire world in on their little plan to leave the planet defenseless. But even then, we'll continue to back the mission, proclaim the necessity of it. We'll kiss every member of the REF good-bye. And by the time they launch, we'll have everyone so paranoid about a second invasion that the UEG will grant us whatever we need to act as Earth's sole protectors. Funding, support, power . . ." Leonard put his hands on hips and rocked on the balls of his feet.

"To the disbanding of the UEG," Moran said, lifting a glass of wine.

Edwards, Petrie, and Zand followed suit. "To the new order," Edwards said.

Leonard acknowledged it with a bow. "I'm only sorry you won't be here to see it happen, Edwards."

Edwards made a dismissive gesture. "One of us has to be aboard the SDF-3 to make sure Hunter and the rest don't strike any separate deals with the Masters." He cut his eyes to Zand, whose nose was bandaged and whose arm was still in a sling. "Unless, of course, the good professor would like to sign on as a member of the plenipotentiary council?"

"No, no, thank you," Zand said quickly, coughing up wine. "I, uh, don't think I have the stomach for space travel." He grinned madly. "Besides, the Shapings require me to be here."

The room grew eerily quiet, but Leonard didn't allow the silence to linger. "Maybe those 'Shapings' will have something to relate about the fate of the Zentraedi, Professor. Because I promise you this much: any aliens who remain on Earth after the SDF-3 launches will wish they hadn't."

* * *

"I'm not saying I don't like it," Rolf Emerson said, standing at the entrance to the Sterlings' high-rise apartment. He inclined his head to one side, staring at Miriya's severly shorn hair. Banged and layered, the new do drew attention to the planes and angles of her face, at once imparting something severe and pious to her features. "It's just going to take some getting used to."

Max ushered him inside. On the way to the living room, Rolf peeked in on Dana, who was sitting on the edge of her bed, lost in a sprite-filled video game. It was Rolf's first visit in months. The last time he'd seen Max or Miriya was at the premission briefing for the raid on the Scavenger base. Since then, his duties as liaison officer to the Southern Cross had kept him hopelessly busy.

"What made you decide to cut it?" Rolf asked Miriya while Max was busy in the kitchen.

"It was something I had to do. An outward sign of my new identity."

The seriousness of her tone threw him. "What new identity?"

"As executioner."

Rolf nodded uncertainly. "I was surprised to hear that Breetai had asked you to fly with him in the *Kara-Thun*."

"He didn't ask me," she snapped. "I asked him."

Rolf was suddenly sorry he had brought it up.

"Marla Stenik thought she could pilot her Battlepod into Breetai's, but I ripped her ship apart before she could reach him," Miriya went on. "Treng crashed his Battlepod and tried to escape into the wastelands on foot, but Breetai chased him down and killed him with his hands." She paused to reflect on something. "It's not something I could expect you to understand, but killing Seloy and . . . others had a powerful effect on me, Rolf. It brought to life something I thought was dead. Something I wish was still dead."

"Rolf understands," Max said, interrupting. "He and Ilan Tinari—"

Miriya shot him an angry look. "Because we live together, you think you understand me?"

Max set a tray of chips and salsa on the table. "Okay,

'understand' is probably the wrong word. Let's say that I don't judge you strictly by Human standards."

"That's good, Max, because I'm *not* Human."

Rolf glanced around uncomfortably, and Miriya picked up on it.

"Rolf, are you aware that Max and I consider you one of our closest friends?"

Rolf relaxed enough to smile. "I'm glad to hear that, Miriya, because I certainly feel that way about you two."

"Do you think you'll be living in Monument now that Venezuela belongs to the Southlands?" Max said, taking a seat opposite Rolf.

"It's beginning to look that way. Especially if Leonard and Moran are going to be dividing their time between Brasília and here. Besides, I've met someone. Her name is Laura." He looked at Max. "Why?"

Max and Miriya traded ambiguous looks. "We're considering joining the REF, Rolf," Miriya said at last.

Rolf was unsuccessful in hiding a frown. "I'm sure Rick and Lisa are thrilled."

Miriya nodded. "They are, but the decision has nothing to do with them. I'm doing this for myself. I'll never be free of the Imperative until I confront the Masters directly, and I think it's important that I do that on Tirol. Something is drawing me there. I don't know how else to explain it."

Rolf studied her, then Max. "Does this have something to do with my living in Monument City?"

Max cleared his throat meaningfully. "Rolf, we can't take Dana with us. We want her to have as normal an upbringing as possible, and the SDF-3 isn't the place for that."

"We want you to think about being Dana's guardian while we're gone," Miriya added.

Rolf was dumbfounded. He gestured to himself. "I don't know anything about raising kids!"

"We know that," Max said. "But Dana's very comfortable around you. She thinks of you as part of the family. There's no one else we can ask, Rolf. Maybe if Jean and Vince weren't going . . ."

"What about her godfathers?"

THE ZENTRAEDI REBELLION 367

"We said *normal*, Rolf," Max said.

"Besides, they're going to be spending a lot of time at the factory."

Rolf started to say something, but laughed instead. "Me and Dana, huh?" He shook his head in self-amusement. "I guess we'll be able to manage for a few months."

"This can only work if you decide to make it work," Catherine Wolff told her husband as he was unpacking their suitcases. The Wolffs were in the bedroom of their small, on-base modular house in the outskirts of Monument City. Johnny was asleep in the second bedroom, pleased with his new surroundings after months of being moved from RDF base to base. "How many times did you ask me to give Cavern City a chance? That's all I'm asking you to do now."

Wolff looked at her. "Yeah, but how long did it take for you to do that?"

"What difference does it make? I found a job, I created a home for us—even if I didn't fit in with your friends and their families."

"Because you never tried to. And you bitched for two years before you took that job."

"Fine. So you have my permission to bitch for two years."

He started to say something but changed his mind. "I just don't know if I can get used to this place."

Catherine folded her arms and frowned "You'd rather be in what's left of Cavern City?"

"I like Cavern. This place is too cold and crowded."

"Do you like it enough to resign from the RDF and enlist in the Southern Cross?"

"I know there's no going back—all I'm saying is that I miss it."

"What you miss is hunting malcontents, Jonathan. And sooner or later you're going to have to accept that that part of your life is also finished."

"That's not so easy, Cath."

She softened somewhat and walked over to him. "I know that. But don't you think you've earned a rest? Haven't

Johnny and I earned a rest? You can't live on the edge forever, and a desk job isn't going to kill you. If you can take some of the energy you brought to the field and apply that to your new position, you'll be a colonel in a year. Then you can start to think about retiring, and we can start a new life for ourselves."

Wolff snorted a laugh. "I won't make colonel for ten years, Cath. Not without a war, and definitely not anchored to a desk or teaching tank tactics to a bunch of recruits."

Catherine blinked. "I'm sorry we can't provide you with a war, *Major*. I'm afraid you'll just have to make the best of peace."

Wolff moved to the window and pressed his face against the cool glass. The night was clear and strewn with stars. Reconciliations were a tricky business, but he knew Catherine was right when she said that any benefits to be gained from their new circumstances would depend on his willingness to embrace change. And that held for their marriage as well: it wouldn't survive unless he wanted it to. But what was he supposed to do about his need for new horizons, action, the camaraderie of combat? Where was he going to find that in Monument City?

He spent a long moment staring at the stars before the truth of his dilemma struck him like ice-cold lightning. By accepting the transfer to Monument—primarily for Catherine's sake—he had bought into a lie. He would never be content here. What he wanted was *upside*, removed from the petty concerns of the planet, to which it owed nothing more than gravitational allegiance. The SDF-3 was where he wanted to be. And if Catherine couldn't understand that, then they didn't belong together. Eight years earlier he'd been left behind by the SDF-1, but this time he wouldn't give fate the chance to cheat him.

"We'll be launch-capable by no later than June 2020," Lang was happy to announce on entering the command bubble of the SDF-3.

Rick, Lisa, and Exedore had arrived only minutes earlier, by tug from level nine of the factory satellite. Outside the eye of the bridge, three hundred feet above the techno-carpeted deck, Breetai sat cross-legged on a retrofitted platform that enabled him to share in briefings held in the command bubble.

"I'm also confident that the fold generators will deliver us to the Valivarre system in a single jump. The ship will manifest three million miles from Fantoma, in its shadow. Tirol will be just emerging from its long night."

Rick and Lisa smiled and hugged. Exedore cast an unreadable, arched-eyebrow look at Breetai. "It still doesn't seem real," Lisa said, looking around the bubble. "Sometimes I'll sit in the command chair, put my hands on the controls, and try to imagine us millions of light-years from Earth, and my mind seems to shut down."

"Soon you won't have to rely on imaginings, Commander," Lang said in a paternal voice. He glanced at Exedore. "How will it feel to be returning home?"

"My mind is also stubbornly silent on that issue, Doctor. I should point out, however, that the Zentraedi have never, and probably will never, associate Tirol with pleasant images. To you, home by and large connotes acceptance and warmth of feeling. But as you will see for yourselves, Tirol is neither warm nor accepting. I will be surprised if the Masters so much as deign to recognize us, let alone entertain our entreaties for peace."

"Don't worry, Exedore, we're not exactly going to show them our belly," Rick said.

Breetai loosed one of his signature growls. "The Masters will find our soft spot, regardless."

"We can't let that happen," Rick argued, "even if it means a fight. But you won't hear me issuing any fire orders until we've stated our case for peace."

Lang was nodding his head in agreement. "We mustn't lose sight of the fact that we are emissaries first, warriors last. Everyone on Earth expects us to demonstrate restraint."

"Everyone but Anatole Leonard," Lisa commented.

Rick cut his eyes to her. "We'll deal with him when we return. He seems to think we've elected him steward of the planet, but the authority we've given him can just as easily be revoked."

"The RDF has encouraged him to think of himself as Earth's protector," Lang said. "And that may prove our greatest failing to date. In fact, I sometimes feel we have more to fear from Leonard than we do the Masters or the Invid."

"Then let's promise ourselves something here and now," Lisa said. "That we keep our first meeting with the Masters as brief as possible, and that when we refold to Earth, we dedicate ourselves to completing the work we began six years ago: restoring our world. Before Leonard or any of his kind succeed in further dividing us against ourselves."

STEEL YOURSELF
FOR COMBAT . . .
PREPARE FOR
NONSTOP ACTION . . .
AND ENTER THE ASTOUNDING
UNIVERSE OF ROBOTECH!

Discover how it all began with FIRST GENERATION:

GENESIS

As the Global Civil War was about to wipe out Humankind, a dying alien genius dispatched the abandoned Super Dimensional Fortress to Earth—and put Humanity's future in the hands of a corps of untried, resolute young men and women: the Robotech Defense Force. Then the most feared conquerors in the universe attacked, and the real war began . . .

BATTLE CRY

Henry Gloval, Human captain of the alien spacecraft called the Super Dimensional Fortress, was a practical man—he only asked himself once or twice a day how in the world he had ended up in command of the stupendously powerful SDF-1. After all, he had more important things on his mind—for now the Zentraedi had come to claim the alien space fortress as their own . . .

HOMECOMING

For more than a year, the Humans aboard the SDF-1 had fought and eluded an endless armada of Zentraedi warships. Now the space fortress would have to battle her way back to Earth. But villains came in Human form as well as alien—and the treachery of power-hungry men might be the most lethal threat of all . . .

BATTLEHYMN

For two years, the SDF-1 had been chased through the Solar system by a race of giant alien warriors, only to be made to feel like unwanted relatives when they finally returned to planet Earth. But after three months of inactivity, the SDF-1's Captain Gloval took matters into his own hands. In direct violation of Council dictates, he ordered the SDF-1 airborne. After all, the fate of the Earth was at stake . . .

FORCE OF ARMS

The giant Zentraedi had given up their efforts to capture the SDF-1 intact. Now they wished only to destroy it—along with its Human crew, the whole Human race and its homeworld, and those aliens who had defected to the Terran side. Supreme Commander Dolza mobilized the largest fleet of Zentraedi warships the universe had ever seen . . . and all their weapons were aimed at Earth.

DOOMSDAY

It was a war without victors—one that had brought two species to the brink of extinction. And it was a war without spoils, save for the devastated Earth itself. After the final battle, Humans began the painstaking process of reconstruction. The Zentraedi would help them—for the two former enemies now shared a common goal: survival. But all was not well in this bravest of new worlds . . . for one Zentraedi had vowed to lead his race back to their former glory—at any cost.

At last the story of the battle for Earth has been told in the new novel of Robotech's LOST GENERATION:

THE ZENTRAEDI REBELLION

Not every Human was eager to share the planet Earth with the Zentraedi survivors of the First Robotech War, and there was little prospect of a lasting peace. The tensions in the Southlands had given rise to two opposing forces: the Army of the Southern Cross, and a loosely organized brigade of Zentraedi insurgents, driven by the Imperative to continue the fight—until one race or the other was eradicated. Caught between those rivals was the Robotech Defense Force, which would play a crucial role in what would be called the Malcontent Uprisings . . .

The adventures of THE SENTINELS begin six years after the final tragedies of the First Robotech War:

THE DEVIL'S HAND
It was 2020, and the Super Dimensional Fortresses 1 and 2 had long been destroyed. But Earth was now on the mend, and the Robotech Defense Force had fashioned a new battle fortress: the SDF-3, tasked with a trip across the galaxy to make peace with Tirol's Robotech Masters. But unknown to Admirals Rick and Lisa Hunter and the SDF-3's crew of thousands, the Robotech Masters were already on their way to Earth. And at Tirol, the SDF-3 would face the galaxy's fiercest warlord: the Invid Regent!

DARK POWERS
Stranded on the far side of the galaxy after battling the Invid hordes, the Robotech Expeditionary Force's chances for survival are slim. But suddenly, a starship unlike any other appeared—manned by an incredible assortment of beings determined to challenge the Invid Regent himself! REF volunteers signed on, their mighty war mecha in tow, for a campaign that would mean their total destruction—or liberty for the planets of the Sentinels!

DEATH DANCE
Four months had passed without a word from the Sentinels, and the members of the Expeditionary mission to Tirol feared the worst—even as they began truce negotiations with the Invid Regent himself. Far away, the surviving Sen-

tinels were hopelessly stranded on Praxis, a planet in cataclysm, at the mercy of the Invid Regis. But deep within that world's core were answers to the Sentinels' prayers—if they could only reach them before Praxis tore itself apart.

WORLD KILLERS

The bearlike Kabarrans and the swashbuckling amazons from Praxis, the feral natives of Garuda and the Human Robotech heroes—these oddly matched champions banded together with yet other species to form the valiant Sentinels. But no fighting force could hope to dislodge the Invid hordes from Haydon IV, ethereal world of superscience, or Spheris, crystalline globe of living minerals and murderous resonances. Nevertheless, the Sentinels launched their attack . . .

RUBICON

Optera—birthplace of the Flower of Life and its agents of retribution, the Invid—was to be the site of the final confrontation between the Sentinels and Edwards and his Invid allies. Edwards, with Lynn-Minmei prisoner and a handful of Invid Inorganics under his control, had fled Tirol for the distant planet. Breetai's Zentraedi were headed there as well—and so were the renegade forces of Tesla, mutated by the fruits of the Flower. The Sentinels themselves were not far behind . . . and it was a battle the Sentinels had to win!

*The beginning of a new age
brings a new war in SECOND GENERATION:*

SOUTHERN CROSS

Twenty years after the First Robotech War, the Robotech Masters came to Earth to finish the conquest their Zentraedi warrior-slaves had begun . . . and a battle-ravaged Earth had to defend itself once more. And young Dana Sterling, half-Human, half-Zentraedi commander of an elite Hovertank unit, stepped into the spotlight of interstellar history!

METAL FIRE
An alien fortress had crashlanded on Earth—brought down deliberately in the struggle between the Robotech Masters and Earth's Human inhabitants. Now the fortress sat silently overlooking Monument City, daring someone to penetrate its dark mysteries. And who better to brave that ship than Dana Sterling's 15th Squadron ATACs—after all, they had brought the thing down to begin with!

THE FINAL NIGHTMARE
The war for Earth had become even more desperate: the Robotech Masters' Protoculture Matrix was degenerating, transforming into the Flower of Life, which was sure to draw the savage, merciless Invid across the galaxy. But the Army of the Southern Cross vowed to wage war for Earth to the bitter end. And Dana Sterling, half-alien commander of an elite Hovertank unit, waged a desperate war of her own to uncover the meaning of her strange visions and the secret of her alien heritage . . .

Robotech's THIRD GENERATION
struggles to reclaim a conquered Earth:

INVID INVASION
The Invid Regis had succeeded where the Robotech Masters had failed—her warrior horde had gained control of Protoculture and laid claim to Earth. It was up to the space-weary Human veterans of the Expeditionary Force to retake the planet—a world most of them had never seen. And the counterinvasion would be more difficult than anyone could imagine . . .

METAMORPHOSIS
There had never been a less conventional band of champions: a downed pilot who was a stranger on his own homeworld . . . a former biker hellion . . . a young Forager obsessed with the vanishing heritage of Humanity's lore . . .

a lethal Robotech warrior ... an irrepressible adolescent convinced that the world owes her a Great Romance ... and a cloned enemy Simulagent who couldn't recall who she was. And somewhere ahead of them lay Reflex Point, nerve center and stronghold of the Invid conquerors—and the destination of the group that was Earth's last hope.

SYMPHONY OF LIGHT

It had been a long, hard road for the ragtag band of Robotech irregulars, but Reflex Point was finally close at hand, and preparations were underway for a full-scale assault on the Invid stronghold. But the Invid Regis would not surrender so easily the world she had come halfway across the galaxy to claim. And no one had thought to ask whether Protoculture might have something to say in these matters. But indeed it did, and the final encounter of the Robotech Wars would be more mystifying than anyone had imagined ...

And finally, the REF's final mission is at hand—
and so is the solution
to the greatest mystery of the universe—in ...

THE END OF THE CIRCLE

The SDF-3 manifested from spacefold, but no one aboard had the slightest idea where they were—the ship appeared to be grounded in some glowing fog, ensnared by the light itself. And the ship's Protoculture drives had disappeared. Meanwhile, in Earthspace, the *Ark Angel* had been spared the destructive fate of the REF main fleet, and a mission set out to locate the SDF-3. Elsewhere, mysterious events were being set into motion, and the ultimate conflict was imminent ...